THE KILLING GIFT

THE KILLING GIFT

A Novel by BARI WOOD

G. P. Putnam's Sons
New York

To Congdon

Part I

1

TWO HOURS to Kennebunkport, and the sun was already in the trees. Tom pushed down on the accelerator . . . too fast for the road, but they'd barely make it by dark as it was, and the road would be impossible at night.

Kate was asleep—passed out, Tom thought, thin rivers of sweat furrowing through the dust on her cheeks, her head rocking against the back of the seat in time with the ruts. He envied her. His eyes burned, his head ached, and he vowed, not for the first time, never to drink bad gin at lunch.

If it had been earlier, he would have pulled over and slept. Too late now. Besides, there was a cool shower, French wine, and one of the Kennet's Inn's first-rate dinners waiting for them only sixty miles south. Maybe he could make it in an hour and a half. His foot pushed until the accelerator pedal only just cleared the floor. The speedometer reached 50; gravel spat against the bottom of the car, the wheels raised a huge puff of dust that blew back into the windows, powdering the leather seats, dashboard, their clothes, coating the isinglass.

The Pierce-Arrow held beautifully around the first curve, even on the gravel. Nothing but the best for the son of Thomas List, Sr. On the straightaway the speedometer hovered at 52, then 55. . . .

He didn't hear the blowout, but he felt it. The car lurched left, hung for a second, then jerked to the right, yanking the steering wheel out of his hands. He hit the brakes too late. The car hurtled across the road, over the dirt shoulder, and smashed against one of the huge old spruces that lined the road.

The windshield splintered. The door on the driver's side smashed open and the back wheels of the car tilted free of the road, still spinning madly, spewing dust from the tires and the spokes of the wheels.

"Not much blood. Husband's banged up a bit. Wife's in pain, pretty bad. . . ." Pause. "Seems to be her hip." Another pause. Tom watched Sheriff Stroud wipe his face and the earpiece of the phone. The town's telephone central was nothing more than a linoleum-floored porch on someone's house. Clean enough, even some plants drooping on the railing. But screens cut off any breeze and the place was sweltering.

"No, their car's out, but I can drive them over." Another pause, then, "Right, as soon as we can."

Tom followed the man down the porch's three slatted steps and back into the dust. By now it was in his eyes and hair, it gritted in his teeth and scratched in his buttocks. A breeze came out of the spruces and the sweat began drying on his face, caking the dust on his forehead and cheeks.

Kate was lying in the back seat of the sheriff's car, her legs drawn up against her body, against the strain of stretching them. Her eyes were open, glazed, Tom thought, and her face was very pale.

"Kate?"

Her eyes shifted to him.

"The hospital's about twenty minutes away," he said. "They're waiting for us." She looked away.

Sheriff Stroud was pumping the fuel pressure.

"Is the road very bad?" Tom asked.

"Not too bad. We'll go easy."

The pressure was up. He started the car, let out the clutch, and eased around the grass, over the shoulder, and onto the road. He was a good driver, steady on the accelerator, gentle on the curves, ready for every rut. Kate's eyes were closed—either asleep or unconscious, no hint of pain.

On their way to the hospital they passed the Pierce-Arrow hunched against the tree, its back wheels still above the ground with the tilt of the chassis, its doors standing open from its sides like broken wings. Tom turned his head as they drove past. It was his first Pierce-Arrow, a wedding present from his father, and he hated leaving it there alone on the empty dusty road in the darkening woods. Then they were around another curve, and the car was out of sight.

The hospital looked better than he'd hoped, clean, fairly modern. To the west, behind the building, the sky was still light, but once out of the car, he saw that the seaward sky had gone dark blue, and out beyond the land-formed breakwater a mist was creeping toward the island of spruce in the bay.

They were waiting on the porch—two men with a stretcher, and another in a white coat. As soon as the car stopped they came across the lawn. The white-coated man—about Tom's age, good-looking but on the short side—opened the back door.

"What are you doing?"

"Going to give her a shot . . . morphine. Otherwise it's going to hurt a lot." He climbed into the back seat of the car and squatted on the floor next to Kate. Tom couldn't hear what he said to her, her eyes were open, sunken now, her answer was very faint. Then she stretched out her arm, and Tom looked away.

The man backed out of the car. "We'll give it a couple of minutes before we try to move her. No sense making it any harder for her."

"What is it?" Tom asked.

"Can't tell till we get an X ray, but the hip might be broken."

Tom looked past the man at Kate. Her face had a little more color, and her body seemed more relaxed.

"Kate?"

She smiled at him. The doctor motioned the men with the stretcher. They eased her onto it and lifted it out of the car. Then they were carrying her across the lawn toward the hospital.

Sheriff Stroud leaned out of the car window.

"You go on, Mr. List. I'll stop in town, and they'll send someone for the car first thing in the morning. Doc More usually has an extra bed, so you can probably spend the night right here."

Tom started to reach for his wallet, but Sheriff Stroud didn't wait, and Tom was left alone on the darkening lawn looking after the puff of road dust, his hand still in his pocket.

The fog had already engulfed the islands and was heading for the shore. Tom turned and walked across the grass to the hospital. Without the late-spring sunlight the air was very chilly, and as he opened the door to the warmth of the hallway, he began to shiver. He sat on one of the wooden benches that lined the walls just as the doctor came back looking for him.

"Let me get you a drink, Mr—"

"List," he said, in the usual tone he used to introduce himself, "Thomas List, Jr."

No special reaction. Apparently the doctor had never heard of the name.

"I'm Dr. Edwin More. Won't you come with me?"

Tom followed into a parlor waiting room with a fireplace and upholstered chairs. The doctor poured colorless liquid from a jug he took from a locked cabinet. Tom took a deep swallow.

"That's pretty good," he said.

Dr. More smiled. "We've got one of the best stills in New England only five miles from here."

Tom took another sip—much better. The trembling had stopped.

"What is this about an X ray?"

"You're lucky, Mr. List, we've got the only one in the county. We'll be able to—"

"I'm not sure I can allow you to do that to my wife." The tone surprised the doctor, made him look closely at Tom. Good tweed under the dust, very good; flannels as fine and soft as silk, and the shoes—no one between Bar Harbor and Kennebunkport could afford such shoes.

"The procedure is perfectly safe, Mr. List. We've been using it for some time. Your wife is in no danger."

"But I've heard about rashes, tumors—"

"I know what you've heard. But those were the early machines. We've almost perfected them now, and we have absolute control over the amount of radiation your wife will receive. Besides, even in the past, the danger was much greater for the radiologist than for the patient."

Tom stood up, tilted his head back so that he seemed to be looking down at Dr. More from a great height. "I said that I cannot allow it, doctor, and I don't intend to argue about it any longer."

He was still young, but Dr. More could already hear unquestioned authority. In a few years, the doctor thought, Thomas List, Jr. would be a difficult man to deal with. But then they all were; the rich who played in Maine.

"I will not treat her without an X ray, Mr. List. She could be crippled if that hip is broken and I don't set it. And if I have to set it without a radiogram, I can't be sure of doing it properly. But of course, she's your wife, and you're free to take her somewhere else—that is, if you think she should be moved again. I don't. But it's entirely your decision, and responsibility."

Tom tried to face the doctor down, but the trembling had started again. He knew his reactions were inappropriate. He didn't want the doctor to think he was arrogant. But it was a shock . . . something had broken under her skin. He could remember the feel of it on the tips of his fingers, against his mouth. The perfect alignment he had sensed through his wife's flesh was shattered.

He sat down again. Apology was out of the question, but he could explain, "It's our honeymoon."

The other man sat down too. "I'm sorry. Headed for Kennebunkport, were you?"

Tom nodded.

"Well, if it's just a pulled muscle or something like that we can tape her up and you'll be on your way in a day or two." He didn't think it was a pulled muscle at all, but he did not want to kill hope before he had to.

"And if it's broken, doctor?"

"We'll have to put one hell of a big cast on her, and she'll be very uncomfortable for a while, but that's the worst. She's young, looks healthy —no reason why she won't be ready for another honeymoon in a few months."

Kate couldn't remember the pain. She knew it had been there, was still there, but she couldn't remember it.

She was lying on her back. Her clothes were gone, but she was draped, crisp cloth that smelled of bleach.

They handled her gently, lifting, then sliding something cold and smooth under her buttocks that made her flesh flatten and spread as they let her down.

Then light bulbs on a pole—no, not light bulbs—something else, incredibly shaped, intricate, like blown glass, enclosed in a black box. Inside the clear glass she could see the filaments, impossibly twisted. As she watched, they moved. Bulbs, box, and all slid past her neck, her shoulders, and out of sight. She wanted to see them again—if she sat up. . . .

"Please don't move."

She started to twist around, to find the source of the voice.

"I said don't move."

The pain plucked at her, and she knew she had to lie still or it would catch up to her.

Someone rolled the sheet down, then moved away. She was alone with the black box. There was a heavy muted click, the black box hummed, another click, and the humming was all around her.

Twenty-five roentgens hit her pelvis in an unseen, unfelt explosion of energy. Piercing skin, fascia, muscle, the rays speared through the ridge of bone to the organs. They flashed around the tiny, grainy, hollow, fertilized ovum only hours old. Stabbing through the cells as they synchronized their differentiation. Inside each cell, inside each chromosome, helices twisted, locked, unlocked, twisted again; coding the billions of messages that would guide the cells from embryo to fetus, from fetus to infant to child to adult. A specialization code for each cell; how to reproduce in harmony with the tissues it would be part of; even a delayed-action message to tell the cells to stop dividing so the organism would deteriorate, then die. Even the rate of the corpse's decay was coded, received, stored.

The instant of radiation added its own message as it fled past and sank away. It was coded, received, and stored too, as the cells divided and the egg grew.

* * *

An ambulance brought Kate to the railroad station. Dr. More, his assistant, and Tom carried her stretcher across the platform and maneuvered it up the steps, through the narrow door and passage, and into the car the Lists had rented to take their son and his wife home again.

They lifted her carefully onto the made-up berth while the porter checked and smoothed the blankets. Dr. More took the crutches they had carried with her and leaned them against the wall.

"A week without the cast isn't very long, Kate, and you only get up for the bathroom. Otherwise you stay right where you are."

She smiled. "I will, Edwin, I promise."

If anything, Tom thought she'd gotten prettier during the past few months. Thinner, paler—much prettier.

They said good-bye. He wanted to be alone with her and he was glad to see them go. But the doctor climbed down the steps to the platform and stayed there watching them through the window. Tom waved, and the doctor waved back, but he did not leave.

Tom tried to forget the man standing under the window. He fussed with Kate's bag, then buzzed for the porter to order tea. Kate lay there, her head resting on the crisp, coarse muslin pillowcase, smiling smugly at him. Tom looked out again. The doctor was still there, caught inside Tom's reflection in the glass. He did not smile this time, or wave, just stared at the window.

Not at him, Tom realized, but at Kate, at the back of Kate's head resting on the pillow next to the window.

Finally the whistle blew, the train lurched, clanked, and began crawling along the track out of town.

The doctor's white figure slipped across the window, out of sight.

Tom smiled. "Not much of a honeymoon," he said, "but we'll make up for it—next summer, I promise."

Kate laughed. "We'd better do it before then."

Something in her voice bothered him; as though she had a secret.

"Why, Kate? Why can't we wait? After all I've got a job—and there's the house. We can't just—"

"Because by next summer the baby'll be a couple of months old, and I don't think either of us will want to leave him."

Tom paled.

"How. . . ."

"The usual way." She was giggling again.

He smiled carefully, as though his mouth were sore, then a little wider—wider still.

The train was at full steam; it fled along the edges of the bays eaten out by the sea, south to Boston and New York.

* * *

Dr. More stood on the platform until the train was only a puff of smoke that blew away in the early autumn sunlight.

"C'mon, doc, we better get back."

He shook himself.

"Anything wrong, doc?"

"No—I guess not. I just wish I'd known."

"Doesn't matter. You'd've had to do the X ray anyway."

The doctor ran his hand through his sun-warmed hair.

"Maybe I should have told them—warned them."

"Ed," his assistant said, "you'd just give that woman seven months of misery, which wouldn't have changed anything."

"You're right. Besides—" The doctor stopped, waiting for his assistant's reassurance which had become part of the dialogue they had been repeating ever since the day he had found out.

"Besides"—his assistant took the cue—"everything might be fine—like as not, it'll be a perfectly normal baby."

2

January 30, 1931

PERFECTLY normal.

Kate examined every inch of her daughter's tiny body.

"Even fingernails!"

Tom laughed with her.

She grew normally. The little body chubbed out, thin blond hair grew thick, coarse, turned reddish, and Kate watched sadly every day as the blue eyes darkened to hazel. Kate kept track of every change in Jennifer's baby book—a sort of diary complete with the footprint and a lock of her hair.

She was unfashionably fond of her and spent most of the day in the nursery. Social obligations suffered until Kate's mother had to be firm. "Now, dear, everyone has babies, you can't let it change your whole life."

"But Mother, it has."

"Of course it has"—Mrs. Compton was fond of contradicting herself—"but there's no reason to make a fetish of it. Now, I've told Lee Fields that we would be there for luncheon on Thursday and I can't think of any more excuses for you. The baby will be perfectly all right. You've got Marjorie, Mrs. Salter. . . ." Kate gave in and began spending at least the afternoons away from Jennifer. But she was always home by four to attend Jennifer's dinner in the nursery.

Her mother was right in a way. Being away from the child made coming home all the sweeter. She couldn't even wait to take her coat off before she ran upstairs to the nursery, where Jennifer seemed to be waiting for her, flopping and gurgling when she saw Kate come in the door.

Then one day she spoke. But when Kate told Tom, "'Mommy,' just as clear as that, not that funny squeaky 'Maaa,'" his face took on a closed look that she'd seen more and more whenever she talked about the baby.

"But isn't that wonderful?"

"I suppose so."

"You suppose!"

"I'm sorry, of course it's wonderful."

"You don't mean it." He didn't mean it; he didn't care.

"Goddamn it, Kate, I said it's wonderful—all right, it's wonderful. Now can we just drop it? I'm sick of coming home to every grunt, every turd—"

She was too shocked to say anything.

"Forget it, Kate, I'm just tired."

Tired, of course, he was tired—she tried to forget it. Then one Saturday when Marjorie brought Jennifer into the library after lunch, Kate saw Tom watching her playing, trying to stand on the blanket Marjorie put down for her, with something in his face that shook her. It was a cool look, measuring, as if Jennifer weren't a child at all, but someone he was going to do business with, get the better of.

She told her mother.

"But darling," said Mrs. Compton, "men never react to babies the way we think they should. They're jealous because the baby takes so much attention. Absolutely normal, I assure you."

Jealous, of course, and tired. Kate felt like an inconsiderate fool. That night she began a new regime. She bought some new dinner gowns, tried not to talk about Jennifer. She listened carefully to what he said about the day's business. She planned and gave several dinner parties, inviting people she knew Tom liked and would feel relaxed with.

She could see he enjoyed the extra attention, spent fewer nights at the club, brought her little gifts on Fridays, a custom that had dwindled after the baby's birth. But his attitude toward Jennifer did not change. If anything, it grew worse as she got older.

Kate did not mention it again. But she realized that this was not the normal jealousy her mother had said it was, it was something else. She decided to ignore it, telling herself that someday Jennifer would do something so delightful that her father would at last be charmed.

Then, the day Jennifer broke the porcelain horse, Kate discovered that Tom wasn't the only one who felt oddly about her little girl.

Jennifer was almost three; it was late winter, the quietest time of day. The morning chores just finished, the maids downstairs and Jennifer in the nursery with Marjorie, Kate thought. Later or earlier in the day she might not have heard the glass break.

When she opened the library door, she saw Jennifer standing alone on the hearthstone, the remains of the horse at her feet, her hand still curved where it had held the statue.

It was a blue porcelain horse that Kate had had since she was a child, one of the few things she took with her from her mother's house when she and Tom moved into the graystone on Seventy-eighth Street.

The horse was in four pieces. Two legs and the tail had broken off the torso, and were lying near it. Jennifer kneeled next to the pieces and gently rolled one of the detached legs back and forth with one finger.

"Oh, Jennifer, what did you do?" She had never raised her voice to the child before, but she was close to tears at the loss of the statue.

Jennifer looked up at her mother, then back at the broken horse. Wanting to help what had unexpectedly become a disaster, she tried to fit the leg back onto the horse's body; her eyebrows knitted as she tried to get the leg back into place, but it wouldn't stay and she began to cry.

Kate sighed, then kneeled next to her, gathering up the pieces, her anger gone.

"Oh, Jennifer," she said, "we can glue it back together again, see?" Jennifer stopped crying and watched while Kate fitted the other leg and then the tail, holding the pieces together so Jennifer could see how the horse would be repaired.

"What is she into now?" Marjorie said as she came into the room. Kate stood up to face the maid.

"You naughty girl." Marjorie waggled her finger at Jennifer who looked first at her mother, then at her nanny, then back to her mother.

"Where have you been, Marjorie? Why did you leave her alone down here?"

"I thought she was in the nursery—I didn't think she could find her way down here—but she's just into everything."

"Of course she's into everything. She's almost three—that's why you're supposed to watch her."

Marjorie's attitude had worried Kate for some time. She was a good worker, and at first she seemed quite fond of the baby, but lately she thought Marjorie was actually avoiding the child.

"I'm sorry," Marjorie said. She didn't sound sorry.

"Marjorie, what is it? Don't you want to work here anymore?" Marjorie looked at the floor and then at Kate.

"No, ma'am, I don't. I'd like to quit."

Kate was shocked. Over twenty girls had applied for the job three years ago, and Marjorie had been pitifully grateful when she was hired. Kate did not know much about the economic situation but she thought that nothing had changed to make it easier for a girl like Marjorie to get a job.

"Do you have someplace else to go?"

Jennifer was humming to herself, tunelessly, loudly, and Kate wanted to tell her to be quiet but stopped herself.

"Well, do you?" when Marjorie did not answer.

"No, ma'am. But I'll find something sooner or later."

Jennifer kept humming. Kate could see that the sound was annoying Marjorie too. Both women began talking louder to cover the noise.

"Marjorie"—Kate tried to sound kind—"what's the matter? You seemed quite happy here."

"Oh, I was. It's nothing you've done, Miz List, you've been just fine—" Marjorie stopped. Kate could see she really did not know what to say next.

"Then why?" Kate prompted.

Marjorie's eyes shifted to the still-humming Jennifer, and away. Very quickly. It was a funny look, unexpected, not a nice look. Kate turned and looked at the child too. Jennifer sat on the Turkey carpet, her head bowed over the pieces of the horse, chestnut curls gleaming in the winter sunlight.

"Is she too much for you, Marjorie? Getting too hard to handle?" Kate expected the girl to jump at the excuse. She always gave people a graceful way out whenever she could. But Marjorie didn't take it.

"No'm. It isn't that exactly. I been around lots of kids all my life. I have seven brothers and sisters, all younger than me. No, I like children"—there was a pause—"usually."

"Usually? Do you mean, Marjorie, that you don't like Jennifer?"

No answer. Kate felt a tiny fluttering in her stomach.

"Are you trying to tell me that you dislike Jennifer?"

"I don't *dislike* her, Miz List. I just think I'd best leave here. I don't think I can take care of her, and you'll all be better off with someone else."

Jennifer sensed altercation. She finally stopped humming and watched the two adults silently.

"You can't take care of *her?* Could you care for another child?" Kate was still speaking reasonably.

"I don't want to say no more, ma'am. I'm going to leave. I'll go tonight if that's all right."

"It's not all right at all." It wasn't the extra work. Kate had taken care of Jennifer many times. She'd bathed her, even changed her diapers. She loved dressing the little pink and white body while the serious hazel eyes watched her button a frilly blouse or tie the snowy shoes. Oh, Jennifer, she thought, and suddenly there were tears in her eyes.

The maid saw them and looked away.

"I'm sorry, ma'am," she said.

"But you haven't explained anything." Kate tried to sound stern, but her voice cracked.

The child heard. Her mother was crying, hurt. It wasn't Marjorie, she hadn't done anything except talk. It was the horse—she had broken the horse and made her mother cry. She hunched her whole body over the broken statue.

"I'm sorry," Marjorie repeated stolidly. Without another word she left the mother and daughter alone together in the sunny front room and went upstairs to pack.

Kate turned around. Jennifer still sat on the carpet, bowed protectively over the pieces of the horse.

"Mommy?" She wanted to tell her mother that she'd never break anything again, but she didn't have the words.

"Yes, darling, we'll fix it." Kate bent and began picking up the pieces.

Tom was home by four thirty. Kate found him in the study and without waiting until he took a sip of his tea she told him about Marjorie's decamping.

"Well," he said, not at all upset, "you weren't too happy with her lately anyway, right?"

"But that's not the point, she's going without any notice, just walked out on us—on *Jennifer!*"

"Is she going or has she gone?"

"She hasn't left yet, but she's upstairs packing. Tom, it's not that I mind being on my own with Jennifer until we find someone else, truly it isn't. It's just the way she's leaving—and she wouldn't give me any reason. As though it were some sort of secret—something that would hurt my feelings—something about Jennifer."

"Jennifer?" He tried to sound surprised but his tone was false. Kate tried to read his expression but he turned away from her.

"Do you want me to talk to her?"

"Yes—oh, don't try to get her to stay, I don't want her to stay now. Just try to find out why she's leaving."

"All right, darling, I'll see her now before she leaves."

"And, Tom, you will tell me what she says—whatever it is?"

"Of course I will."

"There's something strange about her, Mr. List. I know she's your daughter, and Lord knows, I don't mean to be rude, sir." Marjorie faced him in her tiny room, untidy now with clothes and mementos waiting to be packed into the big cardboard suitcases open on the bed.

"Marjorie," he said, "this is a good job. No heavy work. I think we pay well—"

"Oh, yes, sir, the pay's awful good. I make more'n any of my sisters."

"And she really is a sweet child. I know she seems a bit odd, but you'll get used to—"

"No," she interrupted. "I *won't* get used to her. I know she *seems* sweet, never cruel like some kids—at least not that I can tell. And she's smart, ya know, she's real bright. But there's somethin'—I can't tell you in so many words, just something to make me uneasy. And I don't want to . . . no, I *can't* stay near her no more. And that's all."

"Do you have anyplace to go?"

"I'll go home till I find something else. I don't suppose you'll give me a reference." She spoke softly.

"Leave me your address, Marjorie. We'll send you a letter next week. And, Marjorie, please take this—sort of as a severance pay. It'll help you until you find something else."

He took some money from his billfold while she watched him and handed it to her. She held the money, trying not to look at it.

"I don't know what it is either, Marjorie. I wish I did," he said, almost to himself. He went to the door. "Good luck," he said, and walked out.

"Well?" Kate asked as soon as he came back. He looked odd, his face hooded.

"She didn't have much to say." He sounded stilted. "Just that she's not really comfortable here. . . ."

"But Tom, I did everything I could to make her comfortable."

"I know. She's got nothing against you."

"Then I suppose she has something against Jennifer? Against a baby!" Kate's voice was shrilling.

"No. Kate—please, honey, she's got nothing against Jennifer. It's just . . . she says—" Kate waited.

"What difference does it make, Kate? Marjorie's little more than a child herself."

"It's just *what,* Tom? Tell me what Marjorie said."

"She just said that Jennifer made her a bit uncomfortable, that's all. That's all she said—'uneasy.' It's nothing Jennifer did. These things happen." He spoke very quickly, his eyes on the floor, then to the side—looking anywhere but at his wife.

"What does she mean, 'uneasy'?"

"I don't know."

"I think you do know. I think you understand perfectly. You avoid her too, don't you? Your own daughter, and every time she comes into a room, you leave. You never play with her—you never talk about her. You don't even carry her picture—why?"

"Kate, you're working yourself up over nothing. I love Jennifer—but you know how it is—fathers never seem to care enough—" He tried to lighten things. "My mother nagged Dad the same way when we were kids, really she did, Kate. Kate?" He was next to her trying to put his arms around her. "Oh, Kate." She was crying.

"Why, Tom?" she sobbed. "What's wrong with her?"

He did not know what to say. He just held her and let her cry.

3

March 5, 1933

"TOM," KATE called. "Tom." When she reached the landing, she heard the study doors slide back. Breathless, but still running, she reached him, her arms held wide. She stopped suddenly, dead in front of him.

"Kate, what's the matter?"

"Oh dear, I'm pregnant."

Then the outflung arms were around him, hugging him.

"Tom, it's a boy, I know it's a boy."

He held her against him, her face and hair still cold from the outside.

"A boy," he thought. One hand slid under her coat and down her back. "A boy."

Then, over her shoulder, like a small shadow across his joy, he saw his daughter at the door of the study.

"Mommy?"

Oh, Christ, he thought. "Mommy?" He mimicked the tentative tone in his mind. Why the hell can't she just walk into a room?

Jennifer took a few timid steps, almost sidling—because he was there, because her precious Mommy was in his arms.

"What is it, Jennifer?" His voice was sharper than he meant it to be. She almost cringed, and that made him want to hit her. Still, she faced him, her eyes unwavering.

"I heard Mommy. . . ."

"Of course you heard Mommy—she's home."

Kate extricated herself from his arms and he watched while they greeted each other the way they always did, as if they had been apart for years.

Jennifer was four. His early uneasiness had changed—now he disliked her, sometimes even hated her when she hung on to Kate too much. He was a good man, he thought. Honest, plain, and rich. The best family—anyone would be happy to trade places with Thomas List. Only his feeling about his daughter shook the image, and that made him dislike her even more. Nannies had left one after the other, but he found their defection, and the aloofness of the other servants toward the child, reassuring. Their attitude made him feel less unnatural. Now there would be another baby, and maybe he could be a proper father. He felt forgiving.

"Jennifer, you are going to have a baby brother or sister."

"Oh?" She was clutching a fold of Kate's coat.

"Yes, won't that be nice?" As always, when he talked to her he felt that he was giving a formal speech.

"A baby?" She had never gooed or gagaed. She spoke distinctly from the beginning, without any of the little baby mistakes that Tom found so charming in other children.

"Yes, Jennifer. A little boy—you can play with him and help Mommy take care of him."

The gentle tone made her blush. She smiled, let go of Kate's coat, and took a step toward him. He had to stop himself from backing away from her. But she sensed the unmade movement and stood still. He knew it was a long time since he had touched her.

"Darling," Kate was saying, "call the folks and tell them—and call Tonio—he *must* have some champagne."

He walked past Jennifer to his wife. He stroked her hair while the child watched.

"There's got to be champagne somewhere in New York, and I'll find it. And we'll have the folks for dinner—a little party?"

"Yes, we'll have a party." She giggled, and so did he. "Lobster—Tom, we'll have lobster! Send Albert out and tell the cook." He started down the stairs and turned back.

"Kate," he called, "I love you."

"Then lobster and champagne—if you love me."

Jennifer was still standing in the middle of the room. "A baby brother," Kate told her, "a little boy. Oh, Jennifer, it'll be wonderful."

Jennifer laughed at her mother's happiness. Kate laughed too, then she took off her coat, and holding it in one hand she swirled it around in front of her, across her shoulder, and waltzed around the room. A new baby—she whirled, the coat whirled, billowed, faster and faster until the coat's hem hit a small, thin, crystal-bud vase that was standing on Tom's desk. The coat's swirl lifted the vase high, throwing its single flower clear—glass and flower spun in space. Kate reached out instinctively, although she already knew the vase was lost.

Suddenly the air pulsed, her ears went empty of sound, and the room became a vacuum. She was going to faint or be sick. She held onto the desk, legs buckling. The vase seemed to hang right in front of her for a split second and then it settled, not fell, to the floor.

The vacuum broke and Kate could breathe again, but she was shaking and her coat slipped from her trembling hand to the floor. The vase. She leaned over to look at it. It had landed on its base on the bare floor, not on the rug. It was not even chipped. The flower lay close to it and there were several small puddles of water nearby.

She looked at Jennifer, who stood several feet away, on the rug, smiling, very proud of herself. Kate straightened up, looked again at the vase, and back at the smiling child.

"Jennifer?" she whispered.

Jennifer's smile wavered.

Kate went to her daughter slowly. She put her hand under Jennifer's chin, tilted her head back, looked at her intently. The smile was gone.

One last time Kate looked back at the little unbroken vase, glinting in the sun streaming through the window. And then she drew back her hand and slapped Jennifer across the face as hard as she could. The little head jerked to the side and while it was still turned, Kate whipped the back of her hand against the other cheek.

Jennifer hiccuped. Kate slapped her again, then again. There was blood smeared on her mouth from a cut where her lip had smashed against her teeth. She kept hiccuping and tried to cry, but she couldn't catch her breath. Then the hiccups became gasps and Kate stopped hitting her.

Tom found them in Jennifer's bedroom. Kate was sitting in an armchair, Jennifer asleep in her arms. He saw the bandaged lip.

"Kate, what happened?"

"Tom, I beat her," she whispered. She had been crying.

"You *beat* her. Why?"

Kate looked away from him. "She—she—" Kate was stammering. Tom waited. "She broke a vase."

The first lie.

Tom stood looking helplessly down at his wife's bowed head, but she didn't look up and he didn't know what to say. Finally he left them alone together. He was not sorry about the beating, he thought it was a healthy sign—Kate had never hit Jennifer before. But he wondered which of their many vases was so precious to Kate that she would beat her daughter for breaking it.

Part II

1

STAVITSKY FOUND the report on his desk when he came in at nine. For a minute it seemed too good to be true—Amos Roberts was dead. That made Stavitsky's day.

He had first seen Roberts twenty years ago right after a fairly standard gang-fight that left a few blacks and Puerto Ricans in pretty bad shape. No one was killed, and in less than an hour the cops broke the back of the rumble and got the kids in the worst shape to the hospital. Up to that point, everything was predictable.

Then, a couple of hours later, a beat cop found the body of Julio Ososo in the hallway of a building on East 117th Street, and called homicide.

Stavitsky had only been four years on the force, and he had never seen such a mess. Riley, his partner at the time, had ten years in, but even he was sick.

All the boy's teeth were gone—so was his tongue. Burns on the arms, belly, and face. Both legs were broken in several places—probably with a hammer or length of pipe—and he had been castrated.

Stavitsky remembered looking at what was left of Ososo and thinking of the integrity of his own body and how fragile it was—how easily the mouth could become a bloody meaningless hole, how specious the solidity of bones and unbroken skin.

The murder made it a different thing altogether. They rounded up five leaders of the Spanish gang and brought them, silent and sullen, to the morgue at Thirtieth and First. When they were shown their friend's body, the sullenness turned to anger and they gave Stavitsky and Riley eight names and addresses.

Seven of the eight blacks were frightened, defiant, and silent on the subject of Julio Ososo. One was only silent. The others kept glancing at him under their lashes, quickly, and just as quickly away again. But he only looked at the two men who were questioning them.

Even now when he thought of the lightish eyes in the handsome dark face, watching him so coolly, Stavitsky shuddered. He understood then and now why the other boys were more frightened of Amos Roberts than they were of the cops.

They never pinned the Osposo murder on Roberts—although Stavitsky tried for weeks, and after that he followed Roberts' career like a one-man fan club.

Roberts had gone in a year later when he was eighteen, for assault, then four years later for pushing—arrest only, no conviction. Then attempted murder—arrest, no conviction, then murder one—no conviction, and finally pushing again, five years of a fifteen-year sentence, and he was out again—free.

Now he was dead.

Stavitsky unlocked the drawer where he kept Amos Roberts' file. It was one of seventeen that Stavitsky kept separately, locked in his desk. All seventeen were duplicates of originals in the main police file. He had the copies made outside the department at his own expense and he kept each file in chronological order—arrests, charges, convictions, time served—even transcripts of their trials.

He began separating them out a year after he joined the force. At first casually, just because they were special in some way—like Roberts. But as the years went by he kept the files more carefully, found himself looking through them at least once a day. Then, several years ago when they moved into the new building, he hand-carried the drawer across the park to his new office—and sometime during the trip on a slushy path through the brown mud and bare trees, he realized that the file had become an obsession.

The obsession made him different from the others. He knew it, and prized the difference, as his father would have done. His father had been a jeweler—small-time, a concession in the downtown diamond exchange; but he'd enjoyed the work and every few months he'd bring home what he'd call a special. Always a diamond. Sometimes one that was larger than the others, sometimes one whose color or cut was unique. Then, once, when Stavitsky was in high school and his brother just starting college at Queens, his father bought and brought home the queen of all diamonds. Not that big—about 3 1/2 carats—but perfect, his father had told them, absolutely perfect. And the color! They'd all looked at it through the glass while his father told them what to look for. Stavitsky never forgot the thing—color and shine burning up at him from black velvet. A quick profit, his father promised. But it never was sold, and Stavitsky knew after a while that the old man didn't want to sell it. A display piece was his excuse, everyone needs a prize display piece, he told them. He'd kept it the rest of his life. On Sundays, when Stavitsky's mother took them down to their father's stall, he always asked to see it, rolled it in his fingers, stared at it through the glass until his eyes hurt. His mother sold it when his father died. He started to protest, but she wanted to move to Florida, and he tried to understand. He still remembered the pang he felt the day she told him, "Sixty thousand I got for it, Davey—your father was a smart man."

His father would have understood the file's specialness, his son's obsession. He had hated the "nothings" he knew who bought and sold stones without caring about anything except what they paid and what they got. He would not have seen the connection between murderers and diamonds, and the file's horrors would have frightened him and made him sad; but the obsession? He would have liked that—loved it; he would have liked his son's whole life, been proud of him because he was not a nothing, because he cared about the specials.

If the rumors were reliable, and they usually were, Stavitsky would be chief of police in '78 when McGinnis retired; his father would have liked that too, bragged about it. Even now Stavitsky outranked everyone in the building, except Algren, who was chief of detectives. But Algren was a dull, homely man who lived in Queens. No obsessions there. Still, Algren was a good cop, and Stavitsky knew that if he were the short, unhandsome one, he'd have been lucky to make chief of homicide, much less of the whole department. But he looked like everything the politicians and public could want—big, almost but not quite clumsily outsized, and blonder than dark—some Polish mixed with Jewish. The heavy solid Slavic features saved from coarseness by fine wide lips and large dark eyes. Not handsome enough to make anyone uncomfortable, but the few times he'd wanted a woman who wasn't his wife, he'd had no trouble finding one that pleased him and wanted him too.

A good future, and an obsession that set him apart from all the rest. He was feeling pleased with himself as he opened the drawer in which he kept his files.

They were murderers or men who ordered murders—but with a difference, like Roberts, and all of them were free.

Roberts' death left sixteen. Once there had been as many as twenty-five, once only ten, and every time Stavitsky was able to remove one of the files he both hoped and feared that there would be no more to take its place.

He slipped the Roberts file from between its fellows, hefted it on his palms for a moment; then he silently thanked whoever had killed Roberts, and tossed the whole thing into the wastebasket under his desk.

Now, he thought, they're going to hassle some poor junkie bastard that ought to get a medal.

Halfway through the last page of the report on Roberts' death Stavitsky stopped and went back to the top of the page. He read the whole page over slowly, then pushed the "bull pen" button on the intercom on his desk.

"Is Carmichael out there?"

"Yeah."

"Tell him to get in here."

Stavitsky didn't sound pleasant and Carmichael appeared in seconds.

"What the hell is this?" Stavitsky said. "What do you mean 'Cause of death unknown'?"

"Well, it was when I wrote that. There wasn't a mark on Roberts. He wasn't stabbed or shot or beaten—not even a bruise, he was just dead."

"And do you know now?" he asked.

"In a way," said Carmichael. "We got the PM report this morning—about half an hour ago."

Stavitsky licked his lips. He didn't want to seem too anxious, so he made himself wait a moment.

Then he said, "Well?"

"His neck was broken."

Stavitsky waited but Carmichael was through talking.

"Do I have to beg you for every word?" Stavitsky was getting annoyed, but trying to control himself because he didn't want Carmichael to think he was bloodthirsty.

"No," said Carmichael. "I'm sorry, David, I'm not being coy—but that's all there is—Amos Roberts died of a broken neck—separated C_1 and C_2 vertebrae and sectioned spinal column; and that's it. The guy who did the PM 'cannot speculate as to the cause of the injury.'"

"Now let me get this straight. Amos Roberts and two junkies named" —Stavitsky looked at page 2 of the report—"George Hawkins and 'unknown' are robbing an apartment when in walk the tenants. Roberts, who was a walking arsenal, lets them call the police and while they're all standing around waiting for you, Roberts just happens to break his neck and dies. Is that what you're telling me?"

Carmichael looked at his shoes and then at Stavitsky.

"Not exactly. Roberts was dead before they called the police."

"And not one of the witnesses can tell you how he died?"

"They say not. They all, Hawkins and the Gilberts, say they don't know. Look David, read the PM. There wasn't a mark on the guy, he wasn't poisoned, he didn't have a heart attack—nothing—he didn't even trip and fall, he just broke his neck, that's it. And no one knows or will tell how."

"Have you transcribed the interview with this Hawkins yet?"

"No. I don't think they've gotten near it yet. There must be a hundred tapes down there to type. I can get the tape though, and we can listen to it."

"Without losing your place in line?"

"I have friends," Carmichael said, smiling at Stavitsky, who smiled back.

"Let me see the PM report while you get the tape."

The autopsy report on Amos Roberts was no help. The "Conclusion" told him only that Ira Stern, MD, Pathology, etc., could not tell him how Amos Roberts had broken his neck.

By the time he finished reading the report, Carmichael was back with the tapes of his interview with George Hawkins.

He threaded the tape onto the recorder Stavitsky kept in his office, and, after some scratchiness, Carmichael's voice came over the speaker. First he numbered the interview, and the case, identified Hawkins again, informed Hawkins of his rights—for posterity—and the interview began:

George, how do you feel?

Ah'm kinda strung out now. Roberts set up the job for us so's we can pay him. I ain't had nuthin' for a while.

Hawkins' voice was very soft and a little shaky.

Why did you go with Roberts?

Man, you know why—I was inta Roberts for four hundred bucks—he let us owe him for a bit, you see, and then he'd pull the muscle on us, set up a job somewhere and we'd have to do it.

What would he have done to you?

I wasn't gonna find out. I heard what he done to other people.

George, what happened?

We got in there okay—you saw the place, it was easy. Just took the elevator to the roof, roped down to the terrace, broke the glass door, and we was in.

Didn't the doorman see you?

No, we started in the basement, went in through the garage, and took the service elevator—easy as nothin'.

Then?

We just started collecting stuff together. Some cash, silver, jewelry, TV's.

What about the dog?

There was silence. Carmichael asked again.

George, what about the dog?

Roberts killed it. Very softly.

Carmichael waited, then Hawkins went on.

He sliced it—grabbed its front paws, lifted it in the air, and sliced open its underside. It took that li'l dog ten minutes to die—Roberts just left it on the kitchen floor moaning. It was a li'l dog, no bigger 'n that, and he didn't set up much fuss—we coulda just shut him away—I tell you man, I was on my pins or I woulda killed him!

Then what happened?

I wouldn't do no more, just couldn't. Roberts started on me, but Boots said to leave me be, there wasn't time and they could see to me later.

Stavitsky held his breath, if Carmichael missed the question—how could he, the stupid bastard? Then Carmichael asked quite casually,

George, what'd you mean, "I woulda killed him"?

I didn' mean nothing special, just that I woulda but there was no way—that's all I meant, nothin' else. Hawkins' voice was very shaky now.

But you said, "I woulda," not "I woulda." Why, George?

No answer. Carmichael repeated the question several times, but Hawkins would only mumble that he didn't know.

Okay, George, what happened to Boots?

He split, she let him go an he jus ran. He's white, kinda hillbilly, and he had it somethin' terrible.

Why do you think Roberts killed the dog?

Because he was a evil man. Hawkins said this firmly with complete faith. Stavitsky's scalp crawled.

Then Hawkins told Carmichael how the Gilberts had come home, found them, how Dr. Gilbert had mourned her dog. . . .

Stavitsky made Carmichael stop the tape.

"The *woman* is Dr. Gilbert?"

"They're both Dr. Gilbert."

The tape wound on, full of details, carefully elicited by Carmichael, but Stavitsky was getting restless.

Get on with it, he thought. What about Roberts, what the hell happened to Roberts?

Finally.

Roberts hit the husband, then what?

Well, the husband fell down, you know, and his face was cut and bleeding an' . . . ." Hawkins' voice trailed off.

Stavitsky was alert now.

Well?

Well, then . . . Roberts, he just sort of fell over. Very softly now. *Well, he did and I guess that's when he died.*

Just like that?

Yeah. Hawkins' voice was barely audible.

Then, without waiting for Carmichael's next question, Hawkins went on.

N-no one hit him or nothin'. I think Dr. Gilbert, I mean Mr. *Dr. Gilbert, was out cold for a bit and the other one, she was just sort of there, she was way across the room, nowhere near him.* Hawkins spoke very quickly, a little breathless. *No, sir, no one touched that prick—no one—he just died.*

Hawkins had become defensive, even frightened. Stavitsky wondered why. He made Carmichael stop the tape.

"Could Hawkins have broken Roberts' neck?"

"I don't think so," Carmichael said, "at least not without a hell of a fight. He wasn't as big as Roberts and Roberts had the gun."

They listened to the rest of the tape.

According to Hawkins, once Roberts died, the whole thing fell apart. Boots did not even try to stand up to Hawkins and the Gilberts. *So he just ran, and she let him go.*

Why didn't you run, George? Carmichael asked.

Very firmly, very clearly: *Because I'm just through, that's all.*

That was the end of the tape.

"What do the Gilberts say?" Stavitsky asked.

"Complete confirmation. The husband was unconscious when Roberts died, Roberts chopped him a good one, but Mrs. Gilbert saw the whole thing and her story coincides with Hawkins', exactly."

"Too exactly?" Something bothered him.

"No, they both saw the same thing happen, that's all." Now Carmichael was getting annoyed. "What is this? Suppose Hawkins *did* kill Roberts, suppose Boots did, why wouldn't she say so?"

"Maybe they threatened her." But as he said it, Stavitsky knew it was not true. Neither of the junkies had anything to threaten with.

Maybe then they really *didn't* know what happened to him. Was that possible? He remembered reading somewhere how a wrong twist could dislocate something—maybe that's what happened. Roberts had just hit Gilbert, he could have twisted in some freaky way. . . . Stavitsky had long since learned that the simplest, most obvious explanation was almost always the real one. Of course, he had to check, but it seemed clearer and clearer as he held the idea, that there was in fact no great mystery, just a quirk.

When he told Carmichael what he thought, Carmichael started to agree, then he remembered.

"But what about the PM? The guy who did it 'Refused to speculate.' Wouldn't he have said something like that?"

"Maybe. Maybe it just didn't occur to him. I guess it's a once in a million thing—he just may not have thought of it—I think I'll try to see him—see what he says."

"Shit, David, what difference does it make? Roberts is dead. That's *good!* You'd think the bastard was your brother. Why not leave it alone? The Gilberts won't press charges—Hawkins was unarmed, he'll go in for treatment. Let's just wrap it up."

Stavitsky was not going to listen to Carmichael. Nor was he going to tell Carmichael why.

In his twenty years on the police force, fifteen of them in homicide, Stavitsky had seen practically every kind of foolishness and brutality, but few mysteries.

Murders were usually the most obvious of all. Some poor dumb bastard had had enough and shot his wife, or stabbed her, or his girlfriend, or even a stranger during an argument in some bar. They only had to cart him away, still raving and sobbing, and no matter how sorry Stavitsky felt for the victim or killer, murder had become a routine, like any other.

But here was something different. "An evil man" had died in an unexplained way, and Stavitsky wanted to keep it alive, if only in his own mind, and if only for as long as it took the physician who did the autopsy to confirm Stavitsky's "quirk" theory.

"Well, Al, you may have a point—you just may." Stavitsky could be very convincing and even charming when he wanted.

"Tell you what, why don't we see if we can pick up this Boots—we don't want too many loose ends. Let's give it a couple of days and, if we can't find him, we'll just wrap it up—okay?"

"Okay," Carmichael agreed, but he wasn't happy.

"Give it a real try, Al, it'll be a favor." The "to our mutual benefit" gambit. It usually worked.

"Yeah, all right, I'll find him if I can, David."

"Thanks."

As soon as Carmichael left his office, Stavitsky called Dr. Ira Stern and made an appointment to see him at two o'clock. He would have liked to make it later, but Stern said he would be gone after three.

Stavitsky had other work on his desk, but he kept looking through the report—good address the Gilberts had, about the best, and good WASP names—calling-card names; William Ely Gilbert, III, PhD, and his wife, Jennifer List Gilbert, MD.

Stavitsky sighed. He had until two, he thought, and then he must relinquish his mystery.

* * *

He was on time for his appointment with Dr. Stern. He gave his name to one of the women at the reception desk in the main lobby and then sat down in a comfortable plastic chair to wait.

Roberts was here, quiet and harmless, in the basement, in a room as clean and ugly and spacious as this one. Stavitsky thought of the corpse itself, all that was left of Roberts—his mother might still be alive and Stavitsky realized with a sudden stab of shame that he didn't even know if she had been told that her son was dead.

"Captain Stavitsky?" Stavitsky nodded. "I'm Ira Stern."

Dr. Stern was about five feet six with very thick black curly hair, long eyelashes, and a dark beard shadow that began almost just below his close-set brown eyes. He looked no age at all but he must have been between twenty-eight and thirty—he was, after all, an associate in pathology. His white trousers were rainsoaked and he was wearing a sodden trenchcoat that had lost its belt.

Stavitsky felt dapper by comparison.

"Let's go to the cafeteria. We can have some coffee while we talk." He looked as though he needed something hot to drink and Stavitsky followed him to the elevator and along the basement corridor to the cafeteria, four doors beyond the morgue.

Dr. Stern did not try small talk. They made the trip to the cafeteria and got their coffee in easy silence. Then they sat down at one of the many empty tables, took a few sips each, and, in accord, relished the moment of suspension before they began their business.

"Dr. Stern?" Stavitsky broke the silence. It was already two thirty. "I'm here about Amos Roberts. You performed an autopsy on him last night and submitted report, ah"—Stavitsky consulted the report— "number four hundred twenty-five-XB-three."

"That's all right, captain. I remember the case. Not likely to forget."

"I've been trying to understand your 'refusal to speculate' as to what killed him."

Stern drank some more coffee. He was trying to choose his words so that Stavitsky would understand him, and Stavitsky waited politely.

"Well, the first two bones in Roberts' spine, the ones right at the top of his neck, which are very firmly attached to each other and, of course, to the rest of the spine, were completely separated. They are called in the trade C_1 and C_2—the C stands for neck or cervix, and the one and two designate their order. In other words, these are at the very top of the part of the spine that extends up into the neck. Right?"

Stavitsky nodded.

"The bones are formed around a kind of hollow that encloses the spinal cord and protects it. These bones, the vertebrae, are attached to each other by cartilage, or the disks. And the whole business is encapsulated by a sheath of muscle. It's beautifully engineered, made to survive.

"Well, Roberts' vertebrae, C_1 and C_2 vertebrae, were completely separated—completely—and the spinal cord was severed—no, severed isn't the right word—it was pulled apart, not neatly cut, you see?"

Stavitsky saw, or thought he did.

"It would," Stern continued, "take quite enormous force to do that, and as you know, Roberts had no other injury, none. Now that's patently impossible, no way it could have happened."

"But it did, didn't it? I mean, excuse me, doctor, but you couldn't be mistaken?"

"No, I couldn't be mistaken, not about what killed Roberts—but I'm sure you can understand why I was a little reluctant about committing myself to the cause of an impossible injury."

"Of course," Stavitsky said, "but, be patient with me for a minute, let *me* speculate a bit. I've read all the usual crap for laymen, including the believe it or not case histories in the *National Enquirer* of babies with two heads and tumors of the ovary that weigh one hundred pounds or more. And I seem to recall, very dimly, that it's fairly easy or at least possible to break one's neck by, say, twisting a funny way, you know—like you get a crick or. . . ." Stavitsky trailed off. Stern was listening to him, gravely, trying very hard not to look as though he were humoring the huge captain of homicide who sat across from him. There was no light of recognition in Stern's eyes, no "Ah, of course, I should have thought of that." Only patience—Stern was politely waiting for Stavitsky to finish so he could, as gently as possible, tell him how ridiculous his "explanation" was.

Stavitsky was suddenly very happy—his mystery was safe for a while, at least for the rest of the afternoon.

"I guess that's horseshit, isn't it, doctor?"

"Well, yes, you see, it really is," said Stern sadly. He thought Stavitsky would feel like a fool when he realized the enormity of his misunderstanding.

"Let me try to make it clear. The injury that killed Roberts was consistent with a head-on collision at eighty miles an hour or a fall from the top of a twenty-story building, assuming he landed on his head. There is literally nothing less, at least that I can think of, that could have done this to him!"

Stavitsky stared at the young doctor. Then he leaned forward and asked softly, "Have you ever seen anything like this before?"

Something in Stavitsky's tone made Stern answer back softly—almost whisper. "No, captain. Nothing like separation of C_1 and C_2, a split spinal cord, and no other wounds of any kind. But I've only been here eight months and I haven't exactly seen everything. I don't mean to say that it still isn't possible that it happened, just that I'm still fairly new at this."

Stavitsky smiled, then laughed. "Sure, I understand." He paused. "Look, doctor—can I call you Ira?" Dr. Stern nodded. "Ira, would you feel upset if I went, well, sort of over your head?"

"Why, no." Stern smiled. "I think I'd like to know what happened, too."

"Well, then, who *has* seen everything?"

"The head of the department. He's been doing PM's for fifty years, most of them at General. I imagine that what he hasn't seen hasn't happened. His name is Wilbur Galeston, and I guess he's what they call brilliant."

"You don't sound convinced."

"Oh, but I am. You see, he never even got a license to practice medicine and I don't think he's seen a *live* patient since he finished medical school—Harvard, by the way. Galeston is black, and back whenever he went to school, 1920 or so, that was the only school that would take him. It's still a joke around here."

"Did Galeston see your report?"

"He'll probably see it tomorrow, or the next day, maybe."

"You didn't discuss it with him? Something as far-out as this? Weren't you curious?"

"Yes, I *was* curious, and I wanted to talk to him. But it was only last night, and we're stacked to the walls—uh, files, not cadavers." Stavitsky laughed. "And," Stern went on, "I just haven't had a chance to see him yet."

"Where do we find Galeston?"

"He might be in his office; he might have left though, it's after three. Let me call upstairs and find out."

Stern left the table and Stavitsky had a moment to try to understand what he had heard. Unless the doctor was a fool, and Stavitsky knew he wasn't, something completely outlandish had happened to Amos Roberts. The more he thought about it, the more uneasy he became. He had merely hoped for a break in routine, a touch of romance, not an insoluble puzzle. But maybe Galeston could clear it up, at least give him a clue. He'd heard of Galeston but had never met the man.

Stern came back to the table.

"He's at home, but he'll see us." He had his coat on, ready to leave. "I told him I'd come too, with the report, and to help you understand. Galeston's over seventy and he hasn't really spoken to anyone but other physicians for years—he never has to explain anything to his patients, so he's a little hard for a layman to understand. I've heard he was better when his wife was alive, but she's been dead a long time."

When they were in the car, Stern said, "Captain, may I ask you a personal question?"

"Sure. And call me David."

"This Roberts . . . you're so concerned. Was he a friend of yours? If he was, I'm very sorry about what happened to him. I didn't mean to sound cold-blooded before."

Stavitsky had to cough to keep from laughing. After a moment he was able to say, "No, Ira, Amos Roberts wasn't exactly a friend. It's just that I'd known him for many years."

Dr. Wilbur Galeston was an impressive-looking man. Stavitsky himself was six feet two, but he had to look up to Galeston. The old man was still well-built, though thin and stoop-shouldered, and Stavitsky thought that when he was young he must have been huge. He was mostly bald now with just a fringe of gray fuzzy hair around the base of his skull. His face was deeply wrinkled, long vertical lines ran from his nose to the corners of his mouth, and from the pouches beneath his eyes to the sides of his chin. When he smiled, as he was doing now, his face seemed to accordion back from his large yellow teeth. The effect was strange and if Stavitsky had come upon him unexpectedly in a dim light, unable to see the clear, intelligent eyes, he would have been unpleasantly startled.

Galeston led them from the foyer into a large living room, windowed on one wall, that looked over the park. Stavitsky could see the room belonged to a man of extreme orderliness, who took no interest in it other than that it be neat. The carpet and furniture were worn, the tables and desk dusted but unpolished. Everything, books and journals, the odd knickknacks, in the places that were meant for them, but the room, which was really beautiful in its proportion and detail, had a droopy look, like the damp twigs on the bare trees across the street in the park. A sad room.

Then Dr. Galeston said, "I made some coffee and I have some cookies if you'd like."

They accepted, and he left the room.

When he returned with the coffee and cookies on a tray, Stern had the report out ready to show him.

"What was the name?" asked Galeston as he set the tray on a low table and sat across from his guests.

"Roberts, Amos Roberts—male Negro, thirty-four years old, six feet one, weighed about one eighty-five."

"Cause of death?" Galeston poured coffee and passed the cups and a plate of chocolate cookies to his guests.

"Well," said Stavitsky, "that's really what we want to see you about."

"All right, give me a few minutes with your report. Ira—you have X rays?"

Ira nodded.

Galeston put on a pair of half-moon glasses and without another word began going through Ira's postmortem report on Amos Roberts, while Stavitsky and Ira drank his very good coffee and ate the cardboardlike cookies.

When he finished reading, he examined the X rays, photographs, then asked a number of questions. Stavitsky understood neither the questions nor the answers. Finally Galeston turned to him.

"Mr. Stavitsky, I'm afraid I can't help you."

"Do you mean you can't explain it either?"

"I mean more than that. What happened to Mr. Roberts *couldn't* have happened. Now I want to make myself absolutely clear—*couldn't* have happened. This injury is not improbable, it is impossible. I believe that Dr. Stern found what he said he found—he fortunately had the presence of mind to take photographs and X rays, and what they show is incontrovertible. That does not mean that it *could* have happened, it couldn't. And all I can tell you is that it did and I'd give a lot right now to find out how." Galeston was excited, as excited as Stavitsky had been at the beginning of his talk with Ira.

"I'd give a lot, too, doctor."

"Do you understand what *did* happen?"

"I explained to him briefly," said Stern helpfully.

"Ira told me that Roberts would have to have been in a major violent accident of some kind."

"No, sir," said Galeston gleefully, his voice rising a bit. "No sir!" Galeston chuckled and wiped his nose and chuckled again, then laughed aloud. Ira and Stavitsky looked at each other—he was an old man, after all; perhaps he was just a little off. Galeston caught the look and laughed harder.

"Oh, gentlemen," he said, trying to control himself, wiping his streaming eyes. Ira and Stavitsky giggled a bit to keep him company. "No, gentlemen, I'm not senile," still laughing, but now in control. "Ira, this'll be your first paper. Ooo-heee!" Galeston whooped. "You'll read it at some meeting—yessiree—that'll put something up that collection of dead asses! Ira," he crooned, "what an incredible coup. And they'll try to figure it out, you know all of them, they'll try. Then they'll ask me . . . 'Dr. Galeston' or 'Wilbur' depending on which smart-ass it is . . . 'Wilbur,' he'll say, 'what do you think?' And you know what I'll say? Now mark me, Mr. Stavitsky, listen closely—because this is the only way Amos Roberts could've died as he did—I'll say, 'Gentlemen, in my considered opinion, some well-meaning physician injected an extremely small, atomically very dense dwarf into the ring of Roberts' atlas'—that's C_1, captain—'Now this little man carried with him an equally small, heavy lever and a very dull bread knife—yes! A bread knife. The dwarf inserted the lever between the atlas and the axis'—C_1 and C_2, Mr. Stavitsky—'and then pried them apart, like opening a vacuum jar with a press-on lid. Of course he had to apply quite a bit of pressure to do this, about—oh, two or three hundred pounds—no, perhaps not so much after all, he *did* have a lever. Now, he separates C_1 and C_2, exposing his real target, the spinal cord, which he saws apart with the bread knife, shredding the fiber so that it only *looks* as though it had been pulled apart. That, gentlemen, is where we get the appearance of torn undercooked asparagus, which is diagnostic of this rare iatrogenic syndrome!' How's that for a truly brilliant, imaginative diagnosis?"

Galeston's eyes suddenly lost their delighted twinkle.

"Short of what I have just described or some other phenomenon beyond my admittedly limited imagination, nothing I, or anyone else knows, will explain this. And, Mr. Stavitsky, it was not a dwarf—so it must have indeed been something else. But I can promise you, I don't want to be with you when you find it."

Stavitsky finished his coffee in silence and Galeston poured him another cup. Somehow Stern faded into the background and Galeston and Stavitsky faced each other. Stavitsky realized that Galeston, old and revered though he was, was not particularly benevolent—perhaps he was too intelligent for benevolence, he had seen too much. They stared at each other, Galeston thinking about the problem and Stavitsky thinking about Galeston and what he had said.

"What would you suggest, doctor?"

Galeston shook himself a bit and seemed to make a decision.

"I suggest, Mr. Stavitsky, that you forget it. Let Ira and me have our fun and try to consider this a medical and not a police problem."

"I'm not going to do that, sir. I can't."

"Then I'm afraid I've given you all the advice I can. If I were you, Mr. Stavitsky, I'd leave well enough alone."

"But you must have some notion, some clue—"

"Mr. Stavitsky, I've enjoyed our visit, I really have. Believe me, I would also like to help you if I could." Galeston made it clear that the interview was over.

"Just one more thing. You said you didn't want to be with me when I found whatever it was that killed Roberts. What did you mean, exactly? What were you thinking?"

Galeston leaned back and looked over Stavitsky's head, across the room at nothing. "I don't know—just a feeling. You see, this must have been *done,* although I don't know how. I'm just guessing, Mr. Stavitsky, but whoever or whatever did it, it was a pretty precise job. And, believe me, Roberts suffered."

Suffered? No one had said anything about suffering.

"But according to the witnesses—he just—I think the words were 'fell down and died.'"

"Then the witnesses are lying. No, he didn't just fall down and die, he suffered first—it must have taken a bit of time, too, because both his eyes were popped—right, Ira?"

Stern nodded.

"As a matter of fact," Galeston continued, "Roberts died in incredible agony."

Incredible agony. Galeston's words drummed at Stavitsky as he ate. So, he thought, Hawkins and the Gilberts had lied. But why! Suddenly something he had heard Hawkins say during the interview teased at him —he knew it was important—but when he tried to confront it, the knowledge skittered away just out of reach. He purposely emptied his mind for a moment, and tried again—but the memory would not come so he put it aside for the moment, knowing that later that night before he slept or tomorrow at breakfast he would remember.

He could barely finish the Friday night chicken, and, of course, Carole noticed.

"Dave." She always spoke very gently when she thought he was being silly. "So it's a mystery—there've been plenty of others."

Stavitsky fiddled with the silver, drank some coffee. He wanted to explain, to make her understand.

"No," he said, "no mysteries. Lots of crimes, but there's never been a mystery. We usually know everything that happened, we just don't know who did it. And it almost doesn't matter who because the creeps— they're almost interchangeable. They shoot someone, or stab them, whatever; only the name is missing and we could put any one of them away for any one of the murders and it'd be the same because they're all the same. But we know what, where, and how—it's never a mystery.

"Except this time, Carole, I don't know *what* happened. For the first time in twenty years, I don't know what happened."

She didn't like the way his cheeks flushed or the light in his eyes. Too much excitement. She shifted in her chair. Argument would only make things worse.

"Dave, I think you're getting worked up over nothing. I think your pride is hurt and you're curious—that's all. It doesn't even sound like there's been a crime. That doctor said it was a medical problem, didn't he?"

"Yeah, but he also said that Roberts died in incredible agony—his exact words. Which means that the witnesses lied. Now if there's no crime, why did they lie?"

"But from what you told me, nobody actually lied. They were asked what killed Roberts, right?"

He nodded.

"And they didn't know. Did anyone *ask* if he died in pain?"

"No. But if a man dies in incredible agony, someone's bound to notice, and witnesses—*innocent* witnesses—would volunteer information like that. They wouldn't say he just fell down and died. Believe me, Carole, once a witness starts talking, the problem is to shut him up; to try and sift what's important out of all the crap he tells you. And something like this? Christ, you'd have to put a gag on the ordinary witness to keep him from telling you about every single bloody second."

"But you can't expect a man like this Hawkins to behave like an ordinary witness—"

"I'm not talking about Hawkins. Of course he's not going to go into detail unless we pry it out of him. I'm talking about the Gilberts. Nice respectable people—rich from what Carmichael told me. And he said they corroborated Hawkins' testimony exactly—according to them, too, Roberts just fell over and died. But he didn't."

"Didn't you say the man was unconscious?"

"Yeah, okay. But the woman wasn't."

"Maybe she just didn't think of it. Or maybe she isn't the kind who volunteers information. I'm sure some people don't."

The woman—again the memory teased him. What the hell had Hawkins said? But it wouldn't come.

Carole was still talking. "And maybe the memory was painful for her."

"Maybe." Everything Carole said was plausible. But it didn't feel right, and he couldn't let it go; not yet.

Carole said, her voice very soothing now, "Then why not just forget it, honey? You've got so many other things to worry about." All sympathy. He didn't answer. "Come on, Dave, help me with the dishes or we'll be late."

"Late?"

"Yes, dear, it's almost eight. Sam and Arlene will be waiting for us."

Sam and Arlene on the thirteenth floor—bridge. And tomorrow a movie, after dinner at his mother's house. And Sunday the games—all day while Carole ironed and cooked and cooked, and Monday. . . .

Monday Galeston or Ira would call and tell him that the something or other had been overlooked and that Roberts had really done thus and so. The mystery all explained, neat and tidy.

The water was already running in the kitchen, and he began clearing the table: but maybe not, maybe. . . .

2

GALESTON DIDN'T call on Monday morning. The day ground through to twelve, Stavitsky had lunch in the office going over reports. The phone rang and rang, but it was never Galeston, and Stavitsky began to let himself hope that they hadn't found an explanation. Then at three o'clock, Boots—Charles Raines—was picked up at a welfare hotel on Eighty-first and Columbus. . . .

"He's downstairs now," said Patrolman Atkins, very pleased with himself. "Room 209."

Stavitsky was on his feet before Atkins had stopped talking. "I'll be right there."

He didn't wait for the elevator. He ran down the six flights of stairs and arrived on two out of breath and very conscious of the muscles twitching in his calves. He paused in the stairwell to catch his breath and wipe his face. Then, more or less composed, he went out into the hallway and walked as sedately as he could to room 209.

Boots Raines was sitting on the far side of a long table, tilting back so that his weight rocked on the chair's thin back legs.

He was the prototype of what Stavitsky's mother meant when she described someone as *goyish*. His hair and skin were the same pale dishwater color, both thin and a little oily. His faded blue eyes were red-rimmed, his lips thin, and his chin meager. There was matter in the corner of his eyes, clinging to the sparse eyelashes in little white granules, and he was desperately thin. But Stavitsky saw that his clothes were clean and pressed, his boots were shined, and he smelled of a fresh piny aftershave or cologne. Stavitsky realized how much effort it must have cost Raines to keep himself this well; but he fought the sympathy. He had to know what Raines had seen.

"We are not arresting you, you understand. We simply want to ask you a few questions."

"Uh-huh."

"You were with George Hawkins and Amos Roberts at 907 Fifth Avenue last Thursday night, during an attempted robbery?" Raines shifted, then flailed for a moment as his chair teetered backward. He saved himself from falling by grabbing the table. Stavitsky and the two patrolmen who'd brought him in waited while he tried to regain his composure.

"Are you strung out, Raines?" Atkins asked.

"I'm OK."

He didn't look okay, and suddenly Stavitsky smelled his sweat. The man was frightened, very frightened.

"Do you know why you were picked up?"

"No—I thought I was being busted for having some stuff." Raines had a drawl.

"You were at the Gilberts' apartment on Thursday?"

"No one's read me my rights, copper."

"No one's going to. We only want to know if you can tell us any more about what happened to Roberts."

Raines didn't say anything. In the silence, Stavitsky thought of the interview with Hawkins and how much more attractive he sounded than this one.

Then, out of nowhere, as he knew it would, came the memory he had tried to capture on Friday. He heard Hawkins' voice. . . .

She let him go an he jus ran—those were Hawkins' words—*She* let him go! Stavitsky let the memory sink in while he waited for Raines to say something. The silence lengthened—Raines stopped teetering backward and was now sitting four-square, eyes shifting nervously.

"Well, Raines? What happened to Roberts?" Stavitsky's voice hardened and the atmosphere began to tighten.

"He died, that's all."

"How did he die?"

"I don't know." Hawkins' voice had softened when he spoke of Roberts' death, but Raines was growing strident.

"You know his neck was broken? Pulled right apart—did you know that?"

"No."

"He died in pain, right? Incredible agony?"

No answer.

"Well, Raines, let's hear it. Incredible agony, right? Tell me!" Stavitsky's voice had risen too much and the patrolmen looked at each other.

Raines was trembling. He tried to turn away, but Stavitsky followed, standing over him.

"His eyes had popped, hadn't they, Raines? Right out of his head!" The sweat broke out, started running down Raines' face. "They weren't—they weren't supposed to say anything—oh, Christ, I didn't tell you—oh, shit, tell her I didn't tell you."

"Tell who, Raines?"

"Tell her, please, man." Raines grabbed Stavitsky's hand, shaking so hard he could barely hold it.

"You want me to tell the Gilbert woman that you didn't tell us about Roberts—is that it, Raines?"

"That's it, man. You'll do it, won't you, man? Oh, God, please!" His reaction was outlandish but Stavitsky went on.

"You swore you wouldn't tell what killed Roberts, that's why she let you go?"

"Yes. I kept my word—I didn't tell you—that nigger shit must've spilled—make sure she knows that it was Hawkins, not me."

He was breaking. Stavitsky pushed. "Well, Raines, Hawkins didn't tell us. Until this minute we didn't know anything except that she was there—so, you see, it really was you, wasn't it, Boots? You told us. So you'd better tell us the rest."

Incredibly, Raines screamed. His eyes rolled and he screamed again.

He leaped up, upending the chair with a crash. His eyes stopped rolling and he stared fixedly and blindly at Stavitsky as he backed away from the table, still screaming at almost regular intervals. The shrieks tore at his throat, at their ears, smashed against the walls, reverberating until the scream was everywhere. His larynx began to weaken with the strain, and the screams grew hoarse, but he kept on.

The noise was deafening. They grabbed him as men began rushing into the room.

"Get Warner," yelled Stavitsky. "Tell him to bring a hypo."

Raines went on screaming but offered no resistance when they began pulling him back into the center of the room toward the chair. His screams stopped suddenly, and then, without warning, he broke away from them, running not for the door but into a corner of the room. There he collapsed, sobbing, his face pushed into the corner, in shadow away from the light.

The policemen stood without moving, helplessly, watching him. No one spoke. Raines' sobbing was the only sound in the room.

Dr. Warner came in, gave Stavitsky a dirty look and the limp, still weeping Raines a shot. The two ambulance attendants arrived and Raines, quiet now, on the verge of unconsciousness, was carried out. As the door opened, Stavitsky saw the men outside standing around watching as the attendants, Warner, and the stretcher bearing Raines passed them.

The door closed after the little procession, and Stavitsky was left in the room with the two patrolmen. He knew something terrible had happened, but he wanted confirmation.

"Did you see what Raines was doing?" He tried to make the question as neutral as possible.

"Yes," Atkins answered. "He was holding the back of his neck."

That evening after dinner, Stavitsky sat in the small room he and Carole called the den and watched the fish swimming in two aquariums he and his youngest son had established several years before. The room was dark except for the light from the tanks which rippled up the walls and across the ceiling. Stavitsky was alone in the apartment; Carole had gone to visit Mrs. Korn on the eighth floor.

He did not mention Raines or the case to her, and she seemed not to notice anything wrong, so dinner passed smoothly, if with less conversation than usual. Stavitsky was relieved when she left, and now he just sat watching the little brightly colored fish glide back and forth across their glowing glass boxes.

He had seen frightened men before, many of them. He had seen men who knew they were going to die. But he had never seen anyone display the mindless terror that had broken Raines. What kind of woman was she? How had she threatened Raines? What happened to Roberts and what part could she have had in it? The more he thought, the more ominous his vision of Jennifer Gilbert became.

He had to see her.

He let another few minutes pass, then he shook himself, turned on the desk lamp, and dialed the number Carmichael had given him Friday. After a few rings, a man answered the phone, made Stavitsky wait; then another man came on.

"Hello."

"Dr. Gilbert? Dr. William Gilbert?"

"Yes. Who is this, please?"

"I'm Captain David Stavitsky of the New York Police." He did not mention homicide, although he wasn't sure why. "I would like to ask you a few questions about last Thursday night."

"Yes, captain. We were rather expecting to hear from someone, before now as a matter of fact." Dr. Gilbert spoke the standard accentless American that only generations of Yankees and fifty thousand dollars' worth of education can produce.

"Are you free tomorrow—say in the morning?"

"I could come down to headquarters, if you wish, about nine o'clock." Dr. Gilbert sounded pleased at the idea of "coming down to headquarters." He had probably never been inside a police station in his life.

"I'd rather not drag you downtown, doctor—besides, it's difficult to talk there—too much going on. Would you mind if I came to your apartment—say at ten?"

"No, I don't mind, captain—that is, if you're sure the atmosphere won't be too distracting. I mean, I do not have a proper office at home." Dr. Gilbert did sound disappointed, but Stavitsky was firm.

"That'll be fine, doctor—no reason why we can't be comfortable. Then I'll see you at ten."

"Oh, but, captain, my wife isn't here. She's out of town until tomorrow. Perhaps we should wait until—" Not there. He would have to wait to see her . . . just as well; some time to prepare.

"No—that's fine, doctor. We usually find it easier to question husbands and wives separately."

"Oh, quite," said Gilbert. "Well, then, I'll see you at ten, captain—ah, you have the address? It's—"

"Yes, doctor, we have the address."

3

THE ELEVATOR door opened and he faced a small carpeted foyer and large double doors—no hallway, no other apartments. The elevator stayed where it was with the door open and the guard watching until somebody let Stavitsky in.

Stavitsky rang the bell under which a small engraved brass plate discreetly announced GILBERT.

One of the double doors was opened by a handsome middle-aged black man wearing an expensive new dark-blue suit.

"Captain Stavitsky?" Stavitsky had heard the man's voice before but he couldn't remember where.

Stavitsky showed his ID. The man nodded toward the elevator and Stavitsky heard the doors shut behind him and the elevator hum downward. The door was opened wide, the man stood aside, and Stavitsky entered William and Jennifer Gilbert's home—through a marble-floored foyer, down three stairs and into the living room.

The terrace was there, just as Hawkins had said, beyond the huge windows that flanked the room on three sides.

But the terrace was a garden. There was a stone, ivy-colored wall surrounding it, there were trees and what looked like paths—now all lightly covered with snow. No hint of the city beyond, just the garden, sky, and the blowing snow. The room itself must have been fifty feet long, furnished quietly in what Carole would probably have considered "no style at all." And she would have been right. Nothing in the room looked chosen. The furniture belonged to the Gilberts and had belonged to their parents, grandparents, and beyond. It was simply collected through the generations. A few pieces probably from the very beginning, carefully carted from England sometime during the seventeenth century. The rest was a legacy of three hundred years of good taste and solid finances.

Stavitsky was appalled. He had never imagined that such a room could exist without people being able to pay to see it. In the middle of it, looking a little small but not a bit lost, was an almost shabbily dressed man of about fifty. Stavitsky walked quickly toward him to save the man the awkwardness of having to cross the enormous expanse that separated them. But Stavitsky realized halfway across the room that while William Gilbert might sound a bit foolish with a policeman on the phone he was not awkward. They met somewhere in the middle and shook hands.

The entire left side of Gilbert's face was a purple bruise, the eye still almost closed, and a large gauze bandage covered his cheekbone where the split skin had been stitched.

"What did Roberts hit you with?"

"With his gun." No outrage, no bid for sympathy, just a simple statement.

"I've asked to have some coffee served in my study," continued Gilbert without waiting for Stavitsky to comment on the wound. "I thought we'd be more comfortable there."

Stavitsky followed the smaller man up a wide, curving staircase to the second floor, and saw, just before they entered the study, that the staircase kept going, and that the apartment had at least three floors.

The study was two walls of bookcases floor to ceiling, one of windows and one of watercolors of hundreds of different kinds of insects—some extraordinarily beautiful and others grotesque, nightmare creatures.

In his way, Stavitsky was as superb an observer as Wilbur Galeston was in his. It was this talent and his enjoyment of it that was perhaps most responsible for Stavitsky joining the police force. It had been wasted, of course, and Stavitsky often thought that in another time and place he might have been one of the great detectives. But, without regret, he used his gift when he could. Now, sitting across from Gilbert in a huge comfortable armchair, he looked carefully and unashamedly at the other man, ticking off the details as he noticed them, and arranging them almost instantly into a pattern that would tell him a great deal about Gilbert, and perhaps about his wife.

William Gilbert was less than casual about his appearance, but someone close to him was not. He was wearing a very old sportcoat that had been made for him—the tweed was too heavy for this country and must have been brought from England—the standard fabric imports were much finer and lighter to allow for American central heating. But the coat was American cut, so it had been made here, about twenty years ago judging from the style. Despite the excellence of the fabric and the tailoring, it was too worn to look well. But apparently Gilbert had refused to give it up, so someone had taken up the sleeves—they were a fraction too short, which the original tailor never would have allowed— to hide frayed cuffs. The elbows were carefully patched with suede that was much newer than the coat itself, and the pockets and buttonholes were mended, skillfully, but so often that the mends were by now obvious. His trousers, again by the style, were old, though not as old as the jacket, and they too had seen the same careful hand at the pocket edges (which always frayed first) and at the fly. No fabric could stand much American dry cleaning—but the trousers were not very wrinkled, so they had been pressed, probably by hand, and cleaned as infrequently as possible. Only the sportshirt was new, fine cotton fabric with a small monogram just visible beneath the unbuttoned coat—custom made, and William Gilbert was not a man who would bother to have his shirts made.

Stavitsky realized that because Gilbert was a rich man, he could buy all the care he needed or wanted. But his shoes were the real tipoff. They too were old, kept soft and gleaming by countless polishings. Gilbert had not been outside this morning because the shoes were not dulled by the damp streets, but they were scuffed, so they had not been shined for a day or two. The maid was around ("I asked for coffee to be served," etc.) and the butler opened the door. Only his wife was not at home.

Then, thought Stavitsky, she polishes his shoes, mends his clothes, and has taken the trouble to get his measurements and have his shirts made for him.

In the gray light of the snowy morning, Dr. Gilbert himself looked sleek and slightly rosy; his face except for the ghastly bruise was smooth and relaxed. Everything about him was a clue to the care lavished on him. He was well-fed, certainly, but still lean enough. His hands were smooth, the nails neatly trimmed (the wife again?) and he had an air of complete, unarrogant personal confidence.

Stavitsky wanted to mark his discovery in some way, and said, before he could stop himself, "Your wife loves you very much, doesn't she?"

Dr. Gilbert, not at all put out, said in the gentle tone reserved for the less fortunate, "Yes, she does."

Stavitsky wanted to protest, he wanted to say that his wife loved him too, as much as Gilbert's wife loved him, but he knew it was not true. Gilbert was cared for passionately, with attention to the details of his person that would never have occurred to Carole.

Gilbert poured coffee from the silver pot into thin china cups and began to tell Stavitsky his version of what had happened.

He added nothing to what Stavitsky already knew about the scene—Roberts hit him, very hard obviously, and Gilbert was unconscious during the time Roberts died and Jennifer Gilbert "let Raines go." Stavitsky really wanted to know about the woman, and he questioned Gilbert obliquely, trying to find what, in addition to her attention to her husband, formed Jennifer Gilbert's character.

All he learned was that they did not seem to have many friends. Stavitsky kept trying to establish some common acquaintances, someone else who might know her, talk about her. Certainly he and Gilbert were worlds apart socially, but Stavitsky's knowledge of city politics and politicians was extensive, and he mentioned several names that should have been at least familiar to people in Gilbert's position. But if they were, Gilbert gave no sign, nor did he take the opportunity to discuss his own acquaintances. Of course this might have been simple reticence, but the phone on Gilbert's desk did not ring, and there was an air of solitariness about the place.

Stavitsky began to see the Gilberts as a couple apart from the world, concerned with their work and each other, and probably their dog, until the terrible intrusion on Thursday night. But even that probably had little effect. In fact there was something untouchable about William Gilbert. A sort of vagueness that spoke of a basic insensitivity to what went on around him. He was as uninterested in the fate of Roberts and his accomplices as he was in his clothes.

Stavitsky really had only one or two legitimate questions and then he knew he would have to leave.

"Where were you and your wife when they actually broke in?"

"On our way home from Jennifer's mother's house. We go there every Thursday, have dinner, and usually stay for bridge. But my mother-in-law was feeling tired—I think—that was it, and we left early."

"Did any of the men look familiar to you? Had you ever seen any of them before?" It was a hopeless question—Gilbert wouldn't recognize his best friend in a pinch, much less a doorman or handyman who broke into his apartment.

"No—I don't think so," very vaguely. "Why?"

"Someone knew you were going to be away—you usually stayed much later, right?" Gilbert nodded. "And they also knew the layout here pretty well. One of them must have worked here or known someone who did."

"Why, yes," said Gilbert, "that seems quite reasonable."

"But none of them was at all familiar to you or to your wife?"

"No—I don't think Jennifer recognized any of them. At least she didn't say so."

"One more question and then I won't bother you any more, doctor."

"Oh—" Dr. Gilbert sounded a little disappointed.

"Did Mrs. Gilbert tell anyone about what happened?" Stavitsky kept hoping for a lead, any lead back to Jennifer Gilbert. Without it, he must leave this house with nowhere to go, nothing to follow—and would have to face her tomorrow unarmed. Even as he thought it, he realized how odd it was for him to think he needed ammunition.

"I'm sure she told Mrs. Cransten." Stavitsky was surprised at Gilbert's tone—he sounded piqued. "She tells her everything." Very piqued. When Gilbert mentioned Mrs. Cransten he showed more animosity than when he spoke of Roberts, Raines, or Hawkins. Dr. Gilbert had been unable, for some reason, to ignore Mrs. Cransten. She was "Jennifer's best friend. They went to school together, grew up together, etc." All said very coldly. Was Gilbert jealous? Stavitsky wondered. Probably. He seemed the sort of man whose consciousness stopped at his nose and he might resent anything that interfered with his wife's obsession with him. On the other hand, maybe he simply disliked the woman. In any case, he gave Stavitsky the lead he needed—her best friend. Perhaps she would be more aware of Jennifer Gilbert than her husband was.

"Can you give me Mrs. Cransten's full name and address?"

Gilbert looked a little hurt but gave Stavitsky the information.

There was nothing left to ask. Stavitsky and Gilbert shook hands and the butler appeared to see the policeman out. Stavitsky looked back and saw that Gilbert was engrossed with something on his desk. He had forgotten Stavitsky already; in ten minutes he would probably remember little about the last hour, and as soon as the bruise was no longer there to remind him, he would certainly forget the whole episode.

The black man led Stavitsky downstairs and to the front door. Stavitsky reached the door first, opened it himself, turned back, and held out his hand. He knew now where he'd heard the "butler's" voice before. "Good luck, Hawkins," he said. "I hope everything works out for you."

Hawkins made no move to shake Stavitsky's hand—his pleasant face became angry, even threatening.

"You'd do best to keep away from these people, copper. For your own sake."

The voice had that same quiet certainty Stavitsky remembered from the tape: *Because he was a evil man.* And, as before, he felt the skin at the base of his skull crawl.

He faced Hawkins squarely. "Why my own sake? Who could hurt me, George?"

No answer. Hawkins' face shut down and Stavitsky knew he would say no more. The doors shut. Stavitsky stood looking at the carved wood. She'd hired him—bought him—an ex-junkie who'd been caught robbing her apartment. But Stavitsky had to admit he looked more like a butler now than what he had been. He was handsome, dignified, discreet—and obviously loyal to Jennifer Gilbert.

It didn't make sense.

Ellen Olivieri Cransten was the most beautiful woman Stavitsky had ever seen. She was very tall and slim; her almost too-small head perched on a slender, almost too-long neck. Extreme looks that if they were not perfect would have been strange. Her hair was thick, curly, and black; streaked with gray; cut very short to accentuate the neck. Her features were incredibly fine, long thin nose, pinched at the nostrils, and huge heavily fringed eyes as dark as her hair with the kind of shadowed whites that made them look almost blue and as though they glistened with tears. Her skin was very pale and, except for tiny lines around her eyes, it was flawless. She wore no makeup.

She had gone to school with Jennifer Gilbert so she too must be over forty, but she could have been any age from twenty-five to fifty, and Stavitsky knew that even at fifty she would be extraordinary. It was not the kind of beauty that depended on her mood or the weather or her hormone balance. It would not reflect her character whatever that was— it was perfect, immutable, as though she were carved.

Stavitsky did not take his eyes off her from the moment she opened the door to him until he left about an hour later. And he noticed that she watched herself as admiringly as he did. One of the living room walls was mirrored from floor to ceiling and she contrived to face it as often as possible with a graceful, subtle kind of preening.

She divided her attention unequally between him and her own reflection; during most of their conversation her eyes looked past him toward the mirror. He wondered how anyone, no matter how beautiful, could sustain such fascination with their own image.

Yes, Jennifer had told her about what had happened—too awful, especially the dead man. Why yes, she mentioned it, nothing specific—imagine a dead black man in one's living room—ghastly—but she didn't say if there was much of blood or anything. Oh, yes, she had known Jennifer, why it must be forty years. The last was said archly, and Stavitsky gallantly exclaimed his surprise that she should have known *anyone* for forty years. Satisfied, she went on to describe their "friendship"—ever since they were children. But there was little affection for Jennifer in her account. Jennifer was portrayed as Ellen's attendant—a plain girl on whom the beautiful Ellen took pity. Poor Jennifer, until Ellen rescued her she had no friends. No, she never even dated. Very fine family, of course, lots of money—wouldn't you know she'd be the one to marry a rich man—always happens that way.

Stavitsky looked around at the expensively furnished living room, at the severely cut black slack suit Ellen wore, at the diamond bracelet on her wrist. She noticed the appraisal.

"Of course John saw that I was looked after." So the husband was dead, and this incredible-looking woman was the Widow Cransten. "But of course nothing to what the Gilberts have—millions, my dear, literally millions. And except for that palace they live in, they spend nothing—absolutely nothing! I've always said money never goes to the people who know how to enjoy it."

Stavitsky thought of the Gilberts' home, what he had seen of it, and compared it to the starkly modern all-white room he now sat in—white thick carpeting, white upholstered furniture, chrome and glass tables, only the abstract paintings on the walls lent any color, but mutedly, mostly pastels. Ellen herself was the most vivid thing in the room, and Stavitsky thought she'd probably planned it that way.

"Of course she didn't have to marry for money, so she must have loved him—but he's such a pallid little thing—hard to imagine anyone falling in love with him. Frankly, I think she married him because he was the only one who asked her—wanted someone to take care of him—someone he didn't have to pay."

Ellen did not like Gilbert any more than he liked her. Jealousy again? Stavitsky did not think so.

"You and Dr. Gilbert went to school together?"

"No, I went to school with Jennifer—oh, you mean that—well, yes, I guess she is a doctor, of sorts—but she only does research, she never takes care of anyone."

She went on and on in the same vein, picking at the woman she had known for so long. Yes, they had been to school together—several schools. To high school, then to college—Barnard. But the friendship was a burden. Ellen was—well, popular, you know—and Jennifer had no other friends. Ellen tried, she really tried, but nothing worked. She helped Jennifer buy clothes and fixed her up with dates, but they couldn't wait to get rid of her and would never call again. Of course her family didn't help—too snooty. And in spite of all the years that Ellen sacrificed to Jennifer, the Lists had never made any attempt to socialize with the Olivieris. Oh, her father had money, but he made it himself and was not considered good enough to be asked to dinner. Ellen supposed the Lists treated her well enough, but that was because they knew that if Ellen deserted her, Jennifer would have no one else. Jennifer decided to go to medical school, quite right really, because it was apparent that no one was going to marry her. And Ellen, with the entire male student body of Columbia to choose from, married John Cransten—handsome enough, certainly, and lots of fun at first, but only moderately wealthy. Oh, he would have made money, Ellen was sure of that, but he turned out to have a bad heart. Had his first attack at thirty-two, dead at thirty-eight. Incredible luck! And she could have married *anyone*.

At this point Stavitsky tuned out and just let her ramble on until she tired herself out. He maintained an interested look and nodded from time to time.

So this was Jennifer Gilbert's best friend, perhaps her only friend, and when he remembered the vague, coolish, self-centered man he had seen this morning, Stavitsky felt a little jolt of pity for Jennifer Gilbert.

Suddenly he realized Ellen was saying something he wanted to hear.

"Of course, I thought it was all nonsense, some crazy ESP thing—a great waste of time. But Jennifer was fascinated. I don't think she believed any of it but apparently the man who was running the experiment and his assistant were the only people in the world who didn't find her distasteful—"

"Distasteful?" asked Stavitsky. "Did most people find her distasteful?"

"Well, perhaps that's a bit strong, but I don't know what else you'd call it—anyway, whatever it is people think of her, these two didn't seem to. They treated her as if she were some kind of star pupil. I'm sure their grants were running out and they were hoping she'd bankroll the project."

Ellen sounded bitter that there was one situation in which she had not been able to steal all the attention for herself.

"Did she go on with these ESP experiments?"

"I don't know. She finished medical school and was married by the time John and I came back to New York. She never mentioned it."

And, Stavitsky thought, you didn't care enough to ask.

Aloud he asked, "Do you remember their names?"

"No, not the assistant—" Too quickly. She didn't even try to remember it, so Stavitsky knew she did. But why lie? She was talking again.

"The head of it was a psychologist—I think his name was Ching, but I'm not sure. He was at Columbia, where Jennifer went to medical school."

"And she really was interested in this ESP business?"

She laughed. "Even Jennifer's not that foolish. No, they were nice to her, that's all, and she ate it up. I don't know, she probably ended up giving them money."

He'd had enough of Ellen Cransten.

"Thank you very much for your time, Mrs. Cransten." He was on his feet ready to leave, wondering if she would shake hands.

She smiled, showing small, even teeth, translucent at the tips. She wasn't finished with him.

"Then of course there was that strange Nantucket business."

Nantucket. . . . He sat down again, slowly, suddenly unwilling to hear any more about Jennifer Gilbert, suddenly not wanting to hear. Nantucket. . . . At the place-name a hunch whispered across the back of his neck, stirring the hairs.

"We never really knew what happened, but there was talk. So much talk that the Lists decided to take Jennifer out of school for a while," very snide, "which just confirmed the rumors, at least as far as we were concerned."

"What 'we,' Mrs. Cransten?"

"All of us at Miss Masters'. Jennifer and I went to school there, at Dobbs Ferry, except for the year she was away. By the time she came back everyone had forgotten the whole thing." She sounded as if she were still annoyed at her schoolmates' short memories. "But it was a terrible thing, and there must have been some truth to it if even the Lists"—her mouth twisted as she said the name—"couldn't hush it up completely."

"Could you be more specific?"

She could. Right at the beginning of the fall term rumors were going around that Jennifer had done something to a little boy that summer on Nantucket—the girls said some dreadful things about Jennifer. . . .

"What things?" Stavitsky asked.

"That she was sick, that there was something wrong with her, and that she was a danger to us all. At least that's what Miss Wardell, who'd taught art that summer on Nantucket told Mary Craig, and from Mary it had spread all over the school. And the talk went on and on—of course it made things much harder for Jennifer, but she didn't have any friends anyway."

"What was she supposed to have done to this boy?"

"Killed him."

The words echoed off the mirrors. Stavitsky's head pounded.

"How old was she when this happened?"

"Seven or eight."

"Do you remember the boy's name?"

"No, I don't think I ever knew it."

"How did she do it?"

Ellen shrugged, gracefully delighted with the effect she'd created.

The shrug got to him. Before he knew it he was standing over her, his voice tight, angry, too angry, too loud. "C'mon, lady, what was it? An accident—some kind of stupid accident that happens to kids—is that what you all tormented her about?" He was frightening her . . . exciting her, too; she forgot to watch herself in the mirror.

Her excitement pulled. Stavitsky made himself move back.

"When did this happen? What year?" he asked abruptly.

She was looking in the mirror again. "It must be thirty-nine, forty years ago. We were little girls then, both of us."

When he got back to headquarters, the bullpen was quiet—slack time, everyone was eating lunch. The place smelled of French fries; brown paper bags and coffee containers littered desks. He shut the door to his office and dialed the switchboard.

"Lorraine, I want you to get me the chief of police of a place called Nantucket. I think it's in Massachusetts."

It was almost one, but he had no appetite. He looked through the window at the wretched little park huddling between the buildings. It was colder than it had been in the morning, a gray, raw afternoon cold that sent the lunchtime crowds hurrying across the littered cement paths through the bare trees. The snow hadn't left a trace, and the wind rose sharply, scattering the few dead leaves, tearing at the people's coats and scarves, rattling the badly set window. The blower threw hot dry air in his face.

"It's an island," Lorraine told him when she called back. "About thirty miles from the Massachusetts mainland, off of Cape Cod."

No paper bag lunches there, Stavitsky thought.

Then the lines connected, and Stavitsky introduced himself to the chief of police for Nantucket Island, office in Nantucket Town.

"How do you do," the other end answered. "I'm Chief Starbuck. What can I do for you?"

"Chief, you're going to think this is a hell of a request, and I'm not sure exactly what I'm looking for—"

"Zat so," he said, very dryly. "Well, maybe you could give me just a little clue—'twould help."

Stavitsky laughed, and Starbuck chuckled with him. He started again. "There used to be some people lived there many years ago, named List."

"Still do, captain, have a house in 'Sconset, about ten miles from town. But they don't live here, they're summer residents. Come end of May, gone by mid-September."

"How long have they had the place?"

"Since before I was born, and I'm close to forty." He sounded eighty.

"About forty years ago, a boy was killed—some kind of accident, and one of the Lists—the daughter Jennifer—may have been involved in some way."

"Do you know the boy's name?"

"No, we only have her name."

"Not sure we can help without the boy's name, captain, but let me take a look. My daddy was chief here before me, and before that our cousin—all Starbucks, and they kept pretty neat files. Want me to call you back?"

"Maybe I could talk to your father or the cousin, if one of them was chief when it happened."

"Not likely. My dad died a few years ago, and Cousin John's been gone—oh, it must be almost twenty years. We'll have to make do with the files. I'll look tonight, probably give you a call tomorrow."

Tonight, tomorrow. . . . How easily the man spent Stavitsky's time. "Tomorrow!" he wanted to scream into the phone. "What the fuck are you going to do the rest of today?"

Aloud he said simply, "Tomorrow'll be fine, chief."

4

"THERE'S SOMETHING wrong as hell here," he told Carole.

She was quiet at first. Getting dinner, setting the table, moving from kitchen to dining area while he trailed after her trying to explain.

"The Cransten woman lied about not remembering the assistant's name. Why? Hawkins actually threatened me! A very odd thing for a junkie in a bad spot to do. Raines went to pieces when he thought he'd given something away. And the Nantucket thing. . . ."

Finally she stopped moving in the choppy way she had when she was annoyed, sat down with him, and let him tell her everything that had happened.

It was a relief to talk about it, and by bedtime she seemed to have accepted his involvement. When they got undressed and into bed, he held her tighter than usual until sleep eased his grip. He woke in the middle of the night, his arms empty, to find her sitting in her little velvet chair next to the window, staring out into the dimly lit park.

"What's the matter, honey? Can't you sleep?"

"David, what did Hawkins mean? Would he, could he do something to you?"

"No, it's not him."

"But what, then? What was that Raines man so frightened of? Could it, whatever it is, could it hurt you? Is that what Hawkins meant when he told you to stay away for your own good?"

"That's what I have to find out."

"Are you going to see that woman?"

"Yes, tomorrow if I can." Her shoulders sagged against the back of the chair. He waited but she didn't ask him anything else. Finally she sighed and got back into bed. He held her until she was asleep, then he rolled away from her and lay for a long time, thinking about Jennifer Gilbert and what he would say to her when they finally met.

He made himself wait until nine thirty. Then he called her. After a few rings, a Dr. Lambert answered. Yes, Dr. Gilbert was in the office—would he hold on? Yes, he would.

In a second he would hear her voice. His hands began to sweat—and his heart seemed to be beating in his stomach.

"Captain Stavitsky? This is Jennifer Gilbert. What can I do for you?" Connection.

The voice was quiet, even, diffusely timbred. If she were not careful to speak distinctly it would be a difficult voice to understand, but soft, pleasant to listen to.

"I wondered if I could take some of your time today, doctor. About an hour." He felt as though he were talking very loudly. "Just routine. We want to finish up this Amos Roberts business."

"Why, yes, captain." A lovely voice, really—his own sounded harsh by comparison. Most people's voices would sound harsh after listening to Jennifer Gilbert's.

"Are you free around noon? If you can come up here, we can have lunch in the faculty dining room—it's usually quiet."

The sweat was dripping off his palm, around the phone receiver, and trickling up his arm. The lovely, woolly voice waited.

"About twelve fifteen, doctor?"

"Fine, captain, I'll see you then."

Most of Rockefeller University had been built early in the century, but contrived to look as though it had stood overlooking the East River for hundreds of years. The city screeched and hammered around it, but when Stavitsky entered the university grounds, the normal New York bawling was brought to bay and with only a little stretching he could imagine that he was on campus in a small college town—isolated, protected.

She had told him nothing except "the faculty dining room." He entered the first building he came to and found, as he expected, a wood-paneled lobby, complete with oil portraits. The lobby itself was quiet, but there was a sense of distant unseen bustle filtering up hallways that led from the lobby into the heart of the building.

He asked for the faculty dining room and was directed to the double wooden and glass doors at the far end of the room. He pushed through them and entered a large clubby-looking dining room. The wood paneling continued here, gleaming with polish. The tables were covered with spotless white cloths and each table had its own little clear-glass vase with fresh flowers. There were very few people at the tables, but it was still early.

A waiter pointed out Dr. Gilbert's table. She was already there, sitting with her elbows on the table, her head bent over a very thick journal. She had pushed the table setting and the little vase aside to make room for the book and was completely absorbed in what she was reading. He stood there watching her before he went to the table.

The bent head was chestnut, graying, hair parted in the middle and pulled back, tied carelessly at the nape of her neck. Some of it escaped the tie, trailing in wisps down the sides of her cheeks.

"Dr. Gilbert?"

She looked up, and he felt as though he were face to face with someone he had made a very long journey to see.

"Captain Stavitsky." She said his name with a dying fall, as though for her too the meeting were some sort of consummation.

A clear, simple face, regular features, delicate, thin skin. Certainly she looked her age, or older, no, not old really, just worn. Her eyes were hazel, clear enough, set in with a "sooty finger," but the dark underneath them was larger than it should be. She might have been handsome —but she had no style to her, and her clothes were nondescript. But a pleasant-looking woman, the sort a stranger might ask directions of on the street. Suddenly the whole thing started to seem a little silly.

He shook the small warm hand she offered him and sat down. The table stood beside a large, many-paned window that looked out over a garden and beyond, the river. A few flakes of snow drifted by, and then more—she mentioned them. Stavitsky acknowledged them. Then silence.

She closed her book and lit a cigarette. Stavitsky fiddled with the vase. Minutes passed, the waiter brought fruit salad, though no one had ordered it. She killed her cigarette and smiled.

"Lunch is by the day—today is roast beef—no choice—he'll ask you how you want it, but it'll be well done no matter what you say. Mashed potatoes, gummy gravy, and canned green beans—but it *is* quiet."

As she spoke, the sweet warm voice quiet and pleasant, Stavitsky began to feel oddly uneasy. He had not smoked for ten years, and usually did not miss it, but suddenly he wanted a cigarette badly. He tried to respond to her pleasantness, but his discomfort deepened and he spoke more sharply than he meant to.

"Did you recognize any of the men who tried to rob you?"

He sounded almost rude, but she did not seem put out.

"Yes, the man they called Boots. He worked in the building, some sort of handyman. I'm not sure exactly what he did, but I'd seen him around several times."

He forced himself to eat a little of the canned fruit and then spoke carefully, more normally he hoped.

"We've had a hard time figuring out what happened, doctor."

"You mean to the man who died? Yes, it *was* very strange."

Stavitsky watched her very closely. "He was in quite a bit of pain, wasn't he?"

"How did you know that?" No sign of wariness, just a question.

"The physician who did the autopsy, or rather his consultant, told me that Roberts died in great pain."

"You did an autopsy?"

"Yes."

"Why?"

"Because we didn't know what had killed him."

She didn't say anything for a moment, then, "Why did the pathologist need a consultant?"

"Because his report was so strange that a second opinion seemed a good idea." Things were going a little smoother, but his uneasiness was still there—heavy and persistent as though he were coming down with a cold.

"And who was the consultant?"

"Head of the department—a Wilbur Galeston."

"Galeston?" She was jangled at last.

"Yes. But he was just as bewildered as the first man."

"You mean Galeston didn't know what killed him?"

"Oh, he knew all right—he just wouldn't tell me how it happened."

"Well, what *did* kill him?" The question was late, too late.

"His spinal column and cord were separated."

The waiter had not bothered to ask, he just brought two plates of the overdone roast beef, with lumpy mashed potatoes and pale green beans all soaking in cornstarch gravy.

They ate for a moment, or rather she ate. He cut the stringy meat and pushed it around his plate. The discomfort stayed with him, tensing his muscles and making him sweat.

"That's right," he said, too loudly, "broke his neck. Galeston said he died in incredible agony. Funny no one mentioned it."

She did not say anything, just kept eating. He tried again.

"You're a physician—didn't you have any idea what killed him?"

She looked up at him for a moment. He tried to hold her eyes but he was becoming more and more uncomfortable, and finally he had to look down at the table.

She was still calm and pleasant. "I thought the man had probably had a heart attack. At least that would explain the pain and sudden collapse." She was speaking carefully, but she was still on balance.

"According to Dr. Galeston it took him some time to die."

"Perhaps, but he went down very quickly." Stavitsky heard a note of satisfaction in the lovely voice.

"Did you try to help him?"

"No." She was smiling.

Stavitsky wanted to be horrified at the smile, but he understood and in spite of himself he smiled back. The uneasiness receded slightly.

"Why don't you just tell me what happened?" He was trying to be easy with her. It did not work.

"Captain, I don't know what killed the man. I didn't mention that he suffered because it didn't occur to me. Frankly, I didn't care."

"All right, doctor, you and your husband walked in on them, and Roberts got kind of rough—"

Suddenly something happened to her face—she paled, her eyes and lips narrowed, and Stavitsky saw the muscles in her cheeks tighten as she clenched her jaw. Her face was no longer plain or pleasant. Flesh stretched tightly across the bones of her face—she looked at him with distant remembered hatred.

"He hit William, with his gun—because he felt like it. He hit my husband—you saw him, you saw what he did to him."

Stavitsky sat frozen, watching her as she whispered hoarsely at him through clenched teeth, her lips drawn back, almost unmoving. She was leaning toward him over the table, and he wanted to pull back, away from her, but he couldn't move. He was cold and his skin felt tender, as though he were running a high fever.

"He was bleeding, bleeding," the hoarse voice choked on. "His whole cheek was cut open, and he raised the gun to hit him again, even though William was starting to fall." Stavitsky brought all his will to bear on raising his hands—he tried to shut out her words though his eyes were still fixed on her. All the air had left the space he sat in, there were no other sounds, and he knew that he was alone with the rasping, breathless, raging voice—and that he was going to be sick. The dog—it was telling him about the dog—he raised one hand to the edge of the table, then his other hand. With the last of his will, he pushed back. His chair moved and made a slight scraping sound.

The vacuum broke, air rushed around him, and Stavitsky grasped for it. He heard the clink of plates and silverware, the hum of conversation; he was back again. Dr. Gilbert was speaking quite normally now.

"Are you all right, captain?"

The little worn face was as he had first seen it, but now she looked concerned.

He was covered with a film of cold sweat, but he was no longer sick, and most important he was no longer alone with her.

"I know the food here isn't very good, but I've never seen it affect anyone like this before. You really do look ill, captain." All he wanted was to get away from her.

"Captain," she said softly, "I'm sorry. Come upstairs with me and I'll give you something to settle things down."

Her hand reached across to touch one of his, still clutching the table. He snatched it back with sudden instinctive loathing, though he knew the sympathy was real, that she *was* sorry. Sorry for what? he thought. What the hell happened to me?

She looked sadly at the hand, now safely out of her reach, but knowingly, as though it had happened before. She seemed to collect herself, sat back in her chair, and looked at him steadily.

"Do you have any more questions, captain?"

"Just one." His voice was phlegmy. "Why did you call the police?"

They both knew what an odd question it was. What else could she do but call the police? Why did he wonder that she did?

She smiled at him, a cold, secret smile.

"But, captain," she said, "I didn't call the police."

"Then who—"

"Someone in the building, I imagine." Her smile was happy now, and she looked quite pretty. "Someone who heard Amos Roberts screaming."

Stavitsky made it to the men's room, but not quite to the toilet, and he vomited on the floor.

Stavitsky knew he couldn't make it back to the office. Shaking, still sick to his stomach, he went home and called downtown to tell Carmichael he wouldn't be in until morning.

Carmichael grumped, "It's a mess down here. And there's some guy been calling you every half hour from Nantucket." He put the accent on the first syllable. "He sent you a Telex of a report this morning and wants to talk to you about it."

"Get someone to bring it up here—now." He hung up before Carmichael could complain. Then he brewed a cup of tea, made himself drink half of it, and eat a piece of buttered bread before he picked up the phone again. It took some time, the operator had to get codes, then there was a lot of clicking. Finally the phone was ringing on Nantucket Island, thirty miles out to sea.

"Took me all evening to find it," Starbuck twanged. "Still not sure it's what you want but it's all we got that even sort of fits. The date's right, accident, everything. Only thing, the List girl wasn't there when it actually happened—but she was there just before."

"Definitely an accident?" Stavitsky asked.

"Looks like, but they never were sure exactly how it happened."

Stavitsky's nerves jumped and crawled.

"And the boy died?"

"He sure did! Christ, wait till you see the PM on him."

Forty years.

The paper the original report was written on would be old, yellow at the edges. The Telex bond sheets that Carmichael's messenger had left with the doorman were smooth, gray, ink slightly smeared.

John Starbuck had written the report. He had been a careful observer and recorder, and the report was a model.

"Accidental death," according to the medical examiner-coroner. But

John Starbuck never agreed—at least not in print. In fact, especially since there had been no inquest, Stavitsky thought the omission of agreement very marked, as if Starbuck had wanted whoever read the report to note that he, John Starbuck, never committed himself to the accidental death verdict. The "investigation" ended the day it began. Miss Jennifer List had been interviewed, but had added no pertinent information. She had not, Starbuck wrote, even known that the boy was dead until he told her.

Stavitsky read the section concerning her avidly. But, though the rest of the report was extremely detailed, she was mentioned only briefly. Starbuck had even described the other witnesses physically, but not the List girl; only the bare bones of his interview with her recorded. Stavitsky wondered why.

The accident itself was a total mystery. A car or a truck—most likely a truck, according to the medical examiner, but here again Starbuck was silent—no corroboration from the investigating officer.

The witnesses claimed to have seen no car, no truck—still no comment from Starbuck.

No further evidence of the vehicle was ever found.

Stavitsky read the report through twice, and finally turned to the PM report submitted by Joshua Story, MD.

It was horrible; Stavitsky tasted vomit again as he read it.

But the PM ended too. Nothing left now except the Telex image of the signature. He stared at it for a long time as if the handwriting could tell him what had really happened. But it began and ended with itself: JOHN STARBUCK, July 22, 1936.

At about two thirty the same afternoon, Jennifer Gilbert opened a door marked Pathology in the basement of Manhattan General Hospital. The secretary at the desk glanced up, noticed a woman wearing a white coat, a black nametag, and a tweed skirt. Nothing else about the woman caught her attention.

Dr. Gilbert walked past the desk as though she knew where she were going, hesitated after she was beyond the secretary's line of vision, then crossed the brown tile floor to the rows of filing cabinets that lined the walls. Three other people in the room were already looking in the small metal drawers and making notes. All were engrossed in what they were doing, no one noticed the newcomer, no one questioned her.

She walked along the wall past the rows of drawers until she came to the fourth row from the end. There she bent over, finally crouched on her heels, and pulled open the drawer labeled RAY TO RUN. She made sure no one was watching, then she slipped one of the file cards out of

he drawer and put it in her pocket. She shut the drawer and walked
ack the way she had come, out the door, and into the harshly lit green
nd brown cinderblock hallway.

A few steps to the left was another door marked RECORDS. The room
ehind this door was empty. The file cabinets here were much larger
nd arranged in stacks rather than lines against the wall. The drawers
vere numbered, not lettered. She walked along the stack ends, consult-
ng the numbers printed on each, until she found the code 40-700 to
0-900. She turned into the aisle and took the card from her pocket.
The drawer she wanted was at the end of the aisle, almost to the wall.
She pulled the handle, it slid easily, noiselessly. The folders were
rowded together and she had to release the bar at the back of the
drawer before she could see the numbers on each folder easily. She kept
he card out, in front of her as she looked in the drawer, checking the
umber on it against the numbers printed on the large folders in the
drawer. When she found the matching number, she took the folder out
f the drawer, opened it, and examined the contents. Then she put the
ard into the folder, tucked the folder under her arm, and walked back
p the aisle to the front of the stacks. There she paused, stepped partly
ut from behind the cover of the cabinets, and looked around the room.
f anyone else was in the room, they were hidden in the stacks. She
valked to the door, looking down each aisle as she passed. They were
ll empty.

She opened the door to the room and stepped out into the cinderblock hall. Past nurses, doctors in white coats with black nametags
ike the one she wore, past the cafeteria clatter, equipment room, hold-
ng room (morgue), then out the green metal door that opened onto the
arking lot. It was very cold, and she was wearing only the white coat.
She hurried across the lined cement lot to a vintage, ten-year-old black
aguar sedan. She unlocked the door, put the folder on the front seat,
nd slid in behind the wheel, but now her hand was shaking so badly
he had trouble fitting the key into the ignition. She didn't try to start
he car, just sat there holding the file, watching the river, and thinking
bout the captain.

She knew he'd been sick in the men's room, and she felt sorry for
im then. But not now. She'd stolen the file—his fault. She kept holding
t, frightened of what she'd just done, frightened of him. He was pushing
er, and she was frightened. She hadn't been this frightened since she
vas a child, since . . . the Kearney boy. He'd frightened her, too,
ushed her, kept pushing, just like this man.

She hadn't thought of that summer for years. Their first time on the
sland, their first season in the 'Sconset house.

Part III

1

KATE TOLD her that Nantucket was a wonderful island. Far away, off to the left of the bow of the ferry, it looked wonderful—just visible in the twinkling fog. Magic Nantucket, where they were going to spend the whole summer, where there were beaches, swimming, no school, and, best of all, other children to play with.

The beaches *were* there, and she spent days exploring them and collecting shells. The sea on the bay side was calm, inviting, and she swam in it. There were trails through dunes, sand grass and bayberry, and fields of milkweed full of earwigs and butterflies.

There were other children, too, mostly from Boston or New York— summer children like Jennifer. Several of the families in 'Sconset already knew the Lists, and their children were expected to play together. At the beginning the children seemed willing enough. And for a few weeks Kate saw Jennifer playing with small knots of other children on the beach.

It was the first time Jennifer had ever had any friends of her own. There had been her birthday parties in New York, but attendance was forced so they did not count. Besides, the children avoided Jennifer. They came because they had to, presented their gifts, ate cake and ice cream, and then began pestering their mothers to take them home. They did not even play the way they did at the other birthday parties to which Kate took Jennifer. As if being *her* guest cast a pall on them, made them self-conscious. Certainly none of them ever came just to see Jennifer.

But now she was playing with other children and Kate started to hope. Her hope was short-lived. New cliques began to form—without Jennifer. The little girls made pairs, quartets—without Jennifer. By the middle of June she was alone again. Children visited Michael, he visited them, played with them. But Jennifer was always alone.

She developed a routine. Every day after breakfast she walked on the beach for at least an hour or two with a paper bag, collecting shells, pretty rocks, and dried bits of seaweed. Kate bought her a book on shell collecting, and she spent the rest of the morning "desmelling" shells according to the directions in the book. Then she would arrange them on cardboards by size and color, each held in place by a tiny dot of glue. The shells on each cardboard were set in rows, each shell as close as possible in size and color to the one next to it. And Jennifer learned, apparently effortlessly, the species of animals that once inhabited each shell. She could tell you its phylum, order, class, family, genus, and so on.

After lunch she would read, while Michael napped. Sometimes she would stay inside, on the sun porch, sometimes she would take her dark glasses and sit out on the grass verge which ran to the edge of a short sand-cliff that dropped to the beach. Then, when the cook or Kate decided that lunch had had plenty of time to reach the mysterious point in her digestive tract where activity would cause no harm, she was free to swim, roam in the milkweed fields, or ride her bicycle on the narrow, sandy, sunbaked roads and paths.

After a few weeks, she was lean and brown, her freckles disappeared into tan, and her hair lightened from the sun. The lack of supervision, so rare at home, chipped away at her habitual furtiveness.

Then one morning, after only an hour on the beach, Jennifer came home crying, her paper shell-bag torn and empty.

"Jennifer, what happened?"

"Mommy—" The tears cut streaks through the sand that dusted her face. "There were some boys on the beach, and one of them took all my shells, and he broke them and threw them away, and then he pushed me down."

Kate took the remains of the collecting bag from her, led her upstairs, helped her undress and, as a special treat, let her bathe in the master bedroom with some of Kate's scented bubble bath. While she was soaking and splashing in the tub, Kate asked who the boy was that pushed her.

"The others called him Hal," she said, "and he was big, much bigger than me, and bigger even than the other boys."

"Do you know his last name?"

"No."

Kate saw her out of the tub and starting to dress before she went downstairs to the kitchen.

"Mrs. Hussey—" The cook was having her midmorning tea, and Kate poured herself a cup from the ironstone teapot on the table.

"Yes, Mrs. List."

"Do you know a boy named Hal here in 'Sconset who might have picked on Jennifer?"

Mrs. Hussey found her employer reasonable about everything except her daughter. Nantucket-born and bred, Mrs. Hussey had been off the island only five times in her whole life—twice to Falmouth and three times as far as New Bedford. Nantucketers treated their children very differently from the summer people from Boston and New York, and she thought the List children were badly pampered. Still she rather liked the little girl. Of course she knew there was something terribly odd about the child, but she was a Quaker who had never questioned the rectitude of her faith or the existence of God and she found oddness less frightening than most people.

"Did he hurt the little girl?"

"Not really. He frightened her, I think, more than anything. And he took her shells away. Do you know who he might be?"

"It's probably Hal Kearney. Blond boy from the south end of town. Been some talk about him—seems to be kind of a bully. He's supposed to have beaten up a couple of children and there's been some bad feeling between the parents. Course he's much too big for his age—the older boys won't play with him 'cause he's too young, and he's got most of the boys his own age frightened to fits of him. I don't know if they egg him on, or if he beats up the other children for fun. Anyhow he's a problem and Judith Camp—she's the Kearneys' cook—told me the mother's a terrible fool. Won't apologize to the other parents, just keeps defending him. And one boy was hurt so bad his parents had to take him back home. Ruined the tyke's whole summer.

"Easy to understand, though." Mrs. Hussey was a creative talker, and Kate jumped at the opening.

"Why is it so easy to understand? It sounds horrible to me."

Mrs. Hussey poured them both some more tea.

"Well, Mrs. Kearney's over fifty, so's her husband—now Hal's only about eleven, and he's their only child, you see?"

Kate did see then. The Kearneys were in their forties when their son was born—an only child, so late. How terrible that he should be a bully, how impossible it would be for Mrs. Kearney to admit that her only boy was capable of wrongdoing. And of course the boy must have his own problems.

The south end of 'Sconset, above the beach, was nouveau riche only. The better families live at the north end. Snobbery was rife on the island and, as in town, it infected the children. Hal Kearney would be subject to all the subtle slights that the very rich and well-born reserve for the moderately rich whose heredity did not measure up. Suddenly Kate's always ready sympathy went out to the boy who'd broken Jennifer's shells. It made her feel much better. She had no interest in hating anyone, and she certainly did not want to be afraid for Jennifer. Now that she understood, or thought she did, she could forget the boy.

"Let's give Jennifer something a bit special for lunch."

Kate suggested brownies for lunch—Jennifer's favorite—and Mrs. Hussey started to make them.

Jennifer, smelling ridiculously of Chanel, came into the kitchen and sat at the table with Kate while Mrs. Hussey melted chocolate and chopped nuts. The warm sunlight grew soaked with chocolate smell and soon, while Kate and the cook talked quietly about this and that, Jennifer began to doze, her head lying on her arms across the table. Suddenly she sat up with a start.

"He *liked* doing it," she said to the two women, looking from one to the other. "He wasn't just angry or anything like that—he just *wanted* to break my shells . . . to hurt me. And he'll do it again if he finds me—he's a terrible boy."

Jennifer did not go to the beach the next morning, or the next, or the next. She wrapped the shell-covered cardboards in some tissue paper she got from Kate, and put them in the bottom drawer of her bureau, sadly, as though she would never see them again.

From then on she went no closer to the beach than the end of their lawn. She sat as close to the edge as she could, reading or just looking out over the sea. She wore the dark glasses when she was this close to the beach because she thought they would keep him from recognizing her if he happened to walk by on the sand below.

He had frightened her badly but he had also made her angry. A new emotion for Jennifer. She had stood amazed and helpless while he broke her shells against the rocks. He did it quite deliberately, almost carefully, to be sure that every one was ruined. When she saw the shattered pieces, she began to cry and tried to get the paper bag he had taken from her. He had pushed her casually away. There were two other boys with him who just stood and grinned uncomfortably.

"But they're mine," she cried. "Don't break them, please stop, please."

He did not seem to hear her. He just reached in the bag and selected a good-sized sea-urchin shell, bleached white, tissue-thin and perfect. He tossed it lightly in the air a couple of times as though testing its weight, and then pitched it hard, overhand, against a rock where it burst, the shards sprinkling among the other bits of broken shell.

Then she threw herself at him, trying desperately to get the bag back. This time he pushed her hard. She stumbled back several feet and fell down, all the breath knocked out of her. He took the bag, laid it against the rocks, and stomped on it with one foot until he was sure everything inside was broken.

"Dumb little bitch," he said to the other two, and they sniggered appreciatively. But their eyes kept shifting to the fallen Jennifer, and he was surprised at the way they kept edging away from where she sat in the sand. Suddenly he realized that they were more afraid of her than they were impressed with him.

He turned to look at her then, closely, but he saw nothing in the sandy tearstained face.

"C'mon," he yelled. And they ran away over the sand.

Jennifer sat looking after them until they were small dots far away on the long curving beach, wishing more than anything else in the world that she could kill him.

2

THE BEACH NOW off limits, Jennifer began spending more time in the milkweed fields. By the end of June the earwigs were there by the thousands. They clustered up the stalk and on the pods, their little black sleek shining bodies hanging silently in the sun. At first Jennifer was a bit afraid of their pincers and would try to avoid them. But after a while she found that the little pincers were quite harmless, and she began to like the earwigs. They were company in a way, and she began looking forward to seeing them. Sometimes she thought that she could actually tell one from the other, that some of them even recognized her. The fields stretched far under the sun, the milkweed stalks were sharp, the earwigs fierce-looking and the butterflies few, so Jennifer was always alone in the field. She made a small clearing to sit in. Carefully pulling up a few milkweed stalks, and laying them gently—not to disturb the resident earwigs—among their still-standing fellows. She came there every afternoon, leaving her bicycle at the edge of the field and following the same tiny crooked path to her clearing. There she sat and read to herself, and sometimes aloud to thousands of silent earwigs.

She would pick them off the stalks from time to time and look closely at them. They bent their sectioned bodies this way and that, wriggling to escape, but when she put them in her open hand, they explored the palm and fingers slowly, no longer frightened. She always put them back on the stalk that she took them from, so they could rejoin their comrades hanging in the sun.

Finally she would pedal home slowly, hot and dusty, to wash, have milk and cookies or cake, and sit in the afternoon dimness of the sun porch reading again, or dreaming, waiting for supper, and the evening radio programs.

Only on rainy days was she miserable. She sat on the sun porch watching the sea storm soak and bend the dune grass, listening to the wind and worrying about the earwigs. She imagined the ruts in the field turning to tiny streams, and if the storm was bad, to miniature raging rivers. She could see the tiny black bodies, struggling in the torrents, legs and pincers helpless while they drowned in the rivulets or smothered in the mud.

As soon as the storm passed and the rain stopped, she was on her bicycle, pedaling madly over squelchy sand trails and mud roads to the milkweed fields. But no matter how wild the storm, the earwigs survived. Even if the wind broke some of the stalks, when she lifted them carefully from the mud the earwigs were still attached, still alive. Of course there were some casualties, and she found tiny corpses in the puddles, but most lived, hanging silently, shinily as before, waiting for the sun. And Jennifer believed she could sense their relief when it broke through to dry the stalks and the ground.

Tom came to stay for the long July Fourth weekend and she could not get to the field for days. There was no rain so she did not have to worry about them, but she missed them, the field, and her little clearing. The day after he left was Wednesday, her day in town with her mother, so it was Thursday before she could go to the field—almost a week.

It was a perfect day, sunny dry; the sea mist cleared early and the late morning sun bounced back whitely from the sand trail and twinkled on the grass. Her pond glimmered just off the road and except for the pound of the waves, distant, rhythmic, there were no sounds. Blue sky, no clouds.

She left her bicycle at the field's edge, propped on its kickstand, and hurried through the dry, softly blowing stalks, nested with earwigs like little sun-baked shining bits of coal.

"Hello," she murmured as she passed, "hello."

When she approached the clearing she saw four boys, on their knees in a ragged circle, almost hidden by the milkweed. She was curious and a little disturbed and ran the last few yards until she stood over them and could almost see the clearing in the middle of their circle. The boy with his back to her was blond, big, and she realized it was Hal Kearney, too intent on what he was doing to look around. She wanted to run away. Her heart began to jump when she thought he might turn and see her and she took a step back. Then she saw something glint in the sun; a knife. She crept forward and looked over his bowed head at what was happening.

The ground around his and the other boys' knees was littered with earwigs—pieces of earwigs—even as she watched he picked one off a nearby stalk, the knife blade caught the sun as he carefully cut off the lower third of the small black body and all watched while it dragged the top piece of itself, stumbling and tilting, to overturn and die in the pile of its dead and dying fellows, its white grainy insides leaking out behind it.

"No!" she screamed. "No!"

The clear sparkling fresh air carried her scream across the field; two birds rose from the far stalks, circled, their wings shadowing the group, and flapped away.

Startled, the boy dropped his knife and jumped the wrong way, so that the heavy knife cut through his knee socks and nicked his shin. Jennifer's scream and the trickle of his own blood frightened Hal badly. He was pale and shaken—he looked terrible as he faced Jennifer. The other three, delighted with his discomfort, grinned, then giggled, though they kept clear of Jennifer. The grins enraged him, and, because they were three to one, he directed his rage at her.

Jennifer was on her knees, covering the dismembered earwigs with dirt to quicken death for those still alive and to hide the poor sliced bodies from view. She was too sick to cry, and too intent on covering the ghastly piles to notice Hal. Blood rushed to his face. He had never been so angry. The other boys stopped smiling and they all stood around the kneeling girl. The moment of quiet invited, and the birds flew back across the field.

Hal pulled Jennifer up off her knees by the collar of her blouse—buttons popped—for a second she was suspended, her legs still bent from kneeling, her feet in midair. He hit her, closed fist, in the face, then he dropped her and brought his knees up to her chest. Everything went black.

She had never missed lunch before. Kate was frantic and even Mrs. Hussey was worried. Jennifer finally got home about three, pushing her bicycle. She was too sore to ride. Kate caught her breath when she saw her, but managed to stay calm. She called the doctor while Mrs. Hussey took Jennifer upstairs. By the time Kate got there, Mrs. Hussey had her undressed and was washing the caked blood from her face. There was a large red circle on her chest which was beginning to purple, there were early bruises on her legs and buttocks, one eye was beginning to close, her chin was badly cut and would probably need stitching, her nose still trickled blood, but was not, as far as Kate could tell, broken.

By the time the doctor arrived, they had her pretty well cleaned up.

He stitched the chin, painted the other cuts with antiseptic, and taped her chest.

"One of her ribs is broken," he said. "Don't think there was any other real harm, no concussion, far as I can tell, but watch her—if she loses consciousness or has trouble remembering anything—acts funny at all, get her to the hospital—just south of Nantucket Town. It's the only one on the island. I've given her some sulfa and a shot of codeine so she'll sleep." He left some more sulfa with Kate, told her he'd be back the next day, and left.

Kate sat with her while Mrs. Hussey went downstairs to melt some jellied broth and make her some toast. There was an early-evening chill in the air, and Kate put a light quilt over Jennifer and opened the window a bit.

The little face was a mess.

"It was that Kearney boy, wasn't it?"

Jennifer nodded.

"Honey, do you want to tell me what happened?"

"I'm not sure, Mommy. He was cutting up the bugs with a knife, and I screamed at him to stop, and then he just went wild. There were some other boys—but they were afraid of him—they didn't do nothing to me, though."

"Anything, Jennifer," Kate corrected out of habit. "They didn't do anything."

"They didn't. Only him. And, Mommy, he just did it for no reason—he likes to break things—he *likes* it."

Simple words, but as she spoke Kate saw that she was angry, very angry.

"He's just a breaker, that's all, I guess. The shells, the little bugs, I think he was even trying to break me in a way." Something far back in Kate's mind fought to surface. Something from long ago—she almost had it, but then it was gone.

"He's done it to other children too, honey. I think there's something wrong with him. Maybe he can't help himself—and he must be awfully unhappy, Jennifer." Kate was not sure why she was almost defending him. The memory tugged again, but she couldn't catch it.

Mrs. Hussey came in carrying a tray with the broth and toast. They got Jennifer to eat some, then they left her alone. After they were gone, Jennifer snuggled down under the quilt, warm and safe in the cool twilit room, the sound of the waves rhythmic, calming. The earwigs faded from her mind at last, and her anger slipped away. She thought to herself that it would wait in the corner of the room like her clothes, until she woke.

Kate was dreaming, coming up from the dream, almost awake. There was something terribly important that she could not quite make out, a shiny object, hidden in a glistening mist. She was on the ceiling of a familiar room. The object was on the floor far below, glinting in the sunfilled mist. The ceiling opened, she floated up through it, the object below growing smaller in the swirling, gleaming haze. "What is it?" she wondered as she was waking. "What is it?" Suddenly, as daylight filtered through her lids, the mist in the dream room cleared and below her on the waxed parquet floor she saw a tiny crystal-bud vase sitting unbroken in a shaft of sunlight. Unbroken. . . . Kate remembered it suspended in dead air; Jennifer, smiling, proud.

Kate jumped out of bed and almost ran to Jennifer's room. She was still asleep, not heavily, but peacefully, her breathing light and easy. But today in the morning light her face looked ghastly.

Kate sat down in the little chintz-covered chair by the window and looked out at the ocean, just beginning to sparkle as the sun burned away the morning fog. She had to be very careful about what she said to Mrs. Kearney—a warning, just enough to keep the boy away. Because next time. . . . Kate looked at her daughter's swollen, bruised face. What would happen, she wondered, when Jennifer fought back?

3

THE KEARNEYS' maid showed Kate into a large sunny sitting room that made her a little envious. It was "done"—all in yellow—the furniture straight-lined yet delicate, with tall, graceful, yellow shaded lamps on glass-topped tables flanking a linenish yellow couch. Several mirrors framed in simple gilt hung on yellow-painted walls and the drapes were of a printed fabric, yellow and white. It had been a long walk from North 'Sconset with the sun blazing on the white sand road and back in her eyes. She expected the cool dimness of her own house—subdued, antisun colors and dark wood furniture. But this room blazed, the color, glass and mirrors catching and reflecting sunlight. She felt as if she were back outside and put her dark glasses back on while she stood waiting in the new, shining yellow room.

According to Mrs. Hussey, Mrs. Kearney was in her fifties, but Kate thought she seemed older—dry-looking, with wispy thin gray hair. But her eyes were lively and bright. She had too much energy to stay long in one place and circled the room before sitting in one chair, only to rise after a few minutes, circle again, and then sit in another chair. Kate could see that she was usually a cheerful woman, voice a bit too loud perhaps, but she was the sort who always worked the hardest for the bazaars, fashion shows, and balls. A woman without vanity, usually relaxed, happy, and kind. The sort of woman Kate usually liked very much. But wariness overlaid the cheerful vivacity and Kate realized that Hal Kearney must have told his mother what had happened, at least part of it.

Mrs. Kearney chatted about the historical society, ordered tea, then chatted about people they both knew—on and on, trying to forestall the moment when Kate would come to the point.

Kate let the woman talk. Mrs. Kearney kept jumping up, changing chairs, and circling until Kate was almost dizzy. Finally the maid brought tea, and Mrs. Kearney was forced to settle long enough to pour it; and was silent long enough for Kate to say, "Mrs. Kearney, your son beat my daughter very badly yesterday—she was seriously hurt, he even broke one of her ribs. . . ." Kate went on cataloguing Jennifer's wounds, while Mrs. Kearney sat stiller and stiller, began to look as if she were shrinking. Even her bright eyes dulled.

"My son told me about it," she broke in, finally. "He told me that she had crept up behind him and startled him so badly that he cut himself, and that he hit her thoughtlessly, as a reaction almost, if you see what I mean—he was, he says, frightened more than anything."

"Did he tell you about the shells?"

"Shells? No—I don't know anything about any shells."

"I see. Well, this is not the first run-in they've had, Mrs. Kearney—nor is it, I believe, the first time your son has had trouble with other children."

"Excuse me, Mrs. List, but I don't see how that's any concern of yours." Mrs. Kearney's defenses were up.

"You're right, of course, and I really did not come here to discuss any other difficulty your son may have had—only what happened between him and Jennifer. More important, Mrs. Kearney, what will happen in the future." Despite all her efforts, Kate sounded vaguely threatening. Mrs. Kearney flushed.

"I don't really know what you mean, Mrs. List. Harold was certainly not looking to bother your daughter. It was she who frightened him, it was she who started the whole thing. He was with his friends, Mrs. List, with his *friends*—your daughter was alone. Isn't that right, Mrs. List?" The tension had broken but in the way Kate hoped it wouldn't. The woman was angry, too angry and too defensive to listen to any subtle warnings.

"Yes, she was alone, Mrs. Kearney."

"And she frightened him, and the others. As a matter of fact, she seems to frighten most of the other children," Mrs. Kearney said nastily.

Kate tried not to listen, but the woman wouldn't stop. She went on and on cataloguing Jennifer's flaws. Kate's eyes began blinking behind her dark glasses as the woman's voice became more and more insistent. The room was getting yellower, hotter.

"—of course she has no friends," Mrs. Kearney continued, "always sneaking up behind people—that's what Hal said, sneaking up behind them like a little snake. She made him cut himself. You should have seen his leg."

"Snake" was too much. Kate jumped up.

"His leg! He broke one of her ribs, blacked her eye. Her chin was so badly cut that—"

Mrs. Kearney drowned Kate's voice. "He was bleeding." She hadn't heard a word Kate said. "It was awful. And she did it—she deserved exactly what she got!" Triumphantly. There was a moment of quiet. Kate took advantage of it, tried to speak calmly. She knew now that it was senseless to try reasoning with the woman—she tried something else.

"Mrs. Kearney, do you know who I am?"

"Of course." The anger had left her slightly breathless. "You're Mrs. Thomas List."

"Katherine Compton List, Mrs. Kearney." Kate was still standing. She gave the names time to sink in. Then she said, "And while we do not exactly travel in the same circles, Mrs. Kearney, I'm sure you know that I can make things a good deal less pleasant for you. Not only here on Nantucket, but back in New York as well."

It was not an empty threat. Mrs. Kearney swallowed. Kate saw the throat move.

She went on. "Now you are to reprimand your son, and tell him that he is to stay away from my daughter—from North 'Sconset if necessary." Kate tried to use the neutral tone with which she usually gave orders, but she was angry and her voice shook.

The Kearney woman's face turned bright red, splotched in the sunlight that streamed in the French doors. Her frail control slipped altogether.

"I'm not afraid of you and your snooty-arsed friends!" She was shouting and Kate wanted to cover her ears. "And I'm not going to lock my poor son up so that I can go to your snobby little teas. You'd better keep your daughter away from my son, and from all the other children she frightens so much. That's what. Because the next time—"

Something snapped. The too bright room, the strain, the yelling. Suddenly Kate was across the room leaning over the other woman.

"Of course she frightens them, you stupid bitch."

Mrs. Kearney's mouth fell open.

"Have you ever met her? *Have* you?" Kate stood over the woman, her voice rasping. "Have you ever sat in the same room with her? Watched her?"

Mrs. Kearney shrank back in the chair.

"Maybe, Mrs. Kearney, maybe they have good reason to be afraid. Very afraid."

She whispered this last into the woman's face.

"Very afraid."

The yellow walls sucked in the words, threw them back.

"Very afraid."

The effect was devastating in that beautiful sunny summer room where fear seemed so foolish—in a rich, secure house in the richest section of an island choked with money. The fear was strange to the two women, a new visitor that came softly into the sparkling room and sat unfamiliarly with them—uncomfortably—out of place.

Mrs. Kearney waited for Kate to laugh and say that she was being hysterical. But the silence went on, and the fear settled in.

Finally Mrs. Kearney whispered, "What do you want?"

"I want you to keep him away from her—because if you don't I don't know what will happen."

"Why should he be afraid?" Still whispering, "Why should I?"

"Because—because, *I* am."

The two women stared at each other for a long time in the quiet room, then Mrs. Kearney looked away. She stood up and rang for the maid.

"Is Harold home yet?"

"Yes, ma'am, he just came in for lunch," the woman said.

"Please tell him I want to see him at once."

The maid left and the two women waited. The sun was overhead, the room was hot, and Kate felt sweat collecting on her upper lip and trickling down her ribs from her armpits. The yellow room was no longer beautiful—its sparkle hurt her eyes even through the glasses. Mrs. Kearney looked wilted; too worn-out to even try conversation, and Kate was grateful not to have to talk. The silence was almost comfortable.

Then the door opened and Harold Kearney came into the room. Kate had imagined him huge—which he was for his age, much taller than his mother, even taller than Kate. She had also imagined a colorless, doughy face, insensitive, cruel—but his features were clear and delicate, wide-set blue eyes, straight heavy blond hair, clean and shining. He was a beautiful, wholesome-looking boy. Kate could imagine the wonder this dry, wispy woman must feel every time she looked at or touched her son. Kate knew as soon as she saw the boy why the mother loved him so wildly, why the cruelties were ignored and unpunished.

"What is it, Mom?"

"Dear, this is Mrs. List. She's the mother of the little girl who frightened you yesterday."

Kate saw that he was surprised—perhaps this was the first "accuser" he had had to face. His manner changed at once, the sullenness disappeared.

"How do you do, Mrs. List." He stood like a gentleman waiting for her to indicate whether or not she would shake hands. She kept her hands in her lap.

"How do you do, Harold." She had no more to say to him.

"I'm very sorry about your daughter, Mrs. List." He spoke sweetly and seemed genuinely sorry.

Kate nodded.

"Harold, Mrs. List has asked that you stay away from her little girl— she was badly hurt—and I have told her that you would. I want you to promise, both of us, Harold, that you will not go near Jennifer List again." She spoke haltingly; the words were very difficult to say. Harold looked as if she had slapped him.

"Why should I stay away from her? Let her watch out for herself— waddya want me to do, stay in the cellar?" The sweetness slipped badly. Kate could see that he was furious that his mother even implied a reprimand. Mrs. Kearney looked miserable, and Kate felt sorry for the woman caught between the anger of her too-loved son and the weird half-threat from a stranger who meant nothing to her.

Her fear of the unknown won. "I mean what I say, Harold. I don't want you near the Lists, or even that end of town. Do you understand me?"

He looked at Kate.

She looked back, keeping her face blank, but she felt the pull of the child's beauty, sympathy for his obvious shame and bewilderment. The sun caught the golden hairs on his arm; Kate saw that they were thick and that he was close to puberty. What a handsome man he will be, she thought.

"But it wasn't my fault," he said. "She frightened me, made me cut myself, and I lost my head—I didn't mean to hurt her."

"I want you to promise, Harold."

The boy threw his head back arrogantly. "I'm gonna talk to Dad."

Mrs. Kearney looked at Kate, but there was no help there. Then she went to her son and, as though they were alone together she said, almost crooning, "Hal, do this for me—just one little promise. Mrs. List is so upset, and the little girl is hurt. Just for me, sweetheart." She had taken his face in her rough, ropy-looking hands. "Just this one little bitty thing and then maybe we can talk to Dad about teaching you to drive?"

"You mean I can drive if I promise? Can I, Mom?"

"Well, I might be more for it, you know, I might; but, sweetheart, you've got to help me, too." She was cooing, and then she kissed him wetly on the cheek. "C'mon now, just tell Mrs. List that it'll be all right —you won't go near the girl and we'll never mention it again—it'll be just between us."

He looked past his mother to Kate and then rolled his eyes. "See," he seemed to say, "what a fool she is."

"I promise," aloud.

Mrs. Kearney was delighted—she kissed him again on both cheeks. Kate could see that his hands twitched to wipe away the wet her lips left on his face.

Jennifer stayed in bed for the first week. On Friday the doctor told her she could get up for a while every day. He took the stitches out, told Kate the chin was healing well and that the rainbow bruises would fade, the rib heal, and that she would be quite normal before the summer was over.

The first day up was all right—she reexplored the house, read on the sun porch, and thought about the earwigs only intermittently. The second day the cool fog blew away and the sun came out. The lawn and beach invited, the sun glistened on the sea and blazed back from the sand. She got as far as the French doors leading from the sitting room to the lawn and opened the doors wide. The sun slanted in, the sound of the waves became sharp, and the warm sea smell blew gently into the room. But she could not go any farther. He was out there; she knew he was out there somewhere and she could not bring herself to step out the door. She was too afraid. From that moment she realized that she was his prisoner, and she became a miserable little ghost in the house.

Only Mrs. Hussey seemed to understand. She let Jennifer stay in the kitchen as much as she wanted and sometimes let her help with odd chores. At first it passed the time, but the sun blazed in through the windows and doors, across the kitchen garden, mocking the little prisoner, and after a couple of days Jennifer became listless again and even admittance to the kitchen mysteries palled.

By the following Thursday Jennifer had been up six days, and they had had brownies three times. Kate spoke to Mrs. Hussey after Thursday's lunch had ended with the fourth batch of brownies.

"Mrs. Hussey, Jennifer is really on the mend and I think she's doing fine—no need to drown us all in brownies. Not that they aren't delicious, but she's not the only one in the house."

"Mrs. List"—Mrs. Hussey's tone was very firm—"if you think that child's just fine then you haven't eyes to see with." This was very bold, even for Mrs. Hussey.

"I can't imagine why you say that—the doctor says she's doing just fine —and I can see she moves more easily and her bruises are fading."

"Oh, she's *mending* all right, but she's just as wretched as a little girl can be. Do you know she ain't been out of this house since that boy trounced her? She looks out of the window and goes as far as the doorsill, and there she stands, too frightened to go any farther—just standing there turning her face to the sun. It's a sad sight, Mrs. List, a terrible sight. That child did no harm. Why should she suffer so much just for that bully?"

"Mrs. Hussey, there's nothing for her to be frightened of. I went to see Harold Kearney's mother, and she made him promise to keep away from Jennifer, from this house—even from this part of town."

"She made him promise?" Mrs. Hussey was very surprised.

"That's right, Mrs. Hussey. So there's no reason for Jennifer to be afraid."

"But how'd you get that crazy hidebound woman to admit that her son so much as spit against a wall? Well, no matter, 'twas a good job, however done. Then the nipper's got nothing to be afraid of at all. Well then, bless your heart, Mrs. List." She meant it, and Kate was touched. And guilty. It had never occurred to her that Jennifer was frightened of the boy. But of course she was—she did not know anything about her scene with Mrs. Kearney. Kate had not bothered to tell her.

She found Jennifer on the sun porch. Yes, the tan had faded badly, and she had the furtive, almost hunted look that scraped at her mother whenever she saw it.

"Honey, Mrs. Hussey told me that you haven't been out of the house all week. She says you're frightened of Harold Kearney. Is that right?"

"I guess. He could be out there and what if I ran into him? He'll kill me the next time, I know he will." Very matter-of-factly.

"But, honey. I went to talk to his mother, and she made him promise to stay away from you."

"How do you know? She could've just said that."

"I know because I was there and heard him promise."

"Did he mean it?" She sounded doubtful.

"Well, she told him she'd let him learn to drive a car if he promised, so he promised. But if he breaks the promise, if he comes anywhere near you or this house, even this part of town, he won't get to drive, and I think that's very important to him. He'll keep the promise, and you can go anywhere you want to. Jennifer?"

Jennifer was looking at her feet.

"Jennifer—look at me." Kate was getting angry. Her daughter did not believe her.

"Do you think I want you to be hurt? Do you think I'd tell you this if it weren't true?"

"No." Very sullen.

"Then why do you act as if you don't believe me?"

"Because you don't know him. He would say anything." Sullenness gave way to defiance. "But he doesn't mean it. He'll find me if I go out. He's probably waiting now."

"Oh, for heaven's sake, Jennifer, he's a big handsome boy." She remembered his beauty which she could not help contrasting with the plain, willful little face in front of her. "Why should he care about you at all?"

"Because the others are afraid of me and he knows it and he has to prove that they should be more scared of him."

Kate knew it was an amazing bit of insight—not only her assessment of Harold Kearney, but her recognition that the others were frightened of her. Suddenly, without really meaning to, she asked, "Jennifer, do you know why they're afraid of you?"

"Because I'm strange, because there's something wrong with me. But I don't know what. Mommy, do *you* know?"

She'd believe whatever Kate told her, and she waited for an answer. Her face was in shadow, the sun in her mother's eyes. Kate was going to lie—right into the trusting face—she had never lied to her daughter before.

"Jennifer, there's nothing wrong with you and the other children are not frightened—so there's no reason why Harold Kearney should want to hurt you more than he wants to drive a car. Do you understand me, Jennifer?" Kate sounded harsh and Jennifer nodded, but her eyes returned to her feet. She had hoped that her mother would tell her—that the pretending that she was just like the other children would end.

"Jennifer, answer me!" Kate's hand itched to shake her but she remembered the taped ribs.

"Yes, Mommy. He promised, I believe you."

"And I want you out of this house. I don't want you mooning around here anymore bothering Mrs. Hussey."

"Did she say I bothered her?"

"No, of course she didn't. But, honey, we're all getting very tired of brownies."

Jennifer smiled weakly.

"Now, out of the house!"

"Not now, not today. Please, Mommy, please. I'll go out tomorrow. I will—but not today." She was breathless.

Kate looked at the fading bruises and the pleading in her daughter's eyes. "All right, Jennifer. But tomorrow—and no argument. Out you go."

"I promise."

4

MRS. HUSSEY and Kate agreed that they could not simply throw Jennifer out of the house at ten and not let her back in until four. She ate her breakfast in frightened silence, hoping that her mother had forgotten the promise. Then she went onto the sun porch without a word about her threatened loss of sanctuary, leaving Kate and Mrs. Hussey in the kitchen. They discussed several plots to get Jennifer out, until they hit on one that would get her out just long enough to realize there was nothing to be afraid of.

"Jennifer!"

When she heard her mother, she knew the time had come, and she went into the kitchen where the two women waited.

"Jennifer, Mrs. Hussey needs some heavy cream. There wasn't enough on the milk and we forgot to leave the milkman a note about it. Would you go into the village and get a pint from Mr. Storey?"

Jennifer looked from one to the other, and they looked back trying to seem as though she had been asked to do the most ordinary thing. She thought of pleading, of throwing herself at her mother's feet in tears. It wouldn't be hard, she was very close to crying. If she made enough of a scene they would have to let her stay. Kate saw her inhale and hold her breath, and she braced herself for the tantrum. Mrs. Hussey saw it too, and she tensed. Jennifer's face started to turn red. Then, suddenly, she exhaled.

"A pint?" she asked. "Is that all you want?"

They both nodded.

"Okay," Jennifer said, "I'll be back in a bit." And without another word she went out the kitchen door.

"Well," said Mrs. Hussey, "that's a fine bit of nerve if I ever saw it—you've quite a daughter, Mrs. List, quite a daughter."

Kate watched the little figure out of sight. "Yes, Mrs. Hussey, she *is* grand, isn't she?" Kate turned to the other woman and they beamed at each other. "Really grand."

Hal Kearney was waiting on the beach as he had every morning for the past week. He saw her come around the house heading for the drive. She must, then, be heading for the village. He and two other boys were sitting on the piled rock pier that separated the List stretch of beach from the Bordens'. This was the first time any of the boys had watched with him. He had a feeling about today and had been especially persuasive this morning—bribing Johnny Cole, a Nantucketer, with five dollars —an incredible amount to a child from town, and threatening George Borden with a beating unless he agreed to give up his normal activities to sit on the rocks and watch with Hal. Two was all the audience he needed. He would have liked more, but these two would spread the tale of his final triumph over the List girl. Johnny would tell the other town children and George the summer children, and by tonight they would all know about the scene that was about to take place.

For a moment the possible sacrifice of learning to drive and the specter of his mother's whining when she found out that he had broken his promise shadowed his excitement, but the thoughts were ghosts, too unsubstantial to bother him. Then he thought of Mrs. List and the way she had challenged him with her silent dislike—worse than that—as if she thought there was something not quite right about him, like that freaky daughter of hers. The memory and the touch of hatred it brought with it got him going. He jumped off the rocks and started up the beach to follow the figure which had just turned out of the driveway toward 'Sconset Village.

"Well," he called back to the other two, "wanna have a little fun?"

At first Jennifer walked very fast. She wanted to get there and back as quickly as she could, and she steeled herself against the sunny breeze and the outdoor smells and sounds. But the rib began to ache lightly. Then, as she tried not to break her pace, the pain became sharper and she was forced to slow down and walk slightly lopsided.

It had not rained for several days, dust from the road rose around her feet in little puffs that twinkled in the sunlight. The leaves on the poplars and elms that lined the road shimmered silver and the air was salty and smelled of sun. By the time she came to the stone wall that enclosed the Evarts estate, next to the village, the sun and sweet warm air had sucked away some of her fear, made her forget the pain in her ribs, and when she reached the little village circle with its center stone fountain spurting almost noiselessly surrounded by geraniums and trailing rose vines, she was glad they had made her come out. There were few people and no cars or horses on the cobbled village road that circled the fountain and ran south climbing to accommodate the suddenly higher sea cliffs. It was after eleven and most people were home for lunch. The door of Mr. Storey's Village Store was open, and he kept the lamps unlit until about three when the sun was well past the village circle. The store stayed cooler that way—but it was hard for customers to see what was on the shelves. Mr. Storey, who knew the location of every item in the store, was over eighty and unwilling to move much, so he would direct people to what they wanted, and they would follow his directions through the dim store to the "third shelf from the top—count four lines of cans—ayeh, that should be it." And he was always right.

The cream was easy. Jennifer knew where the icebox was, but she politely waited for his direction. "Just around the corner there behind you —it'll be on the top shelf—should be two bowls left."

She took the pint bowl, covered with wax paper held in place by a rubber band, to the counter behind which he sat. He put it in a bag for her and wrote the price in his account book for his weekly billing. Jennifer took her bag, bulging with the bowl of cream, and stepped out of the dim shop into the white sunlight.

Hal Kearney and the two other boys sat on the stones that rimmed the fountain and its little garden. As soon as he saw her he stood up. The sun was still east enough so that he cast a long black shadow across the pink cobblestones dusted with white. He walked toward her lazily, looking so nonchalant that her fear almost choked her. He was not worried that she would get away, he knew she was trapped. Mr. Storey would be no protection. He was an old man, and things would be broken if she went back in there. She started blindly for home.

She kept an even walking gait at first, hoping she was wrong, that he would just cross the road and go into Mr. Storey's or up the south road. But he followed her, and the two boys followed him.

Please, God, she thought, don't let him kill me, please, and she began crying softly to herself. The tensions sharpened the pain in her ribs, but she was closing the distance, walking faster, so she broke into a crooked lope, leaning to the side trying to lessen the pain without losing ground.

She heard him giggle happily and the pad of his Keds on the cobbles quickened as he began to trot. The giggle broke what was left of her control and she started to run full out, clutching her bag, gasping from the pain in her chest. She heard him trot faster and he closed more of the gap between them even though he was not yet running—just trotting easily. She reached the Evarts' stone wall, and a few yards ahead she saw the end of the cobbles and the beginning of the softish dirt road that wound under the elms and pines through North 'Sconset and past her house.

"Please let me make it to the road, oh, please," she prayed.

She knew that she would not be as badly hurt on the road as she would be if he caught her on the cobblestone street. She could already feel the cobblestones digging into her, crushing the wounded rib, breaking more bones.

He knew that she was trying to reach the road. She heard the pound of his feet quicken on the cobbles and suddenly he grabbed the long, thick braid that was flopping up and down on her back in rhythm with her steps, and he jerked it with all his might. The force of his pull wrenched her whole body backward and she stumbled against him. The paper bag flew out from under the protection of her arms and hit the cobbles—the cream-filled bowl broke and the sound of shattering glass cut the still, sunlit air.

She pulled her hair out of his grasp and the moment her head was free, she saw the cream leaking through the torn bag and splintered bits of bowl and spreading lazily between the cobbles. And she could still hear the sound of breaking glass—from long ago, it seemed, and as it stayed with her ringing in her ears, the anger which had joined her like an unexpected ally turned to rage. She turned on him, then circled him, leaning slightly forward, crouching almost, like an animal, until as he circled to face her the stone wall was behind him. He was still grinning, looking forward to the next move. His arms hung loosely at his sides, but he stretched his fingers, and then closed his right hand into a fist. The other two boys were excited and impatient for him to begin. He rocked up onto the balls of his feet feeling the strength and life in his legs and took a light step toward Jennifer. She stood straight. They were very close, and then, perhaps for the first time, he looked at her, closely. The plain little face was vacant, as though she were dreaming—the hazel eyes completely without fear. Under his gaze he saw something move, and when he looked down he saw that she was raising her hands—the movement was quick, but it seemed to go on and on until her hands were even with her chest, the palms up, facing him, white in the sunlight. Still, he saw nothing to fear. He stood his ground and reached to grab the hands facing him. But she was faster, and her palms with all her weight behind them hit him in the midriff.

It was a well-centered push, she felt it strain her shoulders in a satisfying way and the smack as he hit the stone wall behind him had a good, solid sound.

As soon as she saw he was down, she ran. She did not look back until she reached the road and when she did, she saw that he was still down and the two boys were kneeling next to him. She ran for as long as she could and then the strained rib warned her, and she half limped, half hopped through the sunlight. The pain slowed her, but could not dampen her exhilaration. She was alive in the sun, the dust from the road covered her shoes and trousers, sparkling silver, the leaves from the overhead branches cast small coinlike shadows on the road, and a sudden breeze caught some salt and brought the smell of the sea. Despite the pain, she was almost sorry to go inside when she reached the house.

"He chased you and you pushed him. Is that all?"
Jennifer nodded.
"Does your rib hurt?"
"Some."
No one was hurt. Kate fought back tears of relief. She would tell Tom the whole story when he arrived on the five thirty ferry, and then let him handle it.

She was a little worried about the rib and she called the doctor, but he was out—an emergency—and his wife promised that she would tell him as soon as he called or came home, and that he would be there in an hour or so.

Kate insisted that Jennifer take a nap until the doctor arrived. Then she went out on the terrace with a glass of iced coffee. It was peaceful just sitting in the sun, the waves flopping almost quietly against the shore, and she allowed herself an extra cigarette, just to have an excuse to keep sitting there, thinking of nothing.

Barbara, one of the two village girls who came in to clean every day, came out onto the terrace.

"Miz List, there's two men here to see you—from the sheriff's office."
She looked agitated, which annoyed Kate.
"Barbara—ask Mrs. Hussey to see to them, we'll buy ten dollars' worth of whatever they're—"
"No, ma'am," the girl interrupted. "It's not that. They say they need to *question* you and that it's very important. They're in the sitting room."
Suddenly Kate was afraid.
"Thank you, Barbara, I'll be there in a minute."

The girl went back inside the house. Kate forced herself to sit quietly and finish her cigarette. But as she squashed it in the ashtray she saw that her hand was shaking. She lit another and went to the sitting room.

The two men were standing uncomfortably in the middle of the room when she walked in.

"What can I do for you gentlemen?" She did not ask them to sit down.

The older one showed her his badge and card.

"Yes, Mr. Starbuck, I see. Now what do you want?" Kate wondered if the other one was Starbuck too—a beautiful name, she thought.

Why didn't they say something?

"Well?" Her voice was sharp.

"We're sorry about this, Mrs. List."

"Sorry about what?" Tom—had something happened to Tom? "Is it my husband?"

"No, ma'am. Something happened in the village an hour or so ago—a fight, and one of the boys—"

"I can't see what this has to do with me, Mr. Starbuck. Will you please come to the point." Her rudeness was born of fear—she knew the connection without being told.

"Well, from what we've been told, your daughter was involved in some way. Though the story is confusing. Perhaps if we could talk to her, get her version."

"You don't need her version, Mr. Starbuck. The boy, I'm sure, was Harold Kearney, right?" He nodded. The other neither spoke nor moved.

"He has attacked my daughter twice. The second time she was very badly hurt—one of her ribs broken. He chased her again today, and she told me she pushed him and he fell, and that was how she escaped being hurt again. Now I don't know what Mrs. Kearney has told you, but Jennifer was defending herself—the boy is a bully—he's terrorized other children as well, and if he was hurt, well, I'm sorry, but it was bound to happen sooner or later, and I am not going to have my daughter upset again by this awful boy or his awful family, and that's all there is to it. You may accept my word for what happened, and now if you don't mind—" She walked toward the door, signaling the end of the interview.

Neither man moved.

"I'm sorry, ma'am," the younger one finally spoke, gently. "You don't understand. The Kearney boy is dead."

Kate stopped.

"Please, Mrs. List," said the older of the two, "won't you sit down—you look ill."

Kate obeyed.

"Where's the bell, ma'am?" Kate nodded at it, and the younger walked to it and rang. Barbara opened the door at once. She must have been listening outside, Starbuck thought.

"Mrs. List is not well," he said shortly. "Please get some tea."

When she left, Kate said, "Please, Mr. Starbuck"—she did not care which one—"there's some whiskey in the cabinet. Would you mind?"

"Of course not," said the younger. So he was Starbuck, too.

He brought her the bottle and a glass, but her hands were shaking badly, so he took the bottle and poured for her. Suddenly she was in their care. They seemed very kind and truly concerned. She managed to hold the glass without help and sip a little of the whiskey.

"Thank you. Oh, please, sit down." They sat.

"Do you have any idea what happened?" she asked.

"According to the two boys who saw the whole thing, she pushed him into a wall."

"Yes, she told me the same thing—but did he hit his head or something like that?"

The men looked at each other.

"Is that it? He hit his head—fractured his skull or broke his neck?" Oh, God, she thought, that poor woman.

Still the men did not answer. Then the older Starbuck asked, "Is Mr. List at home, ma'am?"

"He'll be here on the five thirty ferry."

"Why don't we come back about seven—after dinner? I think we'll all feel easier to have him in on it all from the start."

"Yes, of course." Kate was relieved. "That's best. And you can talk to Jennifer then, too."

The younger Starbuck started to protest, but the other one took his arm, hoisted him from the chair, and led him to the door.

"We'll see you at seven, ma'am. Thank you."

They went then, the older keeping a firm grip on the younger's arm. When they were outside, Starbuck the younger threw off the other's grip.

"What's the matter with you, John? By seven they'll have told the kid exactly what to say—we'll never find out what happened to him."

"Are your wits fried, boy? What are they going to tell her to say? She's seven years old—probably half his size to boot—could she have done that to him? Now answer me straight—could she?"

Starbuck the younger remembered the state of Hal Kearney's body and the initially bewildered, then horrified doctor trying to retain his composure as he listed the boy's injuries for the police record.

"No, I guess it just doesn't figure any way you look at it."

"No, cousin, it doesn't figure."

Kate told Tom what had happened as soon as he arrived.

"What did Jennifer have to say for herself?" He was more stunned than angry.

"Nothing. I haven't told her yet."

"You haven't told her? But if they're going to question her we've got to discuss it with her—she won't know what to say otherwise."

"Don't be stupid, Tom." The words and her sharpness startled them both. She softened her tone. "She has no idea that he's dead. She would have told me. I know that. And if she doesn't know when they question her she'll be honestly surprised when they tell her, do you see?"

"You mean they actually suspect that Jennifer—"

"I don't know."

Mrs. Hussey brought sandwiches and some coffee, and they ate in silence. At seven sharp the doorbell rang and Barbara showed the Starbucks in.

Tom took over very smoothly; he mixed drinks for them and talked about how well the ferry kept to its schedule until he could see that they were well settled and had each taken a few guilty sips of their drinks.

"Now, gentlemen, my wife told me that there's been a boy killed in town, and that apparently my daughter was there when it happened."

"Yes, Mr. List. We've had some difficulty sorting out what happened. There were two other boys there. One of them, George Borden, lives next door." Tom nodded and the elder Starbuck continued. "Well, from what they told us, Harold Kearney was chasing your daughter and he caught her, just as they were even with the Evarts estate, you know, that big stone wall that runs to the edge of the village. She ran and ran, they say, until he caught her. Then she sort of turned on him. He made a grab for her—missed—she pushed him and, according to both boys, he hit the wall before they even knew what happened. Made quite a smack. She ran away, and by the time they got to him he was dead. Now that part's all pretty straightforward—"

Straightforward? Not the word she would have used at all, Kate thought as she walked to the seaward window.

"And everything gibes—what the boys said, what your wife told us— and we'd leave it as kind of an unfortunate accident except, well, except for—" Starbuck looked significantly at Kate, and then at Tom, as though to say it would be best if she left the room.

"I'll stay," she answered the unspoken request. "I want to know exactly what happened." She spoke too firmly and Starbuck looked sympathetically at Tom.

"Yes, dear." He rallied to her. "It's best you hear it firsthand. Now, Mr. Starbuck, please tell me why this whole thing can't be labeled an accident and forgotten as quickly as possible."

"If you insist. Earlier, Mrs. List asked if the boy's skull had been fractured or his neck broken—and if that'd been all, why, we'd be free to forget the whole thing. I mean, the little girl pushed him in self-defense, that's plain enough. But that wasn't all—I mean his skull was fractured—but practically every other bone in his body was, too. Some of them were sticking out through his skin, oozing the marrow. His whole chest was caved in and so was the back of his head. It was the worst thing I've ever seen, Mr. List. I was in the war, you know, eight months in France, and I never seen nothing like this." He was pale and beginning to sweat at the memory. "There wasn't a whole inch left on that boy's body. Even Doc Storey was sick—and, well, he's a doctor. And we talked to him, tried to find out what could've happened to the boy. At first we thought the other two children must've done it—but Doc said no, he said only something really enormous, with great force, could tear up a body like that. Well, we puzzled and worried at it. But it's no use. Both boys say there was no truck or car that hit him, only that your daughter pushed him—and they swear that's all. You can see, Mr. List, that we just can't leave it at that. His mother's half mad with grief, poor soul, and she's been screaming that your daughter did it. That Mrs. List warned her there was something wrong with your daughter and that your daughter killed her son. Course the woman's raving—no little girl could've done this. But you see our spot, don't you? The dead boy's mother's accused your daughter and we've got to ask questions. Then, too, maybe she can help us in some way, maybe she saw something the others didn't. Anyhow, we've got to ask, you can see that, can't you? And believe me, Mr. List, we understand all that your daughter's been through."

Starbuck sort of ran down, and they all sat quietly for a moment. Then Tom got up, walked out of the room, and Kate heard him calling Jennifer. He came back in and sat down with them to wait for her. No one spoke. The chill evening breeze swept through the room, billowing the curtains. Kate shivered.

Jennifer came in. She was pale, with a streak of dark purple under one eye. The cut on her chin was healing but still looked angry and the marks of the stitches were pale now, but still definite. It was quite obvious that she had been very badly beaten. Kate wanted to be sure they saw it. "See," she wanted to say, "see what he did to her? That's why she pushed him—do you blame her? What would *you* have done?" But she stayed quiet.

"How do you do, Jennifer?" asked the elder Starbuck.

"Fine, thank you, sir."

"We understand you had a bit of trouble with the Kearney boy this morning, and we would like to hear more about it."

"Are you policemen?"

"Yes, we are."

"Are you going to arrest him?"

The Starbucks looked at each other, then the younger asked, "Did he do something that we should arrest him for?"

"Well, I don't know if it's a crime, but he beat me up—broke one of my ribs and broke Mrs. Hussey's bowl of cream. He's an awful boy."

"So we understand. But he won't bother you anymore, Jennifer. He's dead."

The three men watched her very closely.

She looked coolly at the elder Starbuck for a moment.

"Are you sure he's dead?"

"Very sure."

Jennifer nodded, accepting his word as final.

"I'm glad," she said simply.

"Jennifer, that's a terrible thing to say!" Kate said. "You don't mean it."

"Well, I'm not sorry." Kate looked at Tom, hoping he would intercede in some way, but she saw a new look on his face as he watched his daughter.

Starbuck seemed to understand the child's thirst for vengeance.

"We're trying to find out how he died—there were two other boys there and they said that you pushed him against a stone wall. Is that true?"

"Yes, I pushed him as hard as I could." Defiant now, she set her jaw, quite willing to take whatever consequences her rudeness brought on her. Tom smiled.

"Then what happened?"

"I don't know. I pushed him down and I ran away. I thought that he would kill me when he got up and I wanted to get away as fast as I could. But I guess he didn't get up right away because when I looked back he was still down and the other boys were kneeling by him."

As she spoke the elder Starbuck listened more and more carefully, watching her very closely.

"And that's all you know?"

"Yes."

Jennifer and the elder Starbuck stared at each other until she saw the more and more familiar expression of unease on his face and she looked away. He seemed to come to a decision and stood up.

"I think we've found out all we can. Thank you, Jennifer, and thank you, Mr. and Mrs. List. We'll be going now." He looked significantly at his cousin, and he too stood up. "I don't think we'll need to trouble you again. Come on, Jed."

Kate, smiling with relief, saw them out, leaving Tom and Jennifer alone together.

"Jennifer," he said. "Come here."

Still defiant, she crossed to where he sat, but kept a few feet between them. Tom raised his hands and then after a pause quite deliberately he put them on her shoulders and drew her to him. It was the first time in years he had touched her. She watched his face, so close to hers as he examined her, ran his finger down the bruise under her eye, then gently pressed back her lower lip and looked at the cut in the crease of her chin.

"Rib hurt much?"

"Not much."

Then he looked at her. He saw nothing to justify the dislike he had given in to so long ago. She was angry, but he could see the anger dissipating—and under the waning anger, defiance—something he understood and trusted.

"Daddy?"

"Yes, Jennifer."

"What killed him?"

"We don't know yet."

"Was it because I pushed him?"

"No, that couldn't have killed him, Jennifer, no matter how much you hated him. Come on now, time for bed."

"Will you come upstairs with me?"

"Yes."

Suddenly the world turned over for Jennifer. But why, why now? He wondered too. Because she had fought back at last? Maybe, he thought, maybe just that.

He was heir to a tradition that thought meekness despicable, that believed in and had put its money on strength, on arrogance. Until his daughter defied Starbuck he had seen her as gentle, humble—and strange. The strangeness he could forgive. It was still there and he forgave it. But humbleness was contemptible to him. She was, after all, a List.

They went out into the center entrance hall together. Kate had just shut the door.

"That was awful," she said. She saw Tom's hand still on Jennifer's shoulder and the joy on Jennifer's face but said nothing.

"Come on, Jennifer. Time for bed."

"Uh, I'll go upstairs with her tonight, Kate." Tom was blushing.

"Of course, dear, thank you," she said as though it were the most natural thing for Tom to put Jennifer to bed.

They started up the stairs, leaving Kate in the hall, bewildered and delighted.

Suddenly the front door banged open and Mrs. Kearney stood in the hallway.

Her face was blasted, red. The wispy hair was pasted to her skull and her lips were puffed and wet. She looked past Kate and spotted Tom and Jennifer on the stairs. She pointed at Jennifer.

"You!" she shrieked. "You killed him. Stinking, rotten animal," she screamed, "you freak, you killed him." Her voice slammed against the walls, reverberating in the hall, and through the house.

Kate grabbed her and tried to hold her, but she threw her off and started for the stairs looking at Jennifer. Jennifer stared back down into the woman's dry bulging eyes.

"You monster." The words echoed in the stairwell as she reached the first step and stood on it, tottering slightly. "That's what you are, you know"—she was croaking now—"a monster. Your mother knows it. She told me what you are, she warned me about you." Jennifer backed up one step, Mrs. Kearney went up one step. "Even your own mother, you little freak." *Monster, freak* echoed up at the child. "And now you've killed him. You've killed my son." She ended with a dry, racking sob.

Tom was too shocked to move, and Kate too guilty. It was Mrs. Hussey who ended the scene. She had come into the hall during the screaming, dressed to go home. Now she walked up to the dryly gasping woman, grabbed her shoulder roughly, and turned her around away from Jennifer.

"Thee are the monster," she said firmly. "Thee killed the boy and no one else. Now take thy shame out of this house and leave that innocent child be. And remember, thee terrible woman, thee are the whole cause. A year ago, a month ago even, thee might have saved him, but thee chose indulgence and thereby death. Now get out of here and stay away from these people and their child, and pray God to forgive thee."

Kate never heard Mrs. Hussey use the familiar before. It lent more weight to her awful words. Finally, Jennifer gave way and began to cry. Tom picked her up and carried her up the stairs.

Mrs. Kearney stood before Mrs. Hussey, her head bowed, Kate and Jennifer forgotten. Her sobbing was more normal now and Kate saw tears on her cheeks.

"What can I do? Oh, God, how can I go on."

"Go home." Mrs. Hussey's tone had not softened. "Go home and try to be of some use in this life and to God."

She looked for a long time at Mrs. Hussey, who looked back, then turned away from the cook, walked past Kate, not seeing her, and without another word she left the house, closing the door quietly behind her, leaving Mrs. Hussey and Kate alone in the hall.

"How could you say such terrible things to that poor woman?"

"It needed terrible things to stop her." Mrs. Hussey was still angry. "How long will it take the child to forget what she called her? Poor woman? That's a small, selfish woman, and her weakness killed that boy —whatever happened."

"But he'd promised. I heard him."

"So much for promises lightly given and lightly taken, with nothing behind them except wanting to keep everything looking ordinary. But it's the live child that matters now. And there's no evil in your daughter —but maybe something. And thee'd do well to face it, Mrs. List, for all your grandness."

Then Mrs. Hussey walked out of the house and left Kate alone.

When John Starbuck got home at eight thirty his wife was waiting for him with some milky tea ready to be poured and warm biscuits.

"Well, John, what did you find out?"

"I don't know what I can say, Alma."

"That's no answer. They must have told you something. What's the child say?"

"She said that she was glad that he was dead."

"How awful!"

"No, 'twasn't awful. He'd beaten her pretty bad and she spoke in anger—natural enough."

"But was it she—"

"She didn't know that he was dead until we told her."

"Then she couldn't't've done it, right?"

He looked at his handsome, solid wife. He did not think that she had ever, even as a young girl, given way to fancy. She was, as he was, Nantucket born. They had lived with their friends and family and each other on an island only fourteen miles long for nearly fifty years. How could he tell her what he thought; what he had seen for a tiny instant in a child's eyes? Where in their lives was a place for that kind of strangeness? Still, it was there, he had seen it—it had come across the bay with the summer strangers and was with them now in North 'Sconset. But this simple, good woman, what could he say to her that she would understand? He knew he must keep it to himself and that, after a few days, no, a few weeks more likely, the need to share his fear would fade.

"No," he said, "she couldn't've done it. We'll just have to figure it's a mystery and try to forget it."

"That poor, poor woman," said Mrs. Starbuck. "Was the house beautiful?"

"What house?"

"The List house, of course."

"Guess it was nice, but I just saw the hall and their sitting room."

"Tell me about it, everything you can remember. That Hussey woman's as close as a corpse and she never tells us nothing."

Starbuck sighed and composed himself to describe in as much detail as he could the rooms and every piece of furniture he had seen that night.

Part IV

1

December 5, 1976

STAVITSKY STARED at John Starbuck's signature until the letters blurred. Then he turned the last page and shut the folder, smoothing the stiff manila with his fingers. The report led nowhere, a blank.

That left the Richard Ching that Ellen Cransten had mentioned, and if he drew a blank with Ching too. . . . He didn't want to think about that.

He called Ira Stern and told him what he wanted.

"I don't care which of you does what, Ira. Ching was at Columbia twenty years ago—may still be there. Maybe Galeston knows something about him, they're almost contemporaries. Gilbert is Jennifer Gilbert—she's an MD at Rockefeller University—maybe someone at Manhattan's heard of her."

"If she's at Rockefeller," Ira said, "someone's sure to know something about her. Rockefeller's sort of top of the heap."

"OK, OK." His stomach still heaved when he thought of her, and he did not want to hear anything good about Jennifer Gilbert. "It's only two thirty." Amazing, he thought. Only an hour and a half since he had seen her. But the undercurrent of panic seemed to have always been part of him; he couldn't remember what it felt like not to know her. "I want everything you can get—tonight."

"You sound upset, David."

"Yeah—upset. By tonight, Ira."

Carole heard him as she came in; she ran to the den without waiting to take her coat off.

"What's the matter, darling?" She stopped at the door. "David, you look terrible. What happened?"

He forced a smile.

"I think it was something I ate."

Then she was beside him, kneeling, the coat billowing around her on the floor, reaching for him. He was in her arms, dangerously close to tears. He made himself swallow again and again. Finally he was able to say in more or less his normal voice.

"Had a terrible lunch—didn't go down right." He knew he was frightening her; usually nothing bothered his digestion and she saw heart disease or cancer in every physical irregularity, but he didn't know what else to say. She tried to insist on the doctor, but he refused, so she settled for giving him some Pepto-Bismol and her universal cure-all, a hot bath with baking soda.

More to help her forget her worry than because he really felt helpless, he let her undress him. But her hands pulling at his shirt, trousers, then underwear, excited him. He thought she was excited, too, and he lay back naked across the bed and pulled her to him. She went heavy the way she always did when she wanted to make love, and they both pulled at her clothes until she was naked, too.

He was usually a considerate lover, and he started normally enough, stroking her breasts and thighs, as always a little surprised at how much he still loved the way she looked and felt. But suddenly he was too excited to wait until she was ready and almost will-lessly, locked in a new kind of feeling, heaved himself over her, ignoring her gasp at the sudden thrust into her. He couldn't stop because he was coming already—hard, too hard for pleasure—the orgasm went on and on until he thought something inside him would break. And all through it, behind his screwed-shut eyelids, he saw Jennifer Gilbert's pale delicate face, eyes shut too, lips drawn back from her teeth—not this time with rage, but with pleasure, as if she were sharing his orgasm.

Stavitsky couldn't believe what Stern was telling him.

"I tell you, the whole thing's gone. Every copy—X rays, the photo I took, everything." Stern sounded as if he were going to cry.

Stavitsky wanted to scream and shake him. But Galeston said calmly, "Maybe someone took it for study."

"No. Anyone who wanted to study it would only take one copy, and they would have signed for that. But the whole Roberts file is missing, even the code card. Except for the DOA slip in the office we don't have anything to prove that Roberts was even at Manhattan, much less that we did an autopsy, and found—what we found."

Galeston turned to Stavitsky.

"Can we exhume the body and redo the X rays? You still have the police copy of the written report, don't you?"

Stavitsky tried to match the old man's calmness. "We have it, but I can't get a court order to dig up Roberts—not just because of some lost X rays."

"They're not lost," Stern said. "Someone took them."

"I think we have a touch of paranoia here, gentlemen. Who would want it? Who would even know where it was kept, or what it meant?"

"Another physican would know all those things, doctor. A physician would know even more; for instance, without the X rays and photographs, how much is the written report worth?"

"Nothing—even if Ira and I swore that's what we'd seen—nothing."

"And a physician would know that too."

"I assume you have a physician in mind."

"Yes, I have—Dr. Jennifer Gilbert. Ira—what'd you find out about her?"

"Not much," Stern said. "One of the guys I know at Memorial—a sort of celebrity watcher—has heard of her. Said she's an experimental hematologist—mainly leukemia. She'd designed a couple of fairly important clinical studies that were done at Memorial, but he thought she never did any clinical work herself. All basic stuff—how cells respond to chemicals and so on."

"You're sure she doesn't see any patients?" Stavitsky asked.

"No, just cells, mice, and drugs."

Stavitsky was relieved. The thought of her taking care of children with leukemia. . . .

Galeston was watching him very closely. He put his clean bottomed coffee cup back on its dry saucer and leaned across the table toward Stavitsky. "You seem to think this Dr. Gilbert took the Roberts file—very odd, because the only reason she would do that is if she had something to do with Roberts' death. Which as far as *you* know, captain, is impossible."

"What do you mean, as far as *I* know? Do you know something I don't?"

"Oh, quite a few things, I expect."

Galeston's smile widened, creasing the malevolent old face.

"A great many things, one of which may be germane here—at least Dr. Ching might think it germane. But before we get into that, I want to know what *you* suspect—if that's the word—about Dr. Gilbert."

"I don't know what I suspect; it's just—" He hated saying it again, thinking it again, but there were no other words. "There's something wrong, real wrong."

He told them everything then, everything that had happened since the last Friday—the scene with Raines, his interviews with William Gilbert, with Ellen Cransten and what she'd said about Ching, and finally he told them about Jennifer Gilbert. He described what happened to him in the dining room at Rockefeller University as carefully and dispassionately as he could. He even told them about the boy who died on Nantucket, although it sounded so strange.

He realized as he spoke how vaguely founded his suspicions were, and he kept watching the other two men for signs of dismissal. But they listened without interruption, and when he described the fear and sickness he felt when he was with Jennifer Gilbert, Stern bowed his head as though he could not bear to hear about it, while Galeston leaned even closer and his eyes glittered.

He waited for their objection, for Galeston to snipe away at the story, to ask for facts. But no objections—they seemed convinced, as if they already believed in his mystery; as if they wanted to believe it.

Galeston sat as though he were still listening. His eyes narrowed, watchful. He's a match for her, Stavitsky thought. She couldn't do that to him.

"Why do you pussyfoot, captain?" Galeston almost whispered.

"What do you mean?" Stavitsky asked.

"You hint at this, and you hint at that. Why not just say it—you think Jennifer Gilbert killed him. Isn't that right, captain?"

"Yes, doctor, that's exactly what I think."

"But how?" asked Stern. "Roberts was a big man, and even if he weren't how could anyone have—"

"That's what we need to find out, isn't it?" Galeston cut in. "All right, captain, let's assume we know *who,* certainly we know *why.* But what if we *can* prove it? She was still within her rights to do it—he had broken into her home, killed her dog, beaten her husband. . . . Ah, he had a gun?"

Stavitsky nodded.

"Then where's the crime? What business is this of the police?"

"None. And if she had stabbed him, or shot him or clubbed him to death, I'd have forgotten the whole thing. But I believe she did what you described to me. I believe she committed an impossible murder—or killing, whatever you want to call it."

"And if she did what is it to you?" Galeston was not quizzing him, he really wanted to know what Stavitsky thought. "There are hundreds of unjustified murders every year, maybe more for all I know. Why does this quite justified killing upset you so, however it was done?"

Stavitsky chose his words carefully and spoke slowly.

"At first, doctor, I was just curious, at least more curious than anything else. I'm used to knowing what happened. That's my job in a way, and I've always been good at it. I've always been able to make the pieces fit. But the death of Amos Roberts just doesn't fit. Impossible—you told me yourself—and I believe you. So, doctor, my curiosity and need to put things in order aside, I've become pretty well convinced that there is someone walking around who broke a man's neck without touching him. Whatever story I can find, whatever 'solution' I can cook up, that one fact demands something of me."

"As a protector of our safety?" Galeston was almost sneering.

"No, you son of a bitch!" he yelled. He jumped up and leaned as far across the table toward Galeston as he could. The muscles in his jaws twitched and his voice was hoarse again. "I'm facing some sort of—" He searched for the word. Not *mess,* that wasn't the word—*chaos,* that was it. "Some sort of chaos that just walked into my life and into *yours* whether you like it or not."

Stern was embarrassed, but Galeston just sat quietly watching Stavitsky. Stavitsky sank back in his chair, his legs shaking. Chaos, he thought. What do I care, what the hell do I care? What am I doing? He wanted to forget the whole thing now. Aloud he said, "I'm sorry—didn't mean to lose my temper."

"Yes, it's quite a problem," Galeston said, as though the outburst had never happened, "but we may have a sort of clue. An insane one, I think, but a clue nonetheless. You see, I *did* get some information on Dr. Ching. He's seventy, emeritus professor of psychology at Columbia, very good credentials. About twenty years ago he became involved in some studies on parapsychology. Very prestigious investigators—Ford grants—all that sort of thing. Not lunatic stuff at all."

"Parapsychology." The word was not clear at first to Stavitsky.

"Before you ask, David"—Galeston forgave him for the outburst—"that's the sort of general term for ESP, telepathy, spiritualism, clairvoyance, etc."

ESP—Ellen Cransten had told the truth about that much.

"This afternoon in the library I went through the indices for everything Ching's written for the past twenty-five years. And there was one particular thing that might be of interest to us—a report he gave in 1954 on what he thought was some sort of breakthrough. The breakthrough involved only one aspect of his studies and only one subject." Stavitsky tensed. "But it was—or so he said—surprising. And even in as cold and abbreviated a thing as a meeting abstract you could tell that the man was excited."

"What kind of breakthrough?"

"I don't know. The full paper was never published—also very surprising. But something must have happened in 1954 because Ching never reported on anything to do with ESP again. His very next paper several months later was on psychosomatics."

"Where is he now?"

"Still in New York. Retired now. Two years ago he chaired a large, very prestigious conference on the psychosomatics of cancer, so he's keeping his hand in."

"Doctor, it's a little after nine. I want you to call Ching, ask him if we can see him tonight." It was not a request and Galeston chuckled.

"Captain, if you add 'please,' I'll consider it."

Stavitsky smiled. "Please."

Mrs. Ching opened the door to them. She nodded without speaking and led them down a long narrow hallway lined with closed doors and into a room that opened into what must have been a garden, but it was too dark to see outside.

Dr. Ching rose from his desk to welcome them. There were introductions and Mrs. Ching appeared with an extra folding chair. A few minutes while they got settled, then Mrs. Ching was back again with a tea tray. More time while tea was poured and everyone sipped and murmured his thanks. Mrs. Ching nodded again, she still had not spoken a word, and left the room.

"Now, gentlemen." Dr. Ching had a thin reedy voice, and spoke with no trace of an accent. "Our phone conversation was very cryptic, and if your company hadn't combined the best pathologist in America"—Ching nodded to Galeston, who nodded back—"and the head of the New York Homicide Division"—he did not nod at Stavitsky—"I don't think I would have seen you on such short notice. It is late, and while I offer you every courtesy, I would appreciate as brief an explanation as possible." He was smiling pleasantly, despite the admonition to haste.

He was probably, thought Stavitsky, as happy for the break in his routine as the three men in the room.

Stavitsky did not waste time. "Dr. Ching, I am investigating a killing." He outlined the circumstances. Then Stern described the autopsy report. Ching kept on smiling but his head tilted to one side, listening intently. When Stern finished describing the autopsy, Ching turned to Galeston.

"All true, doctor?"

"Every word," Galeston answered.

No one spoke for a moment, and Stavitsky decided to take the plunge.

"Doctor Ching, I think you know one of the people involved. Her name is Gilbert, Jennifer Gilbert, and she's a physician."

Ching began to shake his head slowly, as though he thought not, but could not be sure.

Stavitsky rushed on. "You might know her by her maiden name—List."

Ching's head stopped moving. He sat frozen, his smile an empty grimace straining his face. The three men waited for him to speak. Nothing happened. Then he lowered his head, as though holding it up was too great a strain, and he asked softly, "Was Jennifer List with the man who died—I mean in the same room?"

"Yes," Stavitsky said. "It was her apartment they were robbing."

"Could this have been an accident?" he asked Galeston.

"Accident? No. I still can't believe it happened, but there was a good deal of, well, of a sort of precision involved."

"Then," asked Ching, "would you say it was 'done' actually 'done'?"

"If I had to say anything, then yes, I would say it was 'done.'"

Ching finally raised his head and looked at them. The smile was gone. "Jennifer List." He sighed the name. "I thought I was finished with it—I thought I'd never hear that name again." He stopped. They all sat still; then he said, "I'll tell you what happened, but first I want you to know that I tried to stop it. I tried to warn him, gentlemen, I really tried. But he wouldn't listen. And I've tried not to blame myself for what happened. But through the years. . . ." He trailed off. "God forgive me," he said at last.

Embarrassed silence. The room was getting chilly and Stavitsky began to feel shivery. Stern watched his feet, then shuffled them, and looked at their new alignment. Galeston sat like stone, his eyes full on Ching. A clock somewhere in the house chimed the half hour. It must be ten thirty, Stavitsky thought, but the time did not matter to him—there was no rush, he did not want to hear what Ching was about to say. For the moment they were all safe still and he wanted to stretch it, to go on sitting there silently in the cold room.

Maybe, he thought, maybe it's not too late, we can leave now, we don't have to hear. . . .

But Ching began to talk, and kept on talking. The clock chimed eleven, and then eleven thirty. He told them all he could remember about Jennifer List from the first day he met her and all he had heard about her from Marvin Ross and Chris Haynes. He told them all he knew and all he suspected, and at the end he told them how, in a way, he had blamed himself, through all these years, for what had happened to Marvin Ross.

There was nowhere else Jennifer could hide the folder. Home was out of the question—someone might find it—William might find it. Besides, Rockefeller University was more or less hallowed ground, and the administrators would not like having the police around searching for an autopsy report and, in the process, harassing their director of experimental hematology, who also happened to be Jennifer Compton List Gilbert.

She opened the folder, took out the X rays, and held them up to the fluorescent ceiling lights sky. Amazing. She had never seen anything like them. She wondered what the great Dr. Galeston had made of them. Here was a real problem in forensic pathology—and she could imagine how he would feel when he found that they were gone. Not that it really mattered, because the answer was not in the folder. Of course, he didn't know that; neither did the captain.

The captain. . . .

As if he were already there, watching her, she shoved the X rays back into the folder and pushed the whole thing into the drawer. She shouldn't have taken the report, it would only make him move faster—stupid, stupid, she told herself. But without the report, without the X rays, what did he have? Nothing—nothing that she would have to explain.

Still, he was after her—with or without evidence. There was too much will in his handsome, heavy-featured face, and pride. He'd been sick in the dining room and he'd been frightened, but he'd kept fighting it. What did he think, then? What was he thinking now? How could she lose control like that . . . let him see?

He was the danger, not Galeston.

Unless—

The alternative was always there now; had always been there. The familiar well of coldness opened in her mind. She hated the feeling, but it wouldn't go away. If only he would leave her alone. But she knew he wouldn't—the coldness deepened. It had been there the night Roberts died, and when they told her that Hal Kearney was dead, and finally even Marvin's memory had been buried in it.

Marvin. . . . He'd be older than she. Fifty, fifty-two? If he'd lived. . . .

2

September 29 to November 1, 1954

THE RHESUS monkey's heart was beating. It swelled and pumped while they stood around the table watching and listening to the instructor. Suddenly the rhythm of the beat changed and the dot of light on the oscilloscope hooked up to the small body began to move erratically. The people around the table looked from the heart to the screen, then back to the heart as what they saw was instantly reflected by the movements of the dot.

The heart was in trouble. It seemed to take on a life of its own, independent of its host, struggling for a separate survival. It swelled as they watched, and shrank, and swelled again, each time growing larger as if it were gasping, while the monkey lay helpless, unconscious. The heart swelled again, but the rhythm of the swelling and shrinking became discordant, unpredictable, until it disappeared altogether and the heart began an awful kind of shuddering which seemed to go on and on, while the dot on the screen jittered. Finally the heart swelled again and seemed suspended for an instant while they waited. The instant became seconds, but the heart was frozen in its last pulse. It had failed. The monkey was dead.

"Right," said the instructor. "Now let's see exactly what happened."

Jennifer kept her head down, letting her tears fall straight from her lashes to the floor. She would sob aloud in a second. She had to get out of the room or they would hear her. Eyes still on the floor, she backed away from the ring of people around the table and out the door into the hall. No one noticed.

Safe and alone—the hall was empty—she leaned against the cool plaster and let the threatening sobs break. No one would hear—all the doors were closed. Her shoulders shook and her head turned from side to side worrying with sorrow for the dead heart. Finally, her throat and eyes aching, she made herself stand away from the wall and tried to get the sobs under control. She remembered the handkerchief in her lab-coat pocket, took it out, and held it over her mouth to muffle the sound as she turned away from the wall.

There was a man standing close behind her. "Excuse me." He looked worried.

"Excuse me," he said again, looking nervously up and down the empty hall, hoping someone would come to help him with her.

"It's all right," she said, trying to reassure him. "It's just that this little monkey died—they stopped its heart—and I just wasn't ready. . . ." The tears kept running but she had her voice under control. He seemed relieved to hear her speak. He even smiled.

"Medical student?"

She nodded.

"How will you feel when it's a patient?"

"Oh, God." Her throat started to heave again.

"Oh, my, oh, my." His body twisted at her renewed grief. "I'm sorry, I didn't mean—please, don't cry, that was a terrible thing to say." She pressed the handkerchief harder against her lips, tensed against the sobs, and made herself keep swallowing while he watched helplessly. She kept waiting for him to run away from the terrible scene she was making, but he stood his ground, apparently determined to stay with her until she had regained her control.

The worried eyes watching her were round, gray-green, slightly close-set behind thick glasses. His face was round too, but not pudgy, and his ears stuck out slightly. Thick, bushy, sandy eyebrows, so short they looked like tufts, and an untrimmed mustache the same color as his eyebrows. Impossible to say how old he was—thirty, forty—the thinning, indefinably colored hair gave no clue. The eyebrows, round eyes, whiskers, sleek head, all made him look like a walrus. She smiled, and the tears stopped. He smiled back.

"Better now?"

"Much. Thank you."

"I didn't do anything," he pointed out, reasonably.

"You didn't leave me."

"Uh, yes, I see." She was surprised he didn't have an English accent. "Well, if you're sure you're all right?"

Parting words, but he did not move.

"Yes, I'm fine now, Mr—."

"Dr. Gilbert," he said. "William Gilbert, PhD—entomology."

He kept standing there looking at her. She looked back through swollen lids. Finally, obviously reluctantly, he turned away and began walking down the hall, his tweed jacket flapping with his bumpy gait. He reached the end of the corridor, looked back at her once more, then turned the corner and was gone.

If she ran after him . . . She actually took a step. Too late—the bell rang, doors opened, and the halls began filling. People brushed past her, talking, laughing, a swirl of Friday-afternoon gaiety. The hall stretched ahead of her, full of people. She crossed the stream out of their path and sagged against the wall.

Ten to four, Friday afternoon. Almost time to go home, get dressed, and pick Ellen up, then John, then whomever John had "gotten" for her tonight.

Another Friday-night debacle.

It wasn't Ellen's fault, she thought, or John's. They'd tried. All the boys were nice, some even good-looking, but they all couldn't wait to get away from her.

"I don't know why they go on finding them for me," she had told her mother. Kate knew very well. Jennifer made a good backdrop for Ellen's looks, and John was almost as interested in Jennifer's father as he was in Ellen . . . almost. To Jennifer, she said—the lies had become a habit—"Because they like you, dear. They want your company."

"John hates me."

"Jennifer, you're not to start that again. John doesn't hate you at all." Kate resented the way Ellen and John used Jennifer, but there was nothing she could do about it. Aloud she said, "I'm sure they're very fond of you, dear. And one of the boys is sure to call you." More lies.

Jennifer turned her face back to the wall, away from the stream of students. None of the Friday-night dates ever called her again, none ever would.

She was committed for tonight—no way out. But it would be the last time.

This one was Christopher Haynes: big, good-natured, blond, and very red in the face. He seemed to want Jennifer to like him, the sort who wanted everyone to like him. He listened attentively to whatever nonsense she said, and when he talked, which he did easily, it was to her. At least he didn't sit staring at Ellen the way most of them did. In fact he didn't seem very impressed with Ellen at all. Jennifer felt the pressure of his leg against hers under the table, very gently, and, she couldn't help it, she began to hope that it wouldn't happen the same way.

With the others, it took time—usually about an hour—before they knew something was terribly wrong, and about another half hour before they were certain it was her that was making them uneasy and not too much liquor or something they had eaten.

But it hit Haynes all of a sudden. He began by looking at her as if he'd known her before. A worried kind of look that people get when they're trying to remember something. She was talking and he was watching her with a little frown. Then, in the middle of a sentence, she saw a shock of something like recognition in his eyes. It only lasted a second, then his eyes went blank. He had been leaning toward her, listening; now he leaned away, as far away from her as he could get without moving his chair or falling out of it. He began to sweat. The room was dim, but she could see beads of moisture pop out, gather, run down the side of his face.

"Excuse me." He stood up. "I'm leaving now." He did not make excuses the way others had.

"Hey, man," John said. "It's not even eleven."

"I'm not ready to leave." Ellen was never ready to leave.

Chris looked at Ellen with dislike. "Well, *I* am."

John was disgusted. "All right, all right," he said, a glance of hatred at Jennifer. "I'll drive you home."

"Never mind," Chris said. "I'll take a cab." John started to argue, while Jennifer sat as she always did during the Friday-night denouement; looking at her hands folded in her lap, waiting for them to finish arguing; waiting for the boy to leave so she could take a cab, too, go home, be alone, cry. No, she wouldn't cry anymore: it had happened too often to make her sad, to make her anything except cold—very cold. Even her hands were chilly.

No more argument. Christopher Haynes was firm: his angry voice rose above the pounding of the slow rock. "I said we live in opposite directions. I'll take a cab."

Always polite, Jennifer looked up at him to say good-bye, maybe shake his hand. But he was already walking away, sidling between the tables, his head quickly swallowed up in the almost dark room.

Chris was outwardly calm by the time he got home, but still glad Marvin was there. He did not want to be alone.

Marvin's qualifying exams began on Wednesday and he planned a celibate weekend of studying. He was half lying in their only easy chair, a book propped against his belt, and a half-empty bottle of beer on the table next to him when Chris came in.

"You're home early," he said. He didn't notice Chris' paleness, or the fine tremor in his hands as he unbuttoned his topcoat. "What's the matter, did she have two heads?"

Chris tried to smile. "She might as well have had. It was pretty strange, Marv. I couldn't get away fast enough."

"The ugliest girl in the world, huh?"

Marvin had lost interest and was back to his book.

"No," Chris said. "Not ugly, not ugly at all. But, Christ, she was weird! Too bad too, because she's really kind of pretty and rich as hell."

"Rich?" Marvin rested the book face down on his chest and gave Chris his full attention. "How rich?"

"Jennifer." Ellen was excited. Jennifer braced herself; it was late Monday afternoon, her cadaver seemed to have every organ in the wrong place, and she was very tired. "John just got the nicest phone call from Chris Haynes' roommate. . . ."

"Forget it, Ellen. No more dates."

"Jennifer"—now Ellen was going to nag—"I know Friday was a bore. But John says that Haynes is pretty much of a dud with women. But not this one. John knows who he is, and he says he's very handsome—'foreign-looking,' John says—but I know he means handsome."

Why couldn't they just leave her alone? "Look, Ellen, I know you mean well, and if you need the car anytime. . . ."

Ellen went on as if Jennifer hadn't spoken. "Apparently Chris told him all about you."

"You mean he told him all about my father's money."

"Of course he did. What difference does that make?" Typical Ellen. Jennifer smiled at the phone in spite of herself. "And he's absolutely mad to meet you. Who cares why? So I told John that next Friday would be fine."

"Ellen, I meant what I said, no more—"

"Besides, Jennifer, you never know. He might be the one."

"The one what?" She snorted. But the phrase caught her. The one. And Ellen would not be quiet. She went on, predicting the best night of Jennifer's life with foreign-looking Marvin Ross. "A real stud, John says —women are mad. . . ." Ellen's voice ate away at her, sly, insinuating, sure of its effect. Jennifer sagged, then gave in.

"But this is the last time."

"Of course, darling, but I'm sure you won't be sorry."

She tried to forget it, but the conversation haunted her the rest of the week. "Handsome, foreign-looking, the one . . . Stud, women are mad. . . ."

She tried not to think about him, but she couldn't help herself, and by Wednesday she'd created a shadow figure that lay beside her at night, sat with her in classes during the day. No matter how hard she tried to avoid it, she still thought that maybe, maybe this one. . . .

On Thursday, without telling Ellen, she went to Bergdorf's. Not this time to the more moderate in price and style "Miss Bergdorf" floor, but to the designer's collection, where the lighting was very soft, the air hushed, more like a church than a shop. They showed her to her own dressing room where, in close splendor, a tall beautiful woman brushed past her in one dress after another. Her mother's saleswoman tried to help, but Jennifer wanted to make her own choice . . . and she did. A beautiful dress that the model said was perfect for her. It had a huge crinolined skirt, puffed sleeves, tight bodice arrangement at the top—a queen's dress that stopped at the ankles—a tall blond's dress—and a disaster on short plump Jennifer.

They told her not to worry, it would be altered and at her house by Friday afternoon. Then she left them to count their commissions and walked up the avenue to the Pierre to have her hair done—

—Something they call the Italian Boy. They cut the thick, beautiful chestnut curls, then tried to get the heavy hair to lay softly against her cheeks. But it was too thick and unruly, and stood out in tufts. The hairdresser looked sadly at the spiky head.

"I'm not sure that this is really your style, Miss List."

"Can't you do something to make it stay down?"

He greased and flattened while she watched the process, fighting tears.

On Friday when she came downstairs wearing the dress, hair in points at all directions, Kate tried to look bright.

"You look lovely, dear. Are you going out with John and Ellen?" Kate knew whom she was going with, she never went with anyone else, but she was stalling for time, trying to think of something to hide the dress and maybe draw attention away from the hairdo.

"Yes, standard Friday night." Jennifer tried to sound bored but she couldn't hide the note of excitement which made her mother ache for her. Then Kate remembered Maida Borden—shanty Irish who'd married into Beacon Hill and 'Sconset—who'd told her, "When in doubt, play it for money."

"Jennifer, why don't you take my coat? It's chilly enough."

The coat would certainly hide the dress, at least as long as she was outside.

"Oh, Mommy, I'd love to."

It was brought out. Midcalf sable. Too big for Jennifer, but she looked better with it than without it.

Certainly she looked rich.

At first Ellen was annoyed about the coat, but the dress and hairdo reassured her. Jennifer noticed the flash of satisfaction and spent ten minutes in the Olivieris' huge old-fashioned bathroom in front of the mirror, but only seemed to make things worse. Finally she gave up, and almost amused at the mess she'd made, she went back to the living room just as the bell rang. The Olivieris had no proper servants and Ellen answered the door, while Jennifer crouched in a chair, her hand on her head, trying to hold the hair down.

As soon as Ellen came back into the room, Jennifer saw that something had upset her. John followed her, then Chris' roommate, and Jennifer saw what was bothering Ellen.

Nothing she had imagined equaled Marvin Ross—he was tall, taller than John, heavy boned with straight black hair and a long, dark-skinned face—but his eyes were blue, very light. He was older than they were, even older than John, who was close to thirty—yes, there were strands of gray in his hair.

He didn't even see her at first; he was watching Ellen walking across the room, kept watching as she turned to face him. Jennifer saw Ellen's face change, saw the eyebrows raise and the huge dark eyes open wide. One delicate hand touched her breast, pretending breathlessness. Jennifer saw him look at the hand, the breast, then into Ellen's eyes, and suddenly she knew she'd had enough.

She was going to fight for this one.

She stood up before Ellen could introduce her, walked quickly to the sofa, and swung the sable coat across her shoulders. It swished around her, a magic cape, light, soft, impregnable. She arched her neck and looked at them from a distance that the coat whispered was real and vast. Three hundred years of power and twenty million dollars spoke to Marvin Ross.

"How do you do? I'm Jennifer List."

He smiled, amused at the obvious display of defiance. "And I'm Marvin Ross. How do you do?" But only a little amused. His eyes were on the coat, Ellen's lightly held breast forgotten.

The restaurant Marvin had chosen (he had taken the lead from the beginning) was at the southern end of Little Italy, almost in Chinatown. Not neon like the others, only a discreet storefront with a small sign announcing PATSY'S. Inside, chandeliers—very good ones, she thought—heavy carpets, and a quiet, very large crowd waiting. Jennifer had never seen so many blonds in one place, rings flashed, fur caught the soft light, and the men, as dark skinned as their blond women, were almost as brightly dressed.

"You have to give your names first," a neat, shining fat man told Marvin.

They moved to the front where a huge woman presided over a list on a lecternlike table. A shaft of brighter light glinted on her black hair and pale soft arms.

She looked at them indifferently. "You gotta reservation?"

They did not.

She shook her head, fat rippled and swam back into place. She pretended to consult the list. "We're full up now—no room," with a wave of dismissal.

Behind them the line shifted, reassured. Marvin looked at Jennifer and shrugged. Jennifer moved.

"Excuse me." She edged past Marvin and John and up to the table. "*Excuse me.*" This time a fraction louder. This woman was, after all, a servant, a breed Jennifer understood.

The woman looked up, pretending annoyance. Jennifer did not smile.

The light shone on her shoulders, highlighting the fur. The woman knew sable when she saw it.

"We should have called first, of course." The voice softened again so that the woman had to lean forward to hear, and for the first time Marvin realized how beautiful it was. "But the room is so lovely"—still no smile—"that we thought we'd take a chance, and of course we won't mind waiting for a *few*"—few underlined—"minutes."

Under the softness, both Marvin and the woman heard the command, without hauteur or arrogance, but with the complete certainty of obedience. The woman was shrewd, she recognized the tone. She consulted the list again, this time carefully. Then she heaved her bulk off of the stool.

"I see whatta I can do."

Jennifer turned back to her friends and smiled. A smile Ellen had never seen before. Marvin moved very close to her, to be sure that everyone knew that she was with him. The dim light picked out the red in the messy chestnut hair, showed the streaks of yellow in her hazel eyes, made hollows under the high cheekbones. He took her arm, sliding his hand down the fur until he touched the skin of her palm. She shuddered slightly, he felt it and tightened his hand around hers.

Chris couldn't believe what Marvin was telling him.

"You're going out with her—tonight? Again?"

"She'll be here in a few minutes."

"But didn't you see what I meant, couldn't you feel it?"

Marvin laughed. "Chris, all I saw was ten thousand dollars' worth of sable, and seven thousand dollars' worth of car, and one small, fairly attractive girl."

"Marvin, you must have felt *something.*"

"Look, Chris, maybe you and she were just a bad mix."

"No, Cransten told me—it's like that with every guy he's fixed her up with—it wasn't just me. There's something really wrong with her. John says he feels it too."

"She doesn't seem to bother the queen."

"Nothing bothers Ellen. She doesn't notice anything except whether her hair's in place. John says she blows him and I bet all she's thinking about while she does it is whether it's smearing her lipstick."

Marvin laughed, but the picture set up a little tingle.

"Look, Chris, Jennifer's rich, not ugly"—no, he thought, not ugly at all—"and if she seems strange, I think it's because she's a twenty-three-year-old overprotected virgin who needs a good fuck and a little company."

"You wouldn't *fuck* her?" Absolute horror in his voice.

He looked upset, so boiled, that Marvin laughed. "Don't worry, man. I won't make you watch."

Chris blushed.

The watching was a secret between them, something they rarely talked about. It began a few months after they moved into the apartment on 105th Street. Marvin, claiming greater need, took the bedroom with the double bed, leaving Chris with two singles—"And if I can't fill it three nights a week, I'll let you have it." That rankled at first, especially since Marvin made good on the boast, and most nights when Chris went to the bathroom he would hear low shuddering noises from Marvin's room. He took to leaning his forehead against the connecting door to listen to the sounds rise in intensity—always the woman's voice, never Marvin's. The noises ate at him and he tried to reproduce them in the few women who would let him try, but he didn't know what to do, usually hurting more than exciting them. Finally he couldn't stand it anymore.

"Marv, I want to watch."

"Watch what?"

Deep breath. "What you do with the women."

Marvin was too surprised to say anything. Chris rushed on. "I hear you in there and it's driving me nuts, because I don't know what you're doing to them. I know it's a hell of a thing to ask, but you don't give a shit for any of them. They're in and out of here in a few weeks, you never keep one for very long—and it isn't that I want to do anything except watch."

Marvin looked at him. The fool, he thought, he really means it. But the idea of Chris, maybe even one of Chris' women, watching him gave his insides an excited little twist.

"Okay, Chris."

None of the women ever found out. Marvin left both bathroom doors open, and Chris stayed in his own room, in the dark on the other side of the second door. Marvin always left the lights on anyway, so Chris could see through the darkened bathroom to what was happening on the bed. And by the time Marvin was finished with them, the second door was always closed.

It worked; he began to imitate what he saw Marvin do, though it was painful at first because no matter how excited Marvin was, he always waited . . . smoothed, stroked, licked until they were ready, even if it took an hour. Slowly, very slowly, always easy, as if he had all the time in the world.

Chris copied and found it was worth the effort. Things began to happen with the women that he'd only imagined. Best of all, he began to love them, their feel, their smell, their shaking against him while he went on a gentle kind of hunt into their mouths, across their breasts, and up into them with his tongue, his penis. It was even better, he knew, because he did love them, and after a while, he felt a little bad about Marvin, because Marvin did not feel anything for them, he could see that. With Marvin it was a kind of fight that he always won, holding back, waiting until the body on the bed was helpless, defeated. For all the excitement, a cold business, Chris thought, and he found that he felt a little sorry for his friend, a little superior.

Still, he owed Marvin a lot, too much not to try to protect him from what he had seen in Jennifer List.

"Listen, Marvin," he said, "it isn't the watching."

"Okay. What is it?"

"It's hard to say exactly. I knew there was something happening, but I wasn't sure what—she reminded me of something, something I hadn't thought of for years. At first I didn't know what it was, then, while she was talking to me I really concentrated, really looked at her. And I remembered."

"What did you remember?"

"A sparrow hawk I had when I was a kid," Chris said. He'd never told anyone about the hawk before.

"My dad and I found it in the woods, not far from the house. It wasn't hurt or anything, just too young to look after itself, to hunt. Dad tried to talk me out of it but he was as big a softy as I am, and we both knew we just couldn't leave it there to die. So we took it home with us, and after Dad got my mother calmed down, I fixed up a kind of perch for it in the garage, and we fed it hamburger. Kept it all that winter.

"It was a mean little thing—had to keep it tied or it would've pecked our eyes out, I think—but I didn't mind that, hawks are supposed to be mean. And sometimes I could get near enough to pet it. Then one day— God, I'll never forget—it was early spring and I was in there feeding it. I must've let my guard down, or something startled it. Anyway, it gave me a real peck, good and hard, drew blood. At first that made me kind of happy because I knew that it wasn't a baby anymore, that it was strong enough to survive. But I was worried because I knew if my mother saw the gash, she'd want me to get rid of the hawk.

"I was standing there in front of its perch, winding my handkerchief around my hand, and telling the thing how silly it was to make trouble— you know, the way you sometimes talk to animals.

"I'm not sure what happened, but I guess talking to it like that, and of course being a little miffed about the hand, made me look at it—really look at it for the first time.

"I'll never forget that thing looking back at me. It didn't hate me, I could've understood that. It didn't really know me or care. It was a stranger, and standing there alone in our old garage with it, I was a stranger too. I knew that we'd never know each other. And that we didn't belong anywhere near each other.

"I've never felt so lonely in my life as I did looking at that hawk, knowing that nothing I did, not all the love and care in the world could make us anything but strangers."

So moved, Marvin thought he saw tears threaten.

"And you think Jennifer List's like your hawk?" he asked softly.

"That's right, man. She doesn't belong with other people. She's a stranger to her heart, just as much as that hawk was."

"What did you do with it afterward? Did you keep it?"

"No," Chris said, "I let it go. But you know what?"

"What?"

"I wanted to wring its neck. Because what I saw then, the strangeness, loneness, it scared the shit out of me."

Marvin was impressed with Chris' story. But not as much as he was with the black, chauffeur-driven Rolls that brought Jennifer to West 105th Street, and took them away, while all the people who were out on the street or happened to be looking out of their windows stared after them.

Even so, he looked for signs of Chris' hawk in the pretty, plump woman next to him in the car. After a while, he had to admit that he felt something. But it was the most mild discomfort; it could have come from the beginning of a cold.

Nothing, he decided, that he couldn't handle.

3

DURING DINNER he did most of the talking. He told her about his family in the Bronx. About his overprotective mother and sister, and the father for whom life began and ended in a series of unprofitable deals conducted in Turkish baths from Williamsburg to the Bronx. He told her about the fights, the love-hate with his sister and mother, then about Korea, the shock of violence and fear of death. She watched and listened. He even told her, without details, about the women, how he used them, how much it meant to him to be able to use them, and how unsatisfactory it had grown. He watched for signs of jealousy, for her commitment to saving him from the "others," but whatever she felt did not show.

He wasn't sure why he told her so much. He started the story of his life to charm, but found before long that he was just talking without watching himself or the effect of what he said. It was the way she listened. She never looked away from him, and there was a stillness about her. Her eyes did not widen at appropriate places; there were no expressions of sympathy.

Finally—the table was long cleared and even the late diners were beginning to leave—he said, "And that brings us to the glorious present."

"What are you working on now?" she asked.

"Psychosomatics, mainly, at least in a way. You might be interested—we're gathering data on how emotional makeup influences the development of disease. It's just a baby now—the whole field, I mean—but someday. . . ."

She leaned back in her chair.

"Is there really anything in it?"

"Of course there is. We've built a really solid case, at least statistically, for psychosomatic influence on breast-cancer incidence—and it makes sense." He was really interested now, he never talked about his work to women. "We've found that a woman who has had some serious psychic trauma, her husband's death, her mother's, is more likely to develop breast cancer within a given period of time than other women. There's even some indication of something you could call a cancer personality. That'll be our next project. Right now we've gotten pretty sidetracked, but we'll get back to business soon."

"Who's we?"

"Richard Ching—the head of the whole thing—professor of psychology, et cetera. He's the guy with the grants, and I am number one, very respected assistant."

"How have you gotten sidetracked?"

"About a year ago Ching ran into a Dr. Karp, who'd been working for years on telepathy and psychokinesis. They put their heads together and figured out that there might be some connection between psychosomatics and telepathy, that if the mind can wield enough energy to change our normal physiologic responses—give you ulcers, change the normal pattern of cell growth, make you ill, even kill you—then thought has real physical energy, like light, even like a radio wave that can be sent and received. That's telepathy."

"Do you believe that?"

"No, but Dr. Ching seems to."

"What about the other, the psychokinesis?"

"Same sort of thing. If thoughts can change internal physiological patterns, then why not external physical ones? Why couldn't this same energy act on matter outside the body?"

"Like objects?"

"Like objects."

Something tugged at her. She wanted him to be quiet so she could see what it was—object—some sort of object shimmered behind her eyes. It was longish, made of glass. . . . Then he spoke.

"Of course it's all nonsense."

It was gone. "What?" She was annoyed at him for speaking when she almost had it.

She looked as if she had been asleep, the hazel eyes wide and empty. His pores opened, his ears felt stuffy. For a second the sounds around him stopped, the air emptied—this is what Chris had meant—but he fought. His right knee was shaking. He fought harder, made himself look around. People were walking by. Listen, he told himself, their feet make sounds. Then he heard them. Silver clinked on glass. He'd made it.

Jennifer watched, horrified. Now it would end. Tears filled her eyes. He saw them, something caught at him—unexpected. Nothing hawklike in those tears.

He reached across the table for her hand. It was very small, thin fingers, nails pale, trimmed short. "Hey, baby," he said softly. "It's okay. . . . Too many fried dumplings."

For a moment she looked as if she had heard a foreign language. Two of the tears spilled, then she smiled. The light glowed in her eyes—he had never seen such a smile, and he suddenly thought that she was pretty, quite pretty, and that the smile was beautiful.

He wouldn't let the chauffeur drive him home first, he wanted to see her to the door, he said, and then he'd grab a cab. He knew she'd invite him in, but planned to say no—best to begin very slowly. Just a kiss this time, a good one. He thought they would have an apartment-house hallway to themselves. When they stood on the step of her house—five stories of it, east of Fifth Avenue—his resolve almost left him.

"You live *here?*"

"Yes." She watched him fight awe.

Then he laughed, really laughed. "In the whole thing?"

She laughed with him—sweet, soft laughter, quiet, clear as ice. He looked up at the huge old graystone, and realized that something—the house, her laughter—something excited him.

He pulled her against his erection. She felt it, through his clothes, and right there on the steps she reached for it, grabbed like a child.

He heard her gasp as she touched him, then he kissed her. Her eyes were closed, he saw tears at the corners. He looked as he kissed, past the closed eyes to the street where the huge black car waited.

"Easy," he crooned, "easy, baby."

Just then someone turned on the outside light. The carved wooden door opened behind the glass one.

"Is that you, Miss Jennifer?"

Marvin shrugged, grinned, and stepped away.

"Yes, Albert, it's me. I'll be right in." The door stayed open. A man's figure was backlit by the hall chandelier. Beyond it Marvin saw a polished marble floor, reflecting back the crystal light.

"Next Saturday?" Marvin knew it was a courtesy question. She would see him whenever he wanted.

"Next Saturday?" Why not tomorrow, she wanted to ask, and Monday? Next Saturday was so long to wait.

It was almost light by the time she fell asleep, and after eleven when she awoke. Her hand still remembered the hardness, and she thought her lips looked a little bruised. No one had ever kissed her on the mouth before.

Breakfast was long over, but Albert took her usual Sunday-morning order—oatmeal, eggs, bacon, and grilled tomato—and started for the kitchen.

"Albert." She was looking down at her hips and thighs. "Just bring me some coffee, toast, and orange juice."

They hadn't fixed any time or place to meet. She wasn't even sure that he had her phone number. What if he forgot? She decided she would wait until Friday: if he hadn't called, she would call him—very definite she'd be. "Shall I pick you up?" she'd ask. And he'd be so relieved. "Thank heaven you called. I didn't know how to—"

"Shit." She said it aloud, another first. Albert, returning with a tray, pretended not to hear.

Marvin would have no trouble finding her number if he wanted it—from John, or Ellen.

"Excuse me, miss." Albert again. "Mr. Ross on the telephone for you." Up so quickly she knocked over the coffee cup, left Albert to mop up, and in confusion ran to the phone in the pantry.

"Hi, baby. Did you sleep okay?"

Mrs. Coleman was watching. Jennifer shoved the door closed with her foot.

"After a while. I couldn't—" How could she tell him? ". . . couldn't forget the feel of it against me, in my hand. I can still feel it, and your mouth. . . ."

"Couldn't what?" he asked.

"I couldn't get to sleep at first."

A pause. Then, "What are you doing on Monday afternoon?" She wouldn't have to wait until Saturday. "My last class is over at three. I'm not doing anything after that." A late-afternoon movie? Maybe just coffee, or maybe, maybe he was going to take her home with him—he couldn't just say so, there'd have to be some excuse, they'd have to play the game a little longer. . . .

"You remember what I told you about Ching? The studies?"

She did.

"How would you like to join one of the parapsych study groups? Nothing much to it, just sit there for an hour at most."

Not a word about Saturday, about wanting to see her. She tried to sound cheery.

"Of course." She knew she was being greedy—it was certainly better than spending the whole week wondering if he would call. He told her exactly where, what time, then good-bye.

He sounded perfectly normal, not frightened, not wanting to get rid of her. But hardly anxious. She stood in the closed pantry, the dead receiver in her hand, for a long time. She hung up finally and went to find her mother.

"Hello, dear. You slept late." Kate was in her sitting room, surrounded by the Sunday paper. She'd worked her way to the crossword puzzle, which she always saved for last. The room was full of smoke, a full ashtray sat on the floor next to her.

"Yes, dear?" A little impatiently when Jennifer didn't say anything. Sunday morning was almost the only time Kate had to herself, and she kept it as sacrosanct as possible.

Jennifer opened her mouth. "Help me," she wanted to say, "help me, Mother. If I lose him I'll die, and I know there's something wrong—and he feels it, they all do—tell me what you know." No sounds came. Kate was looking less and less interested.

"Jennifer, say something or close your mouth." She was sorry the minute she said it. She started to apologize when the intercom rang. Kate answered it.

"For you, Jennifer. A Mr. Ross."

Jennifer grabbed the phone—she couldn't go out of the room to talk to him, that would mean too many questions.

"Yes, Marvin."

"Listen, I forgot to say anything before, but Saturday night's still on, right?"

"Of course," very nonchalantly, but Kate was watching and saw the high color and lit eyes.

"Just wanted to be sure, baby. I didn't want to get left out."

"Left out?"

"I didn't want you to make another date."

She sputtered. "No, yes," some silly things, then said good-bye.

"What an extraordinary conversation," Kate said. "Is that the boy you were out with last night?"

"Not boy, Mother." And suddenly very self-assured: "He's over thirty."

Kate thought her eyes looked too bright, too excited.

"Why not ask him to dinner on Saturday? Ask Ellen, too, and John Cransten."

"We might have some other—"

"Yes, I think that would be very nice. We haven't seen Ellen for a while, and Mr. Ross would probably enjoy meeting your family." Kate knew Mr. Ross would probably enjoy nothing less, but Jennifer's manner was unsettling, and she wanted to meet Mr. Ross very much. There was a lot at stake; for Jennifer of course, and for the boy perhaps, too. It had been a long time since Kearney, but Kate knew nothing had really changed. "Yes, dear, I think I shall insist." She was watching very closely. Jennifer tried not to look miserable. "Call Ellen now, before she has a chance to make other plans—I gather Mr. Ross is definitely available."

Ellen accepted at once, she always did. Jennifer thought she liked showing the Lists off to John as her "close friends."

"Marvin will be there, too, Ellie."

Silence.

"Ellie? I said—"

"I heard you. How did this happen?"

She had to tell Ellen—someone—all about it.

"It happened last night. Oh, Ellie, everything happened last night."

"Everything?"

The tone stopped Jennifer. Something underlay the word, something jarring. She covered herself by instinct.

"Well, maybe not *everything*."

Ellen knew she had revealed more than she intended. She backtracked, made her voice light, friendly.

"Something must have happened, baby. At least I hope so—maybe a little squeeze here and there. . . ."

Jennifer was so relieved at the change of tone that she started to tell Ellen all about it.

"He kissed me, Ellen, really kissed me, and he let me—" Her face was getting red and hot. "I can't say it on the phone."

"Never mind, baby, I'm sure my imagination is adequate." They both laughed, finished their plans for Saturday, and hung up, everything normal.

But Jennifer wouldn't have recognized the expression on Ellen's face as she put the phone down. It had a scraped-bare look. Ellen could see Jennifer now, as clearly as if she were there, in that incredible room Kate had "fixed up" for as much money as Ellen's father made in a year. A four-poster they had carted from some uncle's estate in Winter Haven, the Willard clock her grandfather had had in what the Lists called the "old house," a mansion on Fifth Avenue that was torn down when Tom decided that he couldn't afford not to build an apartment building on the site. A floor Tom had shipped from France for his "little girl," drapes of handwoven embroidered wool from Nantucket, bed-cover to match, and a huge antique Chinese carpet dyed a blue Ellen thought only glass could hold. Jennifer could go out of the door of the incredible room into a hallway lined with paintings, down the parquet, thick-runnered stairs, to the huge marble entrance hall under the crystal lights. She had all that.

She was not, Ellen vowed, going to have Marvin Ross too.

4

CHING WATCHED them as they came in and sat down. There didn't seem to be anything remarkable about any of them, there never did, but he couldn't help hoping that as individuals or as a group there might be something. . . .

"First, let me assure you that what we are trying to prove here is not impossible; on the contrary, we already know that it is not only possible, but has in fact happened. So that what we are trying to do here is to confirm evidence."

He went through the same tired speech, repeating made-up data that was supposed to relax them, to convince them that others had already done what he was asking them to do. They listened. Nothing in his manner suggested his own disbelief, his weariness with the business.

At first he thought he did believe in it, at least he knew he wanted to. But now he was just tired of it. He was never sure why he wanted it to be true, why he wanted to be the one that proved it. Maybe, he thought, just because people always want to believe a thing like that, because the mystery makes life more bearable? Maybe. But now he considered the whole project an unequivocal failure, and he was anxious to get on to the next.

He sighed.

He was so used to success. Then he made himself concentrate on the people in front of him.

"Now, the task is very simple. This is just what it looks like, a paper airplane in a catapult." He stepped aside to reveal the rig on the table behind him. When Jennifer saw the bit of folded paper in the makeshift catapult—just a slotted strip of wood fitted with a rubber band, poised like a toy rocket—she felt embarrassed for Marvin. The whole thing looked pretty pitiful.

"When Mr. Ross"—he nodded at Marvin, who stood next to the table like an attendant in a magic show—"releases the rubber band, the plane will take off. It will fly in the direction it is pointing, and unless something changes its course, it will hit the wall or window, and fall. You are going to concentrate on keeping the plane from hitting anything. Watch it as it flies, try to imagine—to actually see it change course." He smiled. "Paper airplanes are quite malleable, so it should be quite simple to keep it away from the wall. But it will take all twelve of you, and you must concentrate on it totally and think of nothing else."

Ching left Marvin alone with the ridiculous equipment, turned off the overhead light, then walked to the back of the room.

Jennifer heard something whir behind her. A shaft of light beamed over their heads to light the plane and catapult. She turned back. The light was coming from a movie camera on a tripod. It was an elaborate-looking thing, obviously expensive and professional-looking enough to make up for the makeshift plane and catapult. Marvin waited until they had all looked at the camera, stopped shuffling, coughing. Soon the room was very quiet.

He released the plane.

It sailed across the room, hit the wall, and fell.

He refitted the catapult with another plane while everyone shifted position. Again he waited until the quiet satisfied him, then he released the second plane. It sailed close to Jennifer, hit the window a few feet away from her, then fell. She saw it hit, saw the nose crumple against the glass. It fell turning, wounded, and she felt sorry for it.

She watched Marvin refit the catapult. The little plane wasn't just a bit of paper. With its folded wings and delicate, pointed nose, it looked vulnerable, and she didn't want to see it smashed against the wall, crumpled, wrinkled, thrown away.

He was ready. He waited again for quiet and he got it. Not just quiet this time, but a kind of stillness that didn't seem possible in a room with fourteen people. He thought they couldn't be more silent if they'd been turned to stone. It was an odd feeling—even the normal, usually unnoticeable currents of air, tiny drafts, seemed to be missing.

He released the plane into the dead air.

It sailed, again for the window. But long before it reached it, the plane turned gracefully, steadily, and headed straight back to the table.

It touched down at the edge, then slid smoothly until it was a few inches from the catapult.

There it stopped, leaned over on its side, and lay still.

There was some rustling as members of the group craned to see if it had really landed, a few excited whispers, one or two nervous giggles.

The bustle started to subside. Marvin held up his hand for quiet and the shuffling and voices stopped altogether. The air became leaden again, totally, without sound or movement. He refitted the catapult, trying to keep his face as impassive as possible, his movements steady.

He paused and held his breath. He had never felt such stillness.

He unhooked the rubber band.

The plane *whooshed* into the vacuum, flew higher and farther than it had before.

A few feet from the wall, it looped, headed back through the unmoving air, landed on the table, slid, and stopped.

"Okay, doc, what happened?"

Ching took his glasses off, wiped his eyes, pinched the bridge of his nose. It was the first time Marvin had ever seen him handle himself in any way before. It was the only sign he gave of his feelings.

"I don't know. But our alternatives are clear. Either those twelve people have some kind of gestalt power that can control the way objects move, or one of them is psychokinetic. Incredible luck—less than two weeks before the conference and we've got something to show them—something they've never seen before. That maybe no one's ever seen before." His voice sounded calm, but he was rubbing the tips of his fingers across his lips.

Marvin snorted.

"Easy, Marvin. We don't know what we're dealing with yet. Unlike Karp, I don't believe in collective power—I think it's an individual, and we have to find whoever it is."

"How do we do that? By asking the one who made the paper airplane land to stand up?" Marvin was angry. He didn't know why.

"We could question them, of course," Ching said slowly, "but I don't think that will do much good, because whoever it is probably doesn't know what he did."

"Why? Seems a hell of a thing to be able to do without knowing it."

"Because anyone who knew that they could do such a thing would never reveal himself so easily."

"Why not? Being psychokinetic isn't against the law."

"Marvin, how do you feel about him? About the one who made that plane land?"

Marvin looked at Ching without answering. Then he stood up and walked across the room to the window that overlooked paths and grass. It was almost dark.

"Answer me. The truth, Marvin. How do you feel about him?"

"I—I envy him."

"Is that all?"

Marvin turned back.

"No."

"Tell me the rest. It's important."

"I'm not sure."

"Do you hate him?"

No answer.

"Maybe a little afraid of him?"

Still no answer.

"I understand," Ching said, "because I feel the same things—envy, hate, fear. That's how most people would feel. He'd know that, wouldn't he? If I know it, he'd know it too, wouldn't he?"

"So, he'd know it; so what?"

"Take the next step, Marvin. Anger. Yes, you're angry. Why?"

"Maybe because—" Ching waited while Marvin thought about his reactions. Then, "Maybe because I can't—"

"That's right, Marvin, you can't. And there's someone who can. A whole new definition of 'can.' And of course that makes you angry—why, look at you; you've clenched your fists. Now, one more step, and you'll see why he can't possibly be aware of what he is, and why we have to try to find him without telling him."

Ching's games. Marvin's jaw ached. He hated Ching, hated the unknown person who had made Marvin Ross into a nobody. He wanted to find him, to face him, to—

"And what would you do with him if you did find him?" Ching asked as though he'd read Marvin's thoughts. "Assuming you were capable of doing anything to him at all."

"I don't know," Marvin said.

"Think, Marvin, think. What if you could control him—control the person with the power? Use him; would you do it?"

"I don't know."

"But you'd *do* something, wouldn't you? You couldn't just forget that he was there, could you? Now, what would you do? If you could, Marvin, if you could. Would you kill him?"

"Maybe, maybe I would."

"Of course you would! Most people would—kill the stranger." Ching sounded pleased, as if Marvin had figured out a puzzle. "And if I know that, he would too. Which means he'll take the next step—he'll be afraid."

"So he's frightened. So what?" Marvin liked the idea that whoever it was would be afraid.

"Marvin, Marvin." Ching shook his head. "You're not thinking. All right—we frighten him, and we would. So you can be sure that if the person knew he had this power, he wouldn't reveal it in a psychology experiment."

"All right, so he doesn't know. So what?"

"Marvin, there's something else. We have to be very careful in all this. You see, if he does find out, what danger are we to him? Really? What do you think you could do to him? Someone with that kind of power? Of course, it could begin and end with paper airplanes. But until we know that, we must take the most ridiculous precautions, because it may be incalculable, beyond anything we can imagine. And if that's true, and he realizes it, what then? What does he have to be afraid of?"

Marvin stared at Ching without blinking as he realized what the man was implying. Danger. In the carpeted office of the chairman of the psychology department of Columbia University, they were talking about danger. Marvin wanted to laugh until he remembered that in the same room, just a few seconds ago, they'd talked about killing.

"You do see now, don't you," Ching said, "in the last analysis, *he* has nothing to fear. Whereas *you*. . . ."

Ching paused and raised his hands, palms up. He was smiling.

That's it, Marvin thought, the little bastard's happy about this whole incredible thing. There's some stinking freak walking around who can turn the whole goddamn order of everything upside down, who might have more power than anyone ever dreamed of having—and he's happy about it!

5

Too much of everything. The table gleamed too brightly. Too many courses—fish, eggs, meat, salad. Too many different wines, one for each dish. It made Marvin a little dizzy. Which piece of silver? Which glass?

Ellen didn't stop looking at him, her lips oily, slightly parted. The mother watched him too, eyes narrowed, measuring. And Jennifer, with a kind of wonder, as if he were something rare and wonderful that she couldn't believe she had captured.

Mr. List and John talked and ate, the only ones who seemed to have something to do besides stare at him.

He thought he did well enough, kept the conversation light, always moving, and he knew no one could see the strain. But they were pulling the strings, and it was beginning to make him angry. Finally they were finished. Then, into the other room—he didn't know what they called it—and had there more to drink, this time out of huge, tissue-thin balloon glasses. A silver coffee service was brought, Kate poured, and he had to hold the cup she gave him. Then a cigar. He was getting queasy.

Finally Tom List did what he did best: He got down to business.

"Well, Marvin." Cold blue eyes looked at him, as measuring as his wife's, but much shrewder. He didn't waste time with preambles. "Has your family been here long?"

Marvin wasn't going to play the game. He'd have Jennifer no matter what Mr. List did or thought. That was going to be clear from the start.

"Not very—about fifty years."

Mr. List was unhappy with the answer. He tried another tack.

"Ross? There's the Grayson Rosses, live out on the island. Any—"

Marvin interrupted. "I'm sure they're no relation. My father's family came here from Russia, about the turn of the century."

"From *Russia?*" Tom's face was swelling, getting red. Ellen was smiling. Marvin couldn't see the others.

"Yes." Marvin was enjoying himself for the first time that evening. "From Russia. Things weren't too healthy for Jews in Russia then, and my grandparents got—"

"*Jews!*" Marvin thought the older man was going to have a stroke.

"That's right," he said. "We're Jewish." The silence was absolute.

Then someone began to laugh. Clear, sweet, it belled across to him. The lovely voice filled the room, soft, full of defiance, the laughter wrapped itself around him. Jennifer almost ran to him, while the others watched, and, still laughing, she leaned toward him until their cheeks touched. Now the laughter was just between them, their private joke.

The sound was irresistible. Kate began to smile, John chuckled, and when Marvin looked up, he saw Tom's mouth twitch, then spread, until, always delighted with his daughter's defiance, he was laughing with them.

Marvin and Jennifer had tears in their eyes as they laughed and looked at each other. Under the tears, he saw her longing and knew that she would do anything to have him, and she saw that he was both happy and surprised at how pleased he was with the prize he'd just won.

Only Ellen sat grim, unsmiling.

When they dropped him off, Ellen memorized the address. He turned to wave at them, the streetlights turning his hair blue. As he walked away from the car, she realized again how big he was, how well made. She would have to plan this very carefully.

In some ways this was not the best night. Everything had gone his way. By the time they left the Lists', after a few minutes of Miss Simp in the hall, mooning over him until Ellen thought she would vomit, he was flushed and happy, the house on Seventy-eighth Street already his domain. And worst of all, the way he treated Jennifer—he liked her! Ellen could see that, he really liked her. And maybe, after tonight, he even wanted her a little—along with the house and the money.

The evening had started out better than she had hoped. She had thought Marvin would hedge, try to ingratiate himself. But he hadn't. He had been too sure of Jennifer to eat the Lists' shit, and she thought it would all come out in the open right then. Wonderful. Tom would throw him out of the house, while Kate counseled patience and little baby Jennifer wrung her hands. It was all there, all ready to happen.

And then that little bitch had to laugh, and everything had changed.

She could still hear the laughter—gay, confident, rising like a song over the collected hatred and envy in that room.

The remembered laughter decided it—it would have to be tonight. She never liked to admit it to herself, but she knew that there was something lovely in Jennifer List, something that the others ran away too fast to see, something that Marvin would find before long, and maybe grow to love . . . if she gave them time. Besides, he would fuck her; maybe tomorrow, maybe Monday, as soon as he could, to consolidate the hold he already had on her. And once that was done the rest was inevitable. She knew that as soon as Jennifer's love and need focused on Marvin, she would forgive him anything—even a lapse with Ellen.

She got rid of John. "Must be something I ate," she said. "I feel really rotten—I think I'm going to be sick."

He was all sympathy. "Probably the salmon. It can go off in no time, especially when they fancy it up like that. Maybe tomorrow?" She heard the hint of begging with satisfaction.

"Of course, sweetheart. Call me in the morning and we'll work something out for tomorrow night. Maybe Jennifer'll let us have the car one more day."

They were in front of her building and he had to let her go.

She waited in the lobby, waving at him through the glass door, until he drove away. She went out on the sidewalk just as Jennifer's car turned the corner. Jennifer's car. For a second she felt sorry for her, even thought about going back, forgetting the whole thing, letting Jennifer have her bit of happiness. But there were ten years of slights behind tonight, ten years of being a member of what Thomas List called "the West Side rich," of not receiving the right invitations, of being Jennifer List's not-quite-acceptable girlfriend.

She hailed a taxi and gave Marvin's address.

He was undressed, just getting into bed, when the doorbell rang. "What are you doing here?"

Ellen walked past him into the living room. He followed. She was still wearing the same gray silk dress. It dripped from her shoulders, clinging to her ribs and hips, suggesting the V in her crotch as she moved.

He saw that the hair on her arms was dark and heavy, and he could imagine the black pubic hair sliding down from her pale flat belly. She was the most beautiful woman he had ever seen.

She waited until he stood still, then she just looked at him, the huge dark eyes shadowed, without expression. She raised her hands, slipped the gray silk from her shoulders. It slid to her waist. Her breasts were small, pale skinned as her face, pointed. Light beige aureoles centered by long, long nipples.

A few steps, the silk moved with her, and she was standing next to him. She took his hands, held the thumbs, and stroked circles with them around the nipples. She let one hand go and began a light scratching on his thigh through the thin cotton pajamas. Then up until she was smoothing the underside of his penis.

"Ellen. . . . Oh, baby." He couldn't help himself. He leaned over, now using the thumb without her help, and took the other nipple in his mouth.

Afterward, she wanted to go right to Jennifer, to make her "confession." But it was after two, and she wanted Jennifer to be awake, aware. The phone wouldn't do, she wanted to see her face. She would have to wait until morning.

***

Jennifer was alone in her room, too happy to study, to do anything but watch the rain soak the back garden, when Albert announced Ellen. It was just after ten.

"Tell her to come up."

She was very glad that Ellen was there. She wanted someone to gloat with. Her mother and father were very quiet at breakfast, obviously repenting last night's tolerance and would now almost certainly try to find some way of extricating her from any further involvement with Marvin.

But she had made up her mind, and, she thought, Marvin had made up his, and now she knew that she was going to marry him. Last night, she saw that for the first time he wanted her too, along with the money. She was certain of that—really wanted her.

Ellen knocked.

"Oh, Ellie." She threw her arms around the other woman, kissed her.

"Did you see the way he stood up to them? He sort of fought for me, didn't he? Wasn't he wonderful?"

Ellen's expression said that nothing was wonderful.

"Ellen, what's the matter? Did you have a fight with John?"

"No, no, nothing like that—it's just that you're so happy." Pause, sigh. "I don't know how to tell you."

"Tell me what?" Her nerves lurched. "Has something happened to Marvin?"

"Oh, *he's* all right. It's you I'm worried about." It was truer than intended. She'd never seen Jennifer look so happy, so pretty. Again, unwanted pity pulled at Ellen. She fought it back.

"Jennifer, you've got to face it." She was doing it for Jennifer's good. After all, he did fuck her last night. "You know nothing about him."

"Of course I don't—well, not nothing." She laughed—last night's laughter. Ellen stiffened.

"I found out that he's a Russian Jew," Jennifer went on, "and I guess I always knew that he had no money. So, you see, I *do* know a couple of things about him. Now—" She took Ellen's hands and led her to the loveseat near the fireplace, set now against the rain. "What don't you know how to tell me?"

"Jennifer, this is so difficult. . . ." Ellen sat down, letting Jennifer keep hold of her hands and wishing that she could bring tears to her eyes. The scene was so perfect for her confession. If only she could cry. Maybe the heat from the fire would make her eyes water. But looking toward the fire meant looking at Jennifer, which she couldn't quite handle, so she kept her eyes on the carpet, abandoning the attempt at tears.

"You know, John and Chris Haynes are fairly good friends, and

Chris has told John a great deal about Marvin. And, well, he's got quite a stable of women. I mean you're hardly the only one—"

"Shit," Jennifer said aloud for the second time in her life. "He's told me all about that."

"But you don't understand." Ellen's voice was beginning to whine with excitement. "They aren't just dates, he—he," as if saying it offended her sensibilities, "sleeps with them."

Jennifer thought of the things Ellen had told her that she had done with John, and laughed again—more laughter. Ellen's stomach muscles tightened, getting ready. No more laughter for Miss List—not for a long time.

"Of course he does," Jennifer said. "It never occurred to me that he did anything else."

"And it doesn't bother you?" Her eyes wide, innocent. She was setting it up perfectly, and Jennifer bit.

"Of course it does. But that was before he met me, before last night."

It was time. Ellen had to consciously relax her mouth to keep from smiling. The whine left her voice, she spoke smoothly, softly.

"I'm talking about last night. About after we left here."

She turned at last from the carpet. Contrite, she told herself, look sorry. If only she could squeeze out a tear—and looked at Jennifer.

The rest stopped in her throat.

Jennifer still had one of her hands—squeezing it, but Ellen felt nothing except the sudden, absolute stillness in the room. The fire leaped silently, the rain spattered against the window in a silent vacuum. She saw nothing of Jennifer List in the dry white face that stretched itself across fine bones, in the huge eyes reflecting the silent fire, reflected in the mirror on the wall. The lips, like a line of ink, moved.

"Don't speak." They formed the words, but Ellen heard nothing. "Don't say anything."

Ellen was gasping, tears finally pouring down her cheeks. She tried to free her hand.

"Jennifer, oh, God, Jennifer, please—"

Snap!

The fire was alive again.

She pulled her hand free, then slipped off of the loveseat to her knees on the carpet.

"Jennifer."

The two women looked at each other for a long time. Then Jennifer put out her hand. Ellen forced herself not to flinch. Very gently Jennifer stroked Ellen's beautiful face, wiping tears away.

"Don't tell me, and I'll never know," she said softly. "Don't ever mention it again. Promise me."

Ellen nodded.

"Oh, Ellie, you're the only friend I have."

Jennifer hadn't meant what had happened, Ellen saw that. She didn't even know. The pain in the hand Jennifer had squeezed rose in throbs, but Ellen made herself move it to take the hand that still touched her cheek—just as gently.

"I promise, Jennifer."

By afternoon the hand was so swollen and painful that Ellen went to the doctor, before her mother saw it.

He examined, "tsked," X rayed.

"Going to have to have a cast, Miss Olivieri. Two of your fingers are broken and four of the bones at the back here. What on earth did you do to it?"

"Slammed it in a door."

That night, hand cast and all, Ellen eloped with John Cransten. Both sets of parents gave their blessings. By the end of the following week they were in Oregon. She did not see Jennifer for almost ten years.

She never saw Marvin again.

6

JENNIFER WAS waiting in the room with the others from last Monday's group. Watching the door. Ellen was gone; she didn't want to think about it. There would be no more visits, no more phone calls. And she hadn't seen Marvin for almost a week. Except for a few formalities to other students, she hadn't talked to anyone except her parents and the servants since last Sunday.

Finally Marvin came in and smiled at her. A few of the other women in the room—all better-looking than she was, she thought—looked over at her. He called a name. One of the members of the group left the room with him. She waited again. Ten minutes and he was back. This time he called her name. She crossed the room—the other women were watching—and just as she reached the door he took her arm.

"What do we do now?" she asked as they walked down the hall.

"Nothing special, just watch a movie. And then we'll be finished with the whole thing."

"But what about the plane? We did make it land, didn't we?"

"You and almost every other group we tested," he lied as Ching had told him to.

She was disappointed. "I thought we were special."

He laughed and squeezed her arm, as if to say she was special even if the others weren't.

Then he was opening a door for her, and Dr. Ching was getting up to shake her hand.

"I'll see you afterward," Marvin whispered, then he left her alone with the little man.

The office was more corporate than academic, and she realized that Dr. Ching had a great deal of stature in the Columbia Graduate School. A carpet muffled her steps as she walked across the room to the chair he nodded at—leather, with arms. A movie screen was set up a few feet in front of it, and behind, almost against the far wall, was another camera set up, just as expensive-looking as the one they'd used last week. This time a projector.

Ching was shaking her hand.

"All we're trying to do today is monitor your physiological reactions while you watch a film we made some time ago," he lied, "of another group which was also able to complete the experiment. I hope you don't mind contraptions?"

She said she didn't.

"Fine, now if you'll just roll up your sleeve." She did as he asked. Then, without protective jelly, he attached an electrode to the inside of her arm. Odd place to do any kind of monitoring, she thought, but he seemed to know what he was doing, so she didn't protest.

She couldn't know that the electrode was attached by a dead wire to an empty box. Only the projector was real.

He turned out the lights, and a picture that she could have sworn was taken last Monday began flickering on the screen. There was the plane they'd saved—at least it looked the same. It sailed, then turned, exactly as last Monday's plane, and flew back to the table, the camera faithful to every move. She was disappointed that another group had done what she was watching. Whenever she thought about it during the week, the plane's salvation seemed peculiarly her property, shared with the other eleven in the group, of course, but theirs alone. Now she knew there were many groups who'd done the same.

Marvin was in the next room with a real paper plane, on a real cata-pult. As soon as Ching turned on the projector, the light they'd rigged the night before came on in the room where Marvin waited. He had exactly seventeen seconds until the film plane took off in the room where Jennifer watched the screen. Thirty seconds to refit the catapult before the scene repeated itself. He and Ching had rehearsed all morning and his timing was perfect, the real and the film plane synchronized almost exactly. The first group member had tested without a hitch, except that of course the real planes crashed again and again into the window or wall.

He thought the scheme was pretty ridiculous.

"How the hell is this going to work?" he growled at Ching as they rehearsed. "Why should watching the damn thing on film in one room make it possible for him to make the real one land in another room?"

Dumb trick, that's all it was, Marvin thought.

"I don't know that it will," Ching answered mildly. "But it's reasonable to expect him to be able to control the plane, even on the other side of a wall. He'll be relaxed enough to repeat whatever unconscious process was triggered last week, and we will not have to reveal anything to him. Yes, I think it has an excellent chance of working. He will not be self-conscious. Most important, he will not even know he's being tested."

Jennifer watched the movie plane. At first it worried her, but its fate was imprisoned on the film and it landed safely again and again. By the fourth time the film ran through the scene she was relaxed, almost sleepy, the fake electrodes forgotten. Again, Marvin's hand released the band, again the plane flew, looped, landed—five times. Ching couldn't hear the projector clicking. It was incredibly quiet, and he was a little out of breath. Six times, starting seven. . . .

The office door crashed open, light streamed in from the hall around Marvin's figure.

"Jennifer."

Ching crossed the room, still breathing harder than normal, and flicked the light switch. Jennifer blinked.

"Jennifer," Marvin said again. He was white.

"Thank you, Miss List." Ching ignored Marvin. He unpinched the electrode. "That will be all for today."

She stood up. Marvin's eyes followed every move, staring as if he'd never seen her before. He was standing in the door, barring her way, staring, staring. Then suddenly the stare changed, took on expression. He grabbed her bare arms—a clutch, almost painful. Excitement was what she saw now in his face, felt in his hands. A naked thing as if he suddenly couldn't control his passion for her.

"Jennifer, I—" No one had ever looked at her like that before.

"Excuse me, Miss List. Please come back this afternoon—about two o'clock?" Dr. Ching's thin voice broke the spell. Marvin let her go and she walked past him out the door, obeying the little man's command.

"Shut the door," Ching said sharply.

Marvin obeyed.

"Now tell me what happened—exactly."

Marvin was still pale, no expression on his face.

"She made the thing land five times."

His voice was shaky.

"Calm down," Ching said. "Get control of yourself. We've got to see the rest of them. Now go back and get the next one on the list. And don't say a word, not a word."

"Why? What difference does it—"

"Cover, Marvin. We still need cover."

"From Jennifer?"

"Later—as soon as we've finished with the rest. I'll talk to her and we'll see."

"But—"

"Alone. I'll see her alone."

"She's—" He stopped himself.

"She's what?"

Mine, he wanted to say, she's mine.

"Nothing." He left Ching and went back to the room where the others were waiting.

An hour later Ching sat facing Jennifer. Her face was fine-boned, he thought. Fine eyes, too. She would be a very beautiful woman in a few years. But that was to come. For now, even though she was attractive enough, quite pretty really, she was not in Marvin's league; it must be the money—a whole house on Seventy-eighth Street, Marvin had told him. Of course now there was a great deal to see in her, but Marvin had only just found that out. He would have to watch that relationship very carefully.

They talked generally for a few minutes. He carefully alluded to the others in the group who had been and would be interviewed, although he had no intention of ever seeing any of them again. Then a little talk of Marvin. She was infatuated with him, that was clear, eyes on her hands, even blushing when Ching mentioned him. Yes, he would have to be careful about Marvin.

He decided there had been sufficient preamble.

"Has there ever been anything especially strange in your life?"

"What do you mean?"

"Just anything odd. For instance, did anything not easily explainable ever happen to you, or around you, when you were a child? Do you remember things being broken when no one was near them, or things moving? A table or lamp, say—anything like that?"

The sense of familiarity she had felt in the restaurant with Marvin closed in on her. She hesitated, but again it was only a feeling, nothing specific.

"No. . . . I don't know. I'm just not sure."

"You mean there might be?"

"Yes, there might. I had an odd kind of *déjà vu* a while ago and it seems to have something to do with an object—something shiny."

"But you can't remember when it was or what happened?"

"No, I can't. Though I've tried, I really have. Maybe it'll come to me one day."

"Do you think it's important?"

She wanted to deny it. "Oh, not really," she wanted to say—then everything would stay ordinary, and she could go on sidestepping his questions until the time was up and she could go home, intact, nothing revealed. But the weight was getting too heavy, the years were piling up on her, and lately a kind of bitter coldness that pushed out the ready sympathy she felt when she was young, even for strangers, even for earwigs.

"I think it's the most important thing in my life." She spoke softly, almost dreamily. Ching suddenly felt uneasy.

"Why do you think it's so important?" he asked. He had to force himself to look at her.

"I don't know."

"I see. Is there anything else? Anything at all that happened to you that no one could understand or explain?"

"Yes, I think so. A little boy I knew was killed after I'd had a fight with him. And no one seemed to know what had killed him."

Ching shifted in his chair. He took his glasses off and pulled his carefully ironed and folded handkerchief out of his breast pocket. He crumpled the smooth bit of cloth and wiped his chin.

"Was he hurt—I mean, did he die of injuries or was it something else?"

"Injuries. They think a truck must have hit him or something like that, because he was broken to pieces."

"Were you with him when he died?"

"No. I'd just pushed him—into a wall, I think, and then I ran away."

Ching felt sick. The handkerchief was sodden in his hand.

"How old were you when this happened?"

"It was our first summer in Nantucket, I must have been seven or eight."

Ching had to keep himself in his chair. He forced himself to sit back.

"Do you know how I feel now?" he asked her.

"Yes," she said, "you want to get away from me."

"That's right. Do you know why?"

"You're afraid of me."

"No." He examined himself mentally. "No, not just afraid—it's more basic than that. It's very deep. It's a generic unease, I think. Perhaps something akin to the way a cat feels about a snake."

She just looked at him. Sweat beaded his forehead, a drop rolled past his eye. He blinked.

"You said you were always alone. Does everyone you know feel this way about you?"

She hated him. But she hid it.

"Most people. My family doesn't. And my friend Ellen doesn't, and I guess Marvin doesn't either."

"But everyone else?"

"Yes—everyone else. Except for Mrs. Hussey, the lady who used to cook for us on Nantucket. But she's dead." Mrs. Hussey—she hadn't been so old, sixty-five, when she died. Jennifer thought she'd have her for a few more years; a little longer, anyway. Now Ellen was gone, and that left—whom did that leave? Whom did she have? The pause had gone on too long. Dr. Ching was waiting, watching. Abruptly she said, "All the rest feel like *you* do." The hatred showed. Ching realized he would have to be more careful about what he said to her. He had to make her his friend.

"What do people who are near you have in common?" he asked as gently as he could.

Jennifer thought for a bit. Ching used the handkerchief to wipe his forehead. "My family couldn't help themselves, they *had* to stand me. Mrs. Hussey—I don't know, she just liked me, always did. I think she felt sorrier for me than afraid. Ellen just never seemed to notice what I'm like—or to care. Besides, she's beautiful, really beautiful, so she's always got men, but not many friends. Actually, not any friends except me. So, I guess, in a way, she and I are in the same spot."

"And Marvin?" he asked softly.

"I don't know. Maybe, maybe he's just different." She sounded hopeful.

As soon as she left, Marvin came into Ching's office.

"Did you hear all of it?"

Marvin nodded and sat down. Lonely woman, the loneliest woman in the world, he thought. The boy in Nantucket bothered him, but that was silly. She'd only been a child. He wondered whether Ching thought she had really killed the kid.

Ching opened his overnight case, put the wrapped film can and his notes inside. The conference began tomorrow morning and Ching was going to make their report.

"Are you going to tell them about the kid in Nantucket, too?"

"No. We don't want her to look like a murderer. I'll just say that the 'subject reported confirmatory phenomena that occurred during childhood,' something like that."

"Then you think she really killed him?"

Ching closed the suitcase and straightened up.

"Maybe. In any case, I'm sure you see now how insane your relationship with her is, how dangerous."

"Why, doc? Even if she did do it, it was an accident."

"Was it? What makes you so sure?"

"Because if it hadn't been, she would never have told you about it. She didn't even know what had happened."

"Marvin, I made you my assistant because you are an exceptionally intelligent man. And now you're acting like a fool. Why did the paper airplane land?"

"Because she made it—"

"No. She didn't know what she was doing then, either. But the paper airplane landed anyway—because she *wanted* it to. Don't forget that."

"You're not going to scare me into not seeing her anymore, doc, I don't care what you say. I've got too much at stake."

"What do you mean at stake? Money? There are plenty of other rich women."

"No," Marvin said, "it isn't just the money."

"You don't love her."

"How do you know that?"

"Because I know you." That rankled, and Marvin started to get angry. He might love her—it was possible that he could love her.

"So, if it isn't the money, and it isn't love," Ching asked, "then what is it? What is keeping you from admitting the most obvious danger—"

"Don't put your fears on me, Ching."

"They're real."

"Of course they are." Marvin's arms hung over the arms of the chair, his fingers stretching and curling with excitement he tried to keep out of his voice. "But it's your fear, not mine. It's you who can't see. Here it is at last, the real thing. Something you have been looking for for years— God knows why—and suddenly here it is. And what're you going to do about it? Take some pictures, collect some data, and then report to that bunch of dried-up jargon pushers you call psychologists that you've seen it—you've seen the other side of the fucking moon and you're scared shitless. And then what? Even if they believe you, what do the brain eaters do? Why, write it up in some musty archive or other that no one ever reads and let it moulder in a library, while you try to forget the whole thing. Not me. It's all there, and I'm going to have it."

"And what," Ching asked calmly, "are you going to do with it? What do you do with power, Marvin?"

Marvin's hands stopped flexing. He sat very quietly.

"Well?" asked Ching.

"Control it," Marvin said softly.

"You're a fool." Ching locked his suitcase and picked it up. He was through arguing. "You'll have to excuse me, I have a train to catch." Then he stopped himself, appeared to soften. Marvin had the upper hand with her now because she wanted him.

But Ching had looked for her for years, and in terms of time, thought, money spent, she belonged to him. He didn't want Marvin on guard against him—against the girl, yes, but not against him, not yet. He tried to regain a tone of friendliness. "Give it some time, Marvin. I'll be back on Monday and we can talk some more. Maybe I'm being a bit of an old woman. But let's do some more work with her and see how far this thing goes. It may be a fluke after all—some strange arrangement of time, place, physiology, that'll never happen again."

"You don't really believe that."

"No, I don't. I think that Jennifer List is a basic genetic variant, as different from us as we are from Neanderthal"—he loved phrases like that—"but we don't know yet. Let's wait and find out."

Marvin didn't say anything, and Ching was late. They were waiting for him in Westchester, Karp and all the others. A standard scientific meeting with golf if it didn't rain, and plenty to drink if it did. And tomorrow, Ching would show the film and tell them something they had never heard before. He couldn't wait to see their faces.

He made one more try. "Remember, Marvin, power is only what you do with it. And in any case, it belongs to her, not to you. It always will." No answer. He had to be content with the last word.

The old fart, Marvin thought as soon as Ching was gone. The hypocritical old fart. He was sure that no matter how much fear Ching professed, the old man wanted her to himself, without Marvin interfering or exercising any control over her. And Marvin knew that the more tractable he seemed, the more secure Ching would feel—until Ching had lost the game altogether.

Tomorrow night would settle things with Jennifer, but not with her family. He didn't have time to win their approval, and he didn't want to try. But a pregnant daughter would make the Lists see things very differently, and once he and Jennifer were married. . . .

The girl, the money . . . the power.

7

THE PERFECT seduction; all planned. He even cleaned the apartment a bit. Then he left and walked several blocks down Broadway until he found a flower stand where he bought a mixed bouquet of autumn flowers. He brought them back and put them in an old, dented pewter cocktail shaker he found in the cabinet under the sink. He put it on the mantel, then he went into the bedroom. It was clean, even clean sheets, but it looked too bare. He remembered a little flowered china bowl that he'd seen in the back of one of the kitchen cabinets while he was looking for something to put the flowers in. He went back, got it down, and washed away the sticky dirt that covered it. It was pretty—delicate china, covered with tiny blue flowers, and shaped like an egg with the small end cut off. He filled it with water, then took a few yellow mums from the large vase and some greens which he tucked into the bowl. He carried it into the bedroom and put it on the table on Jennifer's side, then looked around once more—satisfied with the room, the plan, everything.

It was going to be a perfect evening. A light dinner somewhere, not too fancy, and not too far from the apartment. Not too much to drink or eat, and not too much time traveling. And when they got back, he'd give her a little dry white wine. He had some chilling in the refrigerator. He was already a little excited. He'd be gentle with her, he was always gentle—the master of the light touch. They'd start on the couch, or rather, he'd start. He knew she'd have very little to say about what was going to happen. And after a while, she'd know what power was and she'd be helpless; always the best part, especially tonight, especially with her. He realized as he was getting dressed that he was really looking forward to it, which hadn't happened for a long time. The whole process had become so ritual, the outcome so predictable, that there wasn't any real pleasure in it anymore. But tonight. . . . He smiled at himself in the mirror just clearing from the shower's steam. Ching was wrong, this was a situation he could handle.

They were finished with dinner by nine. Long before either could get tired. Perfect. Then back to the apartment. She didn't hesitate.

"Yes," she'd said, "I want to go with you." Just as simple as that, no coyness, no archness. And no shrill, nervous conversation as they walked the three blocks from the restaurant to his place, no fishing for reassurance or phony changes of heart. She was silent for the most part and he was, too; but it wasn't heavy silence, just two people walking together who'd talk another time. She walked steadily, keeping pace with him until they turned into 105th Street and were at the entrance to his building. Then she stopped. She didn't pull back, and she still didn't say anything. She just stopped and smiled. He wasn't ready for a smile like that. He didn't think anyone had ever been so honestly happy to be with him. He smiled back and took her hand.

Upstairs, he led her to the couch, gave her the wine, took some himself. Then he sat down next to her. He let her sip, then took the glass out of her hand. Everything fine, on schedule, except that he knew vaguely that his usual smile, eyebrows slightly arched, like an actor about to deliver the best line in the play, was missing. He kissed her, tasting wine. The wine tasted lovely from her mouth. She didn't deliberately kiss back, not the way other women did, she didn't put her arms around him. No clutching, no grabbing, no getting ready. Too moved by the touch of him to get a grip on her own passion, she didn't pull away to look at him, didn't arch her back or push with her hips. Her whole body sank into him. He felt his arms tighten around her. He hadn't meant to hold her so tightly, but all of a sudden he couldn't get her close enough to him. Her mouth opened with his, and his tongue touched hers.

Easy, he told himself, trying to stay separate, to hold some control. He made himself loosen his grip, but she pushed closer as she felt his arms relax.

"Easy," he said aloud. "Easy, baby; let me—"

He moved his hand down her back, her hip, and along her thigh. He started rubbing, and she turned her leg out to make it easier for him to reach her. Then she put her hand on him, trying to imitate his stroking, as if she wanted him to feel what she was feeling.

She wasn't watching him, she wasn't watching herself—they were alone together. He thought he'd never been really alone with a woman before without one or both of them standing by, judging his performance.

She wanted to hold him. She was reaching for him the way she had the first time he kissed her. He let her; he leaned back a little so she could, watching her face as her hand found the bulge, slid along it. She pushed gently, her eyebrows pinched in a little frown. Then she found the zipper, started to pull.

"Wait," he said. It was much too soon.

"Please let me."

He couldn't help himself, he had to let her. He unbuckled his belt and pulled his trousers wide open. His erection was free; it felt like glass, and for the first time in years he wondered how long he could hold out. He caught his breath when she leaned over and rubbed her cheek against him, then her lips.

"I'm wet," she said.

He couldn't believe she'd said it.

"Can we now?"

"Oh, Christ." He grabbed her shoulder, pushing her cheek against him for a second. "You're too much, too much. Come on, let's get to bed."

She didn't want to move.

He laughed, shook her gently, holding her away.

"You sweet, dear thing—if you don't stop, I'm going to come all over you, all over the couch. I'm going to leave spots on the ceiling."

She laughed, too, but he could see she wasn't sure what he meant.

"I'll show you," he said, as if she'd asked. "Oh, will I show you!"

He stood up and pulled her to her feet. Then—he couldn't help it—he put his arms around her again, hugged her, kissing all over her face. He wanted to tell her that he loved her, that if he could be alone with her just once a day for the rest of his life something ugly and toxic in him would break up, drain away. But he couldn't say things like that yet.

He had to stop in the hallway, just past Chris' door, and hug her again, running his hands down her body, across her breasts, along her legs. He pushed her against the wall, stroking inside her underwear, letting his finger slip into her. The plan was gone, his usual touch was gone —no sinuous, careful stroking, watching the effect; he was even a little afraid that he might hurt her.

"Here?" she asked him.

"No—Christ, let's get to the bedroom."

She went with him, but the hall would have been fine—on the floor, or even leaning against the wall, she didn't care.

Finally they were in the bedroom. She helped him undress her. Slip, underwear, stockings; he knew it was bad to leave her naked and unattended while he took his own clothes off, but he didn't care. He wanted to look at her, to touch her, he couldn't wait anymore. Her body was prettier without clothes; thin, fair skin, he could see light threads of blue lacing her breasts and thighs. He touched the veins, one arm around her back. The wool of his sweater must be scratching her—bad technique, very bad; but he was helpless against what was happening to him.

Helpless.

He tried to push the feeling away, but he couldn't.

Helpless.

She had everything; a power was closed inside her that he would never be able to reach. She'd taken the control he'd always had over himself, over every woman he'd ever known. The body on the bed wasn't his instrument at all. He tried to hold on to the tenderness, excitement. But it was going, draining away— sucked out of him because she lay there watching him, waiting for him to do what *she* wanted, what she'd wanted all along.

He started getting undressed. He stripped down as if everything were normal. His sweater and trousers were off. He pulled his T-shirt over his head. But it wasn't normal; the erection was gone. His penis was folded against him inside his shorts, no hint of excitement.

But he went on to his usual next step. The old sinuousness had returned to his hands, but the tips of his fingers were numb.

He began rubbing himself, bare now, against her—nothing, no excitement, no sensation at all except for a feeling of dread that spread until he felt it in the tremble of his fingers as they touched her. He kept trying. He pumped against her, nothing. He tried to enter her—impossible.

He was sweating now, the dread turning to panic, and all the time he could sense her excitement cooling as she began to realize what was happening. Still, he would not give up moving her body this way and that, until he was covered with sweat, the muscles in his legs twitching, aching.

Finally she rolled away out of his reach, then off the bed and on her feet. They looked at each other. She tried to smile, to say it was all right —there was time—she understood—it was her fault, but her neck arched with strain and she was standing above him—which made the smile seem arrogant, defiant.

"What the hell are you grinning at?"

His voice was hoarse with anger and it frightened her, but the smile was like a tic she couldn't control.

"Please," she said, "I didn't mean—" She tried to touch him, he was so beautiful, his skin paler and finer than hers, his body hair black, glistening with sweat. He slapped her hand away and stood up, towering over her, his hands flexing. She stepped back, wary, and as she moved he saw past her into the dark bathroom. Both doors were open. Chris— he must have come in while they were out to dinner, and Marvin knew that he was on the other side of the second door—watching—had been there through the whole thing.

"Oh, my God." He almost sobbed. What a joke. They hadn't been alone, not for a second.

She misunderstood and tried to touch him again.

He jumped away from her as if the touch burned.

"Leave me alone, you goddamn freak!"

"Don't." She put her hand in front of her face. "Oh, please don't."

"Get the fuck out of here, you—you monster! Get out," he screamed.

She wanted him to stop yelling at her, she had to stop him. "Please," she said, "please." She was backing away from him toward the bathroom. She was going, but that wasn't enough, he wanted to hurt her. He grabbed the little flowered bowl that he had filled with flowers for her—the china so thin it almost broke in his hands—and he threw it at her. Instinctively she moved aside, the bowl flew past her, lost momentum, fell, and broke on the bathroom floor.

It was delicate china; the sound of it breaking was picked up and magnified by the tiled bathroom walls until it was all she could hear.

Suddenly she was a child again. The air was full of flowers and water and glass. She could see it, the glass caught and reflected it against the droplets of water until the air glistened with water and reflecting glass like the tail of a firecracker.

Then she remembered the rhesus monkey's heart. The spot of light jittering and shining in the screen like a drop of water in the sun. The heart shuddering in its cavity, trying to pump. She saw it so clearly, the dot of light, and the heart itself; helpless, shaking. She saw it swell again, its last try, and freeze. The image stayed on and on in her mind until she bent from the waist and lowered her head and shoulders as far as she could.

Finally the blood came back into her head. The picture was gone; she wasn't going to faint and she knew where she was again. She straightened up carefully and opened her eyes.

Marvin's body was slumped across the bed, half on and half off. As she watched, gravity pulled and the body slipped slowly off of the bed and crumpled to the floor.

Tom was asleep when the intercom rang. Kate reached it and picked up the receiver before it rang again.

It was after midnight and the servants were instructed not to ring after ten thirty unless it was something important.

"Madam, there's a man on the phone for Miss List."

"Well, why ring me? If Jennifer's not home—"

"She's not home, I've tried her room." Albert, usually the model butler, had actually interrupted her. Kate knew then that something must be wrong.

"Well, take a message, Albert. I'm sure she'll be home before long." She kept her voice low not to disturb Tom.

"Yes, ma'am, I'm sure, but it's a policeman, and he says he must speak to Miss List."

The police—but if they wanted to talk to Jennifer then she must be all right. Maybe the car—maybe someone had stolen the car. Jennifer was always parking it on the street and it was bound to be a temptation. Yes, that must be it.

"Albert, I'll speak to the officer. Please connect him."

"Miss List? Is this Miss Jennifer List?"

"No— would you hold on please." Kate put the voice on hold and ran into Michael's empty room. She reconnected.

"Hello," she said, "I'm Mrs. List. My daughter is not at home." It was a relief to stop whispering. "May I help you, Mr.—"

"Mr. Charles, ma'am. I'm a member of the detective bureau of the New York Police Department, Twenty-third Precinct. Would you like my badge number?"

"That won't be necessary, Detective Charles." She always gave people a title if they had one. "What can I do for you?"

"We need to talk to your daughter. Do you know where she is?"

"Not exactly, but she'll be home shortly. Will you please tell me what this is all about? It's late and we're not used to having the police call." It *was* late—almost one o'clock. Kate's politeness was beginning to fray. Where was Jennifer?

"We really need to talk to your daughter."

Was the man a robot?

"I told you she's not here and I *must* ask you to tell me why you have to speak to her."

She could tell from the dead air in the phone that he had covered the mouthpiece—apparently to consult with someone else. It was a long consultation and Kate realized that her hand holding the receiver was beginning to sweat.

"Mrs. List?"

It was the same man.

"Yes, I'm still here."

"Do you know a man named Marvin Ross?"

"Yes. He's a friend of my daughter's."

"Well, there's been some sort of accident here." Kate was looking around for a cigarette. There was an old pack in the drawer of Michael's desk where his phone sat. She managed to get one out of the pack and lighted it with the table lighter on the desk. It was stale and some of the tobacco had fallen out of the end so that the tip flared up when the flame touched it. It tasted awful.

"What sort of accident?" she asked.

"We're not sure, ma'am, but Mr. Ross, he—uh, how well did you know him?"

"I've met him."

"Then you weren't close?"

"Hardly." Get to the point, she thought. Goddammit, get to the point.

"Well, ma'am, he's dead. Apparently your daughter was with him when he died."

Kate sank to her knees. The phone cord uncurled to meet the stretch.

"My daughter—she's—please, is she all right?"

"She was. I mean, she left here okay."

"Where's 'here'?"

"We're at Mr. Ross' apartment now. According to his roommate, your daughter left here less than an hour ago, shortly after Mr. Ross died."

"I see—then the roommate saw the accident?"

"Yes, ma'am, and he tells a pretty wild story."

"Captain Charles—"

"I'm not a captain, ma'am. I'm just a lieutenant."

"Lieutenant Charles"—Kate corrected herself—"exactly where are you now? What address?"

Another consultation.

"Mrs. List, we're at 212 West 105th Street, just off Broadway. We're just about to—"

"Is the body still there?"

"No, ma'am, it's been taken downtown. We've notified his folks and they're on their way down there now."

"Lieutenant"—Kate stood up—"I am Katherine Compton List. My husband and I own our own home at 2 East Seventy-eighth Street. My husband is a member of the New York Stock Exchange and is the president and major shareholder of the Carroll List Company—that is the third largest brokerage house in the world, lieutenant. Do you understand me?"

This time there was no consultation. "Yes, ma'am, I understand."

"Now then, I will be at Mr. Ross' apartment in approximately half an hour. I want you and whoever is with you to stay there until I arrive—I do not want you to do anything more than you have already done. Is that clear?"

"Yes, but—"

"If you do as I ask, lieutenant, I can promise that everything will work out well for all of us."

She hung up before he had a chance to answer.

Jennifer had tried—she and Chris worked on the body together for half an hour until they were both exhausted and covered with sweat. Finally she sat back on her heels and told Chris that it was no use. He went wild then, pushing Marvin's body around, screaming at her to do something. There was nothing to do, he was dead and that was the end of it. She started dressing while Chris kept thumping the stiffening chest. Finally he gave up. He just stayed on his knees next to the body, watching her dress. She was ready in a few minutes, then she went out of the bedroom and called the police from the phone in the living room. When she came back he was still on his knees, watching her. There was nothing to say. She looked one last time at what was left of Marvin. But it was not him at all—Chris had closed the lids over the filmed eyes and even the wonderful blue had gone. The dead face did not resemble him at all.

Now Jennifer was driving east across empty roads that bordered bays, through small towns, silent and unlit, then past Providence, across rivers, down black streets, and back to the main road and its yellow line that stretched ahead into the night. On all sides the world sank into the darkness, ahead and behind nothing except the line. New Bedford next, and the car was squealing through the sleeping city; finally the canal bridge to Buzzard's Bay and she was on the Cape. Nothing left now except the long straight pine-lined road from Falmouth to Wood's Hole. Her foot stayed steady on the accelerator, the car chewed the miles. Little towns raced past, slipped away. Dawn came, then light.

The nine o'clock ferry was getting up steam when she reached it. She drove up the ramp into the huge dim interior and parked the car.

The horn blasted into the mist, then the ferry eased along the dock, left it behind, and headed into the fog.

The image of the filmed blue eyes and pale, flaccid body followed her across the bay. No grief, nothing yet, except horror as her fingers remembered the feel of the dead skin and the compliant limbs flopping as she and Chris moved the body. And his mouth; lips falling slack, tongue lolling until the body began to stiffen and the tongue froze to the roof of his mouth. She ran to the long, narrow ladies' toilet on the second deck and vomited until the gagging tore her throat raw.

She stayed on her knees in the cubicle, swallowing, trying to breathe evenly until the nausea eased. Then she came out into the washroom and splashed her face with cold water until it felt stiff and dry. She looked in the mirror.

She didn't know the face that looked back at her. Pale, eyes rimmed in black, her hair wild, red in the gray sealight that came through the portholes. No trace of Jennifer. Only a pale, beautiful stranger that knew something.

"What?" she asked the reflection. "What happened to him? What did I do?" The reflection crumpled as her face twisted. More cold water. Then to the mirror. The stranger looked back.

"Nothing," she said to it. "Nothing. I didn't even touch him."

It was a terrible cold face. She turned away quickly and went outside into the fog and wind, feeling very light, as if she'd lost a lot of weight. The rest of the trip she stayed on deck until the mist had soaked her clothes.

The ferry landed and she drove down the ramp to the wet parking lot asphalt. Then across Nantucket Town's empty cobbled streets and out the 'Sconset road. Past the turnoff for Mrs. Hussey's old house. Eight more miles and she heard the ocean, then saw it beyond the gray shingled houses of 'Sconset Village. She drove around the village fountain where Hal Kearney and the others had waited for her. The little plot that circled it was unplanted now except for some soaked ivy whipped by the wind. She drove to the end of the village, to the beginning of the wall that enclosed the Evarts estate. She stopped the car next to the wall and got out.

She thought this was the spot, but she couldn't be sure. She remembered trying to reach the dirt road, to get past the cobbles, but the cobbles had been taken up long ago, and the whole road was paved. Had she come all this way to look at a wall? The stones were wet, the grass bordering the wall scraggly. She looked up and down the length of the wall, then took a few steps. This looked more like the place, or maybe even farther along. But what if it was? What would seeing it mean? What could it tell her? She shook her head. The wind was cold and she went back to the car.

The house was cold, too, the furniture dust-covered, and the electricity turned off for the winter. There was water running—cold only, and she knew that there must be some tea and sugar in the kitchen but she was too tired to look for it. She went upstairs to her room and untied and unrolled the mattress. Then she found a quilt in the storage closet, wrapped it around her without taking her clothes off, and lay down on the bare mattress.

Kearney and Ross . . . Marvin.

"I'm sorry," she said to the stiff, empty body that was all she seemed to be able to remember about him. "I'm so sorry." She cried for him until the mattress ticking was soaked and she couldn't cry anymore. Then she fell asleep, her cheek against the damp mattress.

8

THE SUN was shining in the east, right into the window, when Jennifer woke up. She'd slept through the night. She'd been gone almost two days. Her mother and father would be frantic.

The room was freezing. She kept the quilt around her as she went out in the hall to the phone. But it was dead, shut off for the winter. She had to find a phone.

She washed as well as she could with the cold water, but her clothes were wrinkled and dirty, her hair tangled, and there was a mark on her cheek from a mattress button. She combed her hair, then went downstairs to the kitchen to find some tea. But the food cupboards were empty except for a swollen can of something. Her stomach was still tender and she wasn't going to find out what.

She gave up, put on her coat, and went out to the car. The sun was very bright, burning the frost off the grass. The cold burned her cheeks pink, and the wind tangled her hair again. She put the car in gear, and was easing it around the gravel drive to the road when she saw a car parked in front of the Borden house.

It hadn't been the Borden house for several years. The Bordens had moved away after George, the son and heir, had been killed in Korea. He had been with Hal Kearney on the day of their last encounter; the day Kearney died. She got out of the car and stood in the frozen leaves. She hadn't been sorry when she heard that the Borden boy was dead. Not glad the way she was when they told her that Kearney was dead, but not sorry.

Hal Kearney and Marvin Ross. She waited in the wind for a minute until she thought she was calm enough to ask their new next-door neighbor, or whoever was there, if she could use the phone.

The house had been empty for two seasons. Then last year a New York family bought it. She'd heard the name but couldn't remember it. There was an old man—she'd seen him in the garden at the end of last summer. He was supposed to be the major shareholder in the largest trust bank in New York—in the world—with interests, her father had told them, in several hundred industries and businesses. And he had a grandson, but she'd never seen him.

She crossed the two lawns and rang the bell. Someone called, then footsteps, and the door opened.

She knew the man who opened the door and he knew her, but for a second she didn't remember. Then it came back to her. The walrus man who'd stayed with her in the hall the day the rhesus monkey's heart had stopped, the day she met Chris Haynes.

They stood there while the wind swept in the door. Then he said, "I didn't think I'd ever see you again."

"May I use your phone?"

"The phone?"

"Yes, I need to use your phone." He didn't answer for a minute; the wind was sharp, very cold.

"Please, may I come in?" Why were they standing here like this?

"Of course. I—I'm not thinking, please come in."

She followed him inside, to a huge sitting room still furnished with the Bordens' things and looking dusty. The heat was working, and the warmth in the room made her start to shiver.

"I—I'm sorry," she said.

He took her hands.

"You're freezing," he said. "Let me get you something hot."

"Do you have any food?"

"I do. Eggs, bacon, whatever you'd like. I'll scramble some eggs for you while you make your call."

"No, please, don't leave me alone." She held onto his warm hands. "I don't care what you hear, just don't leave me alone, please."

"Of course I won't," he said, as if her outburst were quite normal. "But you'll have to let go of me if you're going to use the phone."

"I'm sorry. Where is it?"

"Over there by the window."

"You won't leave while I'm talking?"

"No. I'll stay until you tell me I can go."

She nodded and went to the phone, then looked back at him. He sat down near the empty fireplace while she gave the operator the number and listened to the clicks that signaled the call's relay. Then the phone was ringing in New York.

"Jennifer, thank God." Kate was crying.

"Mother, oh, please. I'm so sorry. Please, Mommy. I'm okay, but something terrible happened, and I—"

"Jennifer, where are you?"

"Nantucket. I'm calling from next door, the Borden house. I would've called before but I was too tired to think of it, then the phone was dead."

"What are you doing in Nantucket?"

"I started to tell you, Mother. Something happened to Marvin."

"I know, dear. The police called here looking for you."

"The police?"

"Yes, but it's all straightened out now and there's no need for you to speak to them now."

"But I want to speak to them. I want to know what they've found out."

A beat of silence; then Kate asked, "What they found out about what, Jennifer?"

"About what happened to him, about what killed him."

"Oh, they think it might have been a cerebral hemorrhage."

"They *think?* Aren't they going to make sure?"

"What do you mean, dear?"

"An autopsy, Mother. Aren't they going to do an autopsy?"

"Oh dear, no. Nothing like that."

"Why?"

"Why should they? There was no sign of violent death, and apparently unless there is the police can't insist on an autopsy."

Jennifer wondered how her mother had found out so much about it.

"But what about his parents? Don't they want to know what happened? He wasn't sick, Mother, there was nothing wrong with him." Her voice was beginning to break. "And he was a young man. Don't they want to know what killed their son?"

"I spoke to his sister, Jennifer, a very nice reasonable woman, who explained that they will not allow an autopsy unless they're forced to by the courts. And since the police have no further interest—"

"Why did you talk to his sister?"

"I called his sister to extend our condolences and to ask if there was anything we could do to help."

"How did you and his sister get around to discussing autopsies?"

"Quite naturally. I wanted to know if they found out what killed the boy. They're Orthodox Jews, and she told me that her parents had been quite upset at the possibility that their son's body might be violated, but the police assured them that they were not going to ask for an autopsy, and the whole family is very relieved. It would be very cruel of you to start stirring things up now. Besides, what difference does it make? He's just as dead."

"We're a cold bunch, aren't we, Mother?"

"There's no need for that kind of thing, Jennifer. Your father and I have had two terrible nights wondering where you were, what happened to you. I was afraid that you'd do something—" Kate was crying again.

"Mother," Jennifer said, "I love you." Kate hiccuped with shock. They never said such things to each other. She didn't answer.

"Do you love me?" Jennifer asked.

A second passed, then Kate said, very distinctly, "I love you very much, Jennifer."

"Then tell me, Mother, tell me what happened to him."

No answer.

"Mother?"

"Jennifer, I am not going to discuss this with you again. Now get into the car and come home at once."

"But, Mother, you have to tell me. Whatever you know. Don't you see—"

The phone clicked, then went silent. Her mother had hung up.

"And Hal Kearney," she said to the dead phone, "what happened to him? Oh, Mother, Mommy, please. . . ." Silence. She wiped her eyes again and hung up.

He was still sitting there watching her.

"Are you all right?"

She nodded, hoping he couldn't see the tears. He got up and started to leave the room. "I'll make you some eggs now."

She ran after him.

"Can I come to the kitchen with you?"

He smiled at her. "Of course."

He fed her, gave her tea. Clouds were piling up, obscuring the morning sun. The ocean looked dark through the kitchen windows and the house was very quiet.

"Can I stay here with you for a while?"

"As long as you like."

"What are you doing here this time of year?"

"I came up to do some work. I have a lab of sorts upstairs, and it's very quiet. I haven't seen anyone until now."

She was probably interrupting him. She should leave, but she wasn't going to. She couldn't face New York yet, or the empty house next door.

"What kind of work?" She wanted to keep him talking.

"I've been studying the effects of insecticides on spider mites."

"What are they?"

"Arachnids—same class as spiders."

"Oh, bugs."

"No, arachnids." He smiled. "Bugs are quite different. They're rather handsome little things—would you like to see them?"

"I guess so," she said uncertainly.

"They're upstairs. But if you'd rather not. . . ." He hesitated.

"No, I want to."

"Good," he said. "They're just slides. Besides, they're almost microscopic, and they're vegetarians."

She went with him, never letting him get more than a foot or two away.

His workroom was upstairs. The walls were covered with bookshelves, and photographs and paintings of more different kinds of insects than she'd ever imagined. Half of the ceiling had been replaced by a skylight, and one of the windows had been converted to a miniature greenhouse.

"What do you grow in the greenhouse?"

"Roses. I need them for the mites."

He picked a bunch of slides and put one under the microscope on the worktable. Then he turned on the scope light and stepped back so she could look. She adjusted the lenses until the tiny arachnid was in sharp focus. It was lemon yellow, almost round, and had eight delicate legs from which sprouted tiny hairs. More, longer hairs grew out of the fat little body. The mouth parts looked harmless, more like foreshortened legs than like the beaky things she associated with flies and mosquitoes.

"What are the dark spots on its sides?" She asked.

"Just undigested food in her gut."

"*Her?*"

"Yes. The males are much smaller—rather few in comparison to the females, and relatively unimportant."

He showed her several more—all the same shape, all just as harmless-looking, except their colors changed from yellow to orange to deeper orange, and then he put one under the scope that was red.

"Why is she that color?"

"She's a new form. A mutant."

A mutant, she thought. A changeling.

"What caused the change?"

"Insecticide," he said. "Until they were exposed to insecticide, they were all yellow, like the first one, and all sensitive to the toxic effects of the insecticide. When we sprayed them most of them died, of course. But the ones that were left began to produce some slightly orange offspring which were somewhat more resistant to the chemicals than their parents. When we sprayed we kept killing more of the yellow mites —the normals—who were insecticide-sensitive, while we killed fewer of the orange ones who were more resistant to the spray. Then one day, *she* turned up."

Jennifer looked into the scope again. The mutant mite lay imprisoned on the slide, glowing red under the light.

"And," he went on, "she's completely resistant to any of the chemicals we use. Completely."

"Was it the insecticide that caused the mutation, or was it always a recessive trait that became obvious when you killed so many of the normals?"

"I don't know. There's no way to tell. I personally think it's the insecticide. I think she's a chemically induced mutation. I don't think anything like her existed until we started spraying. Can't prove it, though."

Jennifer kept looking at the tiny speck under the microscope.

"The others," she asked finally, "the normals. Do they know that she's different?"

"Yes, they do. It's an interesting thing—quite common with mammals —but rare in lower forms: they avoid her. Of course she's a definite variation and, biologically, ostracizing oddness makes good sense. Preserves the integrity of the species. And I guess that whatever makes the normals certain of their spider-miteness also makes them recognize her variance. Yes," he finished, "very interesting. They leave her as alone as they can."

The creature's isolation closed around her. She wondered as she watched the little red mite frozen on its slide what it must be like for the creature—surrounded by the yellows, but cut off, as alone and enclosed in life as it was now in death, imprisoned in the layers of glass. Unless. . . .

"Do they ever get used to her?"

"No," he answered. "Oh, a few males do, or of course she'd never breed. But only a few, and the rest—" He shrugged.

"Then she's always alone."

"Spider mites don't really think that way," he said quickly, suspecting more tears. "It's not as if—"

"But doesn't she know? Don't you think she realizes that she's not like the rest? Don't you think she wants to be—to be near them, to be part—"

"No," he said as gently as he could, "I don't."

Then she said, not even knowing that she was going to say it, "I'm like her."

"The red mite?"

"Yes."

He looked at her. "Because you're alone?"

"Yes. That. But maybe because I'm a 'definite variation,' too."

That same tender comforting smile. "You're more or less the same color as everyone else."

"I mean it." She did. He stopped smiling.

"You think that because of what happened to that man—the accident you mentioned on the phone—"

"It wasn't an accident."

"Then what happened to him, and to the other one . . . Hal somebody, right?" She nodded. "What happened to them?"

"They died. And I'm—I'm afraid. . . . One was a boy and the other was a young man. There was no reason for their dying except—that I was there."

"I see. So you think you killed them. How did you do that?"

He sounded totally detached. Just asking questions.

"I pushed the Kearney boy into a wall."

"When was that?"

"A long time ago. About fifteen years."

"You were seven or eight?"

"Seven."

"And the other one? What did you do to him?"

"I don't know. He was—" Was it last night? No, the night before last —he'd been dead two days. "He was very angry at me and he—I don't know."

"But you think you killed him because you're like her somehow?"

"Yes."

He walked across the room to the slide boxes, opening too much distance between them; she followed him.

"These boxes are full of insects—arachnids, beetles, all sorts of 'bugs.' Put them under the right stress—chemicals, background radiation, who knows what—and you could get one mutant for every hundred of them, maybe for every ten."

"Then I could be—"

He shrugged. "Maybe. So could I—probably am, in fact; blue eyes, an old, old mutation that got sexually selected and bred true. There's nothing terrible about it—it's wonderful—the variety that's created. The variety and beauty." He was looking at her. "You'll see hundreds of species in this box, all different, all adapted to basically solving the same problem—survival—all in their own unique way. Beautiful." He laughed, shook his head in wonder. "Think of it! We were pond scum until the mutants, and we'd be pond scum yet if something hadn't changed. Become different. Tiny changes that you don't see in the beginning—but startlingly, blindingly clear when you look back along the line of evolution. And the wonderful creatures, the changelings themselves aren't aware of their difference, because even though the change is definite, the mutations that survive are usually not obvious at all. In fact, most of the mutations we can see are deleterious—nightmares, some of them, and they don't reproduce. They just die, or their own kind kill them. It's the subtle alterations that survive and breed that make the difference in the long run. But it's all chance, luck, and it takes time before you can really see that something has changed. For some insects it might take a month, a day, however their generations mark time, and you suddenly realize that you're looking at a new kind of creature. For mammals, it might take a hundred thousand, a million, a hundred million years—who knows?"

His tone, his words spoke comfort and some very old tightness, something she could not remember ever having been without began to loosen a little. "And look at the result of it, the incredibly wonderful variation with which each of us, each species sustains itself, survives. So beautiful. Why, you know, Einstein might be a mutant—just enough of a variation from the norm perhaps so that the difference stretches beyond what we can expect in normal heredity. Maybe his mother was exposed to a drug, or walked too long in the sun, or saw a black cat—and some tiny but definite change took place in the basic cell coding that made him what he is." He stopped. She wanted to hear more, she wanted him to go on talking. "What's your name?" he asked.

"What?"

"Tell me your name."

"Jennifer."

"You see, Jennifer, it's not just spider mites that are expert survivors, but maybe even Einstein. You'd be in good company then, wouldn't you? It would be a gift then, wouldn't it?"

"But what about the Kearney boy? What about Marvin?"

"Your 'victims'? I think it's the silliest thing I've ever heard."

"Please," she said. "I'm alone—I've always been alone. Couldn't it be because people sense something, the way the yellow spider mites do about the mutant? Couldn't it be that they ostracize me because I'm different, like she is?"

"Anything could be, couldn't it? But you don't bother me a bit—and I don't feel at all like ostracizing you. Maybe, though, I'm just one of the maverick males that doesn't mind."

"But don't I frighten you? Don't I make you feel generically uneasy?" How she hated Ching. "Don't you want to get away from me?"

"Not at all. But then, I'm a biologist, and I've seen much stranger things than you."

"Oh." She didn't turn her head or bow her head, or turn away. "Oh." She was crying.

"Oh, God, don't cry like that, please don't cry."

She held out her hand to him, bowing her head finally as if she couldn't bear to watch him not take it. But he did. Then she closed the space between them, getting as close as she could, holding on to him for dear life.

"Shh, it's all right, don't—please don't." But he let her stay where she was.

"Put your arms around me?"

He did; she felt them tighten as she moved against him.

"You don't think I'm strange?"

His hand moved up her back, into her hair. "I think you're the strangest girl in the world."

Part V

1

December 5, 1976 to December 22, 1976

THE FOUR MEN shook hands. It was a solemn business—ritual almost. And Stavitsky thought that they seemed to be making some kind of pact, though he did not know to do what. But the other three looked as if they understood each other's thoughts, and they included him, not suspecting his separateness.

When they finally left Ching it was only a few minutes after midnight, but outside it was dead cold, predawn cold. Nothing registered yet, except that he was exhausted, cold, and frightened. He maneuvered out of the parking space and headed south on Riverside Drive. The buildings hunched to the left of them, and to the right the strip of park, the drive, and beyond the cold black river rushing to the bay.

He looked into the rearview mirror. Galeston sat straight, unmoving, staring between Stavitsky and Stern out through the windshield, alone with his thoughts. The bars of light from the street lamps crossed and lit his face regularly, but between the lamps he sat in darkness.

"Like an old Indian," thought Stavitsky. "Like Queequeg waiting to die."

"What did you say?" Ira asked.

"I said that Wilbur looks like Queequeg waiting to die."

Stavitsky waited but Galeston said nothing. Suddenly he wanted to hear the old man's voice.

"Hey, Wilbur, did you see death in the bones?"

Galeston smiled. Stavitsky could see the accordion grin in the bar of light that streaked across Galeston's face.

"Maybe, maybe I did." The deep voice filled the car. Calm, strong, completely relaxed. Stavitsky took a deep breath. Yes, that was better, much better.

"Well, captain," asked Galeston, "what do we do now?"

The question seemed casual.

Stern turned a pale, frightened face to Stavitsky, waiting for his answer.

What *do* we do now? he wondered. Routine. He took refuge in routine—names, dates, what he could understand, what he'd been doing for years. He was a policeman, routine was what had brought him every success he'd ever had. Check it, habit said, check it out. Routine, habit. It was all he had. "Tomorrow I'll start checking what Ching told me—every word. And if there's some facts to back up what he said, then we'll decide." Decide what? he asked himself. Ching hadn't lied. How could anyone make up a story like that? He could only confirm what he already knew.

Stern nodded, Galeston kept smiling. "Still think this is a medical problem?" Stavitsky asked, looking in the rearview mirror at Galeston.

"No, captain. I wouldn't want to be the one to assign responsibility for this one."

Carole was in bed reading when he got home.

"I left you some cake on the kitchen table, dear. Take a piece and have a glass of milk with it."

He stood looking at her—cake and milk.

When he didn't answer she looked up from her book.

"David, is anything wrong? You don't feel sick again, do you?"

"No, I'm fine." He looked away and started getting undressed. But when he was down to his underwear, he suddenly didn't want to be naked in the same room with her. He'd never felt like that before, but he couldn't help it. He went into the bathroom and closed the door to finish undressing.

When he was naked, he took his pajamas down from the hook behind the door and confronted his body in the full-length mirror. His size filled the mirror and he had to step back to see all of himself. He hadn't looked at himself like this for years; there was gray mixed with the blond body hair, little areas of softness here and there, but all in all not bad. His genitals looked heavy; he stared at them until his penis started to move, thicken. He went closer until it rubbed against the mirror's surface. Then he stepped back—he didn't want Carole now, not at all.

He put on his pajamas and went back to the bedroom. She was just turning off the light.

"Goodnight, dear. Don't forget the cake."

He walked out of the bedroom without answering, but she didn't notice.

He left the lights off and wandered through the dark rooms to the dining room. There was just enough glow from the street for him to find his way. He sat down at the dining room table, rested his elbows on it, and looked out the window.

What had he heard? What the hell had he heard? Incredible.

"Oh, yes," Ching had said, "incredible. We used to speculate about it, Karp and I—before I found her, of course. I never mentioned it afterward. Mind has—is—energy. We can see thoughts, impulses, recorded on screens. So we already know thoughts have physical power of a sort. But how that energy could extend itself to affect objects, to make mass behave—" Ching had stopped, looking past them at the wall. A look so concentrated that for a moment Stavitsky had wondered if someone had come into the room and was standing behind them. *Her* power, Ching had told them, still staring beyond them. So amazing. Remember, he'd said when he'd finally looked back at them, she hadn't just deflected the paper airplane, hadn't just kept it from hitting the wall. She'd *controlled* it—made it turn, fly back to where she'd wanted it to land, and then land there. Yes, incredible. And all without knowing she was doing it.

At first Stavitsky had tried to argue, so had Stern. Not Galeston. But Ching wouldn't argue back—he'd told them what he knew, and they could accept it or not as they chose. Stavitsky could see he wasn't used to being questioned. Only Galeston hadn't said anything, hadn't asked questions. He'd looked from one to the other, whoever was talking, until finally Stavitsky had said it was unthinkable.

"No," Galeston had said then, "not unthinkable at all. I have no difficulty thinking about it."

Then he'd stood up. Too soon. Stavitsky had wanted to ask more, understand more. He wanted something to write down besides the two names Ching had given him, something to record, carry away with him. But suddenly they were shaking hands. The other three men making their pact that Stavitsky stood apart from, didn't understand, even though they included him, made him a part of it.

Part of what?

The headlights of cars coming through the park at Ninety-sixth Street streaked the table with light. He was annoyed at the light. He would have preferred the dark tonight. That was unusual, too. He didn't like the way he felt at all. His hands were sweating, and even though it was almost one A.M. he wasn't even a little tired. He looked out the window— she was just across the park and a few blocks downtown. He could remember her face very clearly, just as she'd looked when whatever it was had happened and he'd gotten sick. But now, thinking about her didn't make him uncomfortable at all. He didn't like that, either. She should make him sick and uncomfortable.

He made himself get up from the table and go into the kitchen and turn on the light. There was the cake wrapped in plastic waiting for him. He cut a wedge, put it on a plate, and poured himself a glass of milk. He put a fork next to the plate and glass on the plastic tablecloth. He would build a net of data, starting tomorrow—he couldn't wait to begin—

a net to trap and hold her. One that she'd never get out of. Facts—everything he could find out about Jennifer List Gilbert. He said her name aloud in the lighted room. It didn't sound sinister, it sounded lovely. Another reaction he didn't like.

He made himself sit down at the table, pick up his fork, and eat the cake. Every mouthful was like sweetened cotton, and he had to swallow hard and gulp the milk to get it down. But it was a normal, routine activity—eating the cake his wife had baked and washing it down with milk—and he thought it was important to eat every bit of it. He even made himself scrape the extra frosting off the plate with his fork and swallow it too.

2

JOEY KAFESTIAN was day shift, and he was already at his desk when Stavitsky walked in at eight. Stavitsky had never been in the office any morning, no matter what time, when Joey wasn't already there. Always with a half-full paper container of coffee and the crumbs of a just-eaten roll. Stavitsky had never seen the roll itself.

"Hi, chief."

"Yeah, Joey, get me a roll too, and some coffee, then come into my office."

"Sure thing, chief." Joey rose slowly and strolled to the door.

"As fast as you can, Joey."

"Sure thing, captain." He ambled out.

The midnight shift, the few that were left, were packing up. Chairs scraping, drawers opening, closing, the telephones going to work. Outside his door, as it got closer to eight thirty, men stretched and yawned, ready to go home, or took their jackets off, got coffee, ready to start the day. Everything normal.

He looked out through the gray-splashed window at the little park. It was cold, sky gray, no clouds and very windy. He watched the people hurrying across it, just like they did every morning, rushing to the entrances of the buildings that flanked the tiny square—to their fluorescent-lit offices, typewriters, computers, stock quotation boards. Usually he watched them carefully. Trying to recognize them—their coats or the way they walked—from the day before. Usually they made him feel good, something worth sympathy in their unselfconscious bustle. Sometimes in the summer he'd take his lunch to the little park to see how the morning people looked close up. He got to know many of them by sight through the years, and he'd watch for them. Even study them a bit. The way their gait changed with the season, the way they dressed, how they looked on Monday, and how they looked on Friday. When one that he'd watched for a while and gotten to know stopped crossing the park, he'd look for him for days, hoping to see him again. If he never saw them again, and they were young, he'd figure they'd gotten another job, on another street. If they were old, he'd always hoped that they had retired and not died.

This morning he looked without seeing any of them.

He had two names—Marvin Ross, dead. And Christopher Haynes. And a strip of film. "Of course," Ching had told him, "you're welcome to it. But you understand it doesn't mean anything—just a paper airplane flying across a room and landing on a table. It doesn't show her, or anyone, except for Marvin Ross, and I think all you can see of him is his hand. But you can have it anytime."

Nothing to tie a net with there. That left the names.

Joey finally came in with the coffee and roll.

"That all, captain?" he asked hopefully.

"No, Joey, that isn't all. I want you to get me a report on this man. Not homicide—natural death. And I don't have a report number. But he died in November, 1954." He gave Joey the precinct number for the 105th Street area.

"But, captain, if it was natural death—"

"There'll be a police report. Shouldn't be too hard to find. Then I want you to find this one for me—Christopher Haynes. Columbia student in 1954. Try their alumni association." It was all he could think of. Over twenty years—Haynes could be anywhere in the country, in the world. "'Substantial sort,'" Ching had said, shouldn't be hard to trace.

"If Columbia doesn't know, then get on to motor vehicles—New York, New Jersey, Connecticut," Stavitsky said.

"'Easterner,'" according to Ching. "'Good clothes, yes, definitely Establishment—for that time, anyway.'"

Lots of Midwesterners, Westerners, foreigners came to New York. Few New Yorkers ever move very far away. The most parochial people in the world, Stavitsky had often thought. So chances were good that Haynes was still in the New York area.

Joey looked at the piece of paper sadly. "Gee, captain, not much to go on. No middle initial, nothing. Hey!" Joey brightened. "Have you tried the phone book?"

For a second Stavitsky thought he was joking, but then he saw that he wasn't.

"Get the fuck out of here," he yelled, "and I don't want to see your ass until you've got the report and that address. And that better be by ten thirty. Got it? Ten thirty."

Joey ran out of the office and slammed the door.

The phone was ringing—Carmichael, to remind him about a luncheon for a retiring inspector from uptown, East Side precinct; good spot, wealthy, well-protected. The mayor was going to be there and he had to go.

Blumenthal brought in last night's reports, slightly thinner than the usual pile. Routine stuff. Then he remembered he'd promised Bob Simon from 200th to call Percy in narcotics and give him the names of four kids who'd been picked up by homicide—all on the balls of their asses. Nothing going for homicide yet, but the kids had been stoned, and they had been holding. Maybe Percy could keep them long enough on narcotics for homicide to get enough to make a charge. They'd knifed another kid in the East Seventies. Hungarian neighborhood, where murder and heroin were uneasy visitors.

Then he took his phone off the hook.

Marvin Ross, Christopher Haynes.

He added names until he had six altogether and two blanks. The blanks were the two detectives Haynes had told Ching about. They had come to his apartment the night Ross died. Stavitsky would get their names from the report, as soon as Joey—

Stavitsky went to the door and looked out. Joey was on the phone, alternately writing and chewing his pencil. Stavitsky closed the door and went back to his list:

Jennifer List Gilbert—he had taken a long time writing her name. It looked as lovely as it sounded. The rest were written in his usual scrawl.

George Hawkins

Charles "Boots" Raines

Ross

Haynes

Harold Kearney (John Starbuck)

Six names, an old police accident report from Massachusetts, Stern's written postmortem—without X rays—to the effect that Amos Roberts had broken his neck without so much as breaking his skin, and a film clip of a paper airplane landing on a table in a classroom twenty years ago. Not one single unbreakable thread from the events to her, certainly nothing to make a net with, yet.

He starred the names of the dead, then numbered all the names except hers. He wouldn't try Hawkins unless he had to. She'd bought him, and it would take pressure to get anything out of him—a lot of pressure. But if he had to. . . .

He still had Raines—safe in Manhattan General. He'd been there too when Roberts died—seen all that Hawkins had seen, and maybe he was calmed down enough to tell a coherent story.

He called Carmichael.

"But Dave, Raines is gone, been gone since Tuesday."

"What do you mean, he's gone? That man was half dead when they carried—*carried* him out of here. What the fuck did Warner do, give him a couple of aspirin and send him home to play with himself?" Stavitsky's heart was pounding. He made himself breathe deeply. "I'll have Warner's head for this."

"Shit, Dave. It's not Warner's fault. One of the social types sprung Raines the next day—a lady lawyer wearing suede Levi's and a mink pea jacket."

"You were there?"

"C'mon, Dave, that was a joke. It was your fault, not Warner's. They had to let him go—you didn't charge him with anything."

Carmichael was right.

"Where'd they pick him up, Al?"

"Warren Hotel," Carmichael said after shuffling papers for a minute. "Eighty-first and Columbus."

"Was he just shooting up or did he have a room there?"

"I don't know. Besides, even if he had a room, he wouldn't go back there."

"Why not? He's got nothing to be afraid of. At least not from us," he amended. Then he realized that she might get to him first, she could have meant the threat. God knows, Raines thought she did, and Stavitsky knew that if the cops had found him as quickly as they had, she wouldn't have any trouble finding him either. He hung up on Carmichael without saying good-bye. He unlocked and opened his bottom desk drawer and took out his revolver, its holster, and ammunition. He wiped it carefully, making himself move deliberately, calmly, against the excitement. He loaded it, then took off his jacket so he could loop the holster around his shoulder. It had been years since he'd worn it and the weight and bulge felt strange. He wasn't quite sure why he was taking it now. To protect Raines? Himself? He rested his arm against it. No, not protection really. Maybe just because it felt good to have it with him again.

He was down in the garage, walking between the mostly unmarked cars, the cold air from outside seeping down the driveway that led to the street, when he realized that for the first time in fifteen years he hadn't checked the reports to see if anyone in his secret file had been involved in anything during the night. He hadn't even opened the drawer to look at the folders.

He'd forgotten all about the file again by the time he was driving up the steep cement ramp to the street.

If he lost Raines. . . .

The Warren Hotel was two blocks south of what had once been the worst street in New York. The surrounding neighborhood had changed—block associations, trees, and a new respect for brownstones—but the Warren stayed loyal to the old days. The lobby was long and narrow, the walls shiny with too many coats of enamel, and a pitted, dirty linoleum floor. There were no tables or chairs, only a long scarred reception desk. Fluorescent lighting fought the gloom. When Stavitsky walked up the three cracked stone steps that led to the lobby, he smelled stale urine and wondered when the floor had been washed last.

Someone not quite as defeated as the place had put a red aluminum tinsel Christmas tree next to the elevator. It stood rumpled and undecorated, a forlorn token to the season.

Stavitsky went up to the counter and pushed the bell. Raines might be upstairs, right now; his connection. He made himself lean on the counter, tried to look casual. It wouldn't help to frighten anyone. A tall, neatly dressed black man opened the door to a room behind the counter and came out. He smiled at Stavitsky.

"Can I help you, sir?" Good-looking man, maybe thirty-five, clean, good accent. Stavitsky wondered what he was doing at the Warren. His shirt had long sleeves, so Stavitsky could not see if they covered needle marks.

"Did you put that tree up?"

The man's smile widened. "Yessir. Haven't had a chance to decorate it, but I got some nice glass balls, and a few of those plastic birds and angels. Expensive, you know, so I could only get a few this year. There'll be more next year." Stavitsky nodded.

"It'll look real nice." Stavitsky pulled out his badge. The man's smile froze. "I'm not looking for trouble here," Stavitsky said. "I just want to talk to a guy who may be staying here, at least he was here on Monday. Name's Raines. Thin, blondish—hillbilly type." The man's face started to close up. Stavitsky leaned very close. "You don't want any problems, baby." The blue eyes were slate and the man saw it. "And there'll be problems, you know that, don't you?" He knew he was frightening him.

The man looked at the badge, kept his eyes on it. He did not want to look at Stavitsky.

"He's upstairs now, I guess. I don't think he's been out of the room since he came back day before yesterday. He looked pretty bad when he came in, and I suppose he's just sacked out. Room 302—third floor." Stavitsky did not insult the man by thanking him.

The elevator left Stavitsky alone in a dark, bad-smelling hallway. There was one grated window at the end of the hall, but it opened on an airshaft, so Stavitsky had to use his pocket flash to read the numbers on the dented metal doors.

Room 302 was two doors beyond the elevator. Stavitsky knocked softly, hoping he would be taken for another tenant or a friend. There was no answer. He knocked again harder. Still no answer. He turned the handle. The door was unlocked, and he walked into the room.

It was very neat. The bed was covered with a clean, flowered spread that was shredding at the edges. Panels of the same cloth were thumbtacked to the wall on either side of the window. Raines had a little tin bucket set in a corner, and a sponge mop hung from a hook just above the bucket. The linoleum floor was the same pattern as the one in the lobby, but here it was clean. A freshly painted dresser stood against one wall with some photographs in standing frames on the top of it next to shaving gear, and a comb and brush neatly arranged on a plastic tray. On the other side of the bed was an alcove with a sink that had a small framed mirror above it.

Everything looked to be in perfect order—a clean little haven. There was even a radio on a wooden chair next to the bed. But the room stank. The smell was worse than it had been in the lobby or the hall. Stavitsky felt his gorge rise and he began breathing through his mouth. When he walked around the end of the bed, he saw what caused the smell.

Boots Raines lay on the floor between the sink and the bed in a pool of jellied blood.

Stavitsky made himself look at the body. Both wrists were slashed and there was a deep gash in the throat. The edges of the wounds were separated, white and rubbery looking. He'd been dead at least a day. There was an open box of single-edged razor blades on the sink, and Raines was still clutching one in his right hand.

Suicides were usually tentative, and made a few preliminary cuts before they could work themselves up to slashing deep enough to kill. But Raines had no such compunction. Each wrist was slashed once very deeply. He must have gotten impatient with the way the blood drained and cut his throat to hurry it up.

Stavitsky walked over to the dresser and looked through the drawers. Clean, neatly folded underwear, socks, and two clean frayed shirts—even a pair of pajamas waited in the middle drawer. The bottom drawer was empty. In the top drawer he found two disposable syringes and a rubber tourniquet, but no junk. There was also a box of stationery and Stavitsky wondered whom the dead man had to write to. Raines' wallet was on the top of the dresser. When Stavitsky unfolded it, an envelope fell out. Stavitsky picked it up; it was unaddressed, and inside was a single folded sheet of the stationery from the top drawer. On it Raines had written:

I did this myself.
CHARLES U. RAINES, JR.

Stavitsky sat down on the edge of the bed. Here it was at last, as he knew it would be . . . blood and stink. A poor miserable bastard who owned two clean shirts and a radio lying in his own blood. Her work, as surely as if she'd held the blade herself.

"Shit," he said to the body. "Shit. Shit. Shit." He slammed his fist against the dresser. He felt cheated. "You could've helped me, you could've stopped her. Why didn't you tell me what happened, at least write it down if you were going to die anyway? Jesus, Raines, what the hell did she do? Was it so terrible, *so* terrible—worse than this?" Raines' slit throat smiled up at him. "You poor, dumb shit. Did you think that she could get you from the other side of the grave?"

There wasn't much else to look at. The photographs on the dresser were old and grainy, two views of what appeared to be the same mountain fronted by a stretch of valley. The wallet had nothing in it except a social security card and seventeen dollars—no pictures, no other identification. Stavitsky went through the motions and got out of the room and into the hallway as quickly as he could. He closed the door on the smell and inhaled through his nose. Then he found the stairway and walked down the three flights. His stomach was queasy, his legs a little shaky.

The man was still behind the desk waiting for Stavitsky to come down.

"I need to use your phone."

Without a word the man lifted a phone from behind the counter. Stavitsky dialed, gave his badge number, the address, and told the operator what had happened. When he hung up he looked down at the man.

"What's your name?" he asked.

"Robert Welles."

"Mr. Welles, you heard what I said just now, so you know what happened. The guy's already dead so they may take their time. Meanwhile, why don't you go upstairs and lock the door. I just pulled it to." The man nodded. "And," Stavitsky went on, "do yourself a favor and don't open it." He turned to go. Then he turned back, put his hand in his pocket and pulled out one of the crumpled bills that he always stuffed in his pocket meaning to put in the wallet later. As he put it on the counter he saw it was a five.

"Here," he said, "buy a string of lights for that tree."

He crossed the street to a bar and took a table near the window through which he could see the museum and the park. He started to order a beer and a sandwich, but he realized that the sight and smell of Raines' body was still with him, and he settled for the beer alone.

A link had broken, one of the few precious, tenuous links with her was gone. He tried to relax against the plastic back of the booth, to drink his beer and empty his mind for a few minutes. But he couldn't—too many deaths collecting around Jennifer Gilbert, and today's was real, not muted by time, not perceived secondhand from some report, but real dead flesh soaking in real blood. He'd seen Charles Raines, Jr., alive, he'd seen his room, the things he owned and used . . . his shirts, poor frayed things, carefully laundered, folded and put away so neatly, waiting to be worn. What she had done was real, not just a story told by an old man on a cold night. Ross, Kearney, Roberts, and now Raines, all real once, all dead, all her work. No more theorizing—no more paper airplanes. If he didn't get to her somehow, and soon, there'd be more. Anger and inaction knotted the muscles in his thighs and abdomen, and made the beer taste like tin. He left most of it and walked out of the tavern.

He knew it would be a long time before he could forget those shirts.

It was there on his desk when he got back to the office. Christopher L. Haynes—address and telephone number. And a dusty old police report made out in the old form. Joey had even pulled the detectives' names out for him so he wouldn't have to do it himself—Samuel Charles (retired), address and telephone number. And Peter S. Gordon (deceased).

Joey hadn't said anything when Stavitsky came in. He waited outside at his desk for the chief's thanks, and he got it. Stavitsky walked out of his office. Everyone looked up as he walked up to Joey's desk.

"Good job, Joey. Thanks." He always made sure that good work was recognized in front of the man's fellow employees, and Stavitsky usually enjoyed doing it. Today it was form only, and hurried. He couldn't wait to get back to his desk to read that report. And the time was going—eleven thirty. He had to be at that damned luncheon by one.

He sat down at his desk, picked up the folder, and held it for a minute. He let the moment of anticipation stretch on as long as he could.

Then he opened it. Not much—not even a PM. But he didn't blame the investigating officers for that; he probably wouldn't have insisted either under the circumstances. Just because a thirty-year-old man drops dead. . . . Then he stopped, ran his finger crossing and recrossing the page. It wasn't there. He'd been looking, waiting to see her name, making himself wait until he read all the way through to the section marked "witnesses," to see it typed in, official—Jennifer List. But it wasn't there. He went back, line by line now. But according to Detectives Charles and Gordon, Christopher Haynes had been the only witness to Marvin Ross' death. But that couldn't be true. Ching had said, "He came to me right after the funeral—a very upset young man, close to raving—saying that the List girl had killed Marvin. Of course, it was the first I knew of it, though I suppose—no—I *know* I suspected. . . ."

But according to Charles, the one who'd signed the report, Christopher Haynes had been the only one there. No mention of another witness. No Jennifer List.

Stavitsky felt something like panic. Nothing, he had nothing. This morning there'd been possibilities, vague, but good bets all of them. Now Raines was dead, and there was nothing on paper to tie her with Ross. No proof that she'd ever been there. Not with Kearney, not with Ross. It was dissolving, his list of names, his mystery dissolving because he had no connection—no way back to her.

He called Ching. It was eleven forty-five, he had fifteen minutes before he had to leave. "Fuck the mayor," he said aloud. He hated the imposition, the time they were taking away from him. He'd never really minded before.

Ching answered the phone himself.

"But that's impossible," he said when Stavitsky told him the report hadn't mentioned the List girl. "Haynes told me himself—"

"Then somebody's lying," Stavitsky challenged.

"Obviously," Ching said, just slightly snide, "but I don't think it was Haynes."

"Why would the cops lie?"

"Never having met the men, it would be difficult for me to say—but Haynes wasn't lying. No—" A pause, while Ching remembered the scene. Haynes trying to control himself, almost in tears, torn with grief, anger. "No," Ching said again, "I'm sure Haynes told me the exact truth."

"Wait a minute. What about the girl? Did the girl ever admit being there? Did she ever say anything?" It was odd to be talking about the worn-looking middle-aged woman he had met the previous day as "the girl." He wondered what Ching would think if he could see her now.

"I never saw her again—I told you that last night. She called, of course—oh, it must have been five or six days after Marvin died. I told her that we were disbanding the entire study—which was true—and that I did not want to discuss Marvin's death. She respected my wishes."

"Did you ever tell her what you suspected or that Haynes had accused her of murder?"

"No."

"Why not?"

"Were you afraid?"

Ching sighed. "Yes, captain, I was afraid."

Stavitsky was usually very good at official functions. He was well liked, laughed a lot; pleasant, deep, natural laughter that set others off. And he was usually funny himself, good at telling jokes, good at listening to them, and always interested in the other guys' problems, listening carefully, offering advice. Good advice. There was always a clump of men around him, and, although there were the usual rivalries, he knew that none of these men would actively enjoy doing him dirt. Of course, they'd do it if they got the chance, but they wouldn't enjoy it, and Stavitsky knew that that was something of a tribute.

Today it was a chore. He prided himself on being as good a listener as he was an observer, but this time no matter how hard he tried, his attention would wander—unconnected thoughts swarming over what the others were saying, obscuring the talk, the jokes, the usual easy camaraderie. Her name, occasionally her face. And Ching's " 'Her power. Incredible.' " And of course Raines' body. He didn't think anyone noticed except Korn, who knew him better than most of the others, had known him since they'd been kids. Every now and then Stavitsky caught his friend looking at him with narrowed eyes, measuring, wondering.

"Hey, Dave," Korn finally said, "you've lost a bit of weight, haven't you?"

Had he? He remembered the soft spots on his body as he'd looked at it last night, and the thought pleased him.

"Yeah," he joked. "A couple of more creamed tuna lunches and I'll be a fucking wraith."

The food at these things used to be pretty good—roast beef, unless the mayor was going to be there, then there'd be filet. Now it was always creamed something, usually unidentifiable, so that when the department bitched about budget cuts and layoffs, the papers couldn't report that the brass had been eating steak while the rank and file got the ax.

Actually the stuff wasn't bad; Stavitsky saw some mushrooms in it, a piece of olive? He couldn't be sure. He couldn't even try to eat. The

morning—Raines' body was still with him. He picked out the mushrooms and ate them, leaving the chunks of white meat, whatever it was.
Korn was watching, and Stavitsky made himself spear a frozen green
pea and eat it. But the rest was beyond him; he knew he wouldn't get it
down. Korn didn't comment when the waiter took Stavitsky's full plate
away and served coffee. He drank the coffee, eschewed the dessert, ice
cream with something over it and probably something under it. Red
sauce on the melting white ball. Raines again; jellied blood. He pushed
the dish away.

"Hey, Dave," Korn asked, "you okay?"

"Sure. Carole's got me on a diet, that's all." In fact, Carole disap-
proved of diets and if Stavitsky had eaten as much as she wanted him
to, the figure in the mirror would look like the others around him—bulging, soft, squishy-looking men. Even Korn, especially Korn, and Korn's
wife—and Carole, and most of the other men's wives. Soft, bulging
thighs through their slack suits, little rolls of fat under their buttocks,
even the V's of their crotches looked bulgy in the too-tight slacks. He
tried not to think about *her*—to compare them to her. Impossible. Jennifer Gilbert was an arrow of a woman, fine bones too thinly covered
with flesh; worn down. He remembered her hand reaching for his, pale,
thin, without color on the short-trimmed nails. Why had he pulled
away? He looked down at his own hand lying on the table, wishing he
had another chance, that her hand was reaching for his now. What was
happening to him? What the hell was happening?

The speeches had started. The guest of honor on his way out, having
reached the magic sixty-five, was trying to look impassive. Most of the
lights had been turned out in the dining room, only the dais was brightly
lit, and, as he had last night, Stavitsky felt more comfortable in the dark.
In the middle of the mayor's eulogy of Inspector Donnelly's long and
undistinguished career, Stavitsky stood up in the dark, pushed his chair
back. A hand grabbed his arm, and his hand balled into a fist. But it
was only Korn. What was happening to him?

"Where're you going, Dave? The old man'll be looking for you."

"To the can," Stavitsky said. "I'll be right back."

The hand released him. And he got out of there into the lobby. He
went at once to the line of phone booths, arranged some change on the
phone stand, and dialed the number for Christopher Haynes that Joey
had given him. Forty cents—about thirty-five miles away, Stavitsky
figured. Two rings and a woman answered. Mrs. Haynes. She reacted
the way people usually did when the police called them, first frightened,
then relieved, then overly cooperative as if they'd done something
wrong. No, Mr. Haynes wasn't home, but of course the captain could

have his office number. She gave it to him—in the city, she said, downtown, she said, he might be out to lunch right now, she said, would he like to know where Mr. Haynes usually ate? He was a member. . . .

Stavitsky was glad of the extra details for once. He took all the numbers, listened to all the information, and he was even a little sorry to break the connection, because he might not be able to reach Haynes and it was even slightly reassuring to know that Haynes really existed, that he had a wife, that Stavitsky could talk to her.

But he was in luck. Haynes was in his office. The secretary consulted him with Stavitsky on hold. But Stavitsky knew that Haynes would talk to him. No one ever refused to talk to the police.

"Yes, sir. This is Christopher Haynes. What can I do for you?"

Stavitsky took a deep breath. A real voice. A connection back to her.

"I wonder if I could take up some of your time, Mr. Haynes. Any time that's convenient. It's in connection with the old case—the death of Marvin Ross." Total silence. Had he hung up?

Then, "I'll be happy to discuss the death of Marvin Ross with you any time at all. Right now if you want. We can have lunch together."

Stavitsky wanted to. He was ready to make the date, then he heard applause from the dining room. The speeches would be over soon. People would be looking for him. Besides, he had to fight whatever it was that was happening to him. He wasn't going to drop everything in his life and run after this thing, and he didn't like any of the reactions he was having. Oh, but he wanted to. . . .

"That's very kind of you." When? he wondered. Tomorrow was too long a wait—he could put it off for a while, but not that long. "I'm afraid this afternoon would be difficult, but what about this evening? I could come to your home if you don't mind, and in the meantime you can call the department and check that I am who I say I am."

They agreed on eight o'clock. Haynes gave him directions and then asked, "What about Marvin? What is it you want to know?"

"I'll tell you tonight, sir. And thank you very much."

He got back to the ballroom just as they were turning the lights back on. No one had missed him except Korn, who seemed relieved that he was back.

3

HAYNES HIMSELF opened the door of the big old Colonial house. "Captain Stavitsky?"

Stavitsky nodded and took his badge out.

"I thought you'd gotten lost," Haynes said.

"I did. I don't really know my way around Connecticut."

"C'mon in, it's cold out there."

Haynes took his coat and led him into a large, brightly lit room. Then he excused himself and left Stavitsky alone. A fire was burning in the stone fireplace. Two long sofas flanked it and Stavitsky eased himself into one. The fire was too warm on his face, his eyes felt heavy, and for a moment he was afraid he would doze off. Then Haynes was back with a bottle of scotch, a bottle of bourbon, and a siphon on a tray. No sign of Mrs. Haynes. He was a big man, as big as Stavitsky. So blond that his eyelashes and eyebrows were almost invisible.

"Would you like a drink?" he asked.

Stavitsky refused.

"Oh. On duty, eh?" Haynes asked uncertainly.

"No." Too abrupt. "It's a long drive back to New York," he explained. He wanted the man to relax—to talk. "But don't mind me, go right ahead."

"Yes, well . . ." Haynes wavered, then he poured himself a little scotch with lots of ice and soda.

"Now, captain . . ." Stavitsky saw that Haynes was trying hard to look nonchalant. He took a long drink, then sat down on the other sofa across from Stavitsky.

Stavitsky put his hand in his pocket and clicked on the transistor tape recorder he had brought with him. He knew that he should tell Haynes that what they said was being recorded. It was his legal duty, but he didn't care anymore; the rules didn't matter. He knew the recorder's controls by heart and turned the volume to full to compensate for the pocket.

"As I told you on the phone, Mr. Haynes, I want to discuss Marvin Ross' death." Ross, and Kearney—and Raines. He wondered how long Raines' body would haunt him. "You see, there's some kind of discrepancy between the information I originally had and the formal police report." Calm, stay calm. Keep the questions routine, and give no answers. Standard interview, he told himself, this is a standard interview.

"Why are you worried about Marvin's death now? That was twenty years ago and no one seemed to give much of a shit at the time." A flash of old, half-forgotten anger.

"I can't tell you why—but I need information about how Marvin Ross died, and who was there when it happened."

"I gave the cop—I can't remember his name—the whole story." Then why wasn't it in the report? Stavitsky wondered. "God," Haynes was saying, "it's been so long. . . ." He shook his head. "The cop wrote everything down, seemed to be quite careful. I'm not really sure I want to go over it all again. I guess in a way it was the worst night of my life."

"You say he wrote down what you said word for word?"

"Well, I don't know about word for word, but he wrote while I talked."

"Was that Detective Lieutenant Charles?"

"Yeah, that was the guy. First two uniformed men came, then the detectives. But the uniforms left with the body. Then there was another detective with Charles—older, I think, but I don't remember his name, either."

"Was it Gordon?"

"I guess so. I'm just not sure."

"Detective Gordon's been dead about five years. Charles is retired." Haynes nodded as though Gordon's death and Charles' retirement were as he would have it. They were both quiet for a moment while Haynes remembered. And Stavitsky watched him do it. He could see an old sorrow, no longer sharp, but still real. Haynes had been there, in the same room with her, could have touched her if he'd wanted to. Stavitsky wondered what she'd looked like twenty years ago.

"Can you tell me how it happened?"

"She killed him." He looked directly at Stavitsky for the first time. Somewhere in the house someone, perhaps one of the children, turned off a radio or a phonograph. In the silence the fire crackled and Stavitsky's nerves jumped at the sound.

"I told them at that time," Haynes went on. "They didn't believe me, of course."

"You told them that she'd killed him?"

"That's right."

"How *did* she kill him, Mr. Haynes?"

Haynes stood up and walked over to the fireplace. "I don't know. I've thought about it again and again, but I don't know."

"Then how can you be so sure?"

"Because I am. Because I saw it happen and I know just as surely as I know anything." Haynes knew—like Ching: "I've told you what I know." Two of them knew.

"Exactly what did happen?"

"Isn't it in the report?"

"I want to hear it from you."

Haynes sighed. "Is it really important?"

"Very important."

"He planned to marry her . . . not just planned to, I think he wanted to. Christ, I don't know, maybe he even fell in love with her in a way."

Haynes' shyness hung on for a while, making the man stammer occasionally, pause to search for words. But soon the story took them both over. Haynes' shyness vanished and he spoke so clearly that Stavitsky began to really see them. Ross, handsome, intelligent, on the surface self-confident, but always in competition—with the women first of all. "He'd sort of beat them down," Haynes was saying, "and he didn't care how long it took—I never saw a woman he couldn't make come; and that was kind of the whole thing for him. He'd get them going, then he'd slow down, then he'd get them going again until they were shaking, helpless."

Then he'd taken on the Lists—wanting, Haynes thought, to beat them down too—and finally their daughter. Stavitsky began to see her too. In spite of Haynes' old dulled hatred, he began to see his quarry as she was twenty years ago—lonely, desperately lonely. ". . . Ellen Olivieri was the only friend she had. And the List girl was a virgin, Marvin was sure of that. But that wasn't it—he'd had plenty of virgins, and said he didn't like it much, too much of a mess. But he wanted her all right. He wanted her more than he knew he did himself. I could see that."

Stavitsky could have listened all night while Haynes told him about Jennifer List, but he tried to hear the words without seeing the picture they described. He was having trouble sitting still while Haynes described how Ross had taken her clothes off, eased her back onto the bed. Haynes told him about Ross' failure, his desperation, calling her names. How Ross threw the vase.

"—and the room sort of pounded, as if all the air were being sucked out of it. No, that's not right, I can't describe the feeling." Stavitsky knew the feeling quite well, but he didn't say so. "And then the air was gone—seemed to be gone. I couldn't hear anything, and, Christ, I couldn't move. And there was Marvin struggling—and I couldn't help him. His mouth was open and I don't know if he was gasping or screaming because I couldn't hear anything. But he was holding himself—pressing his hands against his chest. Then he put out one hand—maybe he was trying to push something away. He must've fallen on the bed, and I couldn't see him anymore. *She* was in the way. I didn't move, but I knew he was thrashing around on the bed. Then she bowed."

"She *what?*"

"She bowed, like to an audience, you know what I mean? And when she did that everything went back to normal. I could hear again; I could move.

"I ran into the room to help him. I pushed her out of the way and tried to get him up. But it was too late, he was dead."

Jennifer Gilbert as a young girl, naked, bowing. He could see it; except that the hair that fell across her face, obscured her profile, was streaked with gray.

He tossed in his chair.

"Okay, Haynes, how did she kill him? You haven't even said that she touched him."

Haynes sat down again, his elbows resting on his knees, his arms dangling between his legs. He looked at the floor and almost moaned, "Shit, shit—that's the question. I don't know. I just don't know."

"She didn't touch him?"

"I didn't see her touch him."

"And there wasn't a mark on him?"

"No, not even a bruise, except on his ankle where he must've bumped it against the bed."

"Then how—"

"Don't ask me that again." Haynes raised his voice. "I told you I don't know. But if you want to know what I think—I think she *thought* him to death."

"Done," Galeston had said, "it was done."

Both men sat staring at each other, Stavitsky trying to look shocked.

"Do you really believe what you've just said to me?"

"Yes. I believe it. And you can take that crazy idea and stick it up your ass for all I care."

"Okay, okay, take it easy, Mr. Haynes. I was just asking. You tried to help him, right?" Haynes nodded. "And when you saw that you couldn't, what did you do?"

"I tried for a long time after she'd stopped."

"You mean she tried to help you bring him around?"

"That's right—but she wasn't really trying and she gave up pretty fast."

"Do you think you might have saved him if she'd tried harder?"

"No. He was dead when we started, I think. Anyway, she starts getting dressed, just as cool as can be, like she was leaving a tea party. Bitch. Then she called the police while I just sat on the floor next to him."

"*She* called the police!" Again a touch of panic. It wasn't making sense. "If she killed him, then why did she call the police?"

"I don't know."

"What did she say to them?"

"Just that there'd been an accident, that someone was dead. Then she gave her name, and the address."

"She told them her name?"

"Yeah. I guess that doesn't jibe with what I've been telling you."

"Murderers don't usually call the police and leave their names."

"But remember what I said—there wasn't a mark on the guy. She knew they weren't going to believe what I'd tell them, what I'd seen. Just like you don't believe me."

Stavitsky wanted to tell the man that he did believe him, that he understood, that he was almost as helpless as Haynes had been twenty years ago, trying to pin something on her. Ching had been right. Haynes was telling the truth, no missing it. That meant Charles and Gordon had lied. Why?

"You don't believe me, do you?" Haynes wasn't angry. He hadn't expected belief.

"Just go on with your story, Mr. Haynes."

"Why are you so interested in her now? Can't you tell me?"

Stavitsky appeared to think before he answered. It was a hard game to play because he really wanted to tell the guy, to give him the satisfaction of being vindicated after so many years, and because then he could ask Haynes other questions—what did she look like then, how far had Ross gotten with her before he lost it. And afterward, when he was dead, how did she look—really look? Cool, triumphant, frightened—what had it meant to her to kill? Raines would have known, Raines had seen her kill, too. Raines could have told him.

Shit. The questions he wanted to ask Haynes would reveal too much about his own feelings about her—about the whole thing—and he wasn't ready to face any of that. Certainly not in front of a stranger.

"Shit."

"What is it, captain?"

He hadn't realized he'd said it aloud.

"I'd like to tell you, Mr. Haynes. I can't. But I promise you, I'm not just wasting your time." There were just too many people who knew, who'd be watching him. Too many people for whom he was in a sense responsible. He didn't want to add to them. "Go on with the story. What did she do after she called the cops?"

"She left—just walked out. The cops turned up about ten minutes later—and I guess you know the rest."

"I guess I do, but I want to hear it from you."

Haynes sighed. "I told them exactly what I told you. They didn't believe me, but they called the detectives. When they came, I went through the story again. They were polite, they listened—but they didn't believe me either. Then I guess I got a little excited and I started yelling about how they were ignoring everything I said and how they were letting a murderer go free without even checking. I said they should autopsy Marvin—maybe she'd poisoned him or something. But I knew she hadn't."

"How did you know?"

"Because she wanted him so much. I could see that." Wanted him—she'd wanted him. He wanted to ask Haynes how he knew that. Was it the expression on her face? The way she lay on the bed? The way she touched Ross? The way she let him touch her? Unsafe ground, he had to get past this part.

"Okay." Stavitsky's voice was hoarse. "Did they agree to do an autopsy?"

"They seemed to go along with it. Hell, I was pretty wild and maybe they hadn't thought of poison. Anyway, they called her house, said they'd question her. But I think they were just humoring me.

"About twenty minutes later, her mother turns up. Terrible thing for her—"

"Wait a minute—wait a minute," Stavitsky said. "Her *mother*? Her mother came to your apartment in the middle of the night?"

"That's right. Neat as a pin, in walks the mother. Oh, and Christ, we all introduced ourselves like we were at a goddamn cocktail party. They'd just carried Marvin's body out of there, and just an hour before her daughter had been lying there on the bed, legs spread, begging for a fuck. And here comes the mother, shaking hands. 'How do you do?' Shit, captain, it was funny." Then Haynes stopped, shook his head. "No, it wasn't funny. I felt sorry for the woman. But I went through my story again—that made three times, only this was the worst, because I was talking about her daughter, and the woman had never done anything to me or to Marvin. And I could see that the things I said hurt like hell, as controlled as she was. But I'll tell you something, captain. As crazy as it all sounded—still sounds—*she* believed me."

Stavitsky stared at Haynes. "She believed you . . ." he asked softly. Then he smiled.

That was it. The mother—so simple, why hadn't he thought of it? What could be more normal, more ordinary? Rich lady pays the cops not to mention her kid trying to get laid in campus love nest. Then he thought of the rest, and that made it even more believable—and more horrible, because she didn't just believe Haynes about the girl wanting to get laid, she believed him about how Ross died. She knew! She probably knew about Kearney, too. And she'd paid off the cops anyway, willing to let it go on. How could she? But he knew very well how she could. He'd seen it before a hundred times. Some little strung-out shit stabs an old couple to death, slices them to pieces and goes on cutting even after they're dead, until both bodies look like sliced bacon, steals the forty-five dollars they have to get through the week, and his mother knows it's true, knows what the creep did—but she defends him. Not my boy, he was at home at the time, I swear it, officer. And if they'd believe her she'd let it go on and on. No matter how many times, no matter how many dead, they'd still get the same story out of her. For a minute, Stavitsky felt weak with hatred. Stupid, selfish, corrupt bitches. *Their* child was all that mattered, no one else was real. The dead hadn't really died—Marvin Ross wasn't *really* dead.

"Of course she didn't say so," Haynes was saying, "but I knew she believed every word I said."

"Then? After you told her and she believed you?"

"Then nothing. They left—left me alone in that place. She offered the cops a lift, and they accepted. Which made me wonder because I thought even back then that they had their own cars."

Of course they did.

"Anyway, they all left together. And the younger cop said that they'd be in touch with me. But I never heard from them again. But I wasn't finished, not then, at least."

"Then you went to Marvin's boss?"

"Yeah. How'd you know that?"

Stavitsky shrugged.

"I'd seen him at the funeral," Haynes said. "God, that was awful—I thought Marvin's mother'd never stop screaming. Marvin used to talk about what a big man Ching was, so I figured he'd have more clout than I did, and after the funeral I went to see him and told him the whole story."

"How did he react?"

"He believed me too. Which surprised the hell out of me. It seemed to have an awful effect on him. He wouldn't say anything for a long time —I remember he just kept shaking his head.

"Then he said the damnedest thing. He said that I should forget it at once, that I shouldn't say another word about it—that I was in *danger*.

"It hit me then. If she killed Marvin, she could kill me just as easily. And if I kept looking for trouble, she might do it.

"Christ, I almost crapped when I saw what the guy meant. I got out of there as fast as I could and I never mentioned it again—until tonight."

"Are you still afraid of what she might do to you?"

Haynes sat looking into his empty glass, then he watched the fire. Finally he looked at Stavitsky.

"Yes," he said quietly. "Yes, I'm afraid. I've thought about this a lot in the past twenty years and I'm scared to death. But I'll help you get her if I can. Only one thing, captain."

"What?" asked Stavitsky.

"What she could do to me, she could do to you."

4

FIRST THING IN the morning he called headquarters.

"Hi, chief." Joey didn't sound very happy to hear his voice.

"Joey, I need some more information. This time about a Mrs. Thomas List. I don't have her first name, but I have her daughter's name—Jennifer, Jennifer List, born sometime in the late twenties—probably twenty-nine. So you can get the mother's name from the daughter's birth certificate."

No answer.

"Joey, are you listening to me?"

"Sure, captain, sure. Just let me get this down. . . ." The silence went on and on while Joey wrote. Stavitsky could see him, the phone receiver tucked between ear and shoulder, chewing the pencil, writing, chewing some more. "OK, captain, what do you want to know about her?"

"Address, where the husband works, what they've both been doing for the last twenty years. I especially want to know where she banked in 1954, and whether she made any unusually large withdrawals in November of that year. And anything else you can find out."

"OK, captain, but—"

"Find out whatever you can, wherever you can. And, Joey, this is kind of on the hush—just between us, OK?"

"Sure." Everyone loved that—a little break in the routine. "Sure thing, captain. When do you need it?"

"By tonight. I'll call you at home."

"But, captain, this is a lot—"

"Tonight, Joey. And don't crap me around. Believe me, you won't be sorry."

"Yeah, OK, captain. I'll do what I can."

A crooked cop. That put Stavitsky on more familiar ground and he felt better. His appetite had returned and he ate breakfast before he left the house. He was going to enjoy interviewing Charles, even without hard facts, because Charles had no way of knowing when Stavitsky would be bluffing about what he actually knew. None of the images—her face, the figure bowing to the body on the bed, Raines' body—had really softened, but there were others to keep them in better proportion—a mother who'd bought two cops, and the cops themselves—things that Stavitsky understood, that could balance the others.

He liked long drives, rarely had a chance to take them, and the weather was good, sunny and not as cold as it had been. On the upper roadway of the Queensboro Bridge, the sun faced the factories on the Queens side, the eastbound traffic was light, and he had time, the whole day if he needed it. As he crossed the river, drove down the sweeping ramp into Long Island City, he felt a little pang at the distance that was growing between him and the woman, but he turned on the radio, made himself listen to the news, and after a few miles of the unrelieved, ordinary ugliness of Queens Boulevard, he was relaxed, feeling more like himself than he had in days.

Finally he was on the expressway then past Kennedy airport and Long Island proper began. It was quiet out here, the trees and houses older, more substantial, but it was still hard to believe that in only another ninety miles on the same road he would reach a rocky coast, the end of the continent, and the open ocean.

Charles lived in a small community called Bethall. There was a sign directing him off the expressway into an established middle-class community. Well-kept houses and small yards that probably blazed with color in the summer. The houses were close to the street—frame or ersatz Tudor stucco.

Charles' house was on a corner lot. It was larger than the others on the street, with a little more land. Stavitsky pulled up in the driveway that ended at a closed two-car garage attached to the house. He walked the cement path that led from the driveway to a glass storm door decorated with curlicued aluminum. The inside door was open.

Stavitsky rang, heard the bell chime down the narrow entrance hall. A woman crossed the hall to the door and looked at him warily through the glass. He took out his badge. She moved closer to see it, her breath leaving a ring of mist on the glass, then she clicked open the door and let him into the foyer. She was medium tall, late fifties or so, with blazing hair teased into a huge fuzz that flowed around her head like a red aura. She wore thick glasses with bright red and blue plaid frames and a clean, starched printed housedress which was just fitted enough to show her still-good figure. Her eyes, slightly distorted behind the glasses, were blue, fringed by thickly mascaraed lashes, and the heavy pancake makeup couldn't quite hide the freckles on her cheeks and nose. Stavitsky thought that she'd probably really been a redhead once.

"What do you want?" She did not ask his name or invite him any farther into the house.

"Mrs. Charles?" She nodded, her mouth a thin impatient line. "I'd like to see your husband."

"Is he expecting you?"

"No, I thought I'd just take a chance. My name is Stavitsky, Captain Stavitsky—chief of homicide." He enjoyed watching her mouth change—fatten out, then try to form itself into something like a smile. But the eyes behind the thick lenses narrowed. Plucked reddish-brown eyebrows drew together.

"Won't you come in?" Her tone was strained.

Stavitsky stepped into a superscrubbed hallway. Green and white rubber tiles gleamed with wax and the place smelled of lemon oil. She took his coat, and as she was hanging it in the hall closet, Stavitsky saw a mink coat, full-length, very dark, hanging with cloth overcoats. She closed the front door then, as though she did not want any of the neighbors to see him and led him into an unused parlor that looked out on the neat brown lawns and bare trees.

The furniture was all in different shades of green and blue silk, covered with clear shiny form-fitting plastic. The rug was shag, newly vacuumed so that she and Stavitsky left footprints as they walked into the room. The wood-trimmed fireplace was spotless, unused, its brass accessories gleaming.

Stavitsky smothered an urge to whisper. "I hope I'm not disturbing you."

"No, no, it's perfectly all right—Sam's just fixing the Christmas lights for the house. He's in the garage." Her accent was thick Bronx and her voice was high-pitched, too loud. "Sit down. I'll get him."

Stavitsky picked the softest-looking chair, but it held him stiffly. Urethane, he thought.

There was a buttery baking smell in the air, and he realized that he hadn't had any lunch. But he was out of luck here—Mrs. Charles would never serve food in this room, probably not even coffee.

"Hell, she brings everybody into this tomb," boomed Charles from the doorway, as if he'd read Stavitsky's thoughts. "C'mon into the den and we can have some coffee and some of those cookies. Mary," he yelled, "we're going into the den—bring us something to eat!"

He was a big, good-looking man with the same coloring as his wife—large blue eyes, freckles. They might have been brother and sister, only Charles' hair was almost yellowish white, with a bit of red around the base of his head. He, too, had a thick Bronx accent, and Stavitsky knew it would be a chore to listen to his voice for very long. But he seemed good-natured, and, unlike his wife, glad to see Stavitsky.

They walked through the hallway to the smaller room. Charles put his arm around Stavitsky's shoulders. "Man," he yelled, "must be five years since I've talked to a real, working cop. Chief of homicide yet! Quite a thrill, captain, quite a thrill!"

The den was "early American"—braided rug, machine-turned maple furniture with plaid flat pillows tied to the seats and backs. It was just as clean as the parlor, but more cluttered and much more comfortable.

When they were finally seated, facing each other, Stavitsky began his usual silent examination. Charles' shirt was the softest wool jersey, part cashmere, Stavitsky thought. His trousers were also of good cloth, very well tailored, and his shoes were fine Italian loafers—$50 or $60 worth. He wore the thin, round, plainly numbered wristwatch that was made only by Tiffany in 18-carat gold. When Mrs. Charles came in with the coffee and cookies, Stavitsky noticed that she wore a diamond ring about 3 carats. He assessed the house at about $80,000 on today's market and figured the taxes in this area were probably twelve to fifteen hundred a year, maybe more.

Very nice on a cop's pension, he thought.

They ate the fresh butter cookies, drank Mrs. Charles' excellent coffee, and made small talk about how much better things had been ten or fifteen years ago. Charles blamed the blacks for crime, litter, high taxes, and he made the usual complaint that they were moving in everywhere, even "out here." But he was just going through the standard tribal rite for middle-class suburbia and the attack had little conviction or viciousness although he conducted it at the top of his lungs.

Stavitsky nodded in apparent agreement because he had not come there to argue with the man and because he did not really care what Charles thought about blacks, or about anything, except the death of Marvin Ross.

Finally Charles ran down and decided to find out why Stavitsky was there. "Well, now," Charles bellowed. Stavitsky felt as though some important nerve endings were beginning to fray. "You didn't come out here to hear me bitch about the boogies. What can I do for you, captain?"

Stavitsky took the folded report from inside his jacket and handed it to Charles. Then he clicked on the tape recorder in his pocket. Charles looked at the report for a long time while Stavitsky watched the good humor waver, then fade altogether. Charles' eyebrows pinched together so that he looked even more like his wife.

"You wrote that report?"

"I guess so, I signed it. But that was a long time ago—don't remember much about it." Charles looked as if he remembered everything about it and the memory did not agree with him.

"Yes, it's been a long time," Stavitsky agreed, "but Ross' death seems to be tied up with another case I've been working on, and some of the information I got from the main witness—Christopher Haynes?"—Charles shrugged as if the name meant nothing to him—"doesn't tally with what your report says."

Charles decided to play dumb. "How do you mean?"

"You say that Haynes was the only one there when Ross died."

"Do I?"

Stavitsky ignored the question and went on. "But Haynes says there was a girl there, a girl named Jennifer List. That he told you she was there, that you wrote it down and even called her house to talk to her. Now there's nothing like that in the report you wrote."

"Sure doesn't seem to be." Charles turned pages, pretending to scan the report.

"Why?"

"I don't know, captain." The first shock was over and Charles was regaining some of his confidence. "Maybe there was no proof, or maybe I thought the guy was lying. Probably that's it—I must've thought he was lying. He was sure the only one there when we got there."

"Oh? It's coming back to you?"

"Yeah, I think I remember the Haynes kid—red-faced, sweated a lot. Yeah—he was lying, captain. Gordon—I think Gordon was with me." He looked at the report again for verification he did not need. "We agreed the kid was lying. Must've had something against the girl. That's how we figured it."

"I see. Then there was no Jennifer List there. You're positive."

"That's right—at least according to our assessment of the information we had available to us." Charles reverted to "cop talk" to give weight to what he said.

"Then how do you explain the fact that it was Jennifer List who called the police the night Ross died?"

Charles paled, and the skin on his face stretched back, making him look younger and frightened.

"What makes you say that?" His voice finally came down a few decibels.

"It's a matter of record, Mr. Charles." Stavitsky wasn't sure and hadn't checked, but Charles would not know that.

Charles did not answer. Stavitsky went on.

"That's interesting, isn't it? She wasn't there but she called the local precinct to report his death and left the address where Ross died, *and* her name. Another odd thing—you and Gordon bummed a ride with *Mrs.* List—the mother of the girl who wasn't there—although you and Gordon had a car. Oh, yes, and what was the mother doing there at all? Real odd, Charles. Makes me awful curious."

Charles still sat without speaking. Stavitsky ate another cookie, then washed it down with coffee.

"Have you anything to say?" Stavitsky asked through the crumbs.

"I know it sounds weird, but this Haynes carried on so we thought'd quiet him down if we at least called the girl's house. When we did, her mother kind of lost her head—I mean here's this guy dead and the police calling up in the middle of the night. She got rattled and came running over there to see what it was all about. And Haynes gave her an earful. Said some pretty rotten things about her daughter. All about he was watching Ross try to screw the girl, and that she was some kind of freak. Said he'd watched Ross screw lots of girls—they had an agreement. Nasty business. Except this Haynes was so red in the face talking about how Ross couldn't get it up—it was really kind of funny.

"The girl's mother knew he was lying, too, and she kept asking him what he had against her daughter. But Haynes had no answer. Me and Gordon, we just wanted an excuse to get out of there, so when the woman offered us a lift we pretended we didn't have a car."

"That's your story?"

"That's *the* story."

"What about the girl calling the station and leaving her name?"

"Doesn't mean a thing. You know how messed up those things get. Haynes was probably the one that called, and when he said that she was the one that killed Ross—that was what Haynes kept saying, you know, even though there wasn't a mark on Ross—they must've written down the girl's name as caller instead of his."

"But the desk man could tell a man's voice from a woman's."

"Sure, but he still could've written it down wrong. How many calls do you think we used to get in that precinct on a Saturday night? Christ, that joint was always hopping. You'd have to find the operator that took the call to be sure—and he might not remember." Charles' voice was booming again and he was smiling. "After all, it's been over twenty years," he finished happily.

Stavitsky sighed and made himself look defeated. He could not help playing cat and mouse.

"Well, I guess that's that," he said.

"Hope you didn't make the trip for nothing." Charles was positively beaming now. Stavitsky almost felt sorry for him.

"No, that's okay. It's a nice ride out here." He moved as if to rise, then, as though he'd just remembered, he asked, "By the way, just for the record, what was the name of your bank back in 1954?"

Charles jumped out of his chair. "I don't have to tell you that!" Mrs. Charles heard the yelling and ran in from the kitchen. He turned on her. "Get the hell out of here, and shut the goddamned door." She did as she was told.

"I know you don't have to tell me"—Stavitsky's voice cooled and hardened—"but I'll find out. You know how excited everyone pretends to get if they think a cop's on the take. Even if it's been twenty years. And I'm checking the List woman's bank, too. Now why don't you save yourself a lot of trouble and tell me what I'm going to find when I look. I'm not looking to hurt you, Charles—a little help from you and I might forget the whole thing."

Charles thought, but not for long.

"Aw, shit—why not? It was her idea, we wasn't even on the make."

"Go on."

"That's it—she paid us to close the case without asking for a PM, which we wouldn't have asked for anyhow. And to leave her daughter's name out of the report. That's the whole story."

"How much?"

Charles sat down, then took a deep breath.

"She gave us a hundred thousand bucks each."

He saw the look on Stavitsky's face. "Yeah, yeah, I know," he said, "but that's what she gave us. Oh, we figured her for a touch all right— she hinted at it when I called her house to talk to the daughter. But no way did I figure that kind of bread."

"What the hell did she give you two hundred thousand bucks for? You can put a hit on the President for that kind of dough."

"Don't you think I know that? But I swear to God, captain, that's all she wanted—no autopsy and no mention of her daughter. And the damnedest thing is all she had to do was ask us. That Haynes bastard was real vicious and he ticked us both off. To hear him tell it, the List girl was some kind of monster. And I felt sorry for the woman, listening to all that shit about her own kid. But she had the checks all made out except for the names.

"I'll never forget it. She led us over to her car, told us to get in with her, so Gordon and me piled into the back seat. She asked us our names and we told her. I didn't even know what she was doing, but she was the sort of woman who you did what she told you to, you know what I mean?"

Stavitsky nodded.

"Well, she handed us these checks—and told us what she wanted. I looked at it and didn't believe it. I thought for a second it must've been one thousand, then ten thousand. That would've been crazy enough—but when I realized how much it was for, I just about conked out. Gordon too. We just sat there like two dummies. Then she said, 'That's all, gentlemen, thank you.' Still can hear that 'Thank you' as if it was yesterday. We just climbed out of the car and stood there with our checks while she drove away. I don't think Gordon and I did anything but nod our heads."

"What assurance did she have that—"

"She wanted us to send her a copy of the official report. She said the bank wouldn't honor the 'drafts' without contacting her, and she said she wouldn't give the OK until she had the report and was sure her daughter's name wasn't mentioned. And that was that."

"And you kept your end?"

"You bet your ass we did. A hundred thousand is a lot of money, captain."

"What'd you do with it?"

"Put it in trust—invested it in a lump. Mainly real-estate trusts. Gordon just stuck his in some blue chips. The money's grown a lot since fifty-four and I'm worth over a half a million now. Luckiest night of my life."

"That was a bribe, Charles."

"Wait a minute, you said that this was between us, that if I spilled you wouldn't—"

"I won't. I don't care what you took." But Stavitsky was disgusted, even though he found it hard to blame Charles.

"Look, captain," Charles said, "I was a good cop. If I'd thought there was any chance at all that the girl had something to do with Ross' death, I'd never've taken that money. Honest to God, I wouldn't've."

"But she *was* there."

"*I* never saw her." Never saw her. Was the woman a ghost?

"But the mother must've thought she'd been there or she'd never have given you that dough. Right?" Stavitsky said. He couldn't keep the growing anger out of his voice.

Charles didn't look at Stavitsky. "Yeah, I guess so," he mumbled. Stavitsky stood up. He walked past Charles without a word, out of the comfortable den, grabbing his coat out of the closet as he walked out the door. He let it slam hard behind him.

He didn't take the expressway back—service roads all the way until he hit Queens Boulevard. The half excitement, half dread was coming back. He kept the radio on, opened the window wide, thought about smoking, anything he could to keep clear of thinking about the fact that he had two logical things to do next—resteal the Roberts report and talk to Mrs. Thomas List.

The first was no problem. In his present mood it seemed simple, if he could find it. He was pretty sure she wouldn't keep it at home, much too dangerous; there were servants at home and her husband. Of course he'd have a hell of a time getting a warrant to search her office. No way. But that didn't bother him. He knew it should have, but it didn't. Seeing Mrs. List was a different matter, because as soon as he saw her, the daughter would know.

"So what?" he asked himself. Once he had the Roberts report back, and with the tapes, the Nantucket report, the film of the airplane, and backing from Galeston and Ching, he'd have her hamstrung. She wouldn't dare hurt any of them then. She couldn't make a move against any of them then and she'd be . . . helpless.

But as he got closer to the city, as he saw the buildings flashing between the pillars of the bridge, and felt the bumps connecting bridge and street that meant he was back on the same island with her, he wasn't sure he wanted her helpless at all—he wasn't sure what he wanted.

He pulled off Third Avenue, headed east to York Avenue, and drove uptown. When he was even with the complex that housed Rockefeller he slowed down and, without planning to, he turned into the drive, then into the parking lot.

He got out of the car and started walking along the paths that led to the main building, to the end of the campus. People were walking ahead and behind. Then he turned and started back, looking into each building entrance he passed. He did not see her.

He went back to the car and drove home.

Galeston was not available. "I'm sorry, Dr. Galeston is not in his office, we can page—"

"Try Dr. Stern, Ira Stern."

"David—we've been wondering why we haven't heard from you."

He didn't sound especially happy to hear from him now. He sounded strained, definitely strained.

"Been checking, Ira, just like I said I would."

"And does it check?"

"Yes, Ira, it checks."

"Oh." Now he sounded upset.

Stavitsky ignored the other man's tone and bulled through, telling him everything. Haynes, Charles, the mother, the payoff. "Think, Ira, two hundred thousand dollars, just not to do an autopsy they wouldn't have done anyway. And Haynes, you should have seen Haynes. He hates her, Ira, Jesus he hates her—still, after twenty years."

"Yeah, Dave, I see what you mean. What're you going to do now? I mean now that you really know what happened. Don't you think we should think about letting it cool down for a while?"

"Cool down? Shit, no."

"Then what—"

"I'm going to steal that report back, Ira. Tonight." Of course, tonight; why wait? Tonight the report, and then he'd have all he needed to see Mrs. List and finally the woman. One last step. . . .

"But once you take the report, she's going to know. She'll know we took it."

"That's right, Ira, she will."

His appetite was definitely back. He'd had no lunch and Mrs. Charles' cookies hadn't helped. Carole had taken leftover pot roast out of the refrigerator for supper. He pulled back the plastic and sniffed at it —he was starving.

"Yes, Ira, she'll know then."

"David, do you think that's a good idea?"

Scalloped potatoes. There was a box of them next to the roast. He couldn't remember ever having been so hungry.

"Who cares, Ira? Besides, what else can I do?" Why was he questioning him? Couldn't he see the most obvious facts?

"Look, Ira—it's all true. Maybe that hasn't sunk in yet—everything Ching told us was true. She can really do what he said she could."

"I think I believed that from the beginning, Dave. So did Galeston."

"Then what are we talking about, 'Letting it cool down'? I've got tapes, Ching's film clip, the Nantucket report, and as soon as I have the Roberts report and the interview with the mother—shit, Ira, I've got her cold."

"You sound very—"

"What?"

"Very excited, Dave. Maybe if you just give yourself a chance to calm down you'll see—"

"What will I see? C'mon, Ira, what the hell are you talking about?"

"Okay. There're three people dead already."

"Four."

"What four?" Stavitsky told him about Raines. For a while Stern didn't say anything, then, "David, what makes you think she'll be squeamish about making it seven?"

"You mean you, me, and Galeston?"

"That's seven, Dave."

"Are you scared, Ira?"

No answer. Stavitsky waited, pulling the plastic wrap off the meat. Where the hell was Carole? He was going to faint from hunger.

Still no answer.

"Well, Ira?"

"OK, Dave, I'm scared."

"Listen to me. It's too late to be scared. We've got to do something. Your name is on that report—you signed it, remember? She knows we talked to Galeston. I told her. Maybe it was stupid, but I didn't know anything then except that no one could tell me how Roberts had died. And she's *seen* me. So she knows about all three of us, Ira, she's known from the beginning."

"Then, wh-what can we do?"

"Take it easy. We lock her in, that's what we do. We make it so that she knows she'll blow herself wide open if she touches any one of us. It's the only way, Ira. And to do that, I'm going to get that report back, and I'm going to see her mother—" He felt himself getting dizzy.

"Can't you do it on the up and up? Get a warrant and search or something?"

"No. No one's going to give me a warrant for this one, Ira."

"Then let me go with you."

"What the hell for?"

"Maybe I can help. Besides, David, you sound a little—well, wild."

"That's a hell of a thing to say." But he was too excited to get angry at Stern. "Besides, if I let you come with me, how do I explain you if I have to? I'm a cop, people put up with a lot from cops, but I couldn't protect you if I got caught." It was four thirty, and he began reading the instructions on the box of scalloped potatoes in earnest.

"You don't have to explain me, I'll explain you. I'm a physician—all sorts of reasons I might be there. I mean, we are going to her office, right? To Rockefeller? You're not talking about breaking into her house?"

"No, her office. Wait a minute, Ira. What the hell are we talking about? You're not coming with me. Why take a chance like that?" He didn't want Ira with him. He wanted to be alone. He was going to her office, he didn't want company.

"David, it really makes more sense. Look. I can take the X ray, get copies right away. It'll work out much better than if you try carrying the only copy around. I think I should come with you, David, definitely."

Why was Ira insisting? Was he afraid that Stavitsky would get into some kind of trouble? Expose them? Maybe he was just frightened in general. Stavitsky *was* sounding a little wild, even to himself; there was an undercurrent in his tone that he didn't remember ever having been there before. Maybe Stern was right—at least he'd keep everything more normal.

"And I can identify the right X rays," Stern was saying. "There might be all sorts of X rays there—you wouldn't even know what you were looking for."

"I thought you said she worked in a lab."

"They take X rays in labs, David. Would you know the difference between one X ray and another?"

"No, I wouldn't."

"You see," Stern said, "it's really much better if I'm with you."

"OK, OK. I'll pick you up at home, at six. Be outside, because I'm not going to ring the bell, or stand around, or any of that shit."

"I'll be there."

Her name was on the wall directory. She worked here, in this building. Every day she came through the door they had just come through. He tried to remember her face and for the first time in days he couldn't. He couldn't really see her. Maybe when they got to her office she would be there, working late. For a moment he thought he would give up the report just to see her again.

The door to her office was locked.

Stavitsky stared at it. 1206, it said, J. GILBERT, MD. She wasn't there, no one was there.

It was a simple latch-type lock; the first key he tried fitted. He took out his flashlight and opened the door. The desk in the inside office—her desk—was cluttered with piles of typescripts, boxes of slides, and a file of thick journals like the one she had been reading the first time he saw her. He turned the beam to the walls. They were lined with file cabinets.

"If it's in one of those cabinets. . . ."

"I know," Stern said, "it could take us all night—if it's here at all."

"Let's get to it. You start with the cabinets, I'll look in the desk." It was probably in the desk, and he wanted to be the one to find it.

"I don't have a flashlight," Stern whispered.

Stavitsky walked back to the door and flicked the switch next to it. Overhead fluorescent lights blinked on in the small room. Then he turned to the shabby desk. The top clutter had a sort of order to it, which he did not disturb. The desk drawers were not locked.

There were some handwritten sheets of paper in the center drawer and a black and white snapshot of William Gilbert smiling shyly at the camera. When he leaned over and shone the flashlight toward the back of the drawer he saw something like a folder pushed to the back. He grinned, reached back, and pulled the flat stiff thing out of the drawer. It was not the manila folder he expected; it was a piece of cardboard, very old, friable, the edges crumbling. It was partly covered with sea shells, each stuck in a heavy dot of long-dried glue. Many of the shells had come off the cardboard, their places marked now by an empty yellow glob of glue. Under both the shells and glue someone had printed the names of the shells. The printing was painstaking, childish, the ink faded, and the empty spaces sad. He reached back into the drawer where he found one shell that had come loose while the cardboard was in the drawer. The others were missing altogether, probably long gone. He looked at the cardboard, holding it carefully in order not to dislodge the remaining shells or crumble the edges. Behind him he heard Ira opening and closing the file drawers. In front of him was her window facing the river. He stood reflected in the glass holding her memento. Beyond his reflection he could see the lights of Long Island City.

Still holding it carefully with two hands, he slid the cardboard back into the drawer.

He opened the side drawers. The top two drawers had nothing in them except slide boxes, some packets of sugar, and a cellophane-wrapped pair of panty hose. The third drawer was deep. He found a few different-sized stoppered glass bottles in it, and, at the back, a folder that held two copies of Ira Stern's postmortem report on Amos Roberts.

The report was intact, X rays and photographs still clipped to the folder.

Ira walked over, took the report out of Stavitsky's hand.

"It's all here, David. Photographs, X rays, everything." Stavitsky's hands felt heavy; he thought he was going to hit Stern. She'd taken it, she'd really taken it—and now this little son of a bitch had it. Stavitsky started to reach for it. Stern stepped back.

"David, what's the matter! We agreed I'd take it, get copies made. That's what we said. David? What's the matter with you?" Stern took another backward step and Stavitsky stood up.

"Little man—" He stopped. What was the matter with him? Why was he frightening the guy? He liked Stern. Stern had turned pale, he was moving back toward the door. Stavitsky stood up.

"Please, David."

"I'm not going to hurt you, Ira. I—I just don't want anything to happen to it. That report's sort of the whole thing. If we don't have it, then the rest doesn't mean much."

"Oh, I'll take care of it. I promise. Just get copies made—first thing tomorrow. Then I'll put the originals back in the files, and they'll always be there if you ever need them. I swear to God, that's what I'll do."

"I'm sorry. I know that. It's just—c'mon, let's get out of here."

They went back to the hallway. Stavitsky started to lock the door, then he stopped.

"Wait a minute, Ira. I just want to make sure I left all the drawers closed."

He went back in through the dark room to her desk. The lights across the river looked brilliant. He wondered if she ever stayed in this room in the dark, watching the lights reflecting on the river.

He opened the center drawer of her desk and reached way back inside until his fingers found the single dislodged shell. He took it out and rolled it between his fingers for a second. Then he put it in his pocket, shut the drawer, and went back to Ira waiting in the hall.

No one saw them leave the building, no one was in the parking lot.

"Hey," Stern said, "is everything OK, David?"

Stavitsky didn't answer.

When they got to Stern's building, and Stern started to open the car door, Stavitsky leaned across him and held the door shut. His face was very close to Stern's.

"You won't let anything happen to that report, will you, Ira?"

"For Christ's sake, David, let me out."

"You'll keep it safe?"

"Yes, yes, yes. Now let me out of here!"

Stavitsky released the door handle and leaned back. Stern got out of the car so fast he almost stumbled.

"Watch out for the dog shit, Ira!"

Jesus Christ, Stavitsky thought, what's happening to me?

Stern ran between the parked cars and into his building. Stavitsky stayed double-parked, looking after him. Then, when Stern was out of sight, he took the shell out of his pocket. It was just a sea snail, very common, worn smooth. He took a piece of Kleenex out of the glove compartment, tore off the edge, and wrapped the shell in it. Then he put it in the little sterling silver box he carried in his pocket for saccharine.

It was after eight. He had to get home and call Joey.

Joey was waiting for Stavitsky's call, and he had a lot to tell about the Lists. The father was dead. The mother, Katherine Compton List, lived in the house they had occupied since 1929—2 East Seventy-eighth Street —right around the corner from the daughter, Stavitsky thought. Mr. List had been the director and major stockholder of the List Investment Company, 80 Broad Street. His son took over in 1968 when the old man died. Joey had gotten most of his dirt from the switchboard operator, an employee who had worked there for twenty-five years and who seemed to dislike the son, pined for the old days, and loved talking about the family. The employee had never met the daughter—heard she'd married an even richer family, money to money, the woman had told Joey. Mr. Thomas List (son's name was Michael) was supposed to have left enough (Joey checked probate—more than enough: all told in the area of $25,000,000). The company had survived the recession, was still surviving, and the woman had to admit that young Mr. List (although Joey explained that he was over forty) seemed to be "managing."

The son had a coin collection which was in the assets of the Bowery Savings Bank, and from which he received interest income of over $100,000 a year. "Coins, yet," Joey said.

But Stavitsky didn't care about the son. "What about her—the daughter?"

Nothing much. There'd been some rumors years and years ago—even the switchboard operator hadn't been there long enough to hear them firsthand—about some nasty incident the daughter had been involved in in Nantucket. Some accident with one of her playmates, but no details. Other than that, all she knew was that she'd been born on March 7, 1929, and that she had married William Ely Gilbert in 1955. She had an operator's license and drove a black Jaguar sedan. Mrs. List had more bank accounts than New York had cops—mostly trusts, but the service account seemed to be kept at something called Banque Internationale at Sixty-eighth and Fifth. Joey'd gone there. But they would barely let him into the place, much less discuss one of their customers. "Fantastic place, chief. Looked more like a whorehouse than a bank. The son—"

"Fuck the son. What about the girl?"

"That's it. That's all I know. I think you'd need an order to get at that bank—they didn't give a shit about my being a cop—don't think they'd unzip for the goddamn President unless they had to."

"You mean that's all you can tell me about the girl?"

"That's it; and she sure ain't no girl anymore. Why don't you talk to Mother if it's the daughter you're interested in?" Jokes—the son of a bitch was making jokes. "Mothers love gassing about their daughters—my wife's sure does."

"Thanks, Joey." Stavitsky kept the anger out of his voice. "I'll do that."

He sat in the kitchen looking at the notes he'd made while Joey talked. So much money, so fucking much money. The amounts fascinated him, made him angry, uncertain, all kinds of feelings that the day had left him too tired to sort out—and he wanted a cigarette. Christ, how he wanted a cigarette.

A house on Seventy-eighth. She'd probably been born there, grew up there, gave parties. *The* Miss List, of *the* Thomas Lists. What the hell did that mean, $25,000,000? What did it really mean? One thing he knew—no matter how much money rich, rich Mommy had, she wouldn't have given two small-time dicks $200,000 to protect a daughter she thought was innocent. No. She'd known, all right, just as Haynes said. She'd believed every word, because one hundred bucks would have kept Miss Jennifer List out of the papers. But for $200,000?

What the hell was he so angry about? Cops had been bought before. Mrs. Thomas List might have been able to buy *him* for that kind of money. He had to have a cigarette. He went to the kitchen cabinet where Carole kept her week's carton—she was upstairs or downstairs, he didn't know which. He tore open one of the packs. His first cigarette in ten years, but the first taste was wonderful—perfect. He took a deep drag. $200,000.

For that kind of money you bought silence on dark secrets, not just a girl trying to get laid and having the bad luck to pick a guy with a dicky heart or a brain tumor. For $200,000 you bought twenty years of silence on something terrible.

Well, Mrs. List, he thought, your investment just ran out.

5

MOST OF THE other houses on the block between Fifth and Madison carried small bronze plaques announcing that they were embassies or foundation headquarters. But Number 2 had no designation except its number. The place unsettled him at first glance and, to fight a growing feeling of insignificance, he walked across to Madison, then uptown until he found a coffee shop where he bought some gum and cigarettes. He planned to chew and smoke uninterruptedly during his visit to Number 2 which he hoped would disgust Mrs. List.

The butler led him upstairs into a very soft-looking book-lined room. An unswept marble fireplace was working and Stavitsky stood near it.

He took the pillbox that contained the shell out of his pocket and held it in his hand, his thumb stroking the smooth surface. Her shell—a talisman of sorts, a tangible connection between them. And now he would see her mother.

She came into the room quietly. A small woman with the same thick wavy hair her daughter had, only grayer, less chestnut, and carefully done. Sweet-faced, like her daughter, but the mother's face was fuller, softer, her eyes and skin fresher. Except for the gray hair she looked her daughter's age, even younger. Stavitsky stood up.

"How do you do—captain, is it?"

Stavitsky nodded.

"Please sit down." He did, and put the manila folder he was carrying on the tea table. She sat across from him on the other side of the fireplace. "I don't have to tell you how strange it is to entertain a policeman at ten in the morning. Or anytime, for that matter. May I offer you some coffee or tea?" Her voice was soft and pleasant, though not nearly as lovely as her daughter's. He tried to recall Jennifer Gilbert's voice while her mother waited for his answer. But, like her face, her voice eluded him. All he could remember was that it was beautiful, the most beautiful voice he had ever heard.

"I would like some coffee." He did not say please or thank you. When she walked across the room to the bellpull, he lit a cigarette. He decided to save the gum until after the coffee and planned to leave the wrapper on the large, polished mahogany coffee table that stood between the two chairs, where she would be sure to see it.

The butler appeared and she ordered the coffee. Then she came back, the skirt of her robe billowing slightly, its hem just clearing the worn Turkish carpet. Stavitsky watched her steadily across the room and back to the chair. She twisted the sleeve end of the robe around her finger and tried to smile, but Stavitsky could see that his unwavering stare made her uncomfortable.

"As I was saying—"

"Yeah, I know, Mrs. List. You're not used to seeing a cop the first thing in the morning."

"Yes. Isn't it usual to call first and make an appointment?"

"Usual, but not necessary. No one's ever too busy to see the cops, Mrs. List. Unless we're collecting for something. But what I told your butler was true. I'm not collecting for anything."

"I see."

The butler came in with the coffee. She poured it and let him fix it himself. The creamer and sugar bowl were heavy, too heavy; he hated their solidness and the fineness of the carving on them that rubbed against his fingers. Even the spoon was heavy, and the china too light. He wanted to drop the spoon into the delicate cup and watch it crack, but he made himself put it carefully in his saucer.

"Well," she said, "I know what you're *not* here for, so perhaps you could tell me—"

He interrupted. "A man was killed at your daughter's home on November 29th. Maybe she mentioned it to you?" His tone was cold, nasty. Kate shifted in her chair, then sipped her coffee, stalling for time, stretching the duration of her own ignorance. The old fear nipped at her.

"Yes, captain." Her coldness matched his, and she could give a twist of superiority that had taken years of practice, and at which he was an amateur. "She 'mentioned' it to me. At the time of his death he was, I believe, assaulting her husband, after robbing their home."

"Right, that's exactly right, Mrs. List. Did she also mention how he died?"

"She told me it was very mysterious and that she suspected it was a brain hemorrhage of some kind."

"I see. She was wrong, Mrs. List. The man died of a broken neck."

"Really. How odd. May I give you some more coffee?" She was praying that he would say no, because she knew that if she had to pour the coffee he would see her hands shaking. She kept them folded as loosely as she could in her lap. She could feel them tremble, small shudders that tightened the fingers against each other.

"No." Again, no "thank you."

"I don't see what this man's death, whatever killed him, has to do with me."

"Mrs. List, do you remember Marvin Ross?"

It was over.

She had been waiting for this moment for forty years, now it had come. In a way it was a relief; she felt the tension, an old tension, unnoticed until this moment, wash out of her body. Her hands lay relaxed in her lap, and her shoulders sagged in a way that she had forgotten they could. She was ready to let go, everything in her wanted to. Then she thought of the child. A ghost child that she had protected so determinedly. And the woman the child had become, no less a ghost, bewildered. The old ties would not loose. She still loved her daughter, alone in a cocoon that no one had spun, owed still her protection for as long as she could give it. She tightened again, her shoulders lifted as she looked at the man who had come to destroy Jennifer.

Stavitsky saw her gather herself. "Yes," she answered finally, "I remember Marvin Ross. He was a friend of my daughter's."

"Just a friend?"

"That's right."

"He died very suddenly."

"Yes. It was quite a shock."

"Your daughter was there when it happened."

Kate thought very quickly, trying to assess how much he knew.

"As it turned out, she was not there. Though Marvin's roommate claimed she was."

"He accused her of killing Ross, didn't he?"

"Yes."

"And you were there to hear him do it."

"Yes. You see, the police had called to talk to her—question her, actually. She wasn't home, and when they told me what happened I panicked and went running over there. Stupid of me, I suppose, but understandable under the circumstances."

"Where was she?"

"She was in Nantucket. We have a summer home there." Like all nonprofessional liars, she added too many details without being asked for them. "She had fallen behind in school because of her relationship with Marvin, and she went up there on Friday to spend the weekend studying. As it turned out, it was a lucky thing she did."

"Why? Because she was out of the way when Ross died?"

"No, because she met her husband there that weekend. They were married soon afterward and have been very happy ever since." This last confidently—she could see Stavitsky was not prepared for that answer.

"So she wasn't even in town when Marvin Ross died?"

"That's right, she was over three hundred miles away. I know you must have been talking to that boy that accused her. I don't remember his name, but he seemed to have something against my daughter, though I never found out what, but he said some very—"

"Cut the crap, Mrs. List." Kate gasped. Stavitsky went on. "The boy is a man now, his name is Haynes, and he remembers everything very clearly. He also didn't strike me as the type who'd carry that kind of grudge for twenty years. And he hasn't budged one inch from the story he told that night."

"How do you know that? How did you even connect him with my daughter or with this Amos Roberts?"

"He has no connection with Amos Roberts. Your daughter is the only connection between Amos Roberts and Marvin Ross."

"And what connection is that, captain?"

"That's what you're going to tell me."

"This is absurd. I told you before, captain, she wasn't even there when Marvin Ross died." She had begun to sweat. Tendrils of fine gray hair curled and stuck in the moisture on her forehead. Her eyes were bright, every inch of her was alive, and Stavitsky thought she looked very handsome. He leaned back in his chair. It was time to spring the trap.

"And you knew, even when you went to Ross' apartment, that Jennifer was far away and had been since the day before?"

"Yes."

"Then why did you go at all?"

Kate assumed an air of reluctance—she did it fairly well. "My daughter was quite fond of the Ross boy. I was afraid that she might have dissembled about going to Nantucket and been planning to spend the weekend with him or something like that."

"How do you know that isn't what happened, and that she didn't go to Nantucket until after he was dead?"

"Because I called Nantucket when I got home that night," Kate lied, "and she was there."

"So your doubts were unfounded?"

"I was foolish to doubt my daughter, captain. She has never lied to me in her life. I told you, the police called in the middle of the night, and I panicked. If I'd been thinking straight, I'd have realized that she told me the truth."

"Then why did you give Detectives Charles and Gordon two hundred thousand dollars not to mention her name in their report and not to recommend an autopsy on Ross' body?"

She did not move, not even a twitch. Stavitsky admired her control. Only one slightly long beat separated his question from her answer.

"I know that seems terribly strange to you, captain—"

"Yes, it does."

She went on as though he had not spoken. "—but we have a certain position and where there are police, there are usually reporters. I didn't want the List name to appear in the *Daily News* the next day. Whatever the *facts,* captain, the newspapers could have made Jennifer look like anything from a promiscuous woman to a murderess. I wouldn't allow that. The two officers were very understanding."

"*Two hundred thousand dollars?* Just to prevent a hint of scandal?"

Kate smiled tolerantly. "You must understand, captain, we are well-to-do people. Two hundred thousand dollars may seem a great deal of money to you, but to us—" She shrugged. She was slipping away from him. He had gone there so certain that he had her, and now she was explaining it all, making it seem ordinary, probable, even though he knew she was lying. He choked on her lies and on his own anger.

"Goddammit, don't you see it's past playing games! OK, OK, she's your daughter. But you've got to have some pity. My God, woman, there's three men dead—"

Then Kate threw it all away. "Three," she cried, "how did you know—"

Everything stopped; he held his coffee cup, she held hers—both frozen as they realized what she'd said.

She tried to recoup. "I mean, what three men? What three?" But it was no use.

Stavitsky stared at her. "OK, lady, let's have it."

"Don't talk to me like that."

He didn't even hear her. He crashed the cup into its saucer, then he was on his feet, around the table. He grabbed her arm and yanked her out of the chair, pulling her against him until their faces almost touched.

"She killed the kid, too, didn't she?" His voice was huge. She flinched, tried to pry her arm loose, but his grip tightened.

"Didn't she?"

No answer.

"I *know* she killed Ross and Roberts." His voice was out of control, raging at the white face in front of him.

"And, goddammit, she killed the little boy too, didn't she? Didn't she?" He shook her until her head snapped back and forth. "You're going to tell me—now," still shaking her. "C'mon, goddammit, spill it."

Still Kate held on through the tears of pain and anger.

"What little boy? What are you talking about?"

Still holding her, he dragged her to the table, opened the manila folder, and grabbed the Telex sheets.

"This little boy, Harold Kearney—eleven years old—smashed to pieces in Nantucket forty years ago. Would you like to read the doctor's report? No? Then I'll read it to you." He snapped the report in her face. "Where would you like to start? Here maybe." He pretended to read: "'Skull fractured in five places.' Mess, Mrs. List, terrible mess—must've been brains all over the—"

"Oh, please, oh, please, no. . . ." She was hanging on to him now for support instead of trying to get away. He held her up, but his voice went on blasting in her face.

"Listen, Mrs. List, I'm good, real good, and by the time I'm finished, I'm going to know every time your daughter went to the toilet since the day she was born. You're going to tell me all of it, Mrs. List." His fingers tightened into her flesh and she whimpered. "Because if you don't I'll find out anyway. And you can bet whoever does tell me won't be as kind about it as you—and the papers are bound to get wind of something this wild. Do you understand me?" He shook her again. "Do you?"

She nodded. He let go of her arm and she massaged it. She sank back into the chair, her legs too weak to stand. She kept her head down, turned away from him.

He stood for a minute looking down at her. Her hands had shrunk into the wide sleeves of the gown and he saw that the hem of one of the cuffs had torn loose, letting the inner lining hang down. There were tear spots on the silk, and the gown was wrinkled at the shoulders where he'd been holding her.

He kneeled down next to the chair, almost sitting on the floor, trying to see her face. "Don't you see," he said softly, "it doesn't matter what proof I have or don't have, it only matters what we know—you and I.

"Look, Amos Roberts deserved to die, I'll give you that. But what about Marvin Ross? If he were alive, he'd still be a fairly young man. Did he deserve to die? Did he?"

"No," she whispered, her head still turned away from him.

"And the other one, the kid. Did he deserve to die?"

"No." Kate sobbed. "He was just a boy, just a young beautiful boy."

"Why don't you tell me about it now." He spoke as gently as he could, holding back the sense of triumph. "Tell me. . . ." He was sure she was beaten; he was going to hear it now. He held his breath.

Then she turned to look at him. Her face was drained, eyes red; nothing of the proud dowager in that face now, and Stavitsky let himself start to feel sorry for her until he saw how thin her lips were, pressed together, corners spread.

"The only thing I'm going to tell you, captain, is that my daughter never knew . . . never consciously hurt anyone in her life. And that's all I'm going to tell you." Her voice was toneless and flat. "Remember that. She never knew—not about Kearney, not about any of them. Write it down, captain—write in that folder you have, because that's the only thing I'm ever going to tell you. Now get out."

He couldn't believe it. "But it's going to happen again. My God, don't you see that? It will happen again. You've got to help me or it's on you, too." He sank back on his haunches. "You can't let it go on—you can't, no matter who she is, no matter what she means to you—you've got to have some pity."

"I don't have to do anything, captain. Just remember what I said. She didn't . . . doesn't know anything."

Their faces were very close, and for a second he was afraid he was going to hit her.

"You bitch. . . . How can you—"

"I'm sure I don't have to take this kind of abuse in my own home. I've asked you to leave. If you don't I shall have to call someone—or are you going to arrest me, captain?"

They stared at each other. Other people always backed down—he was a cop. And he was right—he knew he was right. But she stared and stared. She didn't care who had died, or how many. She really didn't care. Finally he turned away, stood up, and walked back to the table for the folder. His legs felt stiff from kneeling so long, and now other muscles were protesting against the tenseness of his whole body. He picked up the folder and looked back at her. There were still traces of tears, but her face was so composed, so controlled now that he almost couldn't remember how it had looked, twisted and crying.

"You know, Mrs. List," he said, "you're more dangerous than your daughter."

He walked out of the room, down the stairs, and out of the house.

Kate waited until she heard the front door shut, then she closed the study door and dialed Jennifer's office number.

"Jennifer, I hope I'm not disturbing you?"

"No, Mother. But I don't have long to talk—our test animals died during the night."

"Jennifer, you know I don't like to hear about those things."

"I'm sorry, Mother. What do you want?"

She'd spent three months on the drug—three months thrown away. It had done so well in culture and she'd allowed herself to hope. . . . But the first animal trial was a disaster. Seventy-five mice dead. They had died last night, alone in the dark, clumping together against the walls of the cages: little feet curled and stiff, tails twined together, bodies turned over exposing the tiny light pink abdomens under thin fur. Her mother didn't want to hear about it. Warm-blooded animals bored William, and Dr. Lambert, her assistant, still called her Dr. Gilbert after ten years of working together every day. There was no one to mourn the mice with.

"Well, Mother, what is it?" She was impatient and let it show. She was tired, too, and discouraged. Most of all she was frightened. Whenever she thought of the captain, which she did again and again, she was frightened.

"I don't quite know how to tell you. . . ."

Jennifer thought her mother never knew quite how to tell her anything.

"Why not try just saying it?"

"Oh, Jennifer, please. Don't—don't be like that. I've had a very upsetting morning. A man came here . . . a policeman."

A policeman. . . .

"Jennifer, did you hear me?"

"What policeman, Mother?"

"A captain somebody. I don't remember his name. I don't want to.

He was incredibly rude." Rude was her mother's word for everything from using the wrong spoon to committing assault.

"What do you mean rude? What did he want?"

"I mean rude—exactly what I said."

"For God's sake, Mother—what did he want?"

"What's the matter with you, Jennifer? He was a nasty man asking some unpleasant questions. But there's no reason to get excited."

Suddenly Jennifer wanted to hang up, walk out of the office, get into the car, and go away. She never wanted to see them again, not her mother, not William, not Ellen. But then, there was the captain.

"What unpleasant questions, Mother? Questions about the dead man in the apartment? Is that what you mean by unpleasant?"

"Jennifer, you know what I mean. The point is that he was very difficult to deal with, and he—"

"He what?"

"He behaved as if we'd done something wrong."

"We?" Jennifer said, but Kate went right on as if she hadn't heard.

"And I'm calling because I want you to be prepared. I think he may come to see you. He—he's a terrible man." Jennifer thought of how he looked the last time she'd seen him. Pale, fighting his sickness. . . . "He had some sort of file about Hal Kearney. You remember, the little boy. . . ."

"Yes, Mother, I remember." She was holding the phone so tightly that her hand began to cramp. She spread her fingers to ease it, but the cramp tightened and her palm began to sweat.

"And about Marvin," Kate said. "Marvin Ross." Did her mother really wonder if she'd forgotten him?

"I see. Yes, that must have been very unpleasant. And what did you tell him?"

"*Tell* him? What was there to tell?"

"He must have thought there was something to tell, mustn't he? Why else did he come to see you?"

"Yes, he must have—but he was wrong. And when he found out that there was nothing I could tell him he acted like a madman, yelling, calling me names. It was awful. But he finally had to go away."

"And you didn't tell him anything?"

"Why do you keep asking me that?" Kate said sharply. She paused, then very deliberately: "No matter what you think, you and that man"—she was speaking slowly now as if in code—"I have nothing to tell. There was *never* anything to tell. But he didn't believe me and I . . . I'm sure that he will try to see you. Do you understand me? He'll be coming to see you. And—" Kate stopped again. Then, rushing words, "Jennifer, he didn't act like any policeman I've ever met. He doesn't care about the man who died. It's something else."

Jennifer sat with the phone in her hand, listening to her mother breathe. Finally, "Mother, why didn't you just tell him and have done with it?"

"I don't know what you're talking about."

"The truth, Mother. You could have told him the truth. Why not—after so long, after everything. . . ?"

"I told him the truth, Jennifer."

"Did you, Mother? Did you tell him about Hal and Marvin? Did you tell him any of it—any of the things you know? Did you?"

"Stop it. You're not to talk to me that way."

"Tell me, Mother. Tell me the truth. Please. Just say it. It won't hurt. Say, 'Jennifer, there's something wrong. Something I should have told you a long time ago, but it's not too late.' Say it, Mother. Say, 'Jennifer—' "

"Oh, God, you're worse than he is." Kate's voice was cracking. "There is no 'truth,' there's nothing to talk about. Do you hear me? Nothing. I just thought you ought to know that he was here—that he might come to see you. And, Jennifer, be sure someone is with you when he does."

Who? she wanted to ask—who should be with me? But she didn't say anything.

"Jennifer?"

"Yes, Mother. I heard you."

Jennifer hung up without saying any more. She opened the bottom drawer of her desk and reached inside for the file. At first she couldn't believe it was gone. She searched the other drawers, finally taking everything out of them and piling bottles, journals, stationery, even the cardboard of shells on top of the desk until the drawers were empty. But long before she finished, she knew it wasn't there. He'd taken it, he had it now.

She sat back, her face covered with sweat, hair soaked with it, and looked out the window. It was only an autopsy report, that's all; and some strange X rays.

She wondered if he were on his way to her now or if he'd wait. To-night maybe, or tomorrow afternoon. She hoped he wouldn't wait too long.

She stood up and went to the door. The outer office was empty. Then she stopped and looked at the door to the hall that led back to the lab and the dead mice. He could be out there right now. He could turn the knob any second and open the door. She could almost see him standing in the doorway.

It had been the longest afternoon of his life. He had talked to people on the phone, filled out forms, and thought about nothing except what Mrs. List had said about her daughter. That she didn't know. It was crazy. But what if it were true? All afternoon he kept hearing the cool voice, dry after the storm of crying. She didn't know, she never knew. . . .

Finally things were cleared up enough and he could go home, but first he had to give Carmichael a ride to Penn Station. The traffic on the West Side Highway boxed him in, crawling past Eighteenth Street, past Twenty-third. All around him exhaust fumes collected in the windless cold. She didn't know, the mother had said she didn't know. He leaned on the horn and that started a chorus all around him. They inched past Twenty-third, cars lined up from the streets trying to creep into the line. He didn't give way, just stayed as close as he could to the car in front of him. How could she *not* know? It was crazy. But was it? Ching had never confronted her. And God knows that woman on Seventy-eighth Street wouldn't have admitted that her daughter, a member of one of the finest families, etc., etc., might not be exactly like all the other daughters of the finest families. He tried the horn again. They were almost to Twenty-eighth Street.

"Take it easy, David," Carmichael said. "It isn't going to help."

"Fuck you," he said and hit the horn again.

Finally Forty-second Street. He turned off the drive, raced the car down the ramp, and twisted and turned through the traffic, heading back downtown until he pulled up across the street from the station at Thirty-fourth Street. Carmichael was getting out at last, but he turned, holding the door open, and looked back into the car.

"Dave, is something wrong?"

Stavitsky didn't want to look at him. He could hear the concern in the other man's voice and he was afraid that he'd give in; that he'd say yes, something was terribly wrong—that he couldn't stop thinking about her at all anymore. That every minute of his life now was as much hers as it was his, and that he'd become committed to a search he didn't understand for something he was frightened of finding.

"Dave?" Carmichael said.

"Leave me the hell alone. You'll miss your train."

"Look, Dave, if there's anything you need, anything I can do. . . ."

He turned to Carmichael, his face pleasantly blank.

"Go on, you fart—I'm fine."

Carmichael smiled. "That's better," he said. "See you tomorrow." Stavitsky nodded and Carmichael shut the door and walked across the street through the five forty-five crowds to the station entrance.

Good, he thought as he turned west, then north when he reached Tenth Avenue. Very good. That had been a bad moment, and he'd made it. He kept a steady 35 to make the lights—think about making the lights. Small factories lined his way, then parking lots, a big gas station overrun by taxis. He made himself look at everything he passed, pretending that he would have to remember every detail later. He made that light, the next was close but he made it, too. Past the West Side Terminal—blank and abandoned—still good on the lights. The car bumped and shuddered over the potholes, a steady 35. Then he missed a light and had to stop.

It was six. She must be home by now—too early for dinner. He'd read once that the New York East Side never ate dinner before eight. What would she do before dinner? Have sherry—that sounded right—have sherry and talk to Gilbert. He wished he were there. They'd be sipping sherry, all of them, and he'd be saying, so casually, "Oh, by the way— Charles Raines cut his throat yesterday. Wrists, too. Blood everywhere," he would be telling them, sipping sherry. "Blood creeping across the floor until it had spread as far as it could, then gelling at the edges, where it was thinnest." He could see them listening gravely as he described the body. And the part about the clean room—that was the best of it. Flowered curtains tacked to the windows, and a bedspread to match. Then they'd pour more sherry. Some talk about dinner being a few minutes late; then he'd go on, telling them how most suicides were tentative. Oh, yes, just a few experimental cuts before they could work up the will to really slash. But not Raines—he was sure of what he wanted. But, then, he was a man of special instincts—especially for a junkie.

At last the light changed and he pulled away, but the fantasy kept going, light after light, as he kept even speed until Tenth turned to Amsterdam. Special instincts? Her lovely voice . . . Crystal glasses . . . What sort of instincts? Rare delicacy, he would explain. Two clean shirts—the bastard had two clean shirts. Not just laundromated wash and wear, but really ironed. Frayed, of course, but ironed and folded. "Shit." He smashed the side of his hand against the steering wheel. "Shit." She had to have known. How could she have threatened Raines if she hadn't known? Of course the mother lied, and lied, and lied.

But maybe not. Stavitsky's mind shifted again. Raines was a junkie, reason enough to want to die. And, after all, he *might* have misunderstood the threat of a rich powerful woman who didn't want cops and newspaper reporters crawling all over the place. Maybe the threat had nothing to do with Roberts. It was possible. But then he realized that not knowing made her more dangerous, not less. She might do it again, anytime, if she didn't know. But it would also make her innocent, not a murderer. "Check it," he told himself, "check with Ching." Maybe it was true. Maybe she didn't know. He didn't want her to know. At Amsterdam he dropped his speed just right and he didn't miss another light all the way home.

Stavitsky tried to convince Ching that it was possible, but Ching didn't believe Mrs. List.

"Then why would she have taken the postmortem report on Roberts if she didn't know what she'd done." The thin phone voice sliced away at Stavitsky's hopes. He thought for a minute.

"Maybe because I'd frightened her."

"How?"

"The day the report was stolen I'd had lunch with her. I practically accused her of killing Roberts after making a big deal out of the postmortem and the fact that Galeston was looking into it. I tell you I frightened her. Maybe she had to find out what really did happen to Roberts. Can't you see"—he *had* to see—"she might've taken it even if she didn't know what she'd done to Roberts. Besides, I could see the mother was lying about everything, but not about that. She really believed that her daughter didn't know."

"But, captain, the mother might not know the truth. Most mothers know very little about their children, captain."

"But Jennifer was the one who called the police when Ross died— called them and left her name. Would she have done that if she'd knowingly killed him?"

"Did she call the police when Roberts died?"

"No," he said after a while. "She didn't."

"And what does *that* tell you?"

No answer.

"And don't forget, captain, by the time she got to Roberts there were already two dead—two people who had done nothing in this world except cross her. They were not old or sick—nothing to account for their deaths except that in one way or another she wished them dead. Even if the wish were more or less unconscious. She had to *want* these things to happen. She had to *want* the paper airplane to land. And while she may not have actually thought of killing the Kearney boy, she had to have wanted him smashed to pieces. That's what she told me—smashed to pieces."

Stavitsky didn't say anything.

"The same with Marvin," Ching went on, "she had to want him dead. Not just hurt or crippled, but dead. Or he'd still be alive."

"She still could have believed that Ross had a heart attack or something," Stavitsky insisted. "She could even have believed that the Kearney boy was hit by a car and that the other two boys were lying about what happened to him. It's possible."

"At the uppermost surface level, the conscious level, perhaps. But remember—it all, *all* had to be her wish. And Roberts. . . . A broken neck, captain! That's not the result of a vague wish. A precise job, Galeston said. Precision is not subconscious."

Stavitsky kept trying, trying to establish her innocence. "Okay, she might have wanted it to happen. I couldn't blame her for wanting Roberts' neck broken. That doesn't mean she *knew* it was going to happen."

Suddenly Ching was angry. "I told you what I think, captain. Why do you go on with this? Time is running out and it's a little late to be looking for excuses."

"What do you mean? What are you talking about?"

"Don't play games with me, captain. Now if you'll excuse me"—very angry, and something else—"we've discussed this as much as necessary."

Frightened. Ching was frightened.

"What time?" Stavitsky asked.

But the phone clicked. Ching had broken the connection.

Stavitsky thought about calling him back. But the man was too angry, too frightened. And what was the crap about time?

Galeston. He tried to call him but he wasn't home. It was almost seven, and Stavitsky wondered where the old man was.

Stern. He had promised Stavitsky a copy of the report today, but he hadn't heard from him.

The phone rang, rang again. Mrs. Stern answered.

"Oh, captain, you just missed them."

"Them?"

"Ira and Dr. Galeston; they just left."

"Galeston? Galeston was with him?"

"Yes, they just left."

He didn't understand.

"Were they coming here?"

"I don't think so. They were going over some kind of report, then Dr. Galeston called someone—another doctor, I think. I didn't hear the name. Then they left."

"Mrs. Stern," easy, he told himself, "do you have any idea where they went?"

"No, it was all very hush-hush. They stopped talking every time I came into the room."

"Did they have anything with them?"

"Ira had a large brown envelope."

The report.

He slammed the receiver back into its cradle and ran to the bedroom where he kept his old service revolver under his clean pajamas. It had no holster, so he put it in his jacket pocket and headed for the door, pulling his overcoat out of the hall closet on his way.

Carole heard the door slam.

"David?" She ran out of the kitchen to the hall. She opened the door just in time to see him step into the elevator.

"David!"

He didn't answer. The elevator doors closed behind him.

He hit 60 going through the park. If she got that report away from them he had nothing except some weird tapes and the testimony of Galeston and Ching. Galeston would protect it. But why had he let Ira take it there in the first place? What the hell were they doing? Galeston. . . . Galeston would never give it up unless . . . unless she made him. He took the Fifth Avenue turn on two wheels, horn going full blast as he swerved around the corner, just missing the crosstown bus. Eighty-sixth, Seventy-ninth—the car squealed to the left, people stared, other cars got out of the way, drivers mouthing, horns blaring back. Then Seventy-seventh. He pulled up to the curb in front of the building, right at the marquee. An attendant was waving, but Stavitsky pushed past him, ignoring the man at the reception desk, who started after him, and walked straight into the elevator. The operator looked at the badge without saying anything and they started up, leaving the others behind, waving and yelling in the lobby.

The elevator kept its stately pace, past 19, 20. . . . He wanted to throttle the operator, scream, anything to make the thing move faster. Finally the gates slid back and he was facing the double doors. The bell chimed again and again. Then the sound of running feet and the door opened a few inches to show Hawkins' face.

"Open up."

The other man didn't move.

"Open up, you son of a bitch."

"You got a warrant, copper?"

"Open this goddamn door or I'll blow your fucking head off."

For an instant nothing happened. Stavitsky reached for his gun, wondering if he'd have to shoot him. But Hawkins saw and opened the door.

"Where are they? Fast—move."

Hawkins led him through the anteroom and across the thousand-step-long living room, then down a gallery walled on one side by windows that faced east. They changed direction. The apartment took up the entire upper portion of the building and had four exposures.

Hawkins faltered, turned to Stavitsky. "You're making a big mistake, man."

Stavitsky pushed him. "Keep going."

They were all there standing around her desk in an odd-looking line as if they had been waiting for him. Stern stood up straight, Galeston only looked up from the desk, still leaning over. And Jennifer. She was standing between them, facing him. He walked across the room toward them, toward her. He felt as if they were lovers meeting again after a long separation. He wanted to take her in his arms.

She looked as frail as he remembered, even more tired. The circles under her eyes were darker, her skin paler, but he was amazed that he had not noticed before how beautiful she was.

She smiled at him, very widely, firmly, as if she'd been waiting to see him, too. Then she nodded at the envelope on the desk. It was large and had "Manhattan General Hospital, Department of Pathology" printed in the upper left-hand corner.

"Dr. Galeston and Dr. Stern were just returning this to me."

"It isn't theirs to return—if Manhattan General doesn't want it anymore then the New York Homicide division does. In any case, it isn't yours." His tone was almost casual, as if the ownership of the envelope were a technicality that they could dispose of easily.

"I see your point," she said. "But even though, ah, homicide might be interested, in one sense it is mine—my work, which does give me some claim."

"Your work." He stared at her. "Your work." His mouth went dry. "Then you *did* know, you knew exactly what you were doing." He knew that they had to hear the sadness in his voice.

She laughed. "Of course I knew." Galeston raised his hand as if to warn her, to stop her. But either she didn't see the gesture or she didn't care. "You don't really think I could separate a man's spine and tear his spinal cord without knowing what I was doing? It was a neat job, too. Ask Dr. Galeston, he'll show you on the X rays. It's really quite clear, isn't it, doctor?"

"Quite clear." Galeston's voice came tonelessly from the side. Stavitsky didn't look at him, only at her. And she was looking at him, but at the edge of his vision he saw her hand move, reaching for the envelope.

Then he drew the revolver slowly out of his pocket and aimed it, obviously carefully at the spot between her breasts.

"David, don't," Stern was pleading.

Stavitsky ignored him. He walked to the desk, closer to her, closer than they'd been the day he met her. He picked up the envelope. The gun stayed aimed, unwavering. She didn't move or look at it.

"Captain—" Galeston this time. Stavitsky had never heard him speak so gently. "That report isn't going to help you. Even if Roberts had been stabbed or shot you couldn't have made a charge stick. And, captain, under the circumstances. . . ."

"What the hell are you talking about? You said yourself it couldn't have happened—an impossible injury, you said. It doesn't matter about charges, or courts, or any crap like that—it matters that it was *done,* that *she* did it. With this report, and—" The tapes, he was about to tell them about the tapes, but Galeston interrupted.

"All that report shows is that someone was admitted to Manhattan General on November twenty-ninth with a rather neatly broken neck."

"But with no other injury—you said that." What the hell was going on here? What was Galeston trying to pull? "Didn't you say that there wasn't another mark on him? Isn't that it? Not another mark on him?"

Galeston sat down in one of the large green leather chairs next to the desk. He looked at her for a moment, then at Stavitsky. The accordion lines in his face creased as he smiled; "Captain, separation of C_1 and C_2, and no other injury? That's impossible. I think I told you originally that it was impossible, didn't I, captain?"

"No, no," Galeston said, looking up at the ceiling. "It must have been a mistake—a mixup in the files probably."

Stavitsky just stared at him as his voice droned on.

"Yes, a mixup. I seem to remember a terrible accident the same night. Someone fell or jumped from a window, or maybe it was an automobile accident—head-on into a bridge strut or another car. Drunk probably. I'm sure there was something that night to account for those X rays. And it's a big place, Manhattan General. We're all overworked. What could be more natural than that the X rays got switched, and poor Ira here was confused? Here's this set of X rays and a body without any injuries . . . and, of course, he was tired." He turned to Stern. "How many PM's had you done that day, Ira?"

"Seven," he mumbled without looking up.

"There you are, captain. Of course we have a system. But even the best system breaks down, and after seven autopsies. . . ."

"Why are you doing this, Galeston?"

The man was silent.

"Why?" Stavitsky demanded.

Galeston wasn't smiling anymore. There was no expression at all on his face. Except for a faint moist gleam between his almost closed lids there was no life in his face at all. "It doesn't matter now, does it?" he said. Then he opened his eyes and turned to her. "You shouldn't have said it, you know. You didn't have to tell him anything. And without my word that report is meaningless. We'd never have known for sure, Dr. Gilbert, *never.*"

"But I'm going to tell him," she said. She rested her hands on the desk and leaned toward them. Stern stepped back. "I'm going to tell him whatever he wants to know. You came here to find out, didn't you, captain?" She was looking at Stavitsky again and he didn't want her to stop. "You went to my mother and heard the standard forty-year-old string of Mrs. List lies: My daughter? You mean dear sweet ordinary Jennifer? Well, maybe the children do avoid her, maybe she doesn't have all the friends she might, but it's just the usual jealousy. After all, we are who we are. Oh, that Nantucket business? Yes, it *was* terrible, but an accident you know—an automobile, a truck. They never did find out for sure. And of course the Ross thing was unfortunate—but he wasn't our sort, was he? And we did send a whole basket of fruit, quite appropriate.

"That's when I learned that Jews don't send flowers to funerals, captain. Mother told me, so proud of having done the right thing." Suddenly her eyes left his. He saw them go to his hair, he could follow them down the line of cheek and neck to his shoulder across his chest and finally to the hand holding the gun, still aimed. But now it was a meaningless lump growing out of the end of his arm. He wasn't going to shoot.

"You're Jewish, aren't you, captain?"

"Yes." His voice was very soft.

Her eyes left the gun finally, and she looked at him as if they were alone. She leaned even closer. The fine knit fabric of her dress pulled and he could see the line of her collarbone.

"What do you want to know, captain? Mother was so upset. She thought you were mad. Ask me what you asked her—I'll tell you." She spread her hands, arms stretching as she leaned a little closer. The dress fabric outlined her ribs, pulled at her breasts. He looked at the thin body lines helplessly.

"I want to know what happened to Amos Roberts—all of it. What you did, why. What you know." He wanted to know everything. How she'd felt when she'd done it. What it was like to have and use power, to kill, really kill.

"Of course you do." She sounded as though she approved of his wanting to know. "But first I want to tell you that until that night, until that man did what he did, I didn't know."

The wind outside was rising, caught in the updraft, then pulled away out of sight. Her voice was soft against the other sounds and he wanted to lean forward to hear better, but that would bring them very close, nothing but the gun between them.

"You had to *want* them dead." Ching's words. "It had to be what you wanted."

"But only in the way we all want people dead sometimes. I thought the Kearney boy was going to kill me. I was hurt and frightened and I wanted him to die . . . that's true. And Marvin. It was horrible. But he called me a freak, a monster." She looked away.

Look back at me, he thought. Please look back at me.

She did.

"It's true, isn't it? Someone else called me those things too, a long time ago. I can't remember who. So I hated him for that instant, hated him and wanted him to die. But, captain, no matter what I wished, I didn't know! The only difference between me and anyone else was"—the wind was everywhere, shaking the huge windows—"that when I wanted them to die—"

She stopped. Stern sank into a chair and put his face in his hands. Galeston closed his eyes. Only Stavitsky didn't move. He knew he could stand there forever staring at her, that he never wanted to look at anyone or anything again except her face. Then, as deliberately as he'd taken it out, he put the revolver back in his pocket. It made a slight clink as it touched the tape recorder. He turned the machine on and found the volume control as if he were settling the gun, then he turned it all the way up.

"You don't have to." Galeston was talking to her again. Stavitsky wanted to choke him. "You don't have to tell us any more." Still no inflection in his voice. "Until we hear it from you it's conjecture, don't you see that? Nothing but conjecture. You've admitted enough, more than you should have. Stop now. Send us away."

"No, I'm going to tell you." She paused. "Of course, you don't have to listen, doctor. No one's keeping you here. You can go away, out of this room, out of this house. No one will stop you. But I'm finished with the lies."

Galeston didn't move.

"Forty years of lies. That's a long time, almost my whole life," she said, "and now he wants to hear." She was looking at Stavitsky again. "He's got to hear it. Right, captain?"

"Yes."

"And what will you do after you've heard?"

"I don't know."

She smiled at him. He smiled back.

"They're going to betray you, captain. You know that. They're not going to help you at all."

"It looks that way, doesn't it?"

"Without his help"—she nodded toward Galeston—"you'll be pretty helpless, won't you?"

"Maybe." He was still smiling at her. "But I'll try to change their minds."

"You won't though. And without them there's really no way you can hurt me. Hawkins won't say anything. Raines won't either, you know."

"No, Raines won't say anything." The smile was gone. "He's dead."

She turned white and sank into the desk chair. She couldn't look at him. She kept her head up but she avoided his eyes.

"How did—"

"He killed himself." No details. "He was frightened because you threatened him, and he couldn't face what he thought you were going to do to him."

"But I wouldn't— You've got to believe me, I wouldn't have hurt him. I didn't mean it." She stopped, then she said, "That's four, isn't it?"

"Yes."

"But the others—you believe me about them, don't you? You believe I didn't—"

"I don't know what I believe. They're dead, you killed them."

"I only meant to kill once. One man. Not Kearney, not Marvin. And if Amos Roberts had been any other kind of man, *any* other kind, I still wouldn't know. I might never have known." She paused. Then, "You don't know what Roberts was. You can't imagine."

"What was he?" Stavitsky asked.

"Roberts was—" She paused. Stavitsky wouldn't have known how to describe him either. But she did it at last.

"He was absolute," she said.

Stavitsky nodded.

"It was Roberts who made me remember. He was like a key. What he did, what he was. And I'd never have seen him except that we came home too soon."

Hawkins had told her all about his part in it the day after Roberts died, the day he came to work for her. They'd sat together for a while, talking like friends who shared a secret. Then he formally accepted her offer of a job. He'd be in pretty bad shape for a while, he told her, but they'd give him drugs to help, and counseling—two afternoons a week at the treatment center. It wouldn't take long, and he was sure he could make it . . . if she still wanted him. She did. Then he'd told her all about it. He'd told her about Roberts and Raines, how they'd gotten in, and what had happened before she'd come home. He'd blurted it out, words rushing, because he was going to work for her, in her house, and he wanted them to go on trusting each other.

"The story," she told Stavitsky, "his part and mine together, is wonderful, exciting, even beautiful . . . because in the end Roberts was dead." Stavitsky watched her relax as she began. The worn look wavered and her face started looking softer, smoother.

"They met at the white man's place," she was saying. . . .

6

RAINES WAS BRUSHING his hair when Hawkins knocked on the door. He called to him to come in and began putting on his only sport shirt.

"Where's the dragon?" Hawkins asked.

"He should be here any minute."

"He bringing all the stuff?"

"No, it's already there, stashed in the basement."

"I don't know what the hell you need me for."

"He wants you. You can argue with him if you want to, but it won't do any good. I don't want to go either, but I'm strung out. I need a fix. How long have you been?"

"Little over a day. You?"

"About the same, and he's the man, so we're stuck. Besides, George, there'll be some left over after we pay him, enough to keep going for a while anyway."

"Yeah, and then what?"

Raines shrugged. "We do another job or take the cure—not much choice." Hawkins sagged. Raines tried to sound cheerful. "Shit, George, this is an easy one, believe me. And there's plenty there. Besides they're both such crackpots—they probably don't even have a safe. I bet she's got jewelry just lying around the place—probably cash, too."

"You sure they won't be there?"

"Course I am. They ain't been home one Thursday in all the time I been working there."

"He's not even hooked hisself, is he?"

"Roberts? No, I don't think he is. Just likes doing it."

Raines started to put on a shiny, neatly pressed sport coat when Roberts walked in.

Jennifer was dressed, ready to go, but William was still in the shower and would insist on shaving again even though his beard was light and once a day was plenty. She lay back on the bed and let the little dog jump up and lie next to her. William had started singing. "Bo-deoh—do-do" came tunelessly out of the bathroom over the sound of running water. She looked at her watch. Almost six. He'd miss the news.

"William." She stood up and went to the bathroom door. Stellar jumped down, followed her, stopped with her, and put one paw on Jennifer's shoe. Shoes still on at this hour meant that they were going out and Stellar would be left alone. "William, you're going to miss the news."

The water stopped. "Right there, dear."

She went down the hall to William's study where they always watched the news before dinner. The little dog followed. She poured a glass of sherry for William, one for herself, turned on the set, and sat down to watch. Stellar sat next to her, leaning her small body against Jennifer's leg. She scratched the delicate little head, smoothing the fur until the dog put her forepaws on Jennifer's knee.

"Stellar, get down. You'll rip my stocking." The dog sat again, then stretched out and lay on her side with a sigh, her back against Jennifer's feet.

Then William came in, still pink-faced from the hot water. He was wearing the huge terry-cloth kaftan she'd bought a few months ago. He always ignored new things for a few weeks, then he'd try them out once or twice. If he liked it, he'd wear it again and again—grumbling when it was taken away to be cleaned or laundered. The kaftan was a success.

He sat at the other end of the sofa—never next to her. They rarely touched unless there was some purpose—help with a difficult tie or button arrangement, his arm under hers when they crossed the street, and when they made love. Not often even in the beginning, and now . . . she couldn't remember the last time, but she didn't try very hard. She didn't mind, neither did he.

Time went gently, sweetly she thought, very sweetly. And she loved him. Sometimes when she was mending something of his, she would hold it to her face smelling him in the fabric. An odd kind of sensuality that she didn't examine and forgave in herself as harmless. Being with him was still, as it had been from the start, the most comforting thing in her life. He never minded her almost constant presence when they were home. But thinking he might, she fixed up a study for herself at the end of the gallery on the first floor, and she tried to use it. She started out there most evenings. But after no more than a half an hour, she had to leave the empty room and find him, usually in his study, and stay there with him. He never shooed her away. He let her sit there quietly with him, and then she could read, or sew, or catch up on the day's work. But he never made the trip downstairs to her room, just to be with her.

"William, you've got to get dressed, we're going to be late."

"Damn," he said, "it's almost seven." The same words for every Thursday night. He stood up, the terry-cloth robe sweeping the floor. She laughed. "You look like a walrus in a tent."

He loved it when she talked about him like that and he grinned at her.

"I won't be long." He walked out, the terry cloth billowing behind him. The dog looked up when he left, but stayed where it was.

Years ago, she wondered at the lust that had pushed her that night with Marvin. And, sometimes, thinking about it brought back the feeling and she would be more demanding. That seemed to startle William, and excite him too, and during the first five years they were married there were a few nights of a kind of love that left them both drained and a little embarrassed at the memory of how they'd behaved—silent at breakfast, and with a distance between them that she couldn't bear. It didn't happen often then, and never now. She hardly thought about it anymore.

And every evening when she walked past the house on Seventy-eighth Street, just west of Third, and watched the young couple behind the huge uncurtained windows of their living room . . . even then she believed her feelings were tender, romantic. She walked that way every night after work, if the weather was good, and she'd stand in the shadows on the sidewalk and look at them sitting together in the evening. The girl would bring him a drink, or he'd bring her one, and they'd sit very close together on a couch, listening to something or watching television. Sometimes they had other people there, friends, and she'd watch them all talking, sometimes laughing. She allowed herself fifteen minutes of watching, whenever she could. Summer was difficult because the lights came on so late, and it was hard to see through the afternoon reflection of the street on the window. But she could make out their shapes moving apart, moving together. Only she couldn't see their smiles, or their mouths move as they talked.

Once they'd kissed while she was watching—a long kiss, and she'd hurried away before they pulled apart, not wanting to see what would happen next. But she came back the next day, happy enough to see them talk and smile together. Once or twice she'd seen them fight, angry faces, loud voices that carried through the windows and out onto the sidewalk, though she couldn't hear the words. She hurried away then, too.

She'd been watching them most evenings now for about two years. Then there was the time they weren't there. She passed every evening for a week, but the room was dark, no sign of them. She thought they'd moved away, but when she walked up the brownstone's stairs, she saw that it wasn't an apartment house, but a single-family dwelling. There was still a name on the only bell. The front door glass had the usual red, yellow, and blue protection sign that all the private houses seemed to display, and there was no for sale sign. Vacation, she thought. And she kept faith, came back every evening for three weeks until at last the windows were lit again. They'd come home.

She never told William about watching them.

Hawkins' insides always fluttered when he saw Roberts.

He was impressive-looking—Hawkins had to give him that much. About Hawkins' height, but larger, better proportioned, so that he looked shorter. He worked out regularly and had the accentuated rippling muscles that never came from just hard physical labor. But his face was the most impressive thing about him. Hawkins figured he had some white in him from not too long ago, because his skin was lightish—though light black rather than brown—gray, really, and flawless like marble. And his eyes were light, green and yellow, the whites clear, set wide above broad cheekbones. He was very handsome, and women reportedly paid him. Hawkins had even heard that some rich East Side businessmen added to his growing fortune. And that fitted because Hawkins thought Roberts was really a faggot. Women would be too easy—he would get a much bigger thrill cockwhipping a man.

His one physical handicap was his breath. It was horrible—as if something were rotting in his stomach. He seemed to be aware of it, because he was always sucking on something, hard mints or Lifesavers, and whenever he spoke to anyone he kept his face turned slightly away.

Now he turned his face away from Raines and said to him, "Get going. We'll give you half an hour, then we'll be there."

"Where's the truck?" Raines asked.

"Just across the street. You got enough money to take a cab?"

Raines nodded. "But I can get there just's fast on the—"

"Shut your hole—take a cab."

"Sure, sure, Amos. Just let me get my coat."

"You don't need no coat, not with all that pink skin—get going."

"But, Amos, it's only forty degrees—"

"Move your ass, you little shit." He pushed Raines against the door.

"Let him take his coat, Amos," Hawkins said. Roberts turned, ready for more pushing, but Hawkins walked over to the wall hook the coat was hanging from, took it off its wire hanger, and threw it to Raines.

Raines caught it and ducked out the door without waiting to put it on.

Roberts stayed facing Hawkins for a while, and Hawkins stared back. Finally Roberts said, "I'm gonna have trouble with you, ain't I?"

"Maybe. But this isn't the time."

"Yeah, you're right—but there'll be other times."

Hawkins was too physically uncomfortable to care. "Let's get this over with, OK?"

"Why, you hurtin', baby?" Roberts grinned.

"I'm hurtin', all right." That seemed to satisfy Roberts and he sat down on the bed to wait until it was time to leave.

It was cold for a November night in New York. The wind was very sharp, and by the time Jennifer and William rounded the corner of Seventy-eighth, they were both trotting to get inside as fast as they could. The wind pulled the bare tree branches in the park and on the street, making a thrashing noise that made her think of Nantucket. Suddenly the cold and wind, her flapping coat, and their trotting made her feel very gay, and in a burst of exhilaration she broke the trot and started to run. He tried to keep pace, but she was running flat out, her coat waving behind, hair tangling in the wind. He caught her at the door of the house, laughing as he always did, delighted with her odd moments of wildness.

Albert opened the door to them and took their coats. He had seen Mrs. Gilbert's wildness before too; every now and then she would arrive with her always proper husband, looking disheveled, eyes glowing, hair a mess as if the extra energy had reached it and knotted it. He considered her excitement inappropriate and thought of such moments as lapses. Mrs. List did too.

"Jennifer," Kate whispered after their usual greeting—brief hug, dry kiss—William shaking hands with Mr. Reynolds, "Jennifer, go and comb your hair. You look a mess."

"Yes, Mother." But she held her mother tight for a second, kissed her again. Kate pulled away, laughing.

"Oh, Jennifer, stop it. Go ahead, fix yourself up. You'll frighten poor Mr. Reynolds."

Jennifer did as she was told; she went into the huge old powder room with pipes to warm towels and a kaleidoscope of tiles on the ceiling and walls. The tiles were so varicolored that she always had trouble seeing where her hair ended and the wall began. The gray streaks helped, but her hair was still redder than gray, wasn't it? She looked closely in the mirror. "Yes," she whispered at her reflection, "much redder than gray." She pulled a comb through it, composed her face to normal, and went back to join the others.

"Mr. Reynolds, how nice—"

Hawkins stood in the light that spilled out on the terrace from lamps the Gilberts had left burning. The room looked soft, inviting through the glass. He stood looking at it trying to forget the squeaking scrape of Roberts' glass cutter. It only took a minute or two. Roberts pulled the suction cup away, leaving a round empty hole in the glass. Then he turned the handle, opened the door, and they walked in.

"I told you," said Raines. "None of these places have the terrace door wired into security."

Hawkins was not listening, he was looking at the room that stretched ahead of him. The soft light picked out the pattern of the carpet, glossed the upholstery and shining wood, carved shadows on the grandfather clock, gleamed off vases, softened the brightness of the fresh flowers, and the colors of the paintings on the walls in the shadows. The room was alive with color, all soft, muted, inviting. Behind him, beyond the terrace, the city shrank away, its aura helpless against the still beauty of the room.

Raines saw the look on his face.

"Yeah," he said proudly. "It's real nice, ain't it?"

"OK," Roberts broke the spell, "let's get to it."

They went through the first floor quickly, and collected two television sets, several radios, and a brass antique microscope. Hawkins cleared the most ornate bric-a-brac off the tables and mantel and put it carefully together on the carpet.

Then Hawkins left the living room to look in the kitchen. They'd probably have a very nice toaster, maybe even one of those portable electric ovens. He decided he would keep the toaster for his daughter. He found a hallway leading off the dining room to a knobless swinging door. The hallway was dark, but light showed under the door.

He stopped.

Maybe Raines was wrong, maybe all the servants were not out. What if one of the maids were in there now? He turned back as quietly as he could and walked slowly down the short dark hallway. Then he ran through the dining room to the living room. Raines and Roberts had found another radio and a small strongbox that they were trying to pry open.

"I think there's someone in the kitchen," he whispered to Raines.

"But there couldn't be. I told you—Thursday—"

"OK—but there's a light on in there."

"Oh, that's probably where they keep the dog."

"Dog? You didn't tell me they had a dog!" Roberts said in a frightened whisper.

"Sure they do. But it's a little thing. Hardly a guard dog."

Roberts smiled.

"Well, well," he said, "a little dog. Let's go see about it."

Hawkins was suddenly frightened, but he followed them back through the dining room and down the short hall. Light still showed under the door. Roberts had his gun out and Hawkins heard him unlock the safety. Then he pushed open the door.

The room was very long, blazing with light that bounced off the chrome and stainless steel fittings. At the far end, under a heavy wooden worktable, stood a small dog with lots of black and white fur and a long aristocratic face. A dish of water sat on the floor next to it.

As soon as it saw them, it yipped twice, then stepped daintily out from under the table holding its head to one side, wagging its tail uncertainly, just at the tip.

"Well, well," Roberts said again. "A little dog."

Jennifer took a sherry from the tray. Everyone had a drink. Talk about bridge, talk about insects, talk about the market, and about Michael and all the trouble he was having with his wife Barbara. Then back to bridge. Finally dinner. The same Thursday night, pleasant, reliable. More talk, now about Mrs. List's cook, superb, etc., don't know what I'd do if she ever left, and on and on. The sameness must soothe them, Jennifer thought, the same thought she had every Thursday night. And she wondered, as she always did, if it soothed her too, or if she just didn't know any alternatives. But halfway through dinner—sole finished, roast being served—Jennifer could see that her mother didn't feel well. She'd barely eaten and she was pale. By the time dinner was over and they were having dessert, Kate admitted feeling ill.

"I don't know what it is—probably a cold coming. But I have a terrible headache. I'm sorry to disappoint you, Edward, but I'm afraid I just won't be able to play tonight. Actually, I haven't been feeling well all day, but I thought dinner would help and it hasn't. I hope you're not too disappointed."

Mr. Reynolds was very disappointed, but William wasn't. Jennifer was a little worried about Kate. She was very pale.

"Would you like us to stay?"

"No, dear, I'll be fine. I think I just want to go to sleep if you don't mind." For a minute Jennifer wondered what it would be like to look after her mother. Help her into bed, bring her something warm to drink, make sure she was covered; then maybe read to her or sit and talk quietly, just the two of them, until Kate fell asleep.

"I wouldn't mind staying at all, Mother."

"I know, dear, but it isn't necessary. If I'm not better tomorrow I'll call Dr. Kay."

Kate allowed a few more minutes of Jennifer being concerned, then began to sound edgy. Jennifer gave up and they left Kate alone.

Roberts called to the dog. "Here, fella, we wouldn't hurt you." He made his voice very soft. Hawkins had never heard a sound like it, like velvet. "C'mon."

The dog's tail wagged a little more and it took a step out from under the table. "Good boy," Roberts said. "Good dog." The tail kept going, a little black and white plume of fur. The dog was almost clear of the table. Roberts kneeled down, coaxing with his hands. Hawkins wanted to shout, to frighten it into going back. The sound of Roberts' voice, soft, wheedling as the animal came closer was making Hawkins actively sick.

"Leave it alone," Hawkins said. "It won't bother us."

"Thaaaat's right," the voice said. "You wouldn't bother us would you, ol' dog?" The dog was out in the open, the kitchen lights glaring around it, around all of them. Hawkins saw their distorted shapes reflecting in the stainless steel. Roberts and the dog, close to the floor, their reflections bowed out by the curve of sinks. The dog was still moving toward Roberts and Roberts was reaching in his pocket, very slowly not to startle it.

"I've got a goody for you here, dog. Somethin' you're just going to love."

The voice was getting to Raines, too.

"That's enough, Amos. We're wasting time."

But something had happened to Roberts. He didn't even hear them. He was conscious only of the dog. The hand was coming out of his pocket. Hawkins saw the knife.

"Jesus Christ, don't—"

The tone stopped the dog's progress. It stood uncertain for a second, then it tensed, ready to cringe, to run. Too late, it had gotten too close. Roberts grabbed its forepaws, the knife snapped open.

"No!" Hawkins screamed, but the sound the dog made drowned his voice.

He and Raines were holding onto each other. He turned to look at the other man and saw that Raines' cheeks were covered with tears.

Jennifer and William stood in the foyer looking into the living room. Television sets, radios, a little pile of odd silver pieces, and chests of silver sets—even the candelabra—were all piled in the middle of the living room floor. Then they saw Hawkins and he saw them. He started toward them, whispering as he ran across the room.

"Get out. My God, please get out before he sees you." He reached the raised foyer where they stood, his eyes on Gilbert. "Shit, man, get her out of here." Gilbert looked as if he were hearing a foreign language. "Move—now!"

"Where's the dog?" Jennifer managed to keep her voice steady.

"Forget the dog." Hawkins was pleading, ready to cry. "Just get out, please, lady."

"Where's my dog? Stellar?" She started down into the living room calling the dog. "Stellar?"

Hawkins barred her path. "It's as much as your life is worth"—still whispering—"run, go to a neighbor, call for help, but run, run. . . ."

"Your dog? You looking for your dog, lady?" Hawkins froze at the sound of Roberts' voice. He was standing on the stairs to the upper floors, holding her jewel case and a gun.

"Don't mind him," Roberts said. "Every little thing upsets him so. Doesn't it, George?" No answer. "Now," Roberts said, "you were asking about your dog? Little black dog, right? It's around here some place. Isn't it, Boots? Hey, Boots! Come on out, we've got company." Raines appeared from the gallery, his hands empty. "Look at that," Roberts said. "Empty-handed. I do believe the man's heart just ain't in it. Didn't find a thing—in all that big space, not a single thing worth stealing. But you're going to help us. Yes, now we've got help. Mister here'll show us the safe and all the goodies, and then we'll show Missus a real good time. Won't we, fellas? Just lovely."

Neither man said anything.

"If you leave now," William said, "right now, we'll forget—"

"Naw," Roberts said. "We can't leave until we help you find your dog. I think I saw a little black dog in the kitchen—sure I did. Come on." He waved the gun.

Jennifer and Gilbert walked down the foyer steps into the living room. She kept looking back at Roberts and he kept smiling encouragingly, waving the gun. She couldn't miss the joy in his light eyes, so startling in his handsome dark face. She walked past Hawkins, who turned away, and Raines, thin and helpless-looking. Only Roberts followed them through the dining room and into the hallway that led to the kitchen. Jennifer stopped when she got to the kitchen door.

"Go on." Roberts giggled. "Nothing'll bite you."

Jennifer leaned her head against the door for a second, holding the wall.

"Open the door, bitch."

She pushed the door open.

Hawkins watched them come back into the room. Gilbert had his arm around Jennifer, and Hawkins thought it was the only thing holding her up. Her gait was shambling, aimless, tears streamed down her face, and she was shaking her head. Gilbert was pale and there was a tic in his cheek. Hawkins could see it moving in and out as his teeth clenched. She was making a low sobbing sound under her breath as they passed him. Roberts followed, grinning, then trying to straighten the grin, but it kept coming back.

Then, just as she went past him, she turned and looked at Hawkins. Their eyes met and held, then she was past, and he couldn't see her face anymore. But he'd seen something. He started to move, to see her again.

"Stay right there, George darling, or I'll blow your ass off."

Hawkins stopped and looked at Roberts. "Sure, Amos, right."

Whatever he'd seen in the gentle pleasant face made him uneasy, and suddenly he knew that if he were Amos Roberts, he'd be frightened.

Then he found himself smiling at Roberts, which Roberts couldn't understand. The smile made the other man look around as if someone else might have entered the room without his knowing it. Hawkins' smile widened, although he didn't know why.

"Sure, Amos. I'm staying right here."

Roberts looked around again, then walked over to the Gilberts standing together near the foyer railing a few feet from Hawkins. Raines hadn't moved. He stood alone at the far end of the room looking at the floor, then out the window, then back down the gallery. He didn't want to see what was going to happen next. Hawkins didn't either, but he kept watching, hoping to see again whatever it was that he'd seen when she'd passed him. But she was too far away, her eyes in shadow from the chandelier light spilling across the marble foyer.

Roberts ignored Gilbert. He went right to her. Very close. His breath was sickening and she turned her head.

"Look at that," he said to no one. "So modest." The voice was velvet-soft again and Hawkins' skin tingled. Then Roberts put his fine, long-fingered hand in her hair and forced her head around to face him. She looked at him, forcing her fear back to look at this man, to try to see something she could recognize. He was beautiful. More beautiful than Marvin, as beautiful really as Ellen. She breathed through her mouth, so that the smell of his breath wouldn't distract her, and she looked and looked.

"Pretty, ain't I?" he said. She didn't answer. "*Ain't I?*" The fingers tightened in her hair.

"Yes," she said.

"Very pretty?"

"Beautiful," she said.

"Good—good you think so."

He pushed the gun into her belly, very hard. Hawkins saw her flinch at the pain, but the safety was still on—Roberts wasn't through with her yet. "I've got something for you you're really going to like—much prettier than this ol' face—oh, so pretty, lady. And wait till you see what you're going to do with it. Just wait." The gun went deeper and she started to gag, turn white.

He pulled it away and then smoothed her belly in an oddly gentle way with the flat of the gun.

"But that's later. In a little bit. Think you can wait, sugar? Got to, got to. Business first."

It wasn't only a sadistic game. Hawkins could see she sort of turned Roberts on. Maybe if she played it right she'd live, maybe buy her husband's life. Then he thought of what he'd seen in her eyes. What was it? Uneasiness again. Sharper now. Even the air didn't seem right; every sound was very clear, even the slight rustle of the gun against her clothes. Hawkins thought he could hear his heart, even hear all of them breathing, as if other normal sounds had stopped.

"OK," Roberts was saying. His voice sounded very loud in the stillness, but Hawkins knew he was speaking normally. "Let's get this shit packed up."

Hawkins heard Raines moving, the sound of one of the cardboard cartons snap as it unfolded. It sounded like a tree branch cracking with ice. Everything else was very quiet except for his heart and the rasp of his breathing. Roberts let go of her and stepped back, still covering them with the gun.

"You too, Hawkins," he said over his shoulder. "Move it."

Hawkins didn't move.

Roberts turned, the gun aimed low at Hawkins' gut.

"I said move."

"Kiss my ass." Hawkins' voice thundered in his ears. Then Roberts was moving toward him, light, easy steps, graceful. "You know," he was saying. "You know what, George, darlin'? I think I'm gonna shoot your cock off—start the evening off with a bang." Then the giggle. "You'll like that, little lady. Yessir, that'll be lovely. C'mon, George, take it out." The gun was getting closer with Roberts' smooth walk. "C'mon," he was saying, "unzip now, mustn't be shy. . . ."

He was almost to Hawkins when she started to move—as easily as Roberts, smoother, more graceful, and much faster, closer and closer to them. Hawkins saw it now, blazing in her face, in the dreamy eyes, and if the man in front of him had been anyone but Amos Roberts he would have yelled at him to look out. Roberts saw his eyes flicker toward her, and he turned just as she reached him. He stepped back, almost bumped Hawkins, his free hand swinging, and he hit her backhand in the face, his whole body twisting with the blow.

Jennifer stumbled back, lost her balance, and then fell, grabbing for something to hold. She hit a thin marble flower stand with a cut-glass bowl on top full of flowers. The pedestal tilted with her weight. She grabbed at it, and the bowl rocked wildly, its facets catching and reflecting the light, water spilling down her arms, until the bowl looked like thousands of pieces of broken glass—jagged, dancing in the light. She held on to keep it from falling on her, pushing it back until it stopped swaying. The bowl righted itself, the dancing light stopped, and the bowl was still again. Whole—unbroken.

She swallowed. Roberts' knuckle had split the inside of her lip and her mouth was full of blood. She stayed on her knees staring at the bowl, the scene behind her forgotten, while her mouth filled again with blood.

The salt taste was familiar. So was the glittering glass. Blood and glass swam at her from long ago. The blood was the same, only the glass was different—or the light? Yes—the light. It was sunlight, bright, blinding—that was it. She swallowed again and the taste of blood flooded her senses.

Then she remembered.

She saw the little crystal-bud vase clearly, glittering in a bar of sunlight on the floor of her father's study. Like the bowl on the pedestal it was unbroken, and she remembered for the first time how it had gotten there and what had kept it from breaking.

She turned back to them just as Roberts hit Gilbert with the gun. He'd started after Roberts as soon as he had hit Jennifer, to try to help. Hawkins was moving too. But the slashing gun muzzle stopped Gilbert, and now the gun pointed again at Hawkins as Gilbert started to fall. She saw the skin on her husband's face separate, blood spattering, pouring, then soaking his shirt and jacket. He was staring blindly at Roberts. Then his knees buckled, his face level with her. Eyes empty, the whole cheek split, he fell forward.

But Hawkins wasn't looking at Gilbert or at Roberts. He was looking at her. Roberts saw the expression on his face and he turned too. Raines followed, and the three of them stood there watching the woman kneeling on the floor. She was smiling at Roberts. He moved back a step, another step. Hawkins heard the gun's safety pull back.

"I'm going to kill you," she said to Roberts, her voice sweet and clear. "I'm going to kill you now."

Then she laughed. Hawkins heard a little of the laughter, then nothing. He couldn't hear a sound.

Then Roberts was dancing, on his toes, the graceful body swaying, trying to get higher and higher, to leave the ground. His arms moved, hands in rictus, gun falling in silence. He danced and danced, stretching up as high as he could, hands at the back of his neck, swaying and turning on the tips of his toes, profile to Hawkins. His mouth was open, straining in a noiseless screaming. Then clenching, shut, opening, closing. His eyes began bulging, pushing against the enclosing lids while the dance went on. Tiny threads of red ran around the protruding eyeball and back into the socket. Too much strain—the socket emptied as the eye popped, settled outside the socket on his cheek while the slack lids crumpled around the red threads that were still attached to it.

7

No ONE SAID anything for a long time after she finished talking. Then Stavitsky asked, "How long did it take him to die?"

"Only a few minutes really, less than five."

"And the people downstairs called the cops."

"That's right. The noise he made was incredible. I've never heard such sounds before." She was smiling. "I thought his larynx would have to give out, but it didn't. Not until right at the end."

"How did you feel?" he asked softly.

"Wonderful." Her voice was soft, too.

Galeston stood up. Then Stern seemed to crawl out of his chair to his feet. Stavitsky didn't move.

"I'm going to keep this," he said, touching the report.

"I don't think they'll change their minds."

"Don't you? Yesterday they were going to help me. Today—" He shrugged.

"The captain makes us sound very inconstant," Galeston said evenly.

She looked from one to the other. Stavitsky was flushed and he was clutching the envelope, staring and staring at her while Galeston was talking. The excitement of telling them was waning; she was tired.

"All I want is to be left alone," she said.

"Do you? You want me to walk out of here over four corpses and forget the whole thing?"

"I told you why. I told you what happened. Can't you just leave me alone now?"

"No."

"Captain, I think we'd better go." Galeston was at the door.

Jennifer and Stavitsky looked at each other across the desk.

"Captain," Galeston called from the door. Stern was there too. "Captain." Hawkins was in the gallery waiting.

He finally turned away from her and went to the door.

"You won't change your mind?" she called after him.

Stern and Galeston were already in the gallery, and Hawkins was standing sideways, reaching for the knob as Stavitsky passed, shutting the door behind him.

Stavitsky turned back trying to see her one more time, but the door to her study was closing, cutting him off. He kept looking until it was shut altogether and he was facing Hawkins standing guard in front of it. He turned and followed the others across the living room. There was the marble pedestal, and the bowl . . . and there was a rough place in the carpet from which they must have cleaned Gilbert's blood. Up the steps to the foyer—he held the railing Hawkins had held—then to the front door. Hawkins opened it for them, then it closed too. Two doors separated them. Then down in the elevator, no one said anything, and out into the street. Now she was thirty floors away.

There was no question of going home; they had something to settle. They walked to Madison Avenue through the cold and snow, and into the first bar they came to. A singles joint, crowded with young, blue-eyelidded women in the front and empty and dark in the back where the booths were. They all ordered bourbon, then sat hunched and silent over the glass-cupped candle. A few women drifted past, looked, and kept on going.

Stavitsky put the envelope on the table but kept his hand resting on it.

A waitress brought the drinks. Finally Stavitsky couldn't wait any longer.

"OK, Wilbur, let's have it."

Galeston leaned back in the booth.

"Oh, I think you already know. That thing"—nodding at the envelope—"is worthless. And it's going to stay that way."

"You're scared."

"You could say that."

"But of what? You heard her, you heard what the bastard did. OK, she killed him, God knows he deserved it. That doesn't mean she'd kill you or me."

"Doesn't it? You still don't get it, do you, captain? That woman's a killer. She's used her power three times—to kill." He was smiling at Stavitsky. "Yes," he said, "she's a killer." Then he laughed softly. The sound plucked at Stavitsky's scalp.

"But you're saying that she'd knowingly kill all of us—all three of us? For Christ's sake, Galeston, she's not a monster."

Galeston stopped smiling. He leaned across the table toward Stavitsky.

"You fatheaded Jew," he snarled, "what do you think you're playing with here? Of course she's a monster. More dangerous than anyone alive. Don't you know what you heard tonight? Don't you know yet what she is?"

Stavitsky was too taken aback by Galeston's attack to say anything.

"She's a whole new kind of creature—a monster, captain. What she did to Amos Roberts took the most incredible power, the most delicate sophisticated control. She didn't just break his neck, nothing so crude as just breaking something or moving it. She reached—with her mind!—she reached beneath his skin, the fascia, the muscles—without disturbing them in any way, captain. Without so much as an extraneous nick. Remarkable! Do you have any idea of the precision involved? Or of the strength it took to pry those two vertebrae apart? And, as if that weren't enough, she then *tore*—not cut—*tore* the spinal cord in two.

"There are hundreds of ways to kill a man, captain, maybe thousands, and I've seen most of them. And she picked the most brutal. And, captain, you saw her face when she told us. You saw what I saw. What was it, captain? What did you see?"

Stavitsky didn't answer.

"Joy, captain. Exultation. Isn't that right?"

"So she *liked* killing him, she enjoyed it. I would've too. That doesn't mean she's going to kill anyone else."

"But if you believe that," Galeston asked, "then why are you so obsessed with stopping her?"

Stavitsky couldn't answer—he had no answer.

"Why, captain? Or is that really it—are you really trying to stop her?"

Again no answer.

"Maybe you've been thinking you can handle it, control it, use it in some way. Isn't that it? You haven't yet admitted to yourself that there is no way to control that creature up there, no way to use a power like that. You haven't faced that because as soon as you do you'll have to face the rest of it, won't you?"

"What the hell is *that* supposed to mean?"

"It means you're not going to bring Jennifer Gilbert to trial, or put her away, or turn her into a pet like something in a Jack London story, or any of the rest of the shit you've been kidding yourself with."

"Okay, Galeston, you tell me. What *am* I going to do?"

"You are going to kill her, captain."

Nothing moved. He thought the world must have stopped.

Stavitsky looked at Stern. Stern looked at the table.

Galeston was talking again. Stavitsky had to force himself to listen.

"We might have had a chance, a slim one I'll grant, but a chance. I think we might have convinced her we were quite harmless. That's why we went there. To tell her we were sure that there had been a mistake—that we could convince you too—that those couldn't have been Amos Roberts' X rays. Then we were going to leave the thing with her—so she'd feel safe, so she'd see how harmless we were, all three of us. She *was* believing us, I know she was. We could've done it. Then you had to come barging in playing big dick cop waving that fucking gun around."

Galeston leaned back and looked at Stavitsky. "Now, of course, our harmlessness is a dead issue, captain. Not that it really matters, because I think it would have come to the same thing in any case. Yes, now that I think about it, you'd probably have had to kill her anyway. It's the only logical end. You know what kind of man you are—obsessive, wouldn't you say? You can't leave it alone. As long as she's alive you'll push and push. And what does she do when she's pushed, captain? She kills. Simple.

"If it were just you . . . but it isn't. There's Ira here, and Ching, and me. I'm old, but I'm not anxious to die, not yet, and not like Amos Roberts. . . . Come, captain, you look so shocked. Is it possible that this never occurred to you?"

"No," Stavitsky said, "it never occurred to me."

"You'll come to it. I just hope you don't wait until it's too late."

"Too late. . . . What is this too late shit?"

"Well, captain, if I'm right—and I am—then we're on borrowed time and have been ever since she told us about killing Roberts. She's thinking now—thinking about what she told us—just beginning to realize what she's exposed. The exultation is gone, the joy and excitement. No more center stage now. She's just sitting up there now thinking about what we know about her."

"You're asking me to murder that woman we just left."

"That's right. After all, captain, you started this—for all of us. I'm sure you can finish it."

Stavitsky looked at Stern. "Is this what you want, too?"

Stern looked at the table.

"Look at me, goddammit."

Stern obeyed. His face was blank.

"Do you, Ira? Do you want her dead?"

Stern tried to say something. His lips moved, but he didn't make any sound.

Stavitsky stood up, holding the report. Galeston looked at the envelope, then at him.

"It's what she's thinking right now, captain, that matters. She knows as well as I do that you won't leave her alone. Why stop at Amos Roberts? I wouldn't."

Why stop at Amos Roberts? Why stop? The phrase meant something to him, but he couldn't put it together. He had to remember it. *Why stop at Amos Roberts?*

"How long," Galeston was saying, "will it take her to convince herself that we are as much a threat to her as he was? How long would it take you if you were her?"

"You bastard"—Stavitsky was choking—"I'm, I'm not a goddamn assassin you hire to save your ass."

The women in the bar were turning around to see what was causing the commotion.

"You jealous fucking old bastard."

"Jealous? Novel idea," Galeston said coolly. "Jealous of whom? She didn't seem to find you particularly attractive, captain."

Stavitsky ran past the staring women and out of the bar into the snow.

"Galeston wants me to kill her."

Ching sat in the shadows of his long narrow parlor. He was wearing a paisley silk robe, pajamas showed at the bottom and leather slippers on bare feet. Stavitsky couldn't see his eyes behind the thick glasses, but the

dim light threw the bags under them into relief so that they looked
bigger than ever, puffing from the bottom rim of the lenses.

"You sound surprised, captain."

"You're not, are you?"

"No. I thought this was what we all had in mind from the beginning."

"Killing her?"

"Of course."

Stavitsky remembered them all shaking hands that first night, the feeling of ritual. He was the outsider then, unversed in the rationality that
seemed so clear to the others that they didn't have to say it. Kill—the
only logical solution.

"There are other things to do with power besides destroying it."

"For instance?"

"Use it."

"Really. What would you use it for?"

No answer.

"You know, captain, you remind me of Marvin Ross." Ching paused.
Then, "You see, captain, killing Jennifer List is really the most logical
conclusion to your . . . adventure."

Stavitsky exploded. "Jesus, you're a couple of cockless old bastards,
aren't you? All you can think to do is kill. Do your own goddamn
killing."

"And what will *you* do?"

So cool, logical. "Don't you *feel* anything?" Stavitsky asked. "She's a
woman. . . ."

"Oh, yes. Most of all. Right, captain? Tell me, captain, what does she
look like now?"

"She looks . . . OK."

"I thought she'd be a beautiful woman some day. Is she?"

"Yeah. Yes."

Stavitsky knew he couldn't sit still much longer.

"Quite beautiful, I imagine. The sort of beauty that you don't see at
first, right, captain? Very fine, fragile face, nothing really vivid about it
at all. Subtle, gentle beauty. And passion, too. Oh, yes, that was there.
You should have seen her when I talked about Ross. My, how she
wanted him. Big handsome man he was, captain. Not unlike you—prettier, but there are resemblances. And you should have seen her face
when I mentioned Ross. And, of course, the power. That's the main
thing, isn't it? Imagine yourself, captain—and her. Think of it. Just a
woman's body. . . . Is she thin or fat now?"

"Thin," Stavitsky whispered.

"Yes, thin. Imagine it. The fine body, and inside it. . . . Oh, think what's inside it. If you could just touch it." Ching leaned forward. "But forget it. It isn't there. You can't touch it—you can't have it. And as soon as you realize that . . . then of course you'll kill her. What else would a man like you do with a beautiful woman who can break you to pieces just by thinking about it? And believe me, captain, that's a real possibility."

"Christ, you're old, aren't you? You're so fucking old. Are you so scared to die? Is that why we've got to kill her, to save the goddamn hours or days that you two old shits have left—is that it? Answer me."

"No, Mr. Stavitsky," he said at last. "I'm not afraid to die. I'm not interested in death—mine or anybody else's. It's the power. Can you imagine that kind of power festering year after year? Unchecked? *That's* what should frighten you. That's why you have to kill her."

8

HE WAS PARKED at the corner of Seventy-seventh and Fifth when the sun came up. He hadn't shaved or washed, he wasn't even sure whether it was Monday or Tuesday. He certainly didn't know the date. He could see both the entrance to her building and the garage driveway.

It was a weekday, he knew that much, so she would be going to the university. If she came out the front entrance he could see her easily and he'd have no problem spotting a 1957 black Jaguar if she drove.

He wondered if she were awake yet. Seven o'clock—probably. Maybe having breakfast, Hawkins serving. She might be polishing Gilbert's shoes or laying out the baggy trousers and handmade shirt.

It was very cold, last night's snow crusted, already turning gray from the falling soot. But the sun was bright, throwing building shadows across the avenue, sparkling on the still undisturbed white in the park. His eyes burned and he had to keep closing them against the glare of sun on snow. But he wasn't tired. He wasn't anything.

A few people crossed Seventy-seventh. Three boys jumped the wall and disappeared into the park. A bus stopped across the street to leave a lone man on the park side. He walked out of sight behind the buildings. Two black women—maids?—went into the service entrance of her building.

More time, more people, another bus. It was seven thirty. The silencer was making a dent in his belly and he moved the gun butt to ease the pressure.

It was a few minutes before eight when she walked out of the front entrance of the building. She was wearing the standard dark mink coat and boots, but he recognized her hair, red and silver in the morning sunlight.

There was a dog with her, a puppy wearing a coat or sweater. It yipped when it saw the snow and started jumping at the crusty drifts, pulling at the leash. Stavitsky got out of the car and waited with the door open in case she turned toward him and he had to get out of sight. Now the puppy was on its hind legs, forepaws against her boots. She bent down, the fur dipped into the sidewalk slush, and picked the dog up. Then she started walking uptown toward Seventy-ninth.

He shut the car door and followed.

The dog would be a Christmas present, a replacement for the one she'd lost. From Gilbert? From her mother?

At Seventy-ninth the park wall ended. She crossed the street and walked into the park.

He went back to the car and waited. A few minutes later she was back with the dog. She went inside and he waited some more. At nine ten she came down again. This time the doorman hailed a taxi. Stavitsky started his car, eased out into the street. She got into the taxi and they headed south. He followed. East at Sixty-eighth, then all the way crosstown until he could see the sun on the river, then downtown on York to Sixty-sixth. She got out and walked into the university grounds. He pulled into the parking lot and was on the path just in time to see her walk into the building where her office was. He walked up to it and stood there for a few minutes in the cold. Then he walked back to York, bought a newspaper, and found a coffee shop where he ordered breakfast. The place was almost empty and very quiet. He sat there, trying to read, nursing cup after cup of coffee. At eleven thirty the two waitresses began looking nervously at him. The lunch crowds would be in soon and he was taking up space. But his size and the stubble on his chin made them wary. At eleven forty-five he got up, paid for the food, and walked back to the campus.

People were moving about, some already coming out of her building. He walked past the entrance, then turned and stood just off the path waiting. They were coming out in twos and threes. Some with their coats on heading for York Avenue, some with just lab coats running to the cafeteria building or the faculty dining room. No sign of her. Delivery boys plied up and down the paths bringing lunches for those who ordered out. Other people appeared, a small clump of men in business suits walked past, hurrying against the cold to get to the next building. Secretary-types emerged in coats and boots. More lab coats. No Jennifer Gilbert.

At two thirty he gave up and went back to the car. He turned on the motor and heater until he was warm, then turned them off and settled down to wait.

After a while he took his saccharine box out of his coat pocket and opened it. He unwrapped the shell. He remembered the cardboard it had come from, empty glue dots, the careful childish labels—childish, innocent. How many years ago had she found the shell? Thirty? Forty? And what had happened to the girl who'd found it? There was a crack across it where the opening flared. He wondered if it had been there all along or if it had broken since he took it. He touched the flared end and the shell broke apart at the crack. He rolled the two pieces across his palm. Then he fit the pieces back together and carefully set them back in the box.

By three thirty the sun was going, by four, it was almost dark. At four thirty she passed the parking lot, heading for the street. He started the car and followed her around the drive. He thought she'd hail a taxi at York, but she didn't. She turned right at York and started walking uptown. He parked the car next to a hydrant, got out, and followed.

She walked evenly, quickly, not browsing or looking around. As if she knew exactly where she was going. He wondered if she walked this way every night. They went on and on, into the Seventies—a few shops here, but she didn't stop or even glance in the windows as they went by.

At Seventy-eighth Street she crossed York and started walking west. Nothing here but apartments—old, well-kept tenement structures laced with fire escapes. Past First, then Second, still the same steady walk. The brownstones started, and trees. Snow was piled in the gutters but the sidewalks were clear. She crossed Third, and then, about halfway down the block, on the downtown side of the street, he saw her stop, look across the street, and move into the shadow against the stoop of one of the brownstones. He stopped too, and stepped back out of the direct light of the street lamp. She didn't move, and he couldn't imagine why she would stop there.

He eased out of the shadow and looked. The house she stood near was dark. She was still there, he could see the darker patch the coat made against the stone. She was just standing. A little flare; she lit a cigarette. He did the same. He looked across the street. Just houses—mostly unconverted brownstones. He thought that the people in the house opposite should get window shades; their whole living room was visible from the street. It was such an unexpected thing for her to be doing that it took him a few minutes to realize that she was watching them. Jennifer Compton List Gilbert was standing alone on a street in the dark, peeping into someone else's windows.

Suddenly the whole thing was so absurd that he was afraid he would laugh aloud. Here he was, without sleep, unwashed, carrying a goddamn gun and silencer across the city to see for himself if they were right and he'd have to kill her. A whole day watching every movement as half killer, half lover—a whole day on the verge of tears, following the woman like no other woman in the world, and she turns out on top of everything else to be a peeper. And they wanted him to kill her—to put a gun against that crazy red-gray head and pull the trigger. Now there were tears on his face, his cheeks puffed with unsounded laughter. His diamond. His special in all the world and she's watching somebody's window hoping to see a little cock. Too much, too fucking much. . . .

Then he stopped. No, that couldn't be it. No one screws in the living room with bare windows that big and the lights on. Not unless they want to be seen, and if that were the case there'd be a goddamn parade of people. They'd be selling pretzels and chestnuts every night on this street.

She was moving, coming out of the shadows. He looked at his watch —about ten minutes since they'd stopped. He followed again. He didn't have to hide. Most people never expected to be followed and the only trick was not to lose them at lights or in crowds and to try not to actually trip over them. She went west again, across Lexington. There she hailed a taxi. He didn't do the same. He just watched the taillights of her cab turn right at Seventy-seventh Street. She was going home, probably too cold to walk the rest of the way.

He went back the way they'd come, found the brownstone stairs that had sheltered her, and stood there watching the windows across the street, trying to see what brought her there.

All he saw was a couple—not that young, not especially good-looking. He thought the woman was quite plain compared to her. They didn't do much. They sipped drinks, then she got up and came back with a bowl of something—potato chips, he thought, or some kind of dip. They didn't hug or kiss, nothing. They did talk, he could see their mouths moving. Then the man pointed, something on the TV probably, and the woman laughed. It looked like nice laughter, unforced, happy. He could see that. They just sat there. The room wasn't grand, nothing to what she was used to. Nice enough, he thought, very cheerful, very done, very East Side interior decorator—Bloomingdale's probably. Certainly they must have some money—this was an expensive neighborhood. He crossed the street to look at the bells, to find out their name, and found as she had that they were the only ones living there—the whole house. Not bad. He went back across the street and watched some more. But it was the same. More sips of the drinks, crunching the snack, whatever it

was. Then the man got up and walked across the room and bent over—
to turn off the TV? A few more minutes of the same easy conversation,
then the man held out his hand, she took it, stood up, and they left the
room together—probably to the dining room to have dinner. He looked
up the front of the house. There were lights upstairs; children? Or
maybe they dined on the second floor. No way to tell.

He took the Second Avenue bus downtown to get the car.

He was pretty sure that she watched them every night. It was hard to
imagine, standing there alone in the dark, driven to watching a scene as
ordinary as the one he'd just witnessed. What kind of loneliness, he
wondered, could do that?

He followed her for three nights. Leaving the office at three forty-five,
keeping to the streets so he wouldn't get stuck on the East Side Drive,
and getting there with about ten minutes to spare. He got bolder and
began waiting for her on the path, just past her building so he could see
her come out. He noticed that the other men and women usually left in
couples or in groups and that she never did. They talked as they came
out, a little burst of good feeling now that the day was over. Off to have
dinner, or cook it, or maybe go shopping or to the movies. But she was
always silent, always alone. He followed every night, stood there in the
dark with her, watching what she watched, wondering if they were going
to spend the rest of their lives like this in a kind of closeness she never
knew about, standing together in the dark while she watched two
strangers whose lives she could never touch. He wondered if she'd ever
really touched anyone's life except for the killing. Ever acted with people in all the thousands of ways that being with someone could change,
if not your course, then at least a part of a day, a week. But she didn't
even have lunch with anyone. No one said to her, "That sounds good,
I'll have it too." No one bought a dress because she liked it. She dressed
Gilbert, but he thought that would be like dressing a doll—he could
imagine Gilbert's consistent "If you think so, dear." And that was it.

Then, on Friday, the people they watched—the Parkers—had a party
and the whole thing fell apart. It was a cocktail party, about twenty-five
people, the sort of thing you come to at four and are supposed to leave
by eight but never do. Well-dressed Upper East Side people—Second
and Third Avenue, no Union Club, no Fifth Avenue types. A nice
happy party. By the time they were standing on the street watching, a
few were already high, and Stavitsky could see a long decorated buffet
table. Plenty to drink, good food . . . the host and hostess looked very
happy, very much as if they were enjoying themselves. It was a fairly
warm night, slightly drizzly, and one of the floor-to-ceiling windows was

partly open so they—he and Jennifer—could hear party noises, laughter, talking.

He noticed that she wasn't standing as far back as she usually did and she wasn't smoking. She moved forward out of the shadow, almost to the curb, face turned up so that the lights from the windows hit it. What was she doing? Closer, off the curb into the gutter. She was in full view now and her whole body was stiff and tense. He didn't like the way she was standing, he didn't like the way the whole thing felt. The party noises were getting fainter. She moved closer . . . another couple of steps.

Oh, shit, he thought. What's she going to do? He opened his coat, grabbed the gun, started to pull it out. The noise of a gun would stop her. Then he remembered that it still had the silencer. He got it out, started to unscrew the silencer in the dark. He wasn't going to shoot her. . . . He wasn't going to shoot her. . . . She was moving again. He tried to pull the muzzle free but the silencer wouldn't come off.

He looked up desperately. He'd shout. It would mean discovery, but— Then he heard someone scream, a faint but definite scream, and he looked through the window and froze.

A huge, bronze, Chinese-type carved lamp was sailing gently across the Parkers' living room. It didn't hit anyone, it just moved easily, then faster and faster across the room. It was coming for the window. The closer it got the faster it moved, until it was there, smashing through the window with a tremendous crash—glass everywhere, the lamp sailing, holding its momentum, until it fell, metal on asphalt, almost at her feet.

She started to run. He looked once at the mayhem; then he started running after her. The shouts from the house were full volume now, and people up and down the street were looking out of windows, a few coming out of their doors. She ran and ran and he kept after her.

At Lexington she stopped, looked blindly up and down the street. She was confused and he thought he saw tears on her face in the light. Then she started walking very fast downtown. A few feet and she leaned against a brick wall. People looked at her, then hurried past to see what was causing the noise. He stood at the corner, wishing more than anything in the world he could take her in his arms. They just stood there like that a few feet apart until she pushed herself away from the wall and walked wearily downtown to Seventy-seventh Street.

He went home.

Ching was right. It was festering, coming out. Tonight she was a child, spoiling a party, breaking a window. Harmless shit, although he felt very sorry for the Parkers—very nice people, nice party. But what would it turn into? A kid tries to grab her purse in the park, or just insults her, or . . . anything. Maybe the next time the Parkers or somebody like them wouldn't be so lucky. It was the most poisonous combination in the world. He knew it. Power and separation from everything.

He lay back on the couch and looked at the ceiling in the dark, crisscrossed with the lights from the fish tank and from the street. Carole would come in in a second, complain about his always sitting in the dark lately, turn on the lights, then turn on the TV. He closed his eyes. They were right. Tonight she'd hated all those people, not enough to kill or even hurt, but enough to disrupt. And what about tomorrow, and the next day. . . ?

He turned on the couch so that his back was to the room and his face against the upholstery. Roberts. No one on this earth deserved to die more than Roberts, but it wouldn't end there. Ching had said it: You couldn't know a thing like that and then let it go. True, it was true. He hunched his shoulders. Why stop with Roberts?

He rolled over and sat up.

Why stop with Roberts?

He called Si Geller.

"I've got to see you tomorrow morning."

"Up yours—tomorrow's Saturday."

"Right. Tomorrow morning at your office, eleven o'clock."

"C'mon, Dave."

"A favor, Si. I won't forget it."

"OK, OK."

9

HE SLEPT AND woke all night. Once, he got out of bed and looked out the window, thinking about her, across the park, a few blocks downtown. He wondered if she ever thought about him, looked out her window toward him the way he was looking toward her.

He dreamed on and off all night. In one they were all there, Galeston, Stern, Ching, and her. She was covered with a sheet, but he knew she was naked under it, and he was looking for something in her body. The others watched, gave instruction. First in her ears—only so many orifices in a woman's body, Galeston was saying, it had to be in one of them. Then into her mouth. She rolled her tongue back to help him and he pulled the cheeks to one side then the other. He could see her teeth, the uvula at the back of her throat. It wasn't there. Then they spread her legs for him and he was reaching into her. He reached as far as he could, pushing, hurting her, but it wasn't there. In another dream he'd killed her. Shot her in the throat in the park. Blood everywhere, and she fell on the dog. He saw the dog trying to crawl out from under the weight of her body in its mink coat. It looked like a worm, trying to crawl out. He woke up after that one in a cold sweat and had to go wash his face. Finally, about four in the morning, just as he was ready to give up, he fell asleep and stayed asleep until seven.

He spent the hours from eight to ten at the office making copies of everything. Then he stopped at a luggage store and bought an attaché case. Then Si. . . .

"What is this crap?"

"Just keep it for me, that's all." He handed his lawyer a big envelope that he extricated carefully from the case without letting the other man see anything else in it.

"That's it, Si. There's instruction inside—everything you need. And if something happens to me, then open it and do what I ask. Couldn't be easier." A copy of everything to Carmichael and Algren, and one to William Gilbert. He thought they'd make good threats.

"What's this 'something,' Dave, that's supposed to happen to you?"

"If I die, Si. No matter how. If I die."

Simon Geller looked at his friend. He thought he was crazy. He looked crazy. But young, younger and handsomer than he had in years.

It was snowing again, very lightly, not enough to make the roads slippery, and he didn't have to concentrate on driving. He thought he had her boxed in . . . no way out. But as he drove, the plan, everything he tried to think about began to seem less and less important compared with the fact that he was going to see her again. He knew that if it didn't work it would be the last time. The dream of her dead came back to him. He pushed it away but it came back again. It was real and if this didn't work that's how it would end. He'd have to kill her. He pulled over into the parking lot near the lagoon. The snow was building up, almost covering the grass. Sea gulls sat on the thin ice, ignoring the snow. He opened the case and took out the revolver and silencer. They'd picked up the cold even in the case. He screwed the silencer into place and shoved the gun back into his belt. The pressure was leaving a bruise at his beltline and it was painful putting it back, but this would be the last time.

He started the car and drove east through the empty park.

He was at the double door again. Hawkins was opening one. No greeting, no attempt to keep him out.

"I'll see if she's busy."

"Do that, George. You don't mind if I wait in the living room?"

He did mind, but he didn't say anything.

Stavitsky laughed. "Mr. Hawkins," he said, "if you can make that look habitual, you'll be the best butler in history."

No answer. No smile. He was led silently into the vast living room and left there. Same room, only now there was a Christmas tree in one corner, crusted with ornaments. But it didn't help much. The size and solitariness of the place seemed unshakable. It was very quiet, just the snapping of the fire and the wind shaking the foliage on the terrace.

Suddenly he heard a scrabbling sound . . . claws on marble. He turned and saw the small black dog scrambling across the floor of the foyer at the entrance end of the room. The stone floor was slick, so the puppy half ran, half slid. Fur and fat rippled as the puppy swam to the stairs. Then it saw Stavitsky and yipped at him. Stavitsky stood up and the puppy ran and fell down the three stairs into the room. Its paws held on the carpet and it dashed for Stavitsky, every inch wiggling—legs, head, tail, all moving at once—barking and whining.

Hawkins came into the room and started for the puppy.

It was too much. The puppy squatted at once and started to wet the carpet.

"No!" Hawkins yelled.

The yell only excited the puppy more. It rolled over on its back, paws waving, a little stream of urine spouting in the air.

Hawkins, all dignity forgotten, reached the puppy and picked it up. But the puppy went on wetting, right down the front of Hawkins' suit.

Stavitsky was laughing.

Hawkins held the squirming dog away from himself and glared at the policeman, but Stavitsky couldn't stop. He held onto the back of the chair bent with laughter, tears running down his face.

Hawkins tried, but it was no use. His face twitched once, twice, and he started to laugh too. The dog wiggled madly, which made them laugh more.

They rocked back and forth, bent and twisted, held their ribs, helpless with laughter.

Then Stavitsky heard a new sound. Clear, delicate, like a bell, it carried above their voices, cut across it. He turned. She was standing in a doorway leaning against the wall, laughing with them.

Stavitsky stopped. Then Hawkins stopped.

She wiped her eyes and looked at them, straight-faced for a second. Then she started again, which set Hawkins off again. Only Stavitsky had no more laughter.

He followed her. She had little fits of laughing all along the gallery and he could see her shoulders shake. But she kept her back to him. Then she opened the door. He followed her in, closed the door. They were alone. She turned to him. Her face controlled, but there was still some weakness at the corners of her mouth, still wanting to laugh. He waited. Finally she was composed, looking like herself again, worn and solitary.

He put the attaché case on her desk, opened it, and took out a cassette recorder and some tapes.

"We have a lot to talk about." He saw her stiffen. "No," he said, "don't get like that. I've thought about you, about nothing except you, for days and weeks. You've been with me every minute in one way or another, in the most intimate parts of my life, and we have a lot to talk about now."

Then he started taking the papers out of the case. "There's no point in going over the Roberts report, you know I have it. This is a copy. This," he said, "is John Starbuck's report on the death of Hal Kearney. Would you like to read it? Of course there are copies of it, too."

She swayed. Easy, he wanted to say, easy. It won't take long. The pistol's silencer still held the outside cold, rubbing against him as he moved, almost in his groin.

"But I guess you know what it says, don't you?"

She nodded, but he wanted to hear her voice.

"Don't you?"

"Yes," she said, "I know what's in it."

"I think the tapes are really the most important."

She watched his huge hand slide the cassette into the recorder. The light in the room turned the hair on the back of it to gold. The cassette was in place. He pushed the playback button, upped the volume control.

"There are copies of all the tapes—keep that in mind."

There was some silent running, then Christopher Haynes' voice, scratchy but recognizable, began telling them about Marvin Ross' last night.

He played them all and watched her while she listened. She sat like stone through Haynes and Charles, bowed her head during Raines' taped breakdown.

Then her own voice. She listened, apparently impassive, to the absolute testimony she gave against herself.

"How long did it take him to die?" Stavitsky's voice sounded far away on the tape.

"Only a few minutes," said her tape voice. "Less than five."

The tape and the distance it created couldn't hide the satisfaction in her voice. "Less than five." She would have made it ten, or twenty, if she'd had the control.

The tape ended. He turned the machine off and waited. She didn't say anything.

She looked more solitary than ever as she sat looking at the silent machine, like an animal that thinks it is alone and unseen in a forest. He reached into the case for a pile of papers. She watched his hands again—paper, folders, tapes, all from Stavitsky's magic case. She watched his hands collect the thin pile and lift it out.

"This is the police report on Marvin Ross," he said. She watched the hands move the papers. "And," he said, "there's Dr. Ching's film clip—you remember, the paper airplane. He'll let me use it if we need it. And finally, here's the report he gave on you at a meeting in 1954. No name of course, but he'll supply that," Stavitsky lied.

"Why?" she asked, looking at his face at last. "What does he have against me?"

"Marvin Ross. Ching still remembers, still sort of blames himself."

"Yes, I see."

Her shoulders hunched as if she were cold, and she looked away from him again. He couldn't follow her eyes, couldn't get up and stand in front of her, but he wanted to. He looked along the line of her vision: nothing, the rug, the bottom of the bookcase.

"How did you find Dr. Ching?"

"Ellen Cransten." No visible reaction. "She was the one who told me about the boy in Nantucket. She didn't know anything except the rumors, but she told me all about them—as much as she could." Why wasn't she looking at him? "She hates you, you know," he said.

Finally she looked at him. "I suppose she does," she said after a while. She seemed to be waiting.

"Then, of course, Ching told me about Ross and Haynes."

"Of course."

He couldn't stand this worn woman looking at him without seeing him, as if he were a messenger who had no part in what was going to happen.

"You understand," he said, raising his voice, "that these tapes, reports, everything, they're only copies."

"The originals are in a safe place, right, captain?"

A spark at last, a touch of anger. It was better than nothing.

"Right, and you'd have a hell of a time finding them. They're safe." He kept his voice even, but sweat was beginning to collect in the bow of his upper lip. As she watched, a bead broke loose and trickled down his lip. He licked at it. "There are instructions so that no one will see it as long as I am alive. But if anything happens to me—"

She leaned forward. "Yes? If anything happens to you?"

"Your husband will be given one copy of everything you've seen and listened to, and another copy"—he had her full attention now—"will go to my assistant and to the chief of detectives of the New York Police Department." Very impressive. But he could imagine how Algren, Algren of Queens, would react to what was in the envelope he'd given to Si Geller. "Oh, I know they won't believe it, but I am who I am, and they'll have to check. Even if just a little, they'll have to check. And that'll bring them right to Ching. Now, Ching's still pretty big stuff you know."

Threats. The first time in his life he was alone with her and all he could do was threaten. "They can't just ignore Ching. Even if they think I'd gone crazy, they'd have to at least listen to Ching." How could any-one sit so still? "And even if they decide Ching's nuts, there's bound to be talk . . . some whispers here and there. Especially downtown, especially if I'm dead. And there's the reporters. You know, some of them hanging around there night and day. That's their only assignment, to stick with headquarters. You can imagine what will happen, can't you?" Still, so still—her eyes fixed on him. "One'll say, 'Just heard the damndest thing. Word is that some broad murdered that asshole Stavitsky.' And someone'll ask the name and someone'll tell them, and someone'll know that name, won't they? 'Gilbert!' he'll say. 'William Ely Gilbert's wife. Hey, they're the people—he's the one, she's the one.' Then there'll be other names—List, Compton. Then they'll really smell something. 'List, Compton, they're the ones.' So you know what they'll do? At least one will, I promise you. He'll go to Carmichael. That's my assistant. Very junior, but he loves the press and they know it already. He has a terrible time keeping his mouth shut. And he'll talk. Why not? 'Boys,' he'll say, 'it's the goddamndest thing, but old Stavitsky believed.' And they'll listen. He might even give them a look at the evidence. And by the time they're done there won't be a single whole, peaceful second of your life left. They'll get to Ching and even Galeston. Housewives in the Midwest'll read what's on those tapes. And, of course, your hus-band. Can't you see it? Stopping him on the street, or his friends at the club—'Aren't you the man whose wife—'"

"*Stop it.*" Her voice cut his, and she was shaking her head, looking down, shaking it back and forth as if she were worrying something in her teeth. Her hair swished across her face. "I understand. . . . I can't kill you—I won't kill you—I never thought of killing you. Now will you leave me alone?"

"No!"

He unbuttoned his jacket. The gun butt caught the light.

"Ching and Galeston think *I* should kill *you*."

Her head stopped moving, the hair tangled across her forehead, along her cheeks. She looked at the gun, pushing against the firm flesh just above his belt. She was like an animal—an animal watching and waiting. No expression. Stavitsky felt a chill.

Finally, "Ching, too? He wants you to kill me, too?"

"More than Galeston."

"Why? I've never hurt any of them."

"Because they're scared, jealous, leechy little men. Because they think it's the only logical thing to do. That's what they kept saying, both of them. The only logical thing."

"You wouldn't." She was still looking at the gun.

"Don't say that. Oh, don't say that. I would, I will."

He pulled the gun out of his belt. "See," he said, "silencer and everything, all ready to go." The gun gleamed at her, she couldn't look at anything else.

"But I wouldn't hurt them, I wouldn't hurt you."

"That's what I thought, too. Until last night."

"Last night." She was almost whispering, but he could hear her because the room was absolutely still. "What do you mean, last night?"

"The people on Seventy-eighth Street. The party, and that trick with the lamp."

"You followed me. You've been watching." The solitary look was gone. She wasn't alone anymore and she knew it. She looked hunted. "Following me as if I were—"

"A killer. As if you were a killer. That's what Galeston said. Killer, monster—"

"Don't call me that." She was holding onto the edge of the desk.

"No nasty names, right? Never mind what happens . . . what really happens." His voice sounded too loud against the quietness around them. "What do you think I'm going to do? Forget it? Walk out of here and forget it? That case is full of dead men—all your work. And Ching said it would go on—fester, he said—inside you. That you couldn't be what you are and just do nothing. I didn't believe him at first. Didn't want to, because, shit, I don't want to hurt you." He thought of her lying dead in the park, the dog struggling under her. "But last night—"

"No. Stop."

"Why? Why last night? Why those people? How long've you been watching them? A year, six months?"

No answer.

"A long time, right? A long settled habit watching the Parkers." She flinched when he said their name. "Then suddenly it gets to be too much. A party you can't go to, and what the hell do you do? Ruin, break. Why? They must've had other parties in all this time, so why now?"

No answer.

"Because now you know you can. Right? For the first time you know you can. Isn't that it?"

"I don't know. Leave me alone. I didn't hurt them."

"Goddammit, stop saying that. I'm *not* going to leave you alone. I can't. I'll never leave you alone unless I kill you. Don't ever tell me to leave you alone."

Her eyes were moving to the door. But he was between her and it.

"Don't you get it yet?" he was saying. "You did what you did last night because what Ching and Galeston said was true. You did it because those nice normal people had left you out there alone night after night on the sidewalk. Because all the other nice ordinary people have done the same thing. And they'll go on doing it, leaving you out there. Isn't that it?" Except me, he wanted to tell her, except me.

"Isn't that it?"

"No, no," she cried. "It isn't. I'm like they are. I—"

He went on. His voice sounded very loud.

"You're like no one and nothing in this world. And if you don't face it, it really will happen. You really will do it. Galeston, Stern, Ching, me. Maybe worse, maybe even your husband." She was very pale. "Yeah, why not. Dear husband. Look at us sitting here all alone, all this time. Where is he? It's Saturday afternoon. Why aren't you shopping with him, seeing friends, getting dressed to go out to dinner? Where the fuck is your husband?" He couldn't stop.

"How many years do you think you can go on like this? Sitting alone in this room. Walking alone on the streets. A stranger. How many others shut you out every day? Why not them, too? Why not kill them? Who likes you, who wants your company—"

"Get out." She had to stop him. She couldn't listen to any more of it.

"And what do you think they'd do to you if they *did* know? If you make a mistake and do the wrong little trick in the wrong place one day. Because you won't be able to resist that either, you know. What do you think they'd do to you if they found out what you are?"

"Please. Oh, please, stop."

He couldn't.

"They'll tear you to pieces, they'll—"

She was reaching across the desk.

"No." He grabbed her hand. The hunted look was very strong and her palm was wet. There was sweat on her face and neck, too. "Don't call Hawkins." He pointed the gun and let go of her. "I'll kill both of you if I have to. No trouble explaining a dead ex-junkie, and he'll make a good fall guy if I have to kill you. But don't make me. Don't make me. . . ."

He couldn't hear his voice. She was moving away from him, off the carpet, but he couldn't hear her steps on the bare floor. Too far, he'd gone too far. The fire was burning, their shadows jumped against the wall, but he couldn't hear the crackle he'd heard a second ago. Christ. She was going to kill him. She was really going to do it. His thumb was on the safety of the gun, and he was pulling, his fingers turning to huge nerveless cylinders, swelling. She was losing dimension. He opened his mouth, trying to get air. His lungs burned, stretching for air, collapsing for air. Everything was dead, silent. The safety moved and he wrapped one sausage finger around the trigger. He could barely see her, nothing but the thin lines of a woman, and they were fading, rising as he was sinking, bending, knees hitting the carpet. She was near the front of the window, a vague flat form against the light that was spreading luminous gray over the window frames, gray over the walls, lighter and lighter as the shapes softened, giving way. He made the finger squeeze at the metal, on and on with everything he had until he felt the trigger move very, very slowly.

The gun kicked.

He was on his knees, head hanging. Nothing but red, gold, and blue geometry as far as he could see. Then he saw the end of the rug, the floor beyond, walls, window containing the light again. He could breathe. He could hear the fire. Something touched him, held him. She was kneeling next to him, her arm around his shoulders, trying to help him sit up. More red. There was blood on her cheek. Blood seeped down her face to her jaw. There was more at the corner of her mouth. She licked at it absently, then touched the cheek and looked at her hand.

"I didn't know it hit me. I didn't even feel it."

He tried to look closer. She let him. Then he leaned on one hand and touched the cheek, wiped at the blood.

He tried to reach for his handkerchief. But his hands were still numb and he couldn't seem to find his pocket. Her blood was on his clothes. He shook his head. "Just a crease," he said to her. "Just a scratch. No scar. I promise, Jenny, just a scratch."

"The gun's right there," she said. It was, almost touching his knee. He pushed it away.

"Then what?" she asked. "What will you do? I almost killed you. Maybe they're right. Maybe you should do what they want."

"No."

He finally managed to get the handkerchief out of his pocket and held it against her face. She was very close to him. He rose on his knees, still holding the handkerchief against the side of her face, and put his other arm around her until his hand cupped her shoulder. He let himself hold her, pressing her against him while he wiped her cheek. He could feel her breathing. He closed his eyes and rocked slightly, holding her body flat against him. She rocked with him.

"What will you do?" she asked again after a while. He could feel her mouth moving against his cheek.

"It's what *we're* going to do, Jenny." He took the handkerchief away from her face. The blood had slowed to a trickle. "Both of us."

She didn't move.

"It's there in the case. I'm still rocky, just let me stay here for a minute. You get it for me. All that's left in there—sixteen folders. They're men, sixteen men. Roberts was one of them. You got rid of him for me"—his hand went back to her cheek, dabbing at it—"for which I've never thanked you. They're all like him, all like Roberts." She still didn't move. "And you're going to help me with them." His knuckles brushed her hair, fingers touched the lines of her jaw. "Doesn't anyone ever come in here?"

"No."

"Sixteen," he told her, "all special in some way. Like Roberts—even worse, some of them. It's all there, Jenny, all in those folders—who they are, where they've been, what they've done, what they're doing now."

She looked over at the case, then back at him.

"I've been keeping that file for years, Jenny. Sometimes there's more of them, sometimes less—men like that don't live to be very old. You bring the files to me and I'll show you what I mean."

"How am I going to help you?"

"You're going to kill them for me."

She started to move, a quick pulling away, but he held her tight against him.

"Listen to me, Jenny, it's the only way. . . ."

"No . . ." pulling harder.

"There's nothing left for you, Jenny." His voice was very soft. "You can't go back now—not once you've had a taste of it—a taste of power." He thought he'd never looked at anyone so closely before, nor held another body so tightly against his own.

"I can't. . . ."

"You've got to, because if you don't—if it goes on eating at you—then it will be the end of you. And I couldn't stand that, no matter what." He was whispering. He couldn't tell if she was even listening to him. "I'm all you've got," still whispering, "and now you're all I've got too. Nobody else matters. And we'll be together. No more empty rooms, Jenny, no more watching through windows in the dark. Do it." His voice was very soft. "Use the power . . . kill them for me, for both of us. You'll never be alone again."

He stopped talking. Then he held her for a long time without saying anything before he made himself let her go.

She stayed where she was—watching him. He folded the bloody handkerchief and put it back in his pocket. Then he waited. Finally she stood up, went to the case and brought the folders back to him. She kneeled down again, next to him, almost touching him. She put the folders on the floor in front of them.

"Which one should I look at first?"

This book has been read by:-
Barbara Zehn ----- February 1976